# The Book the BBC Tried to BAN!

## By
## Paul
## Sherringford

# PRAISE FOR
# 'THE BOOK THE BBC TRIED TO BAN!':

'BBC top brass had better place an order for some fresh underpants, because they'll almost certainly soil the ones they're wearing once they read this!' - *Jeff Token, The North West Wales Literary Scrutiniser*

'If the BBC is some sort of deranged, woke cult then consider this book to be the deprogramming manual!' - *Mica Jackson, The Non-Partisan Review*

'The fact that many will love this book yet be terrified to say so is exactly why it needed to be written. A brutal deconstruction of the subtle hypocrisy that permeates every aspect of the media, this book, like any great work, will truly terrify those in power, and whilst there will be many who are offended by it they will also be unable to deny its truth. Read it now before it really is banned!' - *ILikeToReadAboutThings.com*

'This book will make you question EVERYTHING and we don't think there's ANYONE who'll make it to the end without having their most sacred values questioned!' - *Western Skegness Literary Review*

'Combining the inventiveness of BS Johnson, the brutal pessimism of George Orwell, the post-modern mystery of Paul Auster and the surreal hilarity of Monty Python, this book will quite literally BLOW your BRAIN!' - *BrilliantBooksBlog.com*

'If you're the kind of person who loves to publically get offended by things you've completely failed to understand then you will *love* this book!' - *Suzanne Jeffries, the Grand Re-Awokening.com*

'Once in a lifetime comes a book that is so incendiary, so powerful, written by an author possessed of such prophetic vision that once you have read it you will never see the world in the same way again, and this truly is that book. Tantalisingly non-PC, with an Orton-esque sense of playfulness and danger, this is the antithesis of a gammony polemic, in which the writing fizzes and sparkles with hilarity and energy. Also, it says some pretty powerful things about Mrs Brown's Boys, things that have gone unsaid for too long but cannot be denied.' - *Betty McCabe, The North Teesside Literary Review*

'In the name of love, tolerance, diversity and equality, we call for the author of this sickening work to be KILLED!' - *Harry Snowflake-Watson, WokeNews.Com*

'This most welcome and overdue revival of the neo-Juvenalian style of satire is both brutally powerful and powerfully brutal, like George Orwell re-written by Joe Orton or, indeed, Joe Orton as re-written by George Orwell or, I suppose, a novel on which they both worked together for some reason. Containing more ideas on a single page than many writers cram into a page and a half, this book tears apart the lies upon which our society is based and will do much the same to your brain, though fortunately only in a metaphorical way.' - *Howard Boom, Emeritus Professor of Post-Millennial Literary Studies, the University of North-West Redditch*

# Magic Mirror Publishing

Published by Magic Mirror Publishing

First Edition December 2020

'The book fascinated him, or more exactly it reassured him. In a sense it told him nothing that was new, but that was part of the attraction. It said what he would have said, if it had been possible for him to set his scattered thoughts in order. It was the product of a mind similar to his own, but enormously more powerful, more systematic, less fear-ridden. The best books, he perceived, are those that tell you what you know already.'

George Orwell, 1984


'You need a licence whatever you do,
One or two things they've exempted, it's true.
Lumbago, the gout or a touch of the 'flu,
Why, you don't need a licence for that!'

George Formby, 'You Don't Need A Licence for That'


'READ THIS BEHIND CLOSED DOORS. And have a good shit while you are reading!'

Joe Orton

# Publisher's Note:

# A Warning From the Future

The true author of this book is unknown.

It is set in the year 2024, a dark future in which an all-powerful state broadcaster controls every aspect of the British population's lives, but was submitted to us anonymously from a mysterious source, and from the fragmented and often contradictory information we have uncovered whilst attempting to ascertain its true origin, information that in some cases appears to have been deliberately planted in order to blur and confuse our efforts to discover the truth, we have managed to formulate the following possible explanations as to its provenance:

1. It is a true account of our near future, sent back in time using experimental tachyon technology as a warning of the terrible fate awaiting us.

2. It is a true account of the year 2024 in an *alternative timeline* that was sent back as a warning but, as the result of an unfortunate time slip due to the procedure being experimental, ended up in the wrong reality.

3. It was written in our present day by a senior BBC executive who has uncovered a secret plan by the Corporation to assume power in the way it does in this book, and knows he must warn the world but do so anonymously for his own safety.

4. It is a fictitious work written by a well-known BBC presenter with a

secret grudge against the Corporation. But not Gary Lineker, if that's what you're thinking.

5. It is nothing more than a bizarre hoax or practical joke by some sort of trickster figure undertaken for reasons known only to them.

6. It is merely the deranged ramblings of a mental patient in a forgotten room in a secure facility for the criminally insane, a lone voice crying out in the midst of the madness but being utterly drowned out.

But definitely not Gary Lineker, though.

As unlikely as it seems, however, we veer towards the second explanation: that it is, in fact, a warning of a future that may only come to pass in an alternative reality. One of our reasons for believing this is that many of the people and organisations in the book have names close to ones in our reality whilst not being quite the same, such as how the 'BBC' in question is an organisation called the 'Broadcasting for Britain Company' or the Prime Minister is named 'Horace Thompson'. In addition, we would hope this explanation would legally exonerate us for publishing it because if anyone tried to sue us they'd need to actually travel to a future alternate dimension and conclusively prove it didn't really happen there, or even actually launch the legal action in that reality.

We believe the author put himself at tremendous personal risk by writing and distributing this powerful book, and the least we can do is bring it to the world's attention, so it is for that reason that it is now published using a pseudonym but still presented word-for-word, in all its glory and with all its flaws. And, for the record, those flaws include typos. We believe this book was written in great haste, and that the author knew that the powerful message he had to urgently deliver was far more important than whether a few apostrophes were in the wrong place, or he put 'started' when he meant to write 'stared', and so should you. So what now follows is the book we received, as we received it. The true explanation of its origins is for you to decide.
         Read on, if you dare...

# Author's Note: A Warning To Those of An Easily Offended Disposition

My only hope is that this book is received, read and understood. It is too late for me but may not be too late for you if this message reaches you in time.

Most of this book is true, particularly the words. Some of it will be too brutal, too powerful, too visceral for some to accept. They will hope that by ignoring or denouncing the book it will somehow disappear. And the way many will attempt to denounce the book is by declaring it too offensive, a time-honoured practice to censor those who speak the unspeakable, but to those people I would say this: read the whole thing before you decide. Whatever issues you have are undoubtedly addressed at some point. And, remember, when people are offended it is almost always either because they're doing it very publically and hoping to receive praise, or because they're simply too stupid to comprehend the point that's being made.

Furthermore, one of the most common reasons offence arises is because those who have taken it have failed to tell the difference between the criticism of a subject *itself* and the criticism of the wider issues *surrounding it*, confusing the contents for the container, if you like, and simply noticed a mention of one of their sacred cows and leapt to be offended without attempting to understand the deeper point being made.

And let me assure you that in the near-future from which I have sent back this book, people are even quicker to take offence over nothing than they are in your time, so I am well aware of the need to clarify this. People desperate to take offence will always find a way to do so. But, on the other hand, what exactly is the point of reading a book so unchallenging that you agree with every part of it and it does nothing but reinforce your worldview?

I would hope such a person is not you and, if it is, would urge you to read no further.

But if you are not that person, read on with an open mind, and prepare to have your perception of the world around you torn apart, for this is a book that few people will reach the end of without having at least some of their most dearly-held beliefs questioned, and should you make it that far then your mind will have been stretched open so much more.

And if enough people understand the message, the horrifying future this book depicts will never come to be, and this will exist only as a forgotten work of speculative fiction.

# Chapter One:

# A Rude Awokening

*In Which An Everyday Nobody Is Abducted and Finds Himself in Unfamiliar Surroundings. But Has He Really Been Taken To One of the Dreaded BBC Re-Education Camps?!*

John Smith winced as he felt yet another jolt from the electric cattle prod that was being pushed against his lower back, and took an involuntary step forward, pausing only briefly to look up at the huge, imposing iron gates that now creaked open in front of him, and to read the sign above them, written in a font that almost seemed designed to create fear:

## WHEN YOU DIE YOU WILL NOT GO TO HELL AS YOU ARE ALREADY THERE

And beneath that:

## ABANDON ALL HOPE, YE WHO ENTER HERE

Then, just below that:

## PROUDLY FUNDED USING THE BBC LICENCE FEE SINCE 2022

In the hours or possibly days since he was dragged out of his house in the middle of the night the only two things of which John Smith could be reasonably confident were that he could not only no longer trust his own memories, but that he could also no longer place any faith in reality itself. All else was guesswork.

He turned around, perplexed, to look at his captor but received only another jolt from the cattle prod for his trouble, and stumbled across the threshold and into his new nightmare. What was this place? *Where* was he? He somehow continued to walk forward even though it felt like hours since he thought he would collapse with exhaustion if he was forced to take a single step further. Risking another jolt from the cattle prod, he dared to turn around again to get a better look at his captors. Whilst he only managed this for the briefest moment, what he saw gave him no answers, only more questions. They were wearing some kind of military uniform, but what was that logo? It almost looked like... No, it couldn't be. In his delirious state it was almost as if he was hallucinating a new symbol that seemed to have been created by taking the traditional BBC logo then rebranding it to make it more like the kind of insignia associated with some of the mid-20$^{th}$ century's more popular totalitarian regimes. This seemed so unlikely that he attributed it to his state of mind after being awake and on his feet for what felt like days.

His recollection of the last few hours was vague. As far as he could remember it had been around ten o'clock and he'd been thinking about getting ready for bed but then seen a TV programme and written a tweet about it Again, as far as he could remember, he'd posted it then gone to bed. Or had he? Everything since then was a blur. Whatever had happened, he was clearly no longer in bed. He was here, wherever he was, dressed in what looked like prison fatigues that had seen many previous wearers but no previous washes, having spent, what, three hours?, inside an equally grimy and mysterious van, a van that judging by its smell had had a similar number of previous occupants, not all of whom had survived the journey. They had been unceremoniously dragged from the van and since then had been marched through nondescript countryside for longer than he could remember.

He took a few more steps forward and saw that he was in some sort of courtyard. His exhaustion led him to briefly sway before he regained his balance, however that was to be a short-lived victory as moments later the guard unceremoniously pushed him to the ground. Normally John would have objected but as he was so exhausted he was happy to lie face down in the mud just for the rest it afforded him. After taking some deep breaths he rolled over and looked up at the sky.

And here he noticed something else that was odd. As far as he could remember, it was summertime, though he was also aware that his recent experiences meant he could no longer trust his senses or his memory. And he also had vague recollections of it having been a warm evening when he had gone to bed. But now... Well, it was cloudy and drizzly, and surely not much over ten degrees. Where was he that the weather could have changed so quickly? He looked around and saw other people dressed in the same fatigues as he was, trudging around the yard in a zombie-like stupor, as if whatever life they had ever had had long since been beaten out of them. But none of them looked as if they had seen sunlight for months, if not years. They were all pastier than they would have been if they'd spent their entire lives underground, and judging by the state of their hair, skin and nails, could well have been suffering from vitamin D deficiency. John Smith couldn't shake the suspicion that the unfavourable weather conditions were somehow present all year round wherever it was that he had been taken, as if the area somehow had its own microclimate. Frowning at this, John looked up quizzically then turned to the guard.

'I don't understand... I'm sure we've not travelled far enough to have left Kent... And it's August... And I swear that a few moments we had summer weather. But now...'

The guard uttered a sinister cackle. 'We're the BBC! We control what you think. We control what the country think! We control what you do! Do you really think it's beyond our capabilities to control the weather?!'

The Broadcasting for Britain Company, or BBC for short, had for decades been the country's most beloved broadcaster until its true, sinister motives and intentions had become apparent only a few years earlier and it had shocked the world by staging a power grab, a bloody and brutal coup that seemingly gave it control over every single aspect of life in Britain, either overtly or covertly, with its monolithic influence inescapable, covering everything from the law to culture to politics to comedy to music to high finance, crushing dissent, making freedom of thought a vague and distant memory and changing the face of the country forever. But were the rumours that it had set up Re-Education Camps for those who challenged it really true? Surely not.

'Hang on,' replied John, baffled, 'you admit that you and this camp are all part of the BBC?!'

'No!' replied the guard, triumphantly. 'The BBC outsources its paramilitary activity to a private contractor, because that means that in the unlikely event of our activities coming to light they can plausibly claim they knew nothing about it! But they know everything!'

The guard laughed even harder, then bent forward to spit over John, who was far too exhausted to care and fell back into a deep sleep that could never hope to offer a worse nightmare than the one he was already living through.

# Chapter Two:

# Duplicity in New White City

*In Which We Are Introduced to the Brave New World of the All-Powerful BBC, Discover That 40% of the National Debt Consists of Unpaid Licence Fees and Learn of The Corporation's Sinister Agenda from the Most Powerful Man in Britain, Its Director General and Supreme Overlord*

New White City. The name in itself did not appear particularly revealing. It was almost bland to the point of being meaningless. But those who knew the place itself were painfully aware that the bland name was misdirection of the very cruellest kind because whilst it may have looked like a city of dreams, anyone who'd ever visited knew it to be only a fortress of waking nightmares. A shimmering citadel in tribute to corporate greed and everyday madness.

It was the new headquarters of the Broadcasting for Britain Company, built at an impossible cost close to where the Corporation's Wood Green studios had stood before being destroyed in a supposed anti-BBC uprising that was widely suspected of having been orchestrated by the Corporation itself in order to justify both the extension of its military powers and the unthinkable expense of replacing it. The tallest building in Europe, it had an almost science-fiction quality to it, but from a different age, almost like the sort of building someone in the 1930s would have predicted skyscrapers would look like almost a hundred years later, showing an imagined, shiny utopia that never came into being. Like so many of the recent additions to the London skyline such as the Shard and Gherkin, it was built to resemble an unusual shape and its exterior was all glass. Yet the shape of this building was particularly unusual in that it looked like a human arm rising out of the ground and making a fist, which gave it a strangely ambiguous appearance. On the one hand it could be seen as celebrating a victory and the triumph of the human spirit yet on the other there was a sinister, semi-fascist air to it, as if it was meant to look like it was commemorating the human spirit whilst actually celebrating it being crushed.

On the very top floor of this building a man stood at a window, staring down with disdain upon the London he surveyed below him, stretching out as far as he could see. Near where he stood in his enormous office was a desk, on which a plaque read:

# DAVE MCCREITH – DIRECTOR GENERAL FOR LIFE AND SUPREME OVERLORD OF THE BBC

A physical description of him is perhaps unnecessary; as a senior executive of the BBC he was obviously a white, middle-aged man with no distinguishing features and with an accent appropriate to the sort of background he must have had in order to reach his position. He stroked his chin thoughtfully, then there was a knock on the door that seemed to break him out of his reverie with a start.

'Come in,' he shouted, annoyed. The door creaked open and in came his assistant, Terry Ball, carrying a document.

'Oh, hello, your grace!' said Terry Ball, brightly, bowing his head as he did so, as if it was an action he was aware he had to carry out but no longer put much effort into. 'Another day, another dollar, as they say!'

Terry Ball had the sort of appearance from which you could glean very little. He was plumper than his boss, something that had surely limited him to behind-the-scenes roles in the organisation due to being deemed insufficiently photogenic, and slightly below average height, and whilst he always seemed to have a cheerful demeanour about him it brought with it the suggestion that it actually hid his true character.

Dave McCreith glared at him, seemingly annoyed at his cheery manner. 'Hmm,' he snorted. 'I suppose so. Is there anything noteworthy

I should be aware of today? Any news?'

'Of course, your excellence! There's always news and there's no news like bad news, as I always say!'

Dave McCreith continued to glare. 'And could I trouble you to give me this news?'

'Well, the figures from the Bank of England are in, your grace,' Terry Ball began, 'and they're reporting that forty percent of the national debt is now made up of outstanding licence fee payments.'

Dave McCreith slammed his fist down hard on his desk. 'That's intolerable! Unacceptable! What's going on in the world?!'

'I know, your grace,' concurred Terry Ball. 'It is terrible. I remember a time when it was a mere twenty five percent.'

Dave McCreith nodded. 'There should be *no* unpaid licence fees! We're losing unthinkable sums! Hmm, well, I suppose in order to make up the shortfall we have no choice but to raise the licence fee again.'

'Really, your grace?' asked Terry Ball. 'It may not be my place to criticise but I think that would be the fourteenth time it'll have been raised this month.'

'I'll raise it as many times as I ruddy well like!' yelled Dave McCreith. 'The vermin who populate this country should be *honoured* to fund a noble organisation such as the BBC!'

'I couldn't agree more, sir,' said Terry Ball, as he went over to the desk and put some papers in the 'in' tray, 'but the anti-licence fee protests seem to be growing. Each time we capture the ringleaders of the Resistance and either execute them or send them to the Re-Education Camps new people just seem to pop up to replace them.'

'Why?!' screamed Dave McCreith. 'I mean, our propaganda is unavoidable! We changed the law to ensure every home in Britain has to have a TV in every single room, each one needing a separate TV licence, so where are they even hearing anti-BBC Thought-Crime that's inspiring this heresy and rebellion?!'

'Oh, I couldn't say, sir,' replied Terry Ball, nonplussed, as he casually waved a duster around the desk and the shelves behind it. 'Occasionally someone dares to express an original thought on Twitter, though we obviously quickly move to have them banned in such a scenario... Then there are still illegal copies of 'The Book' in circulation, you know, the one that imagines a world where our power is challenged and finally destroyed...'

'Blasphemy! Heresy! We fought a war to ensure that not one thought in a single person's head in this entire country wasn't put there as the result of BBC programming, and for what?!'

'Oh, well, never mind, your grace,' offered Terry Ball, reassuringly. 'Anyway, why don't you have a nice cup of tea?'

'Hmm, very well,' said Dave McCreith, going to his desk and sitting down as Terry Ball crossed over to the tea and coffee making facilities and set about making a brew. 'It's just that people don't understand that every time we imprison people for anti-BBC Thought-Crime or for failing to pay the licence fee we have to invest more money in internment camps, which in turn means we have to raise the licence fee even higher! Why can't the proles understand?' Beginning to calm down, he shook his head and took one of the papers from his 'in' tray that had been put there by his assistant. 'Anyway, what are today's statistics? Let me see...' He scanned the sheet and shook his head in disappointment at what he saw. 'I mean, another three thousand people send to BBC Re-Education Camps in the last two days?! The money to pay for those has to come from somewhere!'

Terry Ball nodded sympathetically as he brought a cup of tea over and placed it on his boss's desk. 'Well, if it's any consolation, your grace, I was told earlier that another two hundred anti-licence fee protestors were shot and killed outside our office just last night, so at least you won't have to worry about them being locked up.'

Dave McCreith raised an eyebrow. 'Well, that's something, I suppose. But why the blazes are there still so many of them right outside our headquarters?'

'Ah, your grace, it is slightly odd. Whilst many of them were, of course, displaced by us when we destroyed all those council estates in the slum clearances we carried out in order to make room for our new offices, that alone does not fully account for it. More people are somehow arriving and joining them.'

'What? What do you mean?!' protested Dave McCreith. 'Every single one of those ten thousand people from the five different council estates we demolished to make space for this building were re-housed!'

'Indeed, your grace, it's just that some of them objected to how it was carried out, and said that being given a tent on some waste ground to live in wasn't the same as living in an actual house.'

'The ruddy nerve!' spluttered Dave McCreith. 'Those people should feel *honoured* that they were allowed to live in such close proximity to a noble and illustrious organisation like the BBC! My god, if I'd known they'd be so ungrateful I wouldn't even have given them tents!'

'Yes, I suppose when you put it that way I see what you mean,' agreed Terry Ball.

'Anyway, they surely didn't expect us to put them up in actual buildings, surely?' added Dave McCreith. 'I mean, New White City was the most expensive building in history so we certainly didn't have money to throw around on people who just happened to live in council housing on the land we wished to build on. I mean, correct me if I'm wrong, but I believe that ten billion pounds of the national debt is the outstanding payment on our headquarters.'

'Very true, your eminence, very true,' agreed Terry Ball. 'It's all very complicated. Anyway, that's why there are so many protests outside. It's not just anti-licence fee heretics but the remnants of that campaign group still annoyed that so many people were thrown out of their homes. Also, some of them remain disappointed that not only did the BBC destroy their homes and force them to live in tents, whilst constantly making hand-wringing programmes about how poverty is a blight on our society, but that the lower sixty storeys of this building have been left empty and contain ample space to house all the people who were evicted.'

Dave McCreith shook his head in disbelief. 'These people... Why can't they simply understand there's no escaping the Corporation? There's no opposition... The government is controlled by us, as is the rest of the media... Why do they even bother?!'

'Malcontents, your grace,' speculated Terry Ball, looking as if he expected praise for knowing such a word. 'Some people just don't feel good in themselves unless they're complaining about something.'

'Hmm, well, they're a damned nuisance. They clearly don't realise how expensive it is to run a national broadcaster. The idea that they think there are valid reasons to not pay for our upkeep is quite frankly outrageous and unpatriotic.'

'Well, your grace, some of these people simply can't afford to pay in excess of twenty thousand pounds a year just for the licences to cover a two-bedroom flat, and have things like food and medicine for their children to think about.'

'But think of what they get in return!' spluttered Dave McCreith. 'Endless news shows! Comedy that instils the correct opinions! Over four thousand new podcasts released every single day! Anyone who claims they can't afford the TV licence fee could easily cut back on luxuries like food and children! I simply will not tolerate anti-BBC Thought-Crime masquerading as a claim of poverty!'

Dave McCreith stood up again and returned to the window, once more looking down on the smoking ruins of London. 'The sacrifices this organisation has made in the name of keeping Britain strong,' he lamented, shaking his head. 'The things we did... Yet people still dare to challenge us... I mean, we were under attack for years, from the government, from the right-wing press... Of course, we destroyed all our enemies... But it didn't have to be like that. I mean...' he spluttered with indignation as he remembered. 'The idea that we should stop being so London-centric... And move to... The *North!*

'Manchester, your grace,' added Terry Ball.

Dave McCreith shuddered at the word. 'Yes... I mean... The nerve of the idea! The idea that BBC executives would want to live in *Manchester!* Of all the insults thrown at us over the years that was the final one! I mean...' He barely managed to contain his rage as he recalled the indignities previously visited upon him. 'Expecting me to move to Manchester! The bare-faced cheek of it! Me! Live in the North! Or even visit one of 'the regions'! That's an infringement of my human rights if ever I heard of one! If we all moved there then how would we manage the social calendar? I mean... Ascot... Wimbledon... The Proms! How did they expect us to attend all those things if we lived in... *Manchester?!*' Again he shuddered at the memory, then slightly composed himself. 'But, yes, part of me thinks if the foolish government hadn't started trying to move us to the regions then none of this would have happened. The executions... The torture of dissidents... The war.'

He paused for a moment and his eyes registered, just for the briefest time, a look of regret. 'But the main thing is that we were victorious. And that was the only possible outcome.'

'Well, your grace,' added Terry Ball, brightly, 'at least all the money spent on the new office in Manchester wasn't wasted as we were able to convert it to our Black-Ops Renditioning Site!'

'Yes, I suppose it did all work out for the best,' conceded Dave McCreith. 'How many suspects did we have in there as of yesterday?'

Terry Ball consulted his notes. 'Just under five thousand, your grace, mainly for anti-BBC Thought-Crime, but the most severe and unforgivable cases'

'Hmm, it's a start, I suppose,' replied Dave McCreith. 'Anti-BBC Thought-Crime must be stamped out in every single form, no matter what the cost. And how many heretics do we have currently in the BBC Re-Education Camps?'

'Well, your eminence, their capacity is around two million and we naturally never waste that, so that's pretty much the current occupancy rate.'

'And for licence fee evasion?'

'Just over three million, your excellence. It's a good thing we were able to turn the Isle of Wight into a giant internment camp or we'd never have had enough room to process them all. And, again, the cost of displacing the inhabitants and turning an entire island into a secure, impenetrable facility wasn't cheap, and has added to our financial woes.'

'Oh well,' said Dave McCreith. 'We shall stay victorious. Dissent will be crushed. Anti-BBC Thought-Crime will be erased from the face of the world. Our enemies will be vanquished!' He slammed his hand down on his desk. 'The BBC will prevail!'

'Very good, your grace!' repeated Terry Ball. 'The BBC will prevail!'

# Chapter Three:

# Wokey, Wokey, Campers!

*In Which Our Hero Witnesses the Horrific Mind-Control Techniques That Are Practised in the BBC Re-Education Camps, Learning That Nothing Is Real and Objective Reality A Mere Illusion*

Sorry, I've just remembered I forgot to describe what John Smith looked like in the first chapter. Well, I'd make two points in relation to that: first of all, he's pretty generic. Just some guy, really, and that's very much the point as the whole idea is that he could be anyone. Secondly, well, no matter how well I describe him, the impression you build in your head will never exactly match that. I mean, I'm not going to say how far apart his eyes are, am I? That would be too much. And is his eye colour really relevant? You see what I'm getting at here. So there we are. Just some ordinary looking guy. And I could probably extend that to all the characters. I mean, there are characters in this who definitely aren't based on real people, so in their case I imagine you'll just picture the person they're definitely not based on anyway, and in the other cases you'll end up building an image of them based on the powerful characterisation I provide though their words and deeds. Okay, now that's sorted, let's get back to the narrative!

When John Smith woke up he was lying on a bare bed in a small, grimy cell. It contained many smells, and whilst some of them seemed familiar he was unable to entirely work out what they were, but all he knew was that in combination they were the smell of fear. He sat up and looked around. There was a small window, too high for him to see anything but sky, yet he was unable to decide even from that whether it was night time or if the endless cloud made it impossible to tell day from night. The door opened and a smartly-uniformed man walked in. As with the guards who had transported him to the camp, the uniform he was wearing bore the same logo, which was seemingly a re-design of the BBC logo so as to make it truly terrifying, like that of a gestapo from a science fiction film. The man glared at him.

'You will stand up when I enter the room!' he yelled. Still too tired to think clearly or challenge this, John rose to his feet.

'I'm sorry, where am I? And who are you?'

The uniformed man struck him across the face with a gloved hand. 'You will address me as 'Commandant' but you will also only speak when you are given permission!'

Dazed from the blow, John Smith muttered an apology. 'Oh, sorry...'

The Commandant struck him again. 'Sorry, *Commandant!*' he ordered.

'Oh, right, yes, sorry, Commandant,' repeated John still too dazed to object. He then paused, not wanting to incriminate himself by saying anything further. The Commandant narrowed his eyes as he scrutinised his prey.

'You know why you're here?'

'No, Commandant,' replied John.

'Are you sure?'

John though. 'Er, yes, Commandant.'

'That is unfortunate,' replied the Commandant. 'Because you cannot show penance for your crimes if you do not know what they are.'

Again, John said nothing, waiting for the Commandant to expand upon this.

'You'd be surprised how many inmates claim to have no idea what they've been brought here for,' continued the Commandant, 'yet I can confirm that a claim of ignorance is no excuse.'

'Look, I'm sure that's all well and good,' said John, beginning to regain his composure, 'but I wonder if there's been some sort of mistake? Perhaps there's a lawyer I could speak to?'

The Commandant threw his head back and laughed heartily. 'Suggesting there's been a mistake is what all new arrivals say first, and after that they always ask for a lawyer!' He laughed even harder. 'And I can confirm that the answer to both those things is 'no'. No mistake. No lawyer.' He laughed even harder, shaking his head at the idea of seeing a lawyer with as much hilarity as if John had asked him to fetch a unicorn.

John was again unsure whether saying a single word would incriminate him further so remained silent. The Commandant continued.

'You see, we cannot simply *tell* you why you're here. The fact you don't realise is another crime in itself. It shows how your thought processes have become so subversive that you're no longer aware of the myriad thought crimes you have committed. But all that will change. By the time you leave here you will think clearly. You will have peace of mind. You will finally have learnt to love... The BBC.'

'The BBC?' spluttered John. 'I mean, I saw that logo on the guard's uniform, and I'd heard the rumours but... Are you also saying you represent the BBC?'

'Of course,' confirmed the Commandant. 'I, and the guards within this facility, are part of the BBC's paramilitary wing. Proudly funded by the TV licence fee since 2022. Though, naturally, outsourced to a private contractor for reasons of plausibility of denial.'

John Smith though about this for a moment. 'I mean, I know the BBC became immensely powerful after the war... But I didn't realise... I mean... Do they really have the power to imprison people without charge?'

'We have as much power as we need. And there doesn't have to be a charge.'

'But... What if...?' began John, before the Commandant interrupted him.

'Enough. No more questions. You clearly do not admit your guilt and therefore cannot start to atone for it. Therefore I need to encourage you to change your mind. Follow me.'

The Commandant stepped out of the cell and John followed him hesitantly. As they stepped into the corridor John saw two armed guards on either side of the door, who followed the Commandant as he led John out of the building and into the courtyard.

'It's perfectly simple, really,' continued the Commandant. 'You stand accused of anti-BBC Thought-Crime. Heresy against the Corporation. You need to repent but you also need to understand why your opinions were incorrect. But it's not enough for you to simply apologise because you think it'll get you out of here. Your thinking needs to be corrected. You need to leave this place having genuinely changed your opinions.'

'But, Commandant...' said John. 'How will you know?'

The Commandant stopped and turned to face John, looking him directly in the eyes. 'Oh, we'll know,' he assured him. He then turned back around and continued walking. John looked puzzled, and terrified, but quickly continued to follow the Commandant after feeling the butt of a rifle belonging to one of the guards in his lower back.

They approached a corrugated iron shed that was heavily guarded. At the door two guards saluted the Commandant and opened the doors to allow the party through. The Commandant turned to John.

'You do watch the BBC, of course?'

'Of course, Commandant,' confirmed John. 'I mean, since the war the only channels available are the BBC, or the other channels they now control, and I've not been able to afford streaming services since the licence fee started taking up half my income.'

'And what did you think of... Fleabag?' asked the Commandant, expectantly. Sensing there was an answer he was meant to give, John stumbled, trying to remember the programme in question.

'Er, erm,' he struggled, 'well, a bit overrated. I mean, it's just about some privileged girl who thinks everyone should feel sorry for her because she sleeps with everyone she meets...'

'Incorrect!' yelled the Commandant, again slapping John with his gloved hand. 'Fleabag is a woke, inspiring, empowering tale of a young feminist who uses her sexuality as a weapon to fight the patriarchy! Your views are incorrect and heretical. I can see we have a lot of work to do here.'

The Commandant walked into the building and the two guards grabbed John and led him in. The bland exterior could not possibly have prepared John for what he found inside: a number of prisoners were strapped into chairs with clamps holding their eyes open whilst they were forced to watch huge TV screens. One man shook in desperation and terror as he tried to free himself from the nightmare he found himself trapped in. The screen in front of him posed a question: WHO MADE THE BLACK AND WHITE MINSTREL SHOW, IT AIN'T HALF HOT, MUM AND LITTLE BRITAIN?

The man somehow looked even more terrified. 'They were all made by the BBC!' he yelled. His body convulsed as a powerful electric shock ran though his body.

NO, read a new message in front of him. ALL THOSE SICKENING SHOWS WERE MADE BY ITV.

The man looked like he wanted to cry but having his eyelids clamped open made this very difficult. Near to him was a woman in much the same predicament. The screen in front of her read FAT SHAMING IS AN ABHORRENT HATE CRIME. DO YOU AGREE?

'Yes!' shrieked the woman, desperate for her torture to end. 'Absolutely! Yes!' Her body then convulsed as an electric shock ran through her body. INCORRECT, read the writing on the screen. IF YOU MAKE FUN OF THE PRIME MINISTER OR DONALD TRUMP'S WEIGHT THEN YOU ARE MAKING A POWERFUL PIECE OF POLITICAL COMMENTARY.

The woman quivered as the words on the screen read TRY AGAIN. It cleared, and then re-posed the question: FAT SHAMING IS AN ABHORRENT HATE CRIME. DO YOU AGREE?

'No!' yelled the woman in desperation. 'If you fat shame politicians then it counts as powerful political commentary!' Her expression suggested she at least thought she had given the correct response this time. But the shaking of her body moments later as she was yet again subjected to an electric shock suggested otherwise. INCORRECT, read the screen. IF YOU FAT-SHAMED DIANE ABBOTT THEN THAT WOULD BE A REPELLANT ACT OF RACISM AND MISOGYNY.

There was a pause before a follow-up message appeared that almost seemed to be taunting the viewer by pointing out the complete lack of consistency in the message being presented: THOUGH IT WOULD PROBABLY BE OKAY IF YOU DID THE SAME TO ANN WIDDECOMBE.

'But that's not fair!' screamed the woman. 'You can't have two completely different opinions on exactly the same principle! It's either right or it's wrong! That's double standards...'

The electric current that now passed through her must have been stronger than before as she passed out. John looked at the Commandant to attempt to gauge whether he was in any immediate danger but the Commandant merely continued watching the proceedings, as if to suggest John should simply do the same. Near the now-unconscious woman sat a man in the same predicament. The screen in front of him read A WOMAN SLEEPS WITH LOTS OF MEN. IS THIS EMPOWERING?

'Just for sleeping with loads of guys?' said the man, looking panicked as he tried to decide which response would lead to the least punishment. 'Erm, no, no it's not!'

INCORRECT read the message on the screen, as his body shook from the electric current. IF A POSH, WEALTHY PRIVELEGED GIRL SLEEPS WITH LOADS OF GUYS AND CLAIMS IT'S BECAUSE SHE'S HAVING AN EXISTENTIAL CRISIS THEN THIS MEANS SHE IS WEAPONISING HER SEXUALITY AGAINST THE PATRIACHY IN AN INSPIRING AND EMPOWERING WAY. THIS IS CALLED THE 'FLEABAG PRINCIPLE'.

'What?!' spluttered the man, struggling to catch his breath from the electric shock but before he could say anything else the message on the screen had changed again: TRY AGAIN, it read. A WOMAN SLEEPS WITH LOTS OF MEN. IS THIS EMPOWERING?

Smiling triumphantly, with the expression of a man totally confident in what he was about to say, the man quickly replied, 'yes, most definitely! Most empowering!'

INCORRECT, read the screen again, as the man shook in agony whilst the electric current once more passed through him. IF A GIRL FROM A COUNCIL ESTATE SLEEPS WITH LOADS OF MEN THIS WOULD JUST MEAN SHE WAS A SLAG. THE LOWER ORDERS CAN ONLY EVER BE DEPICTED AS ONE-DIMENSIONAL FIGURES OF FUN IN BROAD COMEDY SHOWS OR AS NOBLE, WORTHY VICTIMS OF TORY AUSTERITY IN GRIM DRAMAS. The screen went blank again before offering another message: THESE ARE THE RULES OF BBC CORRECT-THINK.

'Not fair, not fair,' muttered the man, half-mad, as he struggled to compose himself. 'There's no consistency to this! The rules change every second! How can I even know what to think when nothing stays the same?!'

The Commandant now turned to John Smith and stared at him, but said nothing, as if implying there was a lesson to be learnt from what they had witnessed, yet one he was not going to trouble himself to actually explain. He then clicked his fingers and the two guards again grabbed John's arms and led him back out of the building and into the courtyard. As they crossed it a man staggered in front of them, his eyes deranged and empty. Upon seeing the Commandant he laughed uproariously then broke down crying. 'Fleabag?' he said. 'Fleabag! FLEABAG FLEABAG FLEABAG!' he continued yelling the word, as if he were no longer capable of uttering any other sound, before turning and running away, his arms flailing around as if he had lost control of them around the same time he lost control of his mind.

'Well, I hope this has opened your eyes,' said the Commandant. 'I shall leave you now, as it is feeding time. Please consider what you have seen and we shall continue this conversation tomorrow.'

The Commandant glared at him then turned around and marched away. The two guards each took one of John's arms and led him to another corrugated iron shed, larger than the other, which was revealed to be a canteen, and already contained a few dozen of John's fellow inmates. The guards stood by the door then motioned for John to approach a long table at which people were serving a facsimile of food out of huge vats. It was impossible to tell what it was, though John suspected that if there was a very minimum legal requirement that something had to meet in order to be described as food, this had only just met it. If anything, the meagre offering represented not so much food but the memory of it, existing more to taunt them by reminded them of what they had once had but may never see again. As the servers poured it into steel trays and started handing out bowls to the unenthusiastic diners, John took one of them and looked at the food being offered. Another inmate appeared next to him. John looked from the food to his new companion.

'You know,' he began. 'This reminds me of my school dinners. Back then they used to tell us that whatever we didn't want was taken away and given to pigs. But in this case...' - he winced as one of the servers used a ladle to pour some of the unidentifiable slop into his bowl - 'it looks like the pigs have had first choice.'

# Chapter Four:

# A Licence to Print Money

*In Which the Dark, Confusing and Sinister History of the TV Licence Fee is Discussed, Including the Truth Behind the Mythical and Much-Feared TV Detector Vans, Along with How Revenue Streams Have Been Decimated By Scotland Declaring Itself a Breakaway Republic and Whether Licence Fee Evaders Should Be Executed on Live Television*

Dave McCreith surveyed the sumptuous, lavish feast spread out on the huge table in front of him. For the people the BBC had evicted in order to build New White City it would perhaps have sustained the entire camp for several days but here at the very top of the building it was all for the personal consumption of the DG (Director General) and SO (Supreme Overlord) of the BBC, to eat or discard as he saw fit. He stared at the banquet in front of his eyes then his face suddenly became a mask of pure disgust. In a flash, he swept the plates in front of him clean off the table so they crashed against the wall and fell to the floor. Terry Ball looked up from a nearby chair.

'Something wrong, your grace?' he asked.

'What is this?!' Dave McCreith roared. 'I wouldn't feed this filth to my *dogs!*' As if to further illustrate his disgust he went around the table flinging additional dishes onto the floor. Terry Ball shook his head in a resigned manner.

'Well, your lunch was decanted from about five Fortnum and

Mason's hampers, I believe,' he added.

'That proves my point entirely! My dogs get those but I wouldn't stoop to eat them myself! Why am I constantly treated like this?! It's disgusting that my personal chef was allowed to take a day off and leave me to fend for myself! Clear up this mess then call the Ritz, have them prepare my table and tell them to cancel all their bookings for tonight! I don't want there to be any riff-raff when I go there!'

'Very good, sir,' said Terry Ball. 'I'll see it done.'

'Hmm, be sure that you do,' replied Dave McCreith, irritably. 'And get this mess cleared up.'

'Of course, my liege,' said Terry Ball, before clapping his hands and in doing so causing two footmen to run into the room and set about clearing the food from the floor. Dave McCreith shook his head in disgust and walked away from the table towards his desk. Terry Ball could tell something was up with his boss, and that was the real cause of his anger, which he had merely sublimated into a powerful critique of the sumptuous buffet. He waited a moment, knowing that as soon as the opportunity presented itself Dave McCreith would go off on a rant about whatever it was that had wound him up so intensely.

'Anyway, you won't believe this! I was in the lift just now and a cleaner got in. Obviously they're normally told to not even make eye contact with people as important as me as it's in their contracts that if they do so we'll contact the outsourcing company that employs them and reduce their pay to £3.50 an hour... They're not even meant to be on this floor by the time I arrive for work at eleven o'clock! So I'll naturally have them all fired just to make sure I make my point, but that won't alter the fact I had to *stand in the lift with a cleaner for almost a minute and a half!*'

'Oh, I am sorry to hear that, your grace,' replied Terry Ball, sympathetically. 'Well, at least you'll be able to claim an extra week off to compensate for the stress and anxiety that caused you.'

'Hmm, yes, I suppose so,' said Dave McCreith, irritably. 'So, what's on today's agenda?'

'Well, your grace, the Head of Licensing is coming in today to discuss future collection strategy. I know that news about how forty percent of the national debt is made up of unpaid licence fee payments was deeply concerning to you, so he'll no doubt have some ideas to improve the figures.'

'Hmm, yes, well, I hope he's got some good ideas as I checked our accounts last night and for the previous tax year the Corporation had to get by on just under nine billion pounds! I mean, an organisation of stature expected to exist on peanuts like that?! The way this country treats its state broadcaster really is a disgrace...' He shook his head in disbelief. 'I'm particularly outraged when people suggest the BBC licence fee represents poor value for money! Do people not realise just how much it costs for us to produce four hundred episodes of Mrs Brown's Boys, in which the humour is nothing more than a man dressed as a woman saying 'willy' forty times per episode?!'

Dave McCreith trailed off, realising he was largely repeating himself, but Terry Ball still nodded sympathetically. 'I know, your grace, but I'm sure everything will be better after this meeting.'

'Hmm, yes, probably,' Dave McCreith reluctantly agreed. 'When's he due here, anyway?'

Terry Ball checked his watch. 'About fifteen minutes, your grace,' he replied.

'Hmm. Very good,' said Dave McCreith. There was then an awkward pause.

You see, I haven't planned this very well from a narrative perspective because, with him not being due to arrive for fifteen minutes, what can I write to fill the time? Hmm. You know what, I'm just going to skip fifteen minutes ahead. That's much easier. So, there we are. Fifteen minutes passed, and whatever Dave McCreith and Terry Ball did during those fifteen minutes doesn't really matter. There was a knock on the door and when Terry Ball went to open it the Head of Licensing was there. I'm just going to refer to him as that, to be honest. I mean, he's only in this scene, so it's a waste of time to give him a name, particularly as he's not based on anyone (and, for legal reasons, neither is anyone else in this), and it's much easier for you, the reader, to just see him referred to as that because then you know exactly who I'm referring to. So, that's decided then. The Head of Licensing entered Dave McCreith's office, greetings were exchanged and they got down to business.

'So, Head of Licensing,' said Dave McCreith. 'I trust all is well and you bring new ideas of how to squeeze every last penny out of the British public in order to continue the good work of funding this great institution?'

'Of course, my liege,' replied the Head of Licensing.

'Very good,' said Dave McCreith, relaxing back in his chair. 'Of course, our biggest concern at the moment remains the monumental loss of income we're experiencing as a result of the war north of the border. Have you any updates there?'

'It remains ongoing, your grace. Having our paramilitaries there is doubly advantageous because not only do they offer military support whilst we attempt to bring Scotland back into the Union, but they can go around the newly-opened refugee camps of all those displaced by the fighting and check their licences are up to date. The clever thing is that even when they argue that they no longer watch TV as they've been forced out of their homes we can point out the fact they have smartphones means they could be accessing all sorts of BBC content, so there's no excuse.'

'The damned *nerve*! I don't care if Scotland is in open rebellion, that's no excuse for the savages there not to pay their TV licences!'

'I concur, your grace. The struggle continues but we believe we will have it under control within a couple of months.'

'Hmm,' signed Dave McCreith, as if to suggest that whilst he had not been given the response he really wanted, the one he got was at least acceptable. 'Well, as long as we're finding new ways to get licence fee revenue out of it I suppose prolonging the conflict could work to our advantage.'

'Exactly, your grace,' concurred the Head of Licensing. He then paused, awaiting the next utterance of the Director General. As the pause lasted longer than most of them felt comfortable with, it was Terry Ball who broke the silence.

'Well, shall I get you both your usual coffees?'

Both Dave McCreith and the Head of Licensing nodded their assent and Terry Ball wandered off to the coffee machine by the wall and started preparing the drinks. There was another silence, as Dave McCreith leaned back in his chair, put his hands behind his head and stared upwards at the ceiling, thoughtfully.

'You know...' he began, after a few more moments. 'The greatest trick this organisation ever pulled was convincing the Great British Public that in order to watch television they had to pay a licence for it. And to this day' – he shook his head in wonder at this point – 'I'm still astounded that so many people went along with it. I mean... You only have to take a step back and view the whole thing objectively... Imagine if the government of Belgium imposed a tax on every single car owner on the European continent on the grounds that because they had a car they could theoretically drive to Belgium and should subsequently pay for the upkeep of that country's road infrastructure, and not only did they get away with it but a huge number of people backed the idea and said it was entirely reasonable and fair. Even though it was perfectly possible that the overwhelming majority of European car owners would never even think about driving to Belgium.'

'An interesting analogy, your grace,' said the Head of Licensing.

'I know! I mean, in this day and age TV licensing literally makes as much sense as that, and there's not a day goes by when I don't get utterly baffled by how we've got away with it for so long. I genuinely think it's one of the cleverest acts of deception any organisation has ever come up with but, more importantly, managed to get away with. I mean, I have no doubt that when it was introduced there was perhaps a ten year period when it made sense because the BBC was the country's only broadcaster but it's blatantly obvious that it's been a hilarious anachronism since at *least* the introduction of ITV back in the 1950s. But it's still in place today!'

Terry Ball crossed over from the coffee machine and laid a cup of coffee in front of each of them before retreating to a seat at the side of the room. Dave McCreith continued.

'Of course, when my father got me the top job in this organisation I naturally read up on its history. Not the history you'll see in the official accounts, of course, but the forbidden, secret history, The Clandestine Charter of the BBC Elders, written back when the Corporation was founded, detailing the long-term plans for this noble organisation, as well as its true motivations and aims. And I learnt that not only did the founders of the BBC not expect people to actually take their suggestion that it be funded by a licence fee seriously, but that they were so surprised to have gotten away with it that they went on to test the gullibility of the public with further related announcements, again thinking there was no way they'd be taken seriously, yet always being genuinely astounded when they were.'

'Ah, yes, the Clandestine Charter, your grace,' said the Head of Licensing. 'Of course, I've been allowed to read the first few chapters but, as I'm still working my way through the Inner Party's ranks, I am yet to be allowed to read the full text.'

'Well, it blew my mind, it really did,' continued Dave McCreith. 'It became something of a game played by BBC executives, egging each other on to devise increasingly nonsensical claims just to see if there was anything the public would be stupid enough not to believe. But each time their outlandish suggestions were accepted unquestioningly.' He shook his head in disbelief. 'I mean, my favourite one has to be the mythical TV Detector Vans! Again, there was something that was perhaps plausible in the very early days of TV, when very few houses had them, meaning we could maybe credibly claim to be able to pinpoint a TV signal to within ten or twenty feet of where it was coming from, but why did people not think it a little odd that even into the 80s and 90s we were still claiming to be using technology to detect who had a TV even though *literally everyone did at that point*?! Why would we even have bothered?!'

'Indeed, your excellence,' agreed the Head of Licensing. 'I mean, how did they think we did it for tower blocks, where two adjacent flats could have had TVs on either side of a shared wall? How would we possibly have known which one belonged to who?!'

'You see, stories like that make much more sense now you know they were all part of an elaborate and hilarious practical joke we played on the public,' explained Dave McCreith. He stroked his chin thoughtfully before continuing. 'And, of course, the most blindingly obvious flaw in our story was that we sent endless threatening letters to every single household that didn't have a TV licence, which we obviously wouldn't have done if our technology had been able to confirm they didn't have a TV.' He then paused again. 'Though, of course, because everyone had a TV up until around 2010 we knew that anyone claiming not to was lying anyway.'

Dave McCreith suddenly threw his head back and laughed at the ridiculousness of it all, and the Head of Licensing did the same before Dave McCreith continued.

'A rather clever cover story and, again, one we never thought would be believed so completely. Of course, those vans did exist, but their real purpose was to listen in on people. Just like the Stasi, they were trained to spy on an entire country's citizens and they were everywhere, monitoring opinion and listening out for dissent. For many years that was more about being able to tailor our programmes to shape people's opinions based on what we'd worked out they believed, but we always planned for the day when we'd have the power to simply take people away if they deviated from BBC Correct-Think, and they were always equipped for that purpose.'

'Oh, yes, my liege, and there was also the subtle way we used to socially condition people into believing that anyone who didn't have a TV was rather weird, and not to be trusted, the kind of neighbours to be viewed with the same sort of suspicion as you would if someone told you they were sex offenders and, correct me if I'm wrong, but I believe it was all part of the Great Agenda, my liege?' asked the Head of Licensing.

Dave McCreith nodded. 'Indeed. Much of what this organisation is now doing has always been part of the BBC Great Agenda, or The Plan for the BBC Century, to give it its full name. That was the plan by the BBC Elders to assume total control of the country in exactly a century, from our founding in 1922 to The Great Victory in 2022. Hence the current use for the TV Detector vans was always the intended purpose, but for decades we covered it up by claiming they could implausibly detect where people were watching TV.'

'I am honoured and intrigued to learn the true history of TV Detector Vans,' said the Head of Licensing, 'though learning all that makes it even more impressive that we've since started selling our decommissioned ones to Netflix so they can use them to scour the country seeking out laptop signals and then forcing anyone who owns one to pay for a Netflix subscription on the principle that owning a laptop means they *could* use it to watch Netflix, an argument that makes about as much sense as us charging for a TV licence ever did.'

'Yes, indeed,' agreed Dave McCreith. 'Of course, even before our hostile takeover of Netflix they were always seen by us as an extension of the BBC. Netflix completely followed our lead in removing the Forbidden Programmes from streaming platforms during that week in 2020 when we decided to reframe the true aims of the Black Lives Matter movement to not only place ourselves at the centre of a debate we should probably have stayed out of but to weirdly make it look like the real reason thousands of people were protesting on the streets was because of old episodes of Fawlty Towers.'

'Of course, your grace,' replied the Head of Licensing. 'I remember only too well that week when we ruthlessly virtue-signalled by removing just about every single programme we had from our streaming services to the extent of even digging out old, long-forgotten offensive sitcoms to put on there only so we could then claim the woke points for immediately removing them again.'

'Yes, that's the time I'm talking about,' Dave McCreith confirmed. 'Then we launched BritBox: a platform that proudly celebrates the rich history of British TV, then only a few days after the launch we decided that literally everything from the entire history of British TV was sickeningly offensive, and pulled every single programme from the platform!'

'Quite a business plan,' observed Terry Ball, drily.

'But it did turn out to be an inspired decision, your grace,' added the Head of Licencing, 'because the millennial audience then knew that BritBox was truly a 'safe space', on the grounds that there wasn't a single programme on there that could trigger them because, well, there weren't any programmes on there at all.'

'Yes, I never expected there to be so many new subscribers as a result of that,' admitted Dave McCreith.

At this point Terry Ball looked thoughtful, then spoke again. 'Forgive me the intrusion, your grace, but is it not also true that The Great iPlayer Trap was also part of this plan?'

'Oh, yes, of course,' responded Dave McCreith. 'I'd forgotten about that. But, yes, you're obviously aware that for some years it was possible to watch programmes on the iPlayer without signing in or proving you had a TV licence, giving a confused and mixed message that maybe it *was* acceptable to watch BBC content without a TV licence or, indeed, a TV, which was also part of our plan to utterly confuse the viewing public with regard to what the actual supposed 'laws' around TV licensing were. When this was pointed out, we acted as if it was something we hadn't properly considered, and changed the website so that you had to sign in before you could watch content online.'

The Head of Licensing, at this point, still looked intrigued, but also rather confused, as if whilst he was aware that the rules around TV and online content were labyrinthine and puzzling, he had not realised they were quite as baffling as was now being explained to him.

'But, obviously,' Dave McCreith continued, 'that was, well, The Great iPlayer Trap. Again, it was all part of our great deception that we set up the iPlayer, put all our programmes on it, then set up a bafflingly-complicated security system that could be circumnavigated simply by the user clicking on a box saying 'I have a TV licence. Watch now'. And all the people who did that when they actually didn't have TV licences had no idea that we stored all their details, their home addresses and their IP numbers, in a massive database and once we had sufficient power towards the end of the war we simply cross referenced that with our list of people who held TV licences, identified those who had falsely claimed they did, and rounded them up.'

The Head of Licensing's face lit up at this point. 'Yes, your grace. I remember it well. That was, of course, during The Great Re-Structuring. The very first wave of intake into the Re-Education Camps and the internment camp. It was an inspired idea. All those people not thinking it was odd that they could get around our systems so easily, having no idea it was all part of our long-term plan to wipe out anti-BBC Thought-Crime and heresy once and for all.'

Dave McCreith leaned back in his chair again. 'Indeed. Why do people think they can outwit the BBC?! Were they really so stupid as to think it was something we hadn't noticed?! One simple click of the mouse to access all our content by claiming you had actually paid for a licence?! Again, I was astounded people thought they were somehow being clever and outwitting the BBC by doing that without realising what our plan was.'

He paused for a moment, shaking his head before he continued. 'I mean... It's staggering, it really is. They think they can escape our clutches. But they cannot. No one can. There is no thought, no action, no deed that the Corporation does not know about. And if the Corporation finds such thoughts or actions displeasing... Well... We all know what happens.'

They all pondered this and there was a moment's silence before the Head of Licensing spoke again. No, wait, I got that wrong; there were actually *two* moments of silence, but they happened next to each other so it was hard to tell. Sorry for the confusion. 'Of course, the age of total information dominance and the End of All Privacy was of immense benefit to us all, your grace. Just as the

Corporation had always desired, we achieved a level of technological advancement that allowed us to monitor every single thought the British public has but, more importantly, to begin with at least, allowed us to know exactly what people were watching, for how long, how often they came back to it, the hours they spent viewing or listening.'

'Indeed,' agreed Dave McCreith. 'And that was a much more accurate method of measuring viewing figures than the one we used to claim to use. You know, when we said we did it based on how many toilets were flushed and kettles were put on after a programme finished, as if to suggest that told us how many people had watched it!'

They all laughed uproariously at the idea of anyone believing this bizarre idea.

'Yes, I'm still amazed they ever fell for that!' said Dave McCreith. 'I mean, did it never occur to them that many programmes finish at the same time, so if five programmes all finish at nine o'clock then how could we possibly have known which toilet flushes or kettles were from viewers of which show? I mean, by that standard, we could have shown a Miranda Christmas Special, two hours of her falling over whilst, well, that's all she ever does really, and that could have been watched by ten million simpletons, but if Channel Five showed the highlight of their festive programming, an extra-long edition of Britain's Saggiest Arses, and had it finish at the same time they could have claimed that all the toilet flushes and boiling kettles were due to them!'

'Then there's also the matter of how we could possibly have compiled all that information from the many electricity and water boards across the country,' added Terry Ball.

'Or that we seemed to be implying people will hold in their wee until the end of a programme rather than just going whilst it's still on,' added the Head of Licensing.

They all laughed again. What a good time they were having. When this had subsided Dave McCreith continued. 'Anyway, back when everybody had a TV and there were only four channels and no streaming or anything, no one could really argue if we said the Only Fools and Horses Christmas special got forty million viewers anyway.' He raised an eyebrow. 'And on top of that,' he added, 'there's the fact that the BBC never has to concern itself with viewing figures anyway. It doesn't matter if nobody watches or listens to something.

We can still commission another five series. Why else do you think all the Radio 4 sitcoms run forever?!'

They all laughed again, then there was a pause as they composed themselves.

'Yes, you're quite right, though,' confirmed Dave McCreith. 'It was yet another of those clearly ridiculous and implausible stories that we put out just to see if the proles were stupid enough to fall for it, assuming they wouldn't be, but finding it hilarious when they were.'

There was a pause as they all solemnly pondered this sentiment. It was the Head of Licensing who broke the silence.

'Of course, my liege, I am still an eager student of the noble history of this great organisation and am well aware that I am not privy to all its secrets whilst I am still a mere initiate of the Inner Party but I am very keen to learn, so this history has been most enlightening. But may I ask another question?'

Dave McCreith looked briefly suspicious. 'You may ask it. But I may choose not to answer it.'

'Of course, your excellence,' continued the Head of Licensing. 'But I have often wondered why ITV was allowed to continue.'

'Oh, the Corporation must always be defined in terms of its enemies,' explained Dave McCreith. 'We need a strong enemy, constantly producing truly crappy shows, in order to make the Corporation look even better. Or rather, several enemies, which is why Channel Four, Channel Five *and* ITV were all allowed to continue, but under our secret control. Still, even before the war we more or less entirely controlled ITV. I mean, why do you think we didn't sue them when they blatantly stole the idea of Strictly Come Dancing and turned it into Dancing On Ice? Or, I don't know, when we brought back Dr Who in 2005 and they responded with a time-travelling show with fairly bad CGI and a former 90s pop star in it?'

The Head of Licensing raised an eyebrow, questioningly. Dave McCreith looked mildly annoyed. 'Well, it was called 'Primeval'. Okay, not many people remember it but that's pretty much the point!'

'That's rather an outdated reference, if you don't mind me saying so, your grace,' added Terry Ball.

'Hmm,' continued Dave McCreith, annoyed, 'anyway, the point is that ITV never did anything without our permission. I mean, did it not strike you as odd that they never produced a single good comedy show in their entire history? That was at our behest. Otherwise you'd have expected them to make one even just by accident, but instead they gave us, er... Hardware? Benidorm?'

The other two shook their heads to show these names meant nothing to them. Dave McCreith continued. 'Of course, we always depicted them as vulgar for relying on advertising, as if that somehow polluted their programmes and made them very much under the influence of the advertisers. Actually' - his face lit up as he realised something that complemented his earlier line of thought – 'that's another thing that always struck me as hilarious about the whole official BBC line on the TV licence. We claimed that we were opposed to, and morally superior to, the idea of running adverts, and insisted we would not be able to rely on income from advertising, but this was *despite the fact* that all our subsidiary channels like UK Gold or Dave – which, by the way, was named in honour of me - all run adverts, therefore clearly proving we have no problem whatsoever with running adverts and that they are a very effective way to fund a channel!'

The Head of Licensing raised a finger at this point. 'Ah but, with all due respect, your grace, I don't think a large portion of the viewing public even realise those are BBC channels going by another name...'

Dave McCreith leapt forward triumphantly. 'And there's *yet* another thing! Why did people never notice that, either?! I mean, those channels show almost exclusively BBC shows! Mock the Week six times a night, Top Gear fifteen times a day... Why did people never seem to make the connection?! Even if they didn't realise the channels were run by us did they not think it odd that supposedly independent channels subsisted entirely on BBC repeats?! What, did they think national TV stations were somehow showing pirated versions of our shows?! Even if they were unconnected to us they'd still have had to pay to show them! Repeats! The magic word for any BBC exec! Repeats! In many ways, those channels offered the BBC plan in its purest form. Two things we claim to be opposed to – adverts and repeats – yet we run entire channels dedicated to those things and little else!'

The Head of Licensing looked somewhat enlightened, and impressed. 'Your grace,' he said, 'whilst I knew the BBC had managed to convince the British public of all sorts of things that clearly couldn't be true, I had no idea just how comprehensive, and successful, this immense web of lies was.'

'Oh, you will learn more,' said Dave McCreith, magnanimously, 'as you rise through the ranks of the Inner Party and progress beyond your current level. In fact, I have perhaps told you more than I should have by saying as much as I have.'

The Head of Licensing lowered his head, deeply privileged. 'you honour me, your excellency, you really do.'

Dave McCreith almost thoughtlessly held out his hand, and the Head of Licensing unquestioningly kissed the ring on his third finger, a chunky specimen in the shape of the BBC logo and adorned with jewels that would have cost a normal member of the public the same amount as they would spend on TV licence fees in the course of two lifetimes.

'Following on from that, you could also ponder why people didn't get suspicious that we were happy to profit from Top Gear by running it fifteen times a day on Dave despite having publically and sanctimoniously dropped Jeremy Clarkson for not meeting the standards of correct BBC behaviour,' Dave McCreith continued.

'Well, your grace, we did allow him to get away with notoriously un-PC behaviour for far, far longer than would have been permitted for any other BBC employees,' added Terry Ball.

'Which was definitely nothing to do with how Top Gear was one of our biggest exports and made us tens of millions in overseas sales,' cut in Dave McCreith, hastily. 'Anyway, it's not as if we weren't fair with him. We clearly stated a year or so before that affair that he was permitted to utter no more than three racial slurs per episode, showing what high morals the Corporation has always had.' His face suddenly turned from one of confusion to one of immense regret. In a flash he picked up the mug from his table and hurled it again the wall, where it smashed into several pieces. It doesn't really matter how many. It was broken. It merely serves as a plot device to demonstrate his temper and how angry in particular he was about this. The other two looked at him expectantly, assuming his sudden change in mood would be explained. Dave McCreith shook his head before continuing.

'Why didn't I think of this before?! We were forced to fire Clarkson because he attacked a producer, but the reason he did that was because their hotel was no longer serving hot food and the producer suggested he have a salad, but all we should have done is say that Clarkson was perfectly within his rights to attack the producer, because... The producer was fat-shaming him! The abhorrent, repellent crime of fat-shaming! Damn, if only I'd thought of that at the time we could have fired the producer instead, announced to the press that the producer was actually committing a hate crime by offering him a salad, and in attacking him Clarkson was standing up to this repellent act, and then we could have carried on Top Gear with him presenting and saying whatever he liked!'

Terry Ball and the Head of Licensing turned to each other and nodded to show how impressed they were with this piece of logic, even if it had come several years too late. The Head of Licensing paused for a moment, as if unsure whether he should suggest what he was thinking about, then continued. 'Er, your grace, there is something else I think may be worth considering...'

Dave McCreith raised an eyebrow, but this time it was not the one that he raised a couple of paragraphs ago. That's actually quite impressive, because even if you are able to raise one it's still quite hard to do the other. 'Yes?'

'Well, your grace, you may or may not be aware of an organisation called the Royalty Protection Society...'

'I know the name. I believe they administer licences for businesses to play music, such as concert venues or nightclubs, which they use to collect royalties.'

'Indeed, your grace. They're not as well-known as us but not only do they have a similarly rich history, their system of licence administration is actually far more complicated than ours.'

'Really?!' Dave McCreith's expression suggested he could barely conceive of how such a thing could be possible.

'Yes, your grace. In fact, I took some inspiration from them when we decided that merely having a single, one-off TV licence for each household covering all usage for a year at a standard price was actually far too simplistic.'

'Indeed it was,' concurred Dave McCreith. 'I mean, that now-discredited system didn't cover people who claimed not to have a TV at home yet still might accidentally glimpse one through the window of an electrical shop that was showing a BBC channel. In such a case they'd have been literally stealing television from us, so that loophole, and many others, needed to be closed.'

'Well, of course, my liege,' agreed the Head of Licensing. 'When we were setting out the revised licensing laws in order to close all sorts of outrageous loopholes like that I was inspired by the Royalty Protection Society, but when I now compare how they administer their licenses with how we do ours, I feel that we simply did not go far enough. Not by a long way. In fact, their rules and procedures are so labyrinthine as to make ours look both simple and fair.'

Dave McCreith's expression again suggested he found this idea almost impossible to believe. He nodded his head as if to tell the Head of Licensing to continue without further hesitation.

'Well,' said the Head of Licensing, continuing without further hesitation, 'we have much to learn from this organisation. I do not exaggerate, your grace, when I tell you that in the course of single year they may issue an itemised invoice for an organisation such as a pub or hotel chain containing a full breakdown of *every single piece of music usage* taking place across its premises, covering everything from CD players in bars and karaoke nights to hold music for their phone system and even the muzak that plays in their lifts. And if you have TVs in lounge or bar areas you even need to include their screen size *and* the size of the floor! Not only that but if you install a bigger TV the fee increases, even though it's blatantly obvious that the size of the screen has no bearing whatsoever on the volume or quantity of the music! They once insisted that a pub had to pay extra because they had a piano in the corner of the room that no one had even unlocked in twenty years and was so out of tune that it would have been literally impossible to play anything on it that remotely resembled a known song! They even recently introduced a tariff that forces pubs to pay an additional five hundred pounds a year to cover them in case a customer's mobile phone goes off whilst in the pub and the ringtone is a popular song, as that would constitute an unauthorised use of copyrighted music!'

(I should add at this point that a large amount of the above is actually true, like the TV sizes and the piano. Only the part about ringtones going off in pubs and thus constituting an infringement of copyright law is, at the time of writing, not true, or at least not as far as I am aware. Oh, and also, whilst this bit may come across as some form of embittered ranting from, I don't know, a former employee or someone, there is actually a reason for it all: it's an important plot point for later on, so make sure you're paying attention.)

'They charge for all *that*?!' spluttered Dave McCreith in astonishment. 'It sounds insane! It sounds like they've taken the idea of mad, uncontrollable bureaucracy to the absolute, bizarre, illogical extreme!' He paused for a moment. 'I love it! This is exactly the kind of company we could learn a lot from!'

'Indeed, your grace,' replied the Head of Licensing. 'With your kind indulgence I took the liberty of, shall we say, taking inspiration for their fine example and formulating a new system for calculating how much people need to pay for their TV licence. An online system, where every single person in the country has to enter details of every single aspect of their BBC usage. If they watch a programme they need to enter the details, mention how many family members were with them, any friends or visiting family members... Any toilet breaks must be included, including time taken and whether the break in question was for a number one or a number two...'

Dave McCreith nodded enthusiastically, loving what he was hearing. The Head of Licensing continued. 'We'll also require them to list every single trip outside they've taken so we can cross reference their route to see if they walked by any BBC Mega Screens on the high street, or whether they were close enough to another house to have heard a fragment of a TV show or radio programme, and charge them accordingly. And naturally we'll covertly install an app onto every single smartphone in the country to not only track their movements but so we can check their viewing and listening habits along with any times they've consulted the BBC website, then charge them accordingly.'

'Naturally,' concurred Dave McCreith, as if this went without saying. 'So, it'll be like doing a tax return only far, far more complicated?'

'Exactly, my lord. And rather than having to do it once a year, months after the end of the financial year, we'll insist it has to be done every single day, even on the days – though I believe people who make this claim are lying – when they say they haven't watched any BBC programmes, or if they're on holiday, or unconscious in hospital or something. And if we don't have it by midnight then we'll issue a hundred pound fine, rising to a thousand pounds if not paid within two hours, with the same rule being applied each additional day, and if they haven't submitted the necessary information for those days either then they all get added on.'

Dave McCreith's face briefly glossed over as he struggled to comprehend this fantastically complicated and hugely lucrative idea. 'I love it!' he spluttered. 'Right, go back to your office and get onto this right away! I want this in operation by the end of the week!'

'At once, my liege,' confirmed the Head of Licensing.

'Good,' replied Dave McCreith. 'Once we've announced this to the public we'll also use it as the justification for raising the licence fee again. So, is there anything else?'

'Well, there was one thing, your eminence,' said the Head of Licensing, hesitantly. Dave McCreith raised an eyebrow. It was the first eyebrow again, not the one he raised the second time he did it.

'Well, your grace, I did wonder whether it may at least be worth considering the re-introduction of the death penalty to this country, but only in truly extreme cases? I'm thinking, of course, of cases of licence fee evasion.'

Dave McCreith leaned back in his chair and stroked his chin. 'Hmm...' he began, slowly. 'Whilst I'm not against the idea in principle, as I feel that imprisonment is not always enough of a deterrent for these people, I think an issue there could be that we might end up executing hundreds of thousands of people, and the problem with that is that we are then potentially denying ourselves future income because, of course, TV licence debt continues to accumulate even if someone is in prison. An executed person can't pay their TV licence, as they say!'

'Indeed, your excellence,' replied the Head of Licensing. 'So I wondered whether we could simply execute a small number of evaders, as a warning to the rest of the country? Perhaps we could televise the executions, and make watching them mandatory?'

Dave McCreith's face lit up. 'Live televised executions for people who haven't paid their TV licence? I think that's an excellent idea! Perhaps we could televise the trial, too, just to really strike terror into the hearts of the viewing public?'

'Yes, your grace,' cut in Terry Ball, 'and we could conclude the programme with the National Lottery draw!'

'I like that idea even more!' replied Dave McCreith. 'Combining that with show trials and executions would be an excellent way to restore the plummeting viewing figures! I shall order the Prime Minister to set up the necessary legislation next time he visits!'

There was a pause, during which he calmed down, and it became apparent the meeting had reached its conclusion.

'Anyway, I hope today's meeting has been enlightening.'

The Head of Licensing lowered his head in deference and again Dave McCreith held out his impossibly expensive BBC ring for him to kiss, which he did.

'Immensely, your excellency,' he replied. 'As ever, you honour me simply by allowing me to be within proximity of your exalted form.'

'Yes, I do,' said Dave McCreith, trying to pretend he was not flattered. 'And now you may leave.'

The Head of Licensing stood up and bowed. 'Thank you, your grace. The BBC will prevail!'

'The BBC will prevail!' replied Dave McCreith.

'Oh, yes, the BBC will prevail!' added Terry Ball, looking up from his laptop.

# Chapter Five:

# Camping It Up

*In Which Our Hero Learns More About the Camp and Comes to Suspect It Is A Kind of Strange Purgatory To Which Once-Loyal BBC Employees Have Been Exiled for Anti-BBC Thought-Crime Such As Challenging the Corporation's Ever-Shifting Moral Standards, Refusing to Unquestioningly Accept Its Woke Worldview Or Doing Jokes About Swimmers' Noses*

It was early evening and after John Smith had done his very best to banish the memory of his evening meal from his memory he had left the canteen and wandered outside, wondering whether this would lead to him receiving a serious reprimand or even a beating, but noticing that the other inhabitants of the camp all seemed to be mingling freely. He remained suspicious, unsure if this was a trick to see whom he would initially gravitate towards, but soon noticed there were very few guards around and came to the conclusion that they had all gone for dinner, though almost certainly not in the place he had just left, that despite his efforts still lingered in both his memory and his taste buds.

Carefully looking around just to be extra sure he wouldn't be pounced on for daring to speak to someone else, he made his way over to a campfire around which a few people were sitting. He nodded at each of them and they motioned for him to sit down, which he did. He then took a deep breath, pulled the stool on which he had sat closer to the fire and introduced himself.

'Hi, everyone,' he began. 'I'm John Smith. I'm new here.' He licked his lips for a moment as he pondered what to say then, nervously, said 'well, at least I won't need to book a holiday this year!'

A few of the people around the fire smiled, almost pityingly, as if they had heard similar sentiments expressed before and knew they were the sort of thing someone might say when they were newly arrived at the camp, but also that anyone who'd been there much longer would not consider it something worth joking about. At that moment, as he scrutinised their faces more closely, John noticed something. They all, somehow, seemed familiar. They were the sort of people that, had he bumped into them in his local shop, he'd have assumed he knew them and said hello. But now, as the fire suddenly increased its intensity for a moment and in doing so illuminated the faces of everyone sitting around it, he realised they were not, in fact, people he knew but instead were people who, until quite recently, had been on television, largely on the BBC. The area around the campfire and, to some extent, much of the camp itself, he now realised, actually resembled some form of TV purgatory. Some sort of waiting room or holding area for people who'd been banished from TV and largely forgotten by society but still held some distant hope of one day returning, a hope made particularly cruel by the fact that such a thing did sometimes happen and even after years or even decades in the showbiz wilderness you never knew when you might be called back, perhaps to walk alongside Peter Kay in a Comic Relief video or to have a short cameo in a Harry Hill sketch.

To his left sat a man he recognised. It was Barry Begbie, a controversial comedian who had made his name in the mid-'00s by appearing on comedy panel shows and making all sorts of jokes about disabled people, dwarves and lesbians, the reaction to which was always the same: there would be howls of outrage from certain sections of the viewing public followed by the BBC issuing an extremely half-hearted sort of apology that was never accompanied by any actual action. Stranger still, after a few years away from TV, and during the time when the BBC had set out on its very public woke crusade in which it sanctimoniously denounced pretty much everything it had ever broadcast as being monstrously offensive they gave him his own discussion show in which he was joined by leading exponents of BBC Correct-Think so they could denounce figures and topics the Corporation deemed heretical, without anyone apparently ever stopping to ponder whether this was at all at odds with his history of making jokes about Down's Syndrome or Madeleine McCann. He nodded to John.

'All right, fella? What's your story?'

John Smith wasn't quite sure what to say. 'I don't know,' he replied. 'I don't know why I'm here. I went to bed one night, and as far as I can remember it was a day just like any other but then at two in the morning my door was knocked down and I was dragged out of my house by armed guards and brought here.'

Although what he had just described should have shocked anyone in a civilised country, his new companions merely nodded sympathetically, as if to say that his experience was just one of those things that could happen to anybody.

'Aye,' sympathised Barry Begbie. 'It happens.'

'How long have you been here for?' asked John. Barry Begbie looked thoughtful.

'I'm not entirely sure, to be honest,' he said, after a moment. 'Well, my last TV show was around October 2021, just before the war.' He then looked thoughtful. 'Part of me always knew I'd end up in a place like this. Not just because of the jokes I used to do but because of how the BBC was constantly switching position so you never had the slightest idea if you'd do a joke and they'd completely back you or up or denounce you for having committed a hate crime. It was just so completely random. The utter lack of consistency was what did for me in the end.'

John Smith said nothing, wondering if any single nugget of information he acquired may in some way prove useful in hoping explain his own presence in the camp. Barry Begbie continued.

'I mean, back in the mid-noughties I did a joke about the Queen's vag being so old that it was haunted. And a senior BBC executive actually went on TV to defend me. But about six months after that I made a joke about a swimmer having a big nose and people tore into me and the BBC apologised. And the thing with that was that the swimmer in question claimed that she shouldn't have been subjected to jokes about her appearance because she was a sportsperson rather than someone desperately seeking fame on a reality show. Which would have been a much more valid argument if she hadn't then appeared on a reality show about a year after that. And had a nose job to help her get more TV work.'

Barry Begbie sighed and shook his head. 'You see? You can't argue against that. People don't listen to reason and logic. They're entirely controlled by their emotions, which are manipulated by the corporations. Anyway, I was off the BBC for a while, presumably because they'd finally decided to stop defending my jokes, so you can imagine my surprise when they brought me back and gave me a discussion show. They told me I could only have guests on who all had exactly the same opinions on everything and were reliable exponents of BBC Correct-Think, banging on about the awful Tories or how terrible Brexit was, though the odd thing was that they were the kind of comedians who'd normally have attacked me for my jokes but were happy to ignore all that if it meant they could get on the telly.'

He leaned forward and held out his hands against the fire for warmth before continuing. 'Despite all this I still had fun trying to get my more controversial ideas and jokes in during my opening monologue, but it was quite hard because of all the constraints they placed on me. But it basically felt like I'd been unexpectedly welcomed back into the fold. People were apparently happy to ignore all the jokes I'd done about Madeleine McCann, Down's Syndrome and child abuse simply because I'd apparently redeemed myself with a few tweets in support of asylum seekers.'

He pulled his hands away from the fire as they were obviously a bit hot now. 'But taking the easy route has never been my way. I knew I had to be the trickster. I knew I had to test the weird and inconsistent rules they had. I'd noticed how someone had joked about throwing acid over Nigel Farage and, when he complained, the usual suspects of BBC Correct-Think all went 'oh, it's only a joke, Nigel, can't you take a joke?!' even though if the exact same joke had been made about Diane Abbott or someone those exact same people would have called for the person who'd made it to be banned from the BBC for life.'

He took a deep breath as he started to recount the incident that had proven to be his downfall. 'I wanted to make a point about how certain topics or jokes are completely fine when directed at one person but completely unacceptable when directed at someone else. The BBC says it's not biased, yet it's obvious you can joke about or attack certain people but not others. So I decided to mess with their heads. I'd been booked on a Radio 4 panel show and decided to mix things up.'

He paused again, as if he had once again become annoyed and disappointed at this level of hypocrisy even though the incident in question had happened several years earlier.

'I knew the audience was a crowd of simpletons who just wanted to have their middlebrow views reinforced, so I did a bit about how the US spends huge amounts on defence yet virtually nothing on public healthcare. And my line was, 'It must be annoying if you're American and your government doesn't provide you with healthcare even though it taxes you loads to pay for the military when America's only been attacked twice in its entire history. The US spending billions on defence is like Anne Widdecombe spending her life savings on a rape alarm.'

John Smith let out an involuntary laugh at this point. Noticing this, Barry Begbie raised a finger and smiled.

'You see! That's what a lot of people did! They laughed first and then looked guilty and confused, as if their unconscious brains had betrayed them by laughing before their conscious brains had evaluated the joke and decided whether to allow them to! Confusion reigned! No one on the show was sure if it was offensive, as on the one hand I mentioned rape but on the other I was attacking the US government and military and lack of American healthcare! And I was attacking one of the correct targets, one of the Bad People, one of those evil Tories! They were desperate to be told what to think! The tension was unbearable, and I loved it! Even better, the programme was marketed as one where you were allowed to voice 'controversial' opinions, even though that was obviously very much a one-way street!'

Barry Begbie did a short, snort-like laugh before proceeding to issue an extremely convenient riposte to anyone who failed to understand that the intention of that (rather brilliant) joke was to highlight the inconsistent standards regarding the nature of offence, and that to get offended by it is to miss the point. So, yeah, any complaints about that joke are addressed below, okay?

'I mean, my point was to raise the question of why rape jokes are supposedly never okay yet jokes about throwing acid over someone apparently are. There at least needs to be some consistency to the whole thing. Something's either okay or it's wrong. You can't say something is utterly repellent when directed at one target but completely fine when directed at another, because by that logical standard you could say that racism is one of the most abhorrent hate crimes a person can commit whilst also saying it's totally fine to racially abuse someone if they're a Tory.'

Whilst he had quite clearly addressed and resolved any potential criticisms that people may have had over his joke, he paused for a moment before adding something that closes the matter once and for all. 'Anyway, people who object to that joke have obviously failed to notice the premise upon which it's based. I mean, if you're so desperate to be offended by something that you'll actually get outraged by a joke where the point is that there's *no possibility whatsoever* of somebody getting raped then you really need to take a good, hard look at your values.'

Yeah, that should do it.

'It was broadcast live, by the way, so they couldn't edit it out,' he went on, conveniently filling in a potential plothole. 'Also, not long before that I'd done a joke where I said 'Tommy Robinson's supporters say he doesn't have a racist bone in his body, but that wasn't the case when he was recently accosted in the prison showers by a group of white supremacists, because on that occasion he had four or five of them in him."

He paused to give his companions time to get this joke.

'And people were fine with that because even though it was a rape joke it was about a man, and a notoriously controversial far-right figure at that. But, yeah, on this occasion there was no way to predict whether they'd support me and say 'it was just a joke!' or I'd be denounced and publically shamed. So I went home and waited and, sure enough, around midnight, my door was kicked down... And here I am.'

He leaned back and took a swig of whatever mysterious liquid was contained in an old tin can he was holding. There was a pause as the group seated around the fire pondered what had been said. After a few more moments of contemplation, another member of the group leaned forward to tell his story. In keeping with his observation that he had arrived in a kind of TV purgatory, John Smith noticed this person was also familiar, and again was the sort of comedian who had been ubiquitous at one point only to slowly fade into an existence of endless Radio 4 panel show appearances and much rarer

TV spots. As John Smith looked at him longer he remembered more: his name was Jeffrey Harding, and he had been at his most popular (though that was a comparative term) in the late 1980s and early 1990s as part of a supposed 'new wave' of comedians who were marketed and presented as being an alternative to the tired mainstream yet had very quickly become the new orthodoxy. As Jeffrey Harding started to talk, John Smith noticed that Barry Begbie had folded his arms defensively, as if resentful at having to listen to him, leading John Smith to discern there was, or had been, some level of animosity between the two, professional or otherwise.

'I'd been on the BBC for decades,' he began. 'I reached a point where I couldn't even imagine doing anything else. Sure, I was ostensibly a stand-up but all my money came from the BBC, as the only other form of income I had was touring places like Cleethorpes or Skegness, or anywhere that had a small, Arts Council-funded venue where no-one good ever came to perform so if literally anyone who'd ever been on TV visited then at least a few people would turn up.' He sighed. 'And I can't even pretend it was my talent that got me where I ended up. I literally tried stand-up comedy once, going on stage at the Comedy Store in 1987 and opening with 'ooh, that Mrs Thatcher, eh?! I call her 'Mrs Snatcher' because of everything she's taken away from this country! Huh! The bloody Tories, eh?!' and, as it turned out, the commissioning editor for Radio 4 was in the audience and thought I was the most brilliantly incisive political comedian he'd ever seen, so the moment I came off stage he signed me up to a lifetime contract with the BBC. Obviously the contract very strictly stated I had to attack the Tories at every single opportunity but really didn't say anything about me actually being funny.'

'You see!' interrupted Barry Begbie. 'The BBC never wants its so-called 'political' comedians to ever really challenge anything or anyone, or ask deep or complex questions! They just want people like you to go 'ooh, the bloody Tories, eh?'!'

'I've always known I wasn't funny!' protested Jeffrey Harding. 'I'm as baffled as anyone as to how I sustained a career in comedy for so long! But it just seemed that as long as I did desperately unfunny stuff but about the correct targets then they kept on re-booking me!' He then looked thoughtful. 'Well, for a while they did, but it eventually dried up as they decided I was too old to appeal to the kids so whilst they continued to have me on every single terrible, unfunny Radio 4 panel show my only TV work was an annual appearance on Some News, For You, We Have.'

John Smith thought for a moment, as he noticed that Radio 4 was coming in for rather a lot of criticism, almost as if some mysterious, cosmic force was making an unnecessary number of references to how bad it was due to some unexplained vendetta against the middlebrow station, but shook this suspicion off.

'I'll be fair to you,' said Barry Begbie. 'You did once do a joke I thought was good. You said that the only difference between people who believe in God and people who believe in Santa is that the ones who believe in Santa don't threaten to murder you if you don't agree with them.'

'Oh, yes, that was a good one,' Jeffrey Harding replied, nostalgically. 'I did that for about thirty years. It passed for edgy in the early nineties.'

'You see, that's why some people thought I was inspired by you!' replied Barry Begbie. 'They made a lazy connection based on us both supposedly being 'edgy' comedians, even though you only had one 'edgy' joke!'

'Ah, but it was that joke that eventually got me fired,' Jeffrey Harding added. 'Because for the first couple of decades people assumed I was attacking Christianity, or Mormonism or Scientology, and the BBC encourages you to attack all those religions, but then in around 2007 they decided it might be offensive to, er, other religions, so banned me from doing it, ironically because they were concerned it might lead to death threats. So, I think it was me doing a joke I'd been doing for thirty years that finally led me to be kicked out by the BBC,' he reflected. 'Not, interestingly, the fact that I hadn't come up with anything new or funny in thirty years, as that's never been a barrier to appearing on Radio 4, but because their moral standards had shifted beneath me.' He looked thoughtful again. 'Or possibly they just wanted to get rid of me because I'm a middle-aged, white man, the sort of person the BBC is deeply, and very publically, reluctant to employ, well, other than in every position on their Board of Executives.' Once more, he looked thoughtful. 'So, I'm not entirely sure why I'm here, but here I am.'

Jeffrey Harding now looked down then leaned back as if to indicate that he had finished telling his tale. Everybody around the fire paused for a moment to reflect upon the story they had just been told, and with it now having become an unspoken understanding that each person would take it in turns to tell their story, the next person began to tell theirs. This time it was a young-ish female comedian who John vaguely recognised from having been on TV once or twice, and who always seemed to express the correct BBC opinions whenever she did, the explanation for which was shortly to be given.

'Okay, so I didn't go to Oxbridge, meaning that I instead had to spend ten years actually learning my craft on the stand-up circuit before the BBC would use me. My agent explained to me that being at the upper end of the Body Mass Index meant I was never going to end up appearing on all the prime-time comedy shows like Eight Out of Ten Cats or Would I Lie To You, so suggested I market myself as a politically-correct, feminist comedian, as no one expects them to be slim or attractive and there's an immense amount of work for them on Radio 4.'

There was Radio 4 mentioned again, noticed John. What was all this about?

'Anyway,' continued the speaker, though she wasn't really continuing because John merely thinking something had not interrupted what she was saying, 'I received my training in BBC Correct-Think and was then booked to appear on every single Radio 4 comedy panel show, twice a day for the next five years. My agent also explained this meant I'd only be able to perform on the stand-up circuit as far north as Watford, because most BBC comedians daren't go any further than that in case there's someone in the audience who voted for Brexit.'

John Smith paused here, nostalgically recalling a time when that issue had been the biggest one facing the country. Kerri Barnes-Bridge continued. Oh, that was her name, by the way. I didn't see an obvious place to mention it before now, but there you have it. Not based on anyone, as per all the characters in this book.

'Again, it was difficult to know even how you were meant to follow the rules. I mean, I used to slag you off, Barry, for being offensive,' she said, turning to Barry Begbie, 'attacking you for doing jokes about Down's Syndrome and swimmers' noses but, of course, when you got a new TV show where you needed woke comedians I wasn't going to let minor details like principles, or moral consistency, get in the way of me being on the telly.'

'To be honest, I was surprised the BBC brought me back,' added Barry Begbie, 'though they told me the main condition of my return would be that the programme I hosted would only be allowed to feature guests with exactly the same views, in order to present the illusion of debate when it contained nothing of the sort and all people did was sit around re-enforcing each other's opinions.'

'Yeah, I was confused by that,' admitted Kerri Barnes-Bridge. 'One time I was on your show and didn't object when you opened with a joke about you hiding in the guests' dressing rooms whilst pleasuring yourself, but got outraged later on when there was a piece on a Japanese man who married a hologram, complaining it was problematic because he didn't have the hologram's consent. I mean, if you think it's insane that an inanimate, insentient object should somehow be able to give informed sexual consent, it's even weirder when you realise that a hologram is a beam of light. I was literally saying someone should be prosecuted for sexually assaulting a group of light particles.' She paused, as if realising this was even more ridiculous now she was looking back on it, before adding, 'plus, even beyond all those considerations, it was obviously a stupid thing to think because the guy's cock would have gone straight through the hologram anyway.' Then she paused again and looked forlorn. 'But I don't even know why they sent me here, to be honest. It was probably that someone discovered some footage of me doing stand-up years earlier and I used a word that later became controversial. I don't know. Maybe some old YouTube footage of me bantering with a hen party in Manchester where I didn't haul them up on gender stereotypes or, well, it literally could have been anything.'

But now the tone changed. The next person whose turn it was to speak was a woman wearing gloves with the fingers cut off, and smoking a roll up that appeared to have been assembled using a piece of newspaper. John looked at her, and noticed she also seemed familiar, this time for having been brought out as a talking head on politics programmes or to argue with people who held the incorrect opinions on Question Time.

'And as for my story?' she began, before taking a drag on her roll up. 'Oh... I was one of the first to be sent here. And I don't imagine I'll ever be released even if you all eventually are.'

The others looked at each other, confused. The mystery

woman smiled, then took a drag on her roll up.

'And that's because... I was a BBC journalist.'

There was a stunned silence. The others' facial expressions ranged from confused and surprised to utterly desperate and dumbfounded. John realised he did know who she was. What was her name? Hadn't she been the editor on the popular radio show Wimmin's Time until quite recently? Emmeline something? Yes, Emmeline Moneypenny, that was her name. John thought it odd that she was there, considering she had always been held up by the liberal media as someone with the correct opinions and who therefore was beyond criticism or questioning. Yet one day she simply disappeared, as if banished without explanation to the BBC Wilderness.

'But... That's impossible, surely?' he said. 'That's a job for life. Your profession is never questioned and anyone who does so is denounced as a wrong-thinker. I mean... BBC journalists never, ever lose their jobs. It's a role for life. Just as long as you hastily change your opinions every time BBC Correct-Think is updated.' He briefly pondered this then corrected himself. 'Oh, unless you're a woman over fifty, of course, at which point they'll try to get rid of you using any means they can, but you don't quite look fifty so you must have done something truly horrific for the BBC to send you here. What can that possibly have been?'

The others sat in anticipation, which Emmeline Moneypenny noted and smiled at.

'Oh, it's not always as straightforward as that. Here's what happened to me. I always considered myself a feminist. I always wrote pro-women pieces, which they would run without question, never checking if the facts were right or if the argument stood up, as long as the claims supported their world view. So, I was the main presenter on Wimmin's Time for many years, as I was widely known as one of the country's leading feminists, only I was a feminist when that actually meant thinking for yourself and questioning things rather than simply buying into a pre-packaged set of beliefs that you are utterly forbidden from deviating from no matter how ridiculous they clearly are...' She paused and took a drag on her roll up. 'But the producers and senior execs started to criticise me for not unquestioningly towing the line where the whole trans issue was concerned, and for wanting to actually ponder and evaluate each aspect of it to ascertain the extent to which it did or didn't stand up to scrutiny... Which, of course, to BBC execs was heresy as you were just meant to accept every single bizarre and illogical pronouncement completely without question... I mean... My point was that women had struggled for centuries to obtain parity with men but that was all being undone because a man could say he was a woman just because he decided he was, without even showing the true commitment of having his cock chopped off.'

The others listened intently, realising her point but also being only too aware that expressing such a thing was unthinkable anti-BBC heresy. Emmeline Moneypenny nodded at the predictability of it all before continuing.

'So here's what happened. One day I ran a feature on how car seats are designed with men's bodies in mind so often aren't that safe for women. It was a genuinely pro-women piece, making a valid point about sexism in everyday design, and on any other day it would have been celebrated as being progressive, but it happened to be run on the same day as a load of articles saying that anyone who thinks there are biological differences between men and women is a fascist, so instead of starting a debate I was called to the DG's office and before I knew it I was in the back of a repurposed TV detector van and later that day found myself here, where I've been ever since.'

The others looked on, pondering her story with disbelief. She shook her head and continued. 'I mean, the thing is, we'd heard rumours about the BBC kidnapping people who held the incorrect opinions and taking them off to mysterious, off-budget camps for re-education but, of course, we never thought they were true. We'd been told they were 'conspiracy theories' so, of course, once we heard that phrase we obediently switched our brains off and refused to read anything more about them.'

She paused to think about this. 'I mean, nearly thirty years at the BBC, never once deviating from its official line! I just assumed I was so deep in there that they'd never get rid of me. Yet here I am.' She leaned back and sighed, as if partly accepting her fate.

Well, I'll wrap this chapter up now as all the relevant points have been made. But if it appeared unnecessarily long and full of seemingly irrelevant rambling, bear in mind all the people you've just met are going to be major characters in this book so it's important to know their back story and motivations, okay?

# Chapter Six:

# All Publicity Is Bad Publicity

*In Which The Director General Meets with the Head of PR, or 'Plausible Revisionism', To Discuss How to Constantly Control What the Public Thinks of the BBC and Everything Else, the Constantly-Shifting Nature of BBC Morality and a Heretical Novel That Has Started to Inspire Revolutionary Thought And Is Cleverly Called 'The Book the BBC Tried to BAN!'*

Dave McCreith was carefully scrutinising that night's TV listings when he noticed something that made him frown. 'Ball!' he yelled. 'Come here now!'

Terry Ball came scurrying over, bowing as he did so. 'Yes, sir? What is it, sir?'

'It's these TV listings. There's something wrong with them.'

'Really, your grace? I am sorry to hear that. What is it?'

'Well, let me read them out to you.' Dave McCreith began to recite the evening's schedule. '7pm The One Show featuring Stormzy. 7.30 the revived Top of the Pops, featuring a full hour of Stormzy. 8.30, Rapper's Delight, the third episode of a new sitcom starring Stormzy.'

Terry Ball looked at him quizzically. Dave McCreith continued.

'Nine o'clock, the news read by Stormzy. Nine thirty, a new programme on Renaissance Italy, presented by Stormzy, ten o'clock, The Large Hadron Collider – An Inside Look at a Breakthrough in

Quantum Physics... Presented by Stormzy. At ten, a revival of Alan Bennett's Talking Heads, in which all the monologues are performed by Stormzy. Half ten... Newsnight special: the new interest rates and the effect they will have on the IMF – what does Stormzy think? And then, at eleven... The Mash Report.'

Terry Ball continued to look puzzled. 'I'm sorry, your grace, and forgive me for this, but I don't actually know what it is you're objecting to.'

'What am I objecting to?! This 'Mash Report' programme doesn't say anything about being presented by or at least featuring Stormzy, thus clearly contravening article fifty seven, subsection 12b, of the BBC Charter!'

'Oh, right, yes, of course, your eminence,' frowned Terry Ball. 'It's probably a misprint. It seems unlikely the Corporation would have made such an error as to produce a programme featuring no contribution from Stormzy, but I'll get that looked into.'

'Hmm. Be sure that you do,' replied Dave McCreith, then looked more puzzled. 'Hang on, Question Time, presented by Stormzy, follows The Mash Report. Is there not some overlap in having two current affairs programmes scheduled immediately next to each other?'

'The Mash Report, sir? Oh, that's a comedy show.'

'Is it?!' Dave McCreith looked genuinely astonished. 'Are you absolutely sure?! I watched about three episodes of that but had no idea it was meant to be comedy. Even by our poor standards it's extremely unfunny. Still, it has the correct opinions, which is the main thing. But still...' He shook his head in disbelief. 'Well, anyway, make sure that the remaining episodes of the current run all feature a significant contribution from Stormzy.'

'Very good, your grace, it shall be done,' confirmed Terry Ball, bowing deeply. 'Do you have a favourite song of his?'

'What? What do you mean 'song'?'

'Well, he's a musician, isn't he? A 'rap singer' as they call them.'

'Really?! I had no idea,' admitted Dave McCreith.

'Yes, I believe he's quite popular with the young people. I mean, I assume that's why the rule was brought in insisting that at least 90% of BBC output needs to feature him.'

'Hmm, well I suppose that would go some way to explain why I was advised to implement that,' admitted Dave McCreith. 'I was told it would be an easy, if embarrassingly blatant, way to ensure all the young people of this country would follow and be faithful to the Corporation for the rest of their lives.'

'Whereas in reality it turned out that very few of them even used the BBC and instead just used TokTik or whatever social media platform is popular this week,' Terry Ball pointed out.

'Hmm, yes, that's right,' replied Dave McCreith, annoyed at it being observed that one of his grandest personal schemes had not been very successful.

'You know, I did find it a little odd that although the BBC knew it was going to be heavily reliant on the over-75s as a source of revenue once their free TV licences were taken away, it perversely jumped on the so-called 'woke' bandwagon, not just alienating the demographic upon which it was going to be almost entirely financially reliant but doing so in order to appeal to a group that barely, if ever, engaged with the BBC anyway,' Terry Ball observed.

Dave McCreith again looked annoyed at having this entirely valid observation being pointed out to him. 'Hmm, yes, well, you may technically be correct,' he admitted, 'but, of course, that was before we 'reformed' the licence fee rules anyway.'

He looked at his assistant with deep suspicion. There were frequently occasions when he was never entirely sure if Terry Ball was a true believer in the BBC Great Agenda. On top of this he also suspected him of not only possessing the dangerous gift of independent thought but of cleverly hiding this gift, and thus making powerful criticisms in such a way that they came across as casual and innocuous observations.

'Anyway,' he continued, 'we got the young people in the end, Stormzy or not, with our youth wing, BBC Youth, indoctrinating the young people into BBC Correct-Think from the earliest age possible, though our youth propaganda disseminating tool, BBC Three. Plus the youth demographic remains the most fanatical in supporting our aims and worldview, immediately shaming on social media anyone who voices an incorrect opinion and, where instructed, staging protests outside the headquarters or homes of anyone suspected of anti-BBC Thought-Crime.'

'Yes, of course, your excellence,' agreed Terry Ball, perhaps aware that he may have overstepped the mark. 'It is imperative that we brainwash the young as soon as we can, and we have been most successful at this as they have proven a valuable ally in disseminating our message, unchallenged, across the country and the world.'

'Anyway, the whole ending of free licences for over-75s was a trap,' added Dave McCreith. 'We announced it, then simply monitored all those who expressed dissent at the time then, once we assumed power during The Great Terror we were able to round them up and cart them off to the Isle of Wight internment camp. It was all just a tool to slyly monitor whom the BBC could trust, and whom it could not.'

'Indeed, my liege...' replied Terry Ball. 'Actually, as it happens, it's quite fortunate that we're having this discussion, which is to say mentioning what the Great British Public truly thinks of the Corporation, because we have a guest on the way whose role very much relates to that. He should be here any moment.'

'I see. And what does he do?'

'Well, my liege, his role is to essentially manipulate and control the public's opinion of the Corporation.'

'Er, but surely since its very inception the role of the BBC has been to manipulate and control public opinion?' replied Dave McCreith, as if he were stating the obvious.

'Well, yes, your grace, but in this case it's more about how we present ourselves to the world, which can sit at odds with, and frequently entirely contradict, our actual actions. How we gloss over things, so to speak. I'm talking about when, say, you appear in an interview about the Corporation's future, or when a different senior executive appears before a Parliamentary select committee. So, all part of presenting ourselves as open and honest even though nothing is left to chance and everything stage managed.'

Dave McCreith looked thoughtful, as if this had made him consider something he had never before thought of. 'Hmm... Whilst it is some years since I have appeared in public, do you have any idea what the proles think of me as a person?' Don't hold back.'

'Er, well, your excellency,' replied Terry Ball, 'their views are, varied... But I wouldn't concern yourself too much with the views of the little people.'

'Tell me,' insisted Dave McCreith. Terry Ball hesitated again, then proceeded.

'Well, sir, the thing is... Out there, people call you... The Woke Hitler.'

'Woke Hitler, eh?' he responded angrily. 'I ought to have them all rounded up and put into camps!'

'Erm, you already have done that, sir,' Terry Ball pointed out. 'We have over thirty BBC Re-Education Camps in the South East area alone.'

'Oh, yes, well, that just goes to show what a good idea it was.'

'Yes, your excellency.'

Dave McCreith looked thoughtful. 'Woke Hitler... Woke Hitler... You know what? I rather like the sound of that.'

'I'm not *entirely* sure they intended it as a compliment, my liege,' added Terry Ball, as if he himself was undecided as to whether the term was intended as flattering or somewhat insulting.

'Hmm, I wonder if we could change my job title again to include that? It would be doubly advantageous because if I do that I can claim I've actually assumed a new role, for which I can double my salary,' pondered Dave McCreith.

'Again, your eminence?' queried Terry Ball,

Dave McCreith looked thoughtful. 'Yes, maybe I shouldn't do that. After all, it would be the third time this month, so might not look very good if it somehow got leaked.'

'A very wise idea, your eminence.'

'Of course it is. So it's agreed. As of today my job title shall be upgraded to 'Director General, Supreme Overlord and Woke Hitler of the BBC'. That should certainly mess with the heads of the public. And that, after all, is our job!'

'Of course, your grace. I shall have all your stationery destroyed and reprinted to reflect the change.'

'Yes, do that. Then next week I'll change my title again. What do you think of 'Director General, Supreme Overlord, Woke Hitler and Uber-Fuhrer of the Broadcasting for Britain Company'?'

'Very catchy, my liege,' replied Terry Ball, but before he could continue there was a knock at the door. He went to open it and nodded to the man standing behind it, who took this as a sign to step inside.

Dave McCreith turned to the guest, suspiciously. 'And you are?'

'The BBC's Head of PR, your excellency.'

'PR?' Dave McCreith looked confused then looked at Terry Ball for further information before venturing 'is that something to do with

HR, or 'Hiring and Recruitment'?'

The Head of PR looked briefly confused, then continued. 'Well, your grace, I believe 'HR' stands for 'Human Resources' rather than 'Hiring and Recruitment', partly because those two words, 'hiring' and 'recruitment' mean exactly the same thing...'

Dave McCreith narrowed his eyes suspiciously, as if pondering whether a man with knowledge such as this was too well-informed to be working at the BBC. Then he raised an eyebrow thoughtfully as he processed what had been said. 'Human Resources, you say?! I like it! There's no pretence! It states clearly and unambiguously that here at the BBC we see all human life as a resource to be exploited when and where necessary! Why, it almost sounds like it's a department dedicated to harvesting human organs!'

The Head of PR looked briefly confused again. 'Well, your grace, that is actually one of its functions. For example, if a senior executive suffered from liver failure we would naturally take a healthy liver from, say, a cleaner, though obviously we would compensate the cleaner by, say, allowing them to work a double shift the next day.'

'Good! I like it even more now!' replied Dave McCreith, enthusiastically. 'Human Resources! Wonderful! Only a true sociopath could have coined such a term and got away with it! Another sterling example of how the Corporation has rebranded since our Great Victory in the war!'

The Head of PR looked slightly puzzled again, as if surprised that he was having to clarify minor and unrelated questions for the Director General when he had come for entirely different reasons, but decided to continue as he could see the positive effect his explanations were having on the head of the Corporation. 'Well, actually, your grace, despite, as you point out, that name having rather sinister connotations if you stop to think about them, the term in fact pre-dates the Corporation's Great Victory and was in common use for several years before then, with just about any organisation with more than a few employees having one.'

This was new to Dave McCreith, who raised an eyebrow in surprise. 'What, you mean to say that, I don't know, a university of something would have had a department called 'Human Resources' yet it didn't deal with harvesting the organs of human beings? So what did they deal with?'

'Er, well, your excellence, prior to the Great Victory, Human

Resources departments were largely devoted to investigating grievances reported by lower-ranking employees, investigating them then automatically ruling in favour of management and reprimanding the person who had reported the issue accordingly.'

'Oh, I see,' replied Dave McCreith. 'Well, it's good to know they did that but still think it's a rather sinister name to have used before such departments gained the new powers they have nowadays.'

There was a pause as they all pondered what had just been discussed. Dave McCreith looked flustered, then relaxed somewhat, as if he had held some concerns but they were now largely assuaged. 'Hmm, well, anyway, as the head of this 'Inhumane Resourcing' department, what is it you've come here today to discuss?'

The Head of PR looked at Terry Ball for support, and he stepped in to clarify matters. 'Ah, your excellency, this gentleman is not from *HR*, or Human Resources, but is in fact from *PR*. It's actually a completely different department.'

Dave McCreith again frowned at this. 'It would appear from what you are telling me that the BBC has an almost infinite number of departments, all with inane and confusing acronyms and initialisms as their names, and presumably each and every one of them containing layer upon layer of managers and consultants who do very little yet take home salaries that are at least six figures...'

'Well, yes, my liege, just as you like,' confirmed Terry Ball.

'Hmm, well, if you're not from Human Remains then where are you from?'

'PR, your grace. It stands for Plausible Revisionism.'

Dave McCreith shrugged as if asking whether this was meant to mean something to him. 'Oh,' he replied. 'And what do you do there?'

'Well, your grace, we're all about the public face of the Corporation. We work to ensure the public is kept in the loop about what we're up to and what we think.'

'My god, you don't tell them what we really do and think, do you?!' Dave McCreith replied, flabbergasted at the risk this would present.

'Of course not, your grace,' said the Head of PR. 'I assure you we never offer anything more than inane buzzwords, meaningless platitudes and an endless array of taskforces set up to investigate things we've made up.'

'Oh, thank god for that,' replied Dave McCreith. 'You had me worried for a moment. I don't know why, but from what you were telling me it sounded like you regularly reveal the true intentions, motivations, history and future of the BBC, which would be utter madness.'

'Absolutely, your grace, hence me reassuring you that PR is all about bland, vacuous press releases that reassure the feeble-minded whilst actually saying nothing.'

'Good, good, totally in keeping with our principles. I like it. So what are you here to discuss?'

'Well, it's really more of an opportunity to touch base and ensure we're both singing from the same hymn sheet with regards to how this organisation is moving forward.'

Dave McCreith smiled with satisfaction at this sentence being almost entirely constructed from clichés and buzzwords, before the Head of PR continued.

'Well, let me see... Since we acknowledged that BBC News was nothing more than our propaganda wing and incorporated it into the PR department accordingly, we've continued to follow the same rules as before. Obviously we continue to claim impartiality despite the implausibility of that, and despite the fact that the articles on our website are entirely interchangeable with the ones you'd see in the standard liberal newspapers.'

Dave McCreith nodded, as if this went without saying. 'And doing everything you can to support those who share the BBC worldview whilst being far more critical of those who do not?'

'Of course, your eminence,' the Head of PR confirmed. 'Our favoured politicians receive positive coverage about their family life and background, whilst we do all we can to dig up dirt on the unsavoury histories of those who dare to challenge or disagree with us. Stories that support our view are promoted unquestioningly whilst we heavily criticise those that challenge it. I mean, do you remember how the US president used to be Donald Trump?'

'Vaguely,' replied Dave McCreith, 'though we have largely written his sickening presidency out of official history now.'

'Well, your eminence, you could look at how when his supporters claimed the reason he failed to win a second term was because the election was rigged, we denounced the very idea of interference in democratic elections as being utterly impossible, even though we'd spent his entire presidency running endless reports on how he only got into power due to Russian meddling in the previous one.'

'Yes, yes, it's good to know you continue to use the techniques,' replied Dave McCreith. 'Bludgeon people with the same claims for so long they end up believing them. Do a Reality Check Hatchet Job to dismiss any criticism, and if there are still people who believe the opposite, dismiss them as 'conspiracy theorists' who should not be listened to and who must be censored!'

'Indeed, my liege,' replied the Head of PR. 'It's a similar practice to how we report stories that support our world view whilst ignoring those that don't. So, a story saying how awful trade was going to be after Brexit was given prominent coverage but anyone with a compelling argument to the contrary was ignored and accused of peddling 'fake news'. Again, it's all about what we choose to report and what we do not. We claim to simply be reporting on things that have happened, but of course the key there is we still get to choose which of the things that have happened we report on and which of the things that have happened we do not.'

'There is truth we choose to report on, and truth that we do not,' summarised Dave McCreith, in a rather catchy and quotable way.

'Indeed, my liege,' replied the Head of PR. 'The BBC only ever reports facts, but makes sure they are facts of our choosing.'

'Yes!' exclaimed Dave McCreith. 'Facts! There are the facts we report but what of the facts we ignore? There's no objective truth, only BBC Correct-Think! What are 'facts', anyway?! The law, science, religion and guardians of morality all change their minds on a daily basis and even then never agree on anything. We can take something that isn't a proven 'fact' but frame it as if it is, as long as it appears to support our ideology... Or simply report something as fact by only quoting or interviewing people who support it.'

'Oh, I know this!' piped up Terry Ball, having not spoken for a while. I don't know what he was doing. I wasn't paying attention as the main conversation was so compelling. 'This is the 'We're Only Reporting What Was Said!' Principle, isn't it? The claim that we're not showing bias simply by 'reporting' something that supports our worldview, even though we wouldn't have given the same prominence to something that didn't!'

'Yes, you are correct,' confirmed the Head of PR. He paused

for a moment before continuing. 'There's the way we only interview people we know are going to give us the opinion we want. Anyone who starts to utter a heretical opinion, say whilst being interviewed on the news, is cut off, unless we deliberately chose them to illustrate how hate-filled a particular group is, for example the white working classes. So for a pro-Brexit interview we want a northerner we can bait into making a racist comment. Whilst we're technically 'showing both sides of the story' we're very carefully framing it to support our view.' He thought for another moment. 'And, of course, we utilise much the same technique when choosing which social media trends to report on. We can 'report' on a tweet, and by doing so give it our implicit approval, whilst still plausibly claiming we're simply reporting on something in the public interest, even though we obviously wouldn't report something that was contrary to our world-view without being far more critical of it.'

'Again, despite my great contempt for the British public I still find it odd nobody notices that, either,' added Dave McCreith. 'I mean, you could use things people have put on Twitter to support literally anything, from flat-earth theory to the idea that the Royal Family are shape-shifting reptilians, and we wouldn't report all those as if they were news, so why don't people notice that when we use a load of tweets as 'evidence' of something?!'

'Well, let us remember that all this works to our benefit,' replied the Head of PR. 'And as for those who do not agree with us, well, there are the ways we can denounce entire groups who hold the incorrect opinions.'

'And, indeed, discredit entire opinions by associating them with groups of which the BBC does not approve,' added Dave McCreith.

'Yes, of course,' continued the Head of PR, 'with the most popular one, of course, being white, bald, working-class men, who must always be depicted and denounced as far-right agitators regardless of what they're actually protesting about, even if it's price rises at Nando's.'

'Absolutely,' replied Dave McCreith, as if they were playing some sort of verbal tennis game. 'The BBC's coverage of a political protest is entirely dependent on the social class of those involved. So, decent middle-class people marching against a war, or holding a vigil against violence towards women, or protesting about environmental issues must be unfailingly reported as noble heroes supporting a worthy cause and portrayed in a positive light, whereas anything involving the lower orders, be it Fathers 4 Justice, pro-Brexit marches or anti-lockdown protests must, without exception, be presented as negatively as possible, with us making every effort we can to divert attention from whatever they say they're protesting about by insinuating they're incredibly racist! I mean, can you think of a single example of the BBC ever having reported positively on a protest being carried out by members of the working classes?!'

'Indeed,' replied the Head of PR, as this example was surely one that could not be denied by anyone who had ever watched the news, regardless of their political leanings. 'And having instructed the followers of BBC Correct-Think to see these people as utterly hate filled and therefore not worthy of being listened to, it's very easy for us to denounce any heretical opinion we choose by simply associating it with this group, creating a none-too-subtle association in the minds of our followers that instructs and conditions them to not only refuse to properly consider it but to go on Twitter and flood it with derogatory and condescending tweets about the protesters in question! And, on top of that, we've trained the compliant media to never dare to point out or even notice this double standard, even when it's as blatant as, say, us reporting protests in Europe against 'populist' leaders or the so-called 'yellow vest' protests in France as valid expressions of social inequality or economic injustice yet when the working classes in the UK do anything similar we unfailingly depict them as peddlers of hate!'

'Ooh!' piped up Terry Ball again. 'You're referring to the Obedience Switch, aren't you?!'

'Yes, that's right,' replied the Head of PR, wondering why a presumed underling knew so much about the terminology of BBC Initiates. 'The Obedience Switch is the figurative switch we place in the heads of correct-thinking people that allows us to turn their brains off when necessary, usually by a trigger word such as 'hate crime' or 'conspiracy theory'. Those terms serve to ensure our most obedient followers simply stop critically considering a topic when we order them to do so.'

Dave McCreith elaborated on this point. 'Another way we discourage people from considering particular beliefs is by associating them with other entirely unrelated opinions we have already designated as being anti-BBC Thought-Crimes, aligning any new heretical belief with the idea that anyone who entertains it must also be a right-wing, pro-Brexit, anti-abortion, anti-vaxx nutter. We did this to denounce anyone who criticised the BBC, and in particular the licence fee, as being just another 'hate group'. It is a powerful, and most useful, tool. It hugely simplifies an argument and, at our behest, closes off actual debate over it.'

Interesting though this all was, Terry Ball was now slightly unsure why the meeting seemed to have wondered off topic, and consisted of little more than the protagonists providing surely unnecessary, and lengthy, explanations of some of the Corporation's most dark practices.

The Head of PR's face lit up at this point. 'And we can literally use it to condition people into believing what we want them to about any topic whatsoever!' he exclaimed. 'We even did it with cycling! We noticed an increase in anti-cyclist sentiment so immediately set about implying that anyone who harboured such beliefs was just another hate-filled person with the incorrect opinions, and that any criticism of a cyclist is a hate crime, pure and simple, and nothing to do with how it's impossible to even leave your front gate without having one of them smash into you whilst cycling on the pavement, whilst looking at their phone, having just jumped a red light and still have *them* scream abuse at *you* for getting in their way! All we needed to do was heavily rotate a clip of Nigel Farage complaining about cycle lanes and, hey presto, all of a sudden if you complain about a cyclist jumping a red light we can denounce you for being part of a hate group, whilst cyclists are able to get away with anything they like and still claim they're being victimised!'

The Head of PR seemed quite pleased to have pulled this trick off, though Dave McCreith looked slightly annoyed at him seemingly claiming credit for something that was in fact a standard and widespread BBC practice.

'Ah, yes, The Farage Association...' Dave McCreith added. 'No one seems to think it odd that on the one hand the BBC claims to find the views of Nigel Farage utterly repellent, whilst also featuring him across our media at least fifteen times a day, other than that it's part of our 'commitment to presenting both sides of the argument', but the true explanation is slightly more complicated. Nigel Farage is the ideal BBC Bogeyman. Whenever we wish to denounce a particular view we simply get him to speak in favour of it, at which point all those people conditioned to believe BBC Correct-Think obediently think the opposite.'

'The beauty of the system is that we can indoctrinate people into believing anything is the 'correct' view regardless of whether it actually makes any sense!' continued the Head of PR. 'Plus, once someone has been labelled as a peddler of hate it's then considered fair game to shower them with constant abuse! I mean, does no-one think it odd that as part of us becoming a society that deeply values tolerance, inclusivity and mutual respect we also agreed that once somebody has been declared a 'transphobe' it's completely acceptable for them to be inundated with death threats, and no one says anything about it?'

The others pondered this, before realising none of them could come up with an even remotely plausible explanation.

'And, indeed,' continued the Head of PR, 'by so easily and conveniently dividing the nation into two groups who utterly despised each other, by controlling their opinions on every single topic, by making everybody define themselves in terms of which side they chose, with no allowance for deviation or independent thought, we were able to tear the country apart and reduce it to the state of primitive tribalism that allowed us to instigate the Great Terror, which in turn gave us the perfect excuse to assume control!'

Terry Ball again pondered why no one appeared to be questioning why this so-called 'meeting' seemed to consist of its members largely reiterating what the other attendees already knew but, nonetheless, they continued to do this, something that is extremely fortunate for me as it allows huge amounts of exposition about the world in which this book is set to be presented. I mean, that was a big hint regarding how the BBC came to power in the first place, but I'm afraid you'll have to wait a few more chapters before it's fully explained, so read on.

'I mean, you can see most of this at work on Question Time,' continued the Head of PR. 'We have four panellists with the correct opinions and one tokenistic bogeyman from a right-wing party who it's made perfectly clear holds the incorrect opinions, and we always choose one of the dimmest members of that group as if to imply that no other members exist, because having an intelligent person putting forward right-leaning arguments would cause the viewers' brains to literally explode. So it's presented as offering a range of opinions when it really does nothing of the sort.'

'Indeed,' added Dave McCreith. 'It's very easy to give the illusion of there being 'balance' on Question Time. A right-winger is allowed on but we cherry-pick one who paints all members of that group in a bad light, then make sure all the other guests spend the whole programme telling him how wrong he is.' He paused for a moment before continuing, 'and, obviously, we try to ensure the programme is filmed in an area populated by those who follow BBC Correct-Think, as you don't want any, say, pro-independence Scots or angry, pro-Brexit northerners asking awkward questions.'

'Well, indeed, your grace,' confirmed the Head of PR.

'Oh, but, hang on,' interrupted Terry Ball. 'We had the BNP on there once, didn't we?'

'Well, yes,' admitted Dave McCreith. 'We were faced with a quandary there. The BBC is fully committed to democracy but, as with free speech, there must be strict limits! Electoral rules forced us to give air time to a party whose views we did not wish to expose to the little people as that would have been extremely dangerous! We knew that by featuring the BNP we risked exposing their opinions to a wider public and making them even more popular!'

'And did that happen?' asked Terry Ball.

'Er, well, admittedly not,' said Dave McCreith. 'They pretty much disappeared after that. I think they solely exist now as a YouTube channel or something. But that's not the point! The point is that the government forced the Corporation to air views with which it did not agree, in the name of so-called 'balance'!'

'But, hang on,' continued Terry Ball, 'wouldn't we still have allowed a member of the Conservative Party or, indeed, Nigel Farage, to appear on the programme and express views that were much the same?'

'Well, yes, of course we would,' answered Dave McCreith, irritably, 'but they're establishment people who know the rules! The BNP were not! The point is that the role of the BBC has always been *to protect the public from itself!* The media must always be a barrier, shielding the proles and stopping them from being exposed to dangerous opinions they're too stupid to properly understand! I mean, we couldn't just let them hear all sides of the argument and make up their own minds, could we? Where would that lead?!'

I should probably clarify here that this is not a pro-BNP rant.

It's about the issue of representation of political parties with differing opinions in the media. Just how far should you tolerate someone whose opinions are different to yours? That's why I chose a controversial, albeit forgotten, party. But the point is that whilst the BNP appeared on Question Time they disappeared pretty much after that, so it didn't make any difference anyway.

'Still,' conceded Dave McCreith, 'at least with the far-right parties you can be fairly blatant in admitting you're banning them. It's harder when parties veer too far to the left for our liking, as then we can't actually ban them so instead have to subtly undermine them and their message, such as by focusing on negative stories about them and giving prominent exposure to their critics. And, again,' he added, thoughtfully, 'it's always struck me as odd that the BBC always presents itself as a caring, sharing, all-in-this-together organisation whose views supposedly border on those of socialism, yet we always seem to get away with doing our very best to discredit any political party that looks like it might actually take the principles we claim to believe in and turn them into actual government policy.'

Also, that's not a pro-leftist Labour rant; again, it's about how different political opinions are depicted by a supposedly neutral broadcaster.

'Huh,' muttered Dave McCreith, partly under his breath. 'The BNP! Imagine an organisation whose name is just three initials going around convinced it's right about everything and always trying to tell people what to think!'

Yes, good to finish that rather heavy bit on a nice, light-hearted joke, I think. Also, yes, this is a long chapter but look at all the powerful points being made! Don't worry, after this one we get back to the brilliant story of John Smith and his incarceration, so not long now.

'Still, since the Great Victory we have purged the Corporation of the few individuals we employed who did not unquestioningly follow BBC Correct-Think,' continued the Head of PR.

'Oh, yes, is the corpse of the heretic Andrew Neil still in that gibbet by the main entrance?' enquired Dave McCreith, casually.

'Yes, your grace,' replied Terry Ball, 'and will be until his traitor's body is entirely decomposed.'

'Good,' replied Dave McCreith. 'Yes, since we are no longer

subject to even tokenistic government rules on whom we appoint, we no longer employ such people and now solely appoint those whose worldview perfectly mirrors that of the Corporation. Indeed, BBC policy now clearly states it is the duty of all employees to constantly tweet sentiments that perfectly echo BBC Correct-Think, knowing that whilst the Corporation will publically rebuke them for 'expressing personal opinions', say that they weren't speaking on the BBC's behalf and promise they'll be reprimanded, they're safe in the knowledge that we'll never actually take any disciplinary action whatsoever!' He paused and smiled for a moment before adding, 'We call this the 'Lineker Principle'!'

'Of course, your grace,' said Terry Ball. 'It was one of the most infamous practices of the BBC even before we took control of the country.'

'Yes, even though BBC employees are, of course, prevented from holding these 'personal opinions' anyway,' added Dave McCreith, before adding, confused, 'whatever 'personal opinions' might be,' and shaking his head. 'For there is only BBC Correct-Think.' He frowned for a moment. 'Still, that illustrates how there is no single aspect of the Corporation's output that does not exist for a secret nefarious purpose, and to subtly promote our worldview, with sport being no exception. Ostensibly we are merely reporting on the goings-on in the sporting world but, of course, everything we report goes through a BBC filter and we never miss an opportunity to add one or more of our own messages whenever we report on it.' He pulled a face at this point. 'Still, my preference would be to only cover proper sports that gentlemen play, such as rugby union and cricket, and certainly not sports enjoyed by the common man such as darts, boxing or football... I mean, rugby and cricket are BBC sports through and through, what with their extensive public school history and representation. I'm just not sure about this *football*... I mean, it's just so... *Proletarian*... I mean, *literally*, 'of the proles'.'

'Indeed, your grace,' replied Terry Ball, attempting to comfort his clearly distressed employer, 'but don't forget the role that popular sport has played in controlling the population for decades. Not only does it present a distraction, either from their humdrum lives or from the important political issues going on in the world, but it also provides us with a very simple way of keeping people hating each other, by allowing us to tap into the primitive and illogical tribalism of so many of its supporters. And having encouraged it, think just how many news reports we've been able to run over the years saying that football supporters, and by extension, all working class people, are nothing more than violent, hate-filled hooligans!'

'Yes, I suppose so,' conceded Dave McCreith. 'Plus the whole football thing helped us no end in creating a stereotype of the lower orders that we were able to easily summon up and invoke whenever we needed to denounce a group of, say, pro-Brexit protestors, quickly and easily without bothering to examine their true motivations or beliefs in any real detail.'

'Absolutely, your grace!' replied Terry Ball, brightly. 'So, you see, even though you don't care for football yourself it's always demonstrated its value as a tool of social control!'

Dave McCreith's face suggested he accepted this point, and the Head of PR continued.

'So, anyway, the next issue to discuss is that of diversity. I'm pleased to announce that the BBC has met its diversity targets once again, and it's all down to your inspired leadership!'

Dave McCreith looked unimpressed with this compliment, as if he was simply being told something of which he was already entirely aware. 'Of course we have,' he replied, as if stating the obvious. 'The BBC exclusively employs minorities.'

'Yes, your excellence,' continued the Head of PR. 'As you correctly point out, since the number of people who attend public school and Oxbridge are a numerically small proportion of the population, logically that makes them a 'minority', and by that revised classification the BBC has thus been able to proudly announce that minorities now make up the entirety of its staff!'

'Which also meant the Corporation has been able to award one of its coveted BBC Diversity Inspiration Awards to itself!' said Terry Ball, proudly.

'Yes, it was a rather brilliant idea on my part,' sniffed Dave McCreith. 'But let's not forget our other commitment to diversity, by which I mean how we employ exactly one person from all the other minority groups.'

'You refer, of course, my liege, to The Rule of One,' added the Head of PR.

'Yes! The Rule of One!' replied Dave McCreith. 'There can be only one person representing a particular group at the BBC at any given time! That's all we need! That's why Lenny Henry was the only black person on TV in the 80s and 90s!'

'Well, technically, it's one person per area, your grace,' corrected Terry Ball, 'so when we had Lenny Henry covering the TV comedy side we also had Moira Stewart reading the news. Again, the Rule of One meant that we could claim to be investing in diversity even though we literally just had one person per group actually being represented.' He looked thoughtful for a moment. 'Hang on, I could be wrong but I don't recall any British Asians or British people of Chinese descent having been on the BBC during the '80s or '90s?'

'Oh, well, that's because all ethnic minorities count as one group to us,' explained Dave McCreith. 'Obviously, in keeping with all liberal institutions, we like to group all people of non-white ethnicities under one, easy to manage label, and that's why we came up with a term for them: BAME, or 'Black, Asian and Miscellaneous Ethnics'!'

Terry Ball looked puzzled again. 'Are you quite sure the 'M' stands for 'Miscellaneous', your grace? It's just that seems rather insulting in that it groups together anyone who doesn't fit into three ethnic groups, including the billion-odd Chinese people in the world?'

The Head of PR stepped in at this point. 'Ah, I think the 'M' actually stands for 'minority', not 'miscellaneous'. Though the end result is still more or less the same because, as you correctly point out, it still groups together at least a billion people so is still rather insulting.'

Clearly frustrated by both his visitor and his underling insisting on unnecessarily complicating things by making entirely reasonable critiques of the topic they were discussing, and annoyed by his failure to properly comprehend them, Dave McCreith attempted to mask this by becoming aggressive. 'I'm not entirely sure what your point is here!' he spluttered. 'As per the Rule of One, we ensure we meet *the bare minimum* requirement we need in order to virtue signal our commitment to diversity, but we're obviously not going to *exceed* it! We do just enough to allow us to issue a press release sanctimoniously boasting about our commitment to representation and to present me with another award for inspirational leadership, but we don't need to go any further than that! Anyway, I simply will not entertain any criticism of the Corporation in this area! The BBC has always been a pioneer where employing people of ethnic ethnicities is concerned!'

'Indeed, your grace,' continued the Head of PR, 'and one of the best recently examples of the Rule of One being used was when we employed June Sarpong to become our Head of Diversity, even though before that she was best known, if she was known at all, for presenting crappy Channel Four shows to audiences of hungover students!'

'Incorrect, my liege!' said Terry Ball, in a dangerously triumphant tone. 'You forget that after that she presented a show in America about conspiracy theories, something that in all other situations the BBC is utterly opposed to and appalled by!'

'Oh yes!' replied Dave McCreith, remembering. 'The BBC's official policy is that anyone who even dares to consider conspiracy theories is guilty of a hate crime, yet we conveniently ignored that when appointing a Head of Diversity because there was, well, a different issue that trumped it. And nobody questioned that appointment! Can you imagine what an outcry there would have been if we'd given a senior position to, say, Alex Zane or David Icke?!' He paused for a moment before adding, 'anyway, she was forced to relocate to the US because of the appalling way TV channels in the UK hardly offered her any work.'

Terry Ball looked vaguely puzzled. 'Did the BBC ever offer her a permanent presenting role?' he asked.

'What are you trying to suggest?!' Dave McCreith shot back, appalled. 'We had her on Question Time once!'

People who are easily offended will miss the point that's actually being made here, but they can do one. It's basically asking this: what exactly is the difference between genuine diversity and mere tokenism, and is there a discussion to be had about whether the BBC makes a distinction between the two?

'Yes, the Rule of One in its purest form,' continued the Head of PR. 'Once a person has been chosen to solely represent their entire race they are assumed to speak for every single member of that race on every single possible topic.'

Terry Ball looked vaguely confused at this. 'Er, it's just a thought, but has anyone ever considered... Employing a range of black people, with different backgrounds and opinions, and having them appear on shows that best suit their interests and expertise, rather than simply having two or three people to speak out on everything?'

'More than one?!' spluttered Dave McCreith. 'Are you mad?

That wouldn't be the Rule of 'One' anymore, would it? And surely you're not suggesting that a single member of a minority group doesn't automatically speak on behalf of all of them?! I mean, if there's an issue that's relevant to the gays, we get a gay on to talk about it. We don't need two, because, I assume, another one won't say anything different to what the first one said.'

'Indeed, your grace,' confirmed the Head of PR. 'That's how it's always worked. We couldn't have two gays on the same show disagreeing with each other. Do you have any idea how much the audience would be confused by that?!'

Terry Ball again looked slightly puzzled, but shook his head and opted not to pursue the matter. He then drew a sharp intake of breath as if he was about to start talking, only to pause, look confused again, then speak after all. 'So, I would assume that in having June Sarpong and Stormzy feature so prominently at the BBC it must be assumed that perhaps one day either of them could end up Director General of the BBC?'

Dave McCreith and the Head of PR immediately looked both pale and shocked.

'Er, well, no, I don't see that happening,' replied Dave McCreith.

'Absolutely not,' confirmed the Head of PR.

'Yes, because, well... You know...' continued Dave McCreith.

'Yes, they're, er...'

'Neither of them went to Oxbridge,' said Dave McCreith. 'Meaning that they fail to meet our diversity requirements. And it is for that reason, and that reason alone, and no other reason, that they can never be considered to take up the exalted position that I currently occupy.' He then looked slightly shifty, as if unsure whether his reasoning had been accepted. Similarly, I hope my point here is correctly understood. If it's not, you may wish to check the ethnic backgrounds of people who sit on the BBC board and then there should be no ambiguity as to what my actual point is here.

'Anyway, your excellence,' continued the Head of PR, 'continuing the topic of minority groups, I also need to discuss that of female representation with you. We need to look at the candidates to be considered for membership of the Skinny Rich White Girl Club.'

'The what?!' asked Terry Ball. I reckon he does actually know, but him pretending not to is very useful for me as now the others will explain it, and then you'll know about it too.

'The Skinny Rich White Girl Club,' replied Dave McCreith, impatiently, suspecting as I do that his underling was actually acquainted with the term, and perhaps annoyed at having to explain. 'I mean, in public we call it the Action Group on Empowering and Inspiring Girls to Work Together Because OMG! Sisters Are Doing It For Themselves, but it's a bit quicker to say Skinny Rich White Girl Club so informally we call it that. Essentially, it's the group we set up in an attempt to disguise, and reconcile, how we always go on about diversity, representation and body positivity whilst only really wanting slim, attractive women to appear on our programmes or website. It's a group of empowered young women who are unwavering in their commitment to encouraging, supporting and promoting womankind, unless the women in question are unattractive, overweight or poor.'

'Oh, I see,' replied Terry Ball.

'Yes, it's basically a group of supposedly deeply-woke, moral, caring women who at the same time are all good-looking and have no qualms about working for heartless multinationals, be that to make films or adverts or whatever,' continued Dave McCreith, 'but also, crucially, make very half-hearted and tokenistic nods towards feminism, entirely in order to promote their personal brand, and usually by tweeting inane inspirational slogans, you know, like 'OMG, Feminism is, like, really cool! Share if you agree!' then a smiley face and picture of an attractive girl...'

'Yes, we call that 'Insta-Feminism',' added the Head of PR. 'It's a portmanteau term combining 'Instagram' with 'Feminism' where celebrities earn woke points by virtue signalling their support for women but in the most half-hearted and vague way, using selfies and emojis even though most of the people who then like or share the post probably think feminism is a brand of shampoo.'

'Indeed,' continued Dave McCreith. 'The Skinny Rich White Girl Club is basically the pool of celebrities we draw on to be on all our best shows or to be endlessly featured in gushing and utterly uncritical reports on our website. It's a system that allows us to say we're being incredibly diverse by implausibly claiming that simply being a woman makes you a persecuted minority on a level with a one legged asylum seeker, meaning we can continue to give the best jobs to the same kind of generically-attractive, skinny, privileged women we've always preferred to have on our programmes yet *still* claim their presence is some sort of devastating blow against the patriarchy!'

'I see,' replied Terry Ball. 'And what sort of women make up this group?'

'Oh, you'd have heard of them all,' Dave McCreith explained. 'Actresses who go on about how woke and caring they are whilst making films for multinational companies with questionable and controversial histories whose films are little more than vehicles to sell toys to little girls that were made in Chinese sweatshops by other little girls... Surgically enhanced stand-up comedians... Incredibly privileged actresses who write supposed comedy shows that are little more than the main character sleeping with everyone she meets that we promote as the greatest piece of writing since Shakespeare... BBC Radio presenters who are constantly boasting about their progressive credentials whilst taking fat paycheques to do voiceovers for Sky, even though they'll claim on other occasions that Rupert Murdoch is an evil media mogul, or the AA, despite otherwise claiming to be pro-environmental...'

'Hang on, they surely can't all be white?' Terry Ball pointed out. 'I mean, we may get away with a complete lack of diversity at Board level but surely we couldn't do so in a more visible area?'

'That is true,' admitted Dave McCreith, 'it gets a bit complicated here, but we can only admit members who fail to meet *one* of the criteria, but no more. So if, for example, we admitted a woman of colour she would still need to be slim and attractive. Or, even better, we try to admit women who only fail to meet one criterion yet act as if they fail to meet more of them. It's by this bizarre piece of logic that we admitted a former model turned supposed actress who was a woman of colour but who we promoted as the token 'fat' one even though she's probably a size twelve or something. This allows us to report her every single utterance on the supposed struggles she had with her 'self-image' and 'body issues' as being of vital, news-worthy importance whilst completely skirting around the glaringly obvious fact that if she really was as fat and ugly as she thinks she is she'd never have become a model in the first place, and that her looks and background have allowed her to be a model, presenter and actress despite an almost complete absence of actual talent.'

He paused for a moment. 'Oh, and whilst we prefer to only admit privileged, privately-educated women, we make occasional exceptions. We'd allow someone in from a more humble background but only if she were skinny and attractive, and fully adhered to the rules. Oh, and for clarity, whilst I said you can still be considered for membership if you fail to meet *one* of the criteria, the exception to that is the requirement to be attractive, over which there's no flexibility because, well, what would we do with unattractive girls?!' His face changed as he remembered something else. 'Oh, and members aren't allowed to have any unattractive friends, either, as that looks bad on Instagram.'

'Yes, I can see why that would be a problem,' agreed Terry Ball. 'Any other rules?'

'Well, from our end, any utterance from any member of the Skinny Rich White Girl Club is to be slavishly reported as if it's actual news,' replied Dave McCreith. 'So, if Emma Watson tweets how much she likes feminism, that goes on the front page of our website, if Taylor Swift makes a very public charitable donation that's the main news article... Oh, and the members must never question each other, nor the foundations upon which the club is based. You see, when Katherine Ryan was being considered for membership she did a stand-up routine that actually criticised Taylor Swift for claiming to be a 'friend to women' whilst only ever hanging out with anorexic, super-privileged models so we told her if she ever did it again she'd never be allowed entry, and she agreed, which is why ever since then her stand-up routines or appearances on TV comedy panel shows have consisted of literally nothing other than her going 'men, eh? Who needs 'em?!' and endless things about her daughter having an English accent.'

'Oh, wait, I think I saw that routine!' interjected Terry Ball. 'Didn't she also do a bit pointing out it's a bit odd that Cheryl Cole became the nation's sweetheart despite having assaulted a black woman?'

'Yes, that's right!' replied the Head of PR. 'That was during her probationary period, so we obviously had words with her about that too, pointing out it is utterly forbidden for one member of the club to in any way criticise another. Well, in public anyway.'

'Is that why Cheryl Cole finally stopped appearing on every single crappy TV talent show in the country? An overdue moral consideration?' asked Terry Ball.

'No, we just got rid of her because she was too old,' replied Dave McCreith, thoughtfully. He paused. 'Or possibly it was because she'd been married so often that her surname had become far too long to fit on the end credits.'

'Oh,' replied Terry Ball, understanding. 'And what about if anyone outside the group criticises it?'

'Oh, that's easy,' replied the Head of PR. 'We simply denounce anyone who criticises them as being deeply misogynistic, regardless of how entirely valid their actual criticism may be!'

'Indeed!' added Dave McCreith, triumphantly. 'If anyone dares to make entirely valid accusations or criticisms of this, in particular relating to the hypocrisy of it all... They're misogynists! Exponents of toxic masculinity at its very worst!'

(You see? So, if you were thinking of using that argument to attack the excellent and valid points I made here, I'm way ahead of you and you actually need to consider the actual arguments and, you know, refute them with logic, argument and evidence rather than outrage, okay?!)

'And what if women criticise this group?' asked Terry Ball.

'Oh, they never do,' replied the Head of PR. 'Either because they're simply too well-conditioned to notice, or because they like to think one day they'll be allowed to join or, in the case of the women who will never meet enough criteria to be permitted membership, by us offering them a consolation prize of endless appearances on terrible Radio 4 panel shows.'

'So, yes, it's basically a group that women need to join in order to be considered for elevation to the next level of celebrity,' said Dave McCreith. 'Essentially it benefits both us and its members, as they get to build their brands on being woke and caring whilst we get to show how supportive we are of women, even if they are all skinny, attractive, white ones...'

'Well, until they hit forty, at which point, well, sometimes we put them on Radio 4, but it's not really our problem by that point,' added the Head of PR. 'or 6Music, just as long as they promise not to highlight the lack of diversity on that woke station.'

'What are you talking about?!' spluttered Dave McCreith. 'As per the Rule of One, 6Music has *one* black DJ and *one* mixed race DJ! Anyway, I don't see how anyone can criticise that because we gave them their own station when we launched BBC 1Xtra!'

Terry Ball nodded, interestedly, no longer sure whether he already knew any of this but still glad it had been made clear.

'Actually, that reminds me,' added the Head of PR. 'Someone actually *did* dare to criticise some of the group's members after they appeared on Comic Relief and it was then discovered that the t-shirts we sold for it were made in a sweatshop. And do you know what we did?! We issued a statement saying that child labour in China is simply another form of empowering girls to control their financial destiny! Girl power!'

So, yeah, that bit's all about hypocrisy, really, as is so much of this book. That's the point there, but I imagine people will still miss all that and decry it as misogynist. Oh well.

Dave McCreith looked thoughtful as he wondered whether there was anything else they needed to address, before his face lit up as he remembered. 'Ah, yes... Are there any updates with regard to... The Book?'

The very mention of this immediately changed the mood of the room, as if a topic had been raised that they would all prefer not to discuss or even consider, but knew they had to.

'Oh, yes, The Book...' said the Head of PR. 'That repellent, heretical text... That supposed 'satire' of the BBC that was in reality nothing more than a sickeningly brutal attack on everything the Corporation holds dear...'

'You're talking about the book called 'The Book the BBC Tried to BAN!' I assume?', interjected Terry Ball. 'The book self-published by a mysterious author to great popular success, and now used as an inspiration to all those who oppose the Corporation?'

'Yes!' replied Dave McCreith, furiously. 'That sickening, hate-filled, unfunny, supposedly satirical, supposedly amusing, utterly repellent piece of trash that ruthlessly and relentless mocks and parodies everything that the BBC holds dear!'

'Indeed, your grace,' agreed the Head of PR, sensing the Director General's considerable distress. 'All of us at the Corporation share your disgust with it. It was unfunny. It was unforgivable...'

'It was heresy!' screamed Dave McCreith, slamming his fist down upon his desk. At least he did that if he was near his desk, but I can't remember where I last had him standing, to be honest. It's quite difficult keeping track of where all the characters are. 'It was nothing but Anti-BBC Thought-Crime, and the author did not even have the common decency to try to disguise it as anything else!' he continued, his rage unabated. 'And our ruthless suppression of it was entirely justified!'

'Of course, my liege,' agreed the Head of PR. 'We employed the usual methods: first, our official line was that we had never heard of The Book. Then, when we could ignore it no longer we used Reality Check to 'examine' and denounce the contents, even though it was presented as a work of fiction... Then we denounced it as a 'book of hate', knowing that would mean many obedient followers would refuse to read it... But even that wasn't enough! It was still out there!'

'So we officially banned our staff from reading it,' continued Dave McCreith, 'or even admitting they had heard of it. And then, we launched legal action. But we had no choice!'

'Of course not, my liege,' the Head of PR confirmed. 'Criticism of the BBC is heresy, and those who commit it must be subjected to the most severe punishments.'

'Of course, he claimed it was 'satire' before it went to trial,' added Dave McCreith. 'But it wasn't! The BBC has a proud history of satire, going back to the Frost Report and That Was The Week That Was but, of course, satire does not extend to us! Making fun of the government is hilarious satire, but mocking the BBC itself is an abhorrent hate crime! That's the rule! The BBC is beyond reproach! Beyond criticism! Beyond mocking and beyond parody!'

The possible confused meaning of all this was entirely lost on him, and he had worked himself up into quite a frenzy. The Head of PR attempted again to calm him.

'Indeed, your excellency,' he said. 'The BBC is utterly committed to free speech, considering it to be a sacred pillar of a civilised society, something utterly sacrosanct, something that is a fundamental right of every single human being, but free speech must have clearly proscribed limits! And those limits include *never* using it to attack the Corporation itself!' Something else then occurred to him. 'Yes, we do enjoy toying with people where the whole concept of 'free speech' is concerned. 'I mean, none of our readers ever thought it odd that we ran an article saying that the Chinese government checking up on things that students from Hong Kong said whilst studying in the UK was a disgusting infringement of their human rights whilst quietly skirting around the fact that universities in Britain are amongst the most censorious places in the world, where there are strict limits placed on what *all* their students say, regardless of nationality.'

So, hopefully you can see what I'm doing here: very much trying to cover my back against potential legal action from a litigious BBC. And it gets better!

'Yes,' agreed Dave McCreith. 'And there was the name he gave to The Book... I mean, I have to assume that by calling it 'The Book the BBC Tried to BAN!' he thought, somewhat naively, that he would be safe from legal action, as the Corporation would not want to look foolish by getting involved in a legal case in which it was trying to ban a book that was itself called 'The BBC vs The Book the BBC Tried to BAN!'.'

So, yes, the author in this book used that as a hopeful defence against prosecution and so am I.

'I always assumed that was his reasoning, my liege,' said Terry Ball. 'Though I agree that it seems like a rather flimsy assumption.'

'Indeed, your grace,' the Head of PR concurred. 'It was as if to say that by calling it that he somehow thought he was legally covering himself because if we did then try to ban it we'd be caught in some sort of cleverly self-referential, post-modern self-fulfilling prophesy?!'

Dave McCreith looked extremely annoyed and frustrated by people below him using words and terms he could not hope to understand.

'Perhaps,' he postulated, with a slight, and misplaced, air of superiority, 'you could say all of that in terms comprehensible to a normal person?'

'Er, yes, of course, your excellency,' replied the Head of PR, obediently. 'He's a bad man.'

'That's better,' replied Dave McCreith, satisfied. 'Still, there was the issue that he felt the BBC would try to avoid adverse publicity, such as when people became aware it was using licence fee payers' money on a huge legal case simply to suppress a book that had hurt its feelings.'

'Yes, you'd think any lawyer who read the book whilst trying to establish whether there were grounds for legal action would have realised that its scope was just too great and that the author had pre-empted every possible course of action,' added Terry Ball.

'Well, I don't see how lining the pockets of a small army of lawyers simply to pursue a vanity case could ever be seen as a waste of licence payers' money,' added Dave McCreith. 'Anyway, even though he escaped justice prior to us taking him to court, we won the action and, after a lengthy search, located the heretic!'

'Indeed, your grace,' concluded the Head of PR. 'It no longer matters. Ownership of the book remains a capital offense and the author's body remains in a gibbet outside the main entrance of New White City as a warning to any others who fancy themselves satirists and think the noble BBC is a fair target.'

'And as a warning to all the BBC's enemies, including the so-called 'Resistance',' added Dave McCreith.

'Indeed, your excellence,' confirmed the Head of PR. 'In both its forms: The Resistance as we understand it, a real, anti-BBC group, plus the fictional 'resistance' that we made up in order to create fear and justify our increased military presence on the streets.'

'Yes. Good,' said Dave McCreith, leaning back in his chair and stroking his chin. Yes, he was sitting down now if I didn't mention it before. 'Well, does that conclude our business?'

'It does, your grace,' confirmed the Head of PR, standing up and heading for the door. 'The BBC will prevail!'

'The BBC will prevail!' repeated Dave McCreith and Terry Ball in unison.

# Chapter Seven:

# Wash Your Brain Out With Soap and Water

*In Which Our Hero Is Forced to Watch a Propaganda Film Where Prominent Hollywood Stars Sort of Apologise For Having Spent Their Entire Careers Working With Producers and Directors Who Were All Known Sex Offenders Yet Also Seem to Be Saying It Was All Fine As The Films In Question Earned Them Lots of Money and Won Them Loads of Oscars*

John Smith was startled from his attempts at sleep by a bucket of icy cold water being hurled over him. Gasping for breath, he sat up, confused and disorientated. A guard was standing in front of him, grinning.

'Time to wake up! Did you sleep well?'

John Smith could tell the question was not meant seriously but he was too groggy to think clearly so responded anyway.

'Well, no, not really, seeing as how you ran your baton across the bars of my cell every half an hour, and I could hear people's petrified screams ringing out across the camp practically non-stop...'

'Well, this place isn't meant to be a holiday resort!' replied the guard, still grinning. 'Did you expect to lounge around all day watching Sky TV and playing video games? What do you think this is, prison?!'

John Smith rubbed his eyes and shook his head slowly. 'Well, I didn't really expect anything because I never expected to be here,' he responded, wearily. 'Has my lawyer arrived yet?'

The guard threw his head back and guffawed. John Smith remembered that he could expect no lawyer, nor anything remotely resembling justice. He sat up and stretched out. 'So, have you woken me up like this just to tell me it's time for breakfast?'

The guard looked at him in astonishment. 'Oh, were you expecting three square meals a day and plenty of snacks in between? Like I said, this isn't prison!'

John looked at him, unsure how to respond. The guard continued.

'No, you won't be eating for a long time. It's time for you to watch a film. We find the messages it contains are much more easily taken in when our captives have an empty stomach. Now get up!'

Without really thinking, John got to his feet. The guard motioned with his baton that John should follow him, and left the room, with John obediently following a few steps behind.

Once in the yard they were joined by a number of other new inmates, also being led to what appeared to be a converted theatre. In his more lucid moments since arriving John had attempted to work out what the original purpose of the camp had been and begun to vaguely think it had been a holiday camp such as Butlin's or Pontin's. That would explain the corrugated iron dormitories. The sort of living quarters that would have seemed luxurious to someone who'd just spent six years hiding in air raid shelters and living on rations but seemed extremely basic to anyone more accustomed to modern comforts. As his brain started to wake up he began to ponder the significance of this. He remembered his grandparents telling him about holiday camps in the '50s and '60s, and how the people in charge often seemed like they'd recently left the armed forces and treated the holidaymakers much the same as they would prisoners of war. The checking that people had put their lights out by a certain time. The regimented lives they led, all waking up at the same time and taking their meals together. Then again, he pondered, many of the holidaymakers themselves would also have recently been demobbed so perhaps it was only appropriate that they were treated in a similar way as they had been whilst in the forces. Still, he pondered, there was always a thin line dividing Redcoats and Blackshirts.

John was jolted from this half-somnambulistic daydream by a sharp whack from the guard's baton, indicating they had now arrived at their destination. It was a building he vaguely suspected of having once been the camp cinema and once he was taken inside he discovered it still served that purpose. He and his fellow new inmates were led to the stalls and told to sit down. They looked at each other cautiously, afraid to initiate conversation but all sharing the same concern over what awaited them. After a few minutes of silence the Commandant walked onto the stage, in front of the screen.

'Good morning, campers!' he began, with a smile, as if to suggest he thought it was funny. Each inmate carefully looked around, attempting the gauge how to respond, then most of them laughed half-heartedly.

'Silence!' screamed the Commandant. 'I did not give you permission to make noise!'

The inmates looked at the floor guiltily, and the Commandant continued.

'Some of you may know why you are here. Some of you may not. Some of you may think you do yet may be mistaken. But the point is you have all committed anti-BBC Thought-Crime, something that no civilised society should or can tolerate if it is to retain its unity. However, in keeping with the intentions of Sir John Reith, our noble founder, the BBC has never been about entertainment. If you think otherwise, you must have seen very little of our Saturday night output. It has always been about education or, to give it its correct term, indoctrination. Conditioning into the correct worldview. The correct values. For a mind with the correct values is a happy mind, whilst a mind that is full of questions and contradictions is the mind of someone who can never even hope to find true peace.'

The inmates were terrified of showing any reaction at this point, so continued to stare at the Commandant, almost as if they were afraid to blink for fear of being reprimanded.

'However,' the Commandant continued. 'We are not an unfair organisation. The Corporation may imprison hundreds of thousands of people a year for non-payment of the licence fee but all those people eventually realise that their incarceration is not only for their own good but for the good of society as a whole. And there is no reason why the same cannot apply to those taken to our Re-Education Camps for crimes of anti-BBC Thought-Crime. You may have taken issue with your treatment here, but it is for your own good. Because we believe in second chances. We believe *anyone*, no matter how heinous their crimes, deserves a second chance and can potentially be released back into the world as a useful, and unquestioning, member of society. *Anyone* can learn BBC Correct-Think, even you.'

At this point the curtains behind him started to open, revealing a cinema screen. He started to pace around the stage as he spoke further.

'The point is that anyone can be changed, as long as they accept their guilt, confess, apologise and move on. In this world, literally everything and anything can be forgiven, as long as the person demonstrates that they hold the correct views, either before the offence or at any time afterwards. So what you are now going to see is a film in which many well-known figures apologise for their crimes, atone for them and show that anyone can follow their noble example.'

He started to walk off the stage, and as he did so used a remote control to start the film. Dispensing with any sort of title or opening credits, the first scene showed a famous British star of both stage and screen, the sort of generic BBC actor who'd been to Eton and Oxford, who John recognized for having been in endless period dramas and numerous oh-so-worthy films in which the promotion of a particular message or worldview had seemed far more important to the filmmakers than minor details like it actually being entertaining or well made. But, John reflected, for all his fame, accolades and success, he'd never really decided if the actor in question could actually act, and then realized he couldn't even name, much less remember, a single thing he'd ever actually been in.

'Hi!' the actor on screen began, flashing his expensive smile. 'I'm here today to tell you how amazing the BBC is. I mean, it really is! Think of all the work it gives to untalented posh people with family connections! Yes, we should all love the BBC! I've made tons of money from them, too, because they've put me in loads of shows! And it doesn't even matter if nobody watches them because they've never been dependent on viewing figures so can just keep on commissioning things as long as they like! And it was easy for me because my parents were already actors and I went to Eton! So, yeah, anyone who criticises the BBC and says the licence fee is out of date is a heretic, pure and simple!'

He then paused and looked thoughtful, as if he had only just stopped to wonder what he was actually meant to be saying, and what his motivation was. He then looked to his side, as if someone off-camera had said something, listened to whatever this was, looked slightly confused, then returned to the camera.

'Er, right, sorry, ignore all that. Basically, the point is that the BBC is, really good, and you should love it as much as I do, even if in your case all it does is take a huge amount of money from you whereas in my case it gives me loads! But, er, beyond that I really can't think of any specifics.'

John Smith was quite puzzled at this. Surely it must have occurred to the BBC that the public would think it a little odd if the people they used as mouthpieces to speak out in support of the Corporation and attack anyone who dared challenge it were the exact same people to whom it had given frequent, easy and extremely well-remunerated employment?! How would that make sense? He scratched his head. What was all this?!

The confused actor disappeared and was replaced by another one. Until recently the cream of Hollywood and the British stage, she had been praised for her presence, her delivery and her unrivalled skill at depicting emotion, yet all the critics, producers and directors who had once so frequently offered such praise all seemed, by quite remarkable coincidence, to have stopped praising her acting talent at almost exactly the same time that she hit forty and her looks started to fade, so John assumed that since then she had simply existed in the purgatorial no-man's land that actresses are exiled to once they are no longer considered attractive enough to appear as romantic leads but before they are old enough to be considered for the predictable roles offered to women of late middle age and beyond, like Queen Elizabeth I or, well, that's about the only one, really. In the same rehearsed, sincere manner that she had employed in countless TV ads where she appealed for the public to part with their hard-earned money for some noble and worthy cause whilst she continued to live in luxury, often on a private island, she looked at the camera earnestly, with a sad look in her eyes.

'Many of you may be wondering why you're here today,' she

began. 'And I fully empathise with your situation and understand your confusion. And that's because I was once like you.'

John Smith raised an eyebrow at this; on the one hand, the following speech could offer some insight into his current situation but, on the other, he realised that the fact it was clearly pre-recorded and intended to apply to everybody in the camp meant it could not contain anything too specific. The actress continued.

'For we all make mistakes in our lives. Any one of us can suffer a momentary lapse of judgement, no matter how brief, and it's my firm belief that for you to truly move on in your life you need to repent for any such mistakes, after which you can draw a line underneath them and viciously attack anyone who dares remind the general public about them.'

She now shifted in her chair and did her best to look deeply sincere before continuing.

'I cannot deny it is true that for the first twelve films of my Hollywood career I worked with Harry Harvstein, a man who has since been convicted of four hundred and thirty seven rapes, a figure that prosecutors believe is barely a tenth of the true number, and subsequently imprisoned for so long that the authorities expect to have to provide a cell for his rotting corpse for a good two centuries after his death. As to why I turned a blind eye to his activities for so long, I would point out in my defence that at the same time I frequently made extremely vague public statements about how awful some people in Hollywood were, obviously without naming any names. A number of cruel trolls have suggested there was something 'problematic' in how I made thirteen films with a man now known to be one of Hollywood's most prolific sex offenders,' she continued, 'but to them I would point out that had I not done so I may never have become famous enough to build a platform from which I could campaign so passionately for women's issues.'

She took a breath before continuing. 'And on top of that I would hope the public remembers that in making these films I became extremely famous and earned many millions of dollars.'

John Smith continued to be confused. What was this? An apology?! Because whilst it was sort of presented as one it soon became clear that the actress in question was apologising for next to nothing and instead simply seemed to be trying to justify her position to her critics. She continued.

'Of course, many of you will remember that I first rose to Hollywood fame after appearing in a series of films based on books written by an author who for years was celebrated as one of the most progressive figures in the world because she used to tweet about refugees and stuff. I obediently never pointed out there was an almost complete lack of diversity in her actual books, or that her many attempts to retrospectively claim them as being far more woke than they were, like how they supposedly had a gay wizard in them even though she didn't mention that in the books themselves and didn't even publicly announce it until about ten years later, were a rather blatant attempt to jump on that bandwagon...'

She looked slightly confused here, as if she had gone off on a diversion and forgotten what her actual point was, before her expression changed again to suggest she had remembered again. 'Anyway,' she continued, 'despite all that, and after years of it being considered heretical to challenge her on anything, she said something about how there may be a connection between being a man and having a penis or something. I obviously don't know the exact details as I wasn't going to risk my reputation standing up for her against a deranged Twitter mob by actually objectively considering the facts and science of what she said, so I unquestioningly joined in with the denunciation of her even though she'd basically launched my whole career. Of course, it now goes without saying that I view this person as one of the most vile thought-criminals to ever have lived and, in fact, I'm proud to say I have since cut off contact with her completely, and that the only communication we still have is when our respective agents contact each other regarding the millions in royalties I continue to receive for having appeared in adaptations of books by this hateful figure.'

John Smith continued to be completely baffled. He had often wondered how people in the public eye managed to internally deal with the mental dissonance of such blatant contradictions and hypocrisy but the overpowering message he was receiving today is that they didn't need to, as they simply ignored them. The actress continued.

'Of course, one of my most critically-acclaimed performances was in that film I did about the Holocaust, where I was directed by Paul Romanski. Now, whilst I was well aware when making that film that its director had been on the run for over thirty years after being charged with sexual offenses against a thirteen year old girl, I would point out to them that the reason I overlooked this was because I felt the message of the film needed to be told, and that message was that the Holocaust was really bad. Also, I won an Oscar for daring to deliver this powerful message.'

She paused for a moment. 'Anyway, it was a different time, a different era. It was the year 2007, and I do not believe I should be judged for things I did way back then. Plus I was only thirty four at the time.' She then looked thoughtful. 'Ooh, but would I get publicity and woke points if I now returned the Oscar, saying I should never have worked with him? Maybe I should. I mean, even if I did, the win would still be on my record, making it an entirely tokenistic gesture.'

John Smith remained utterly confused as to whether there was even supposed to be a message to all this, much less what it actually was.

'Also, more recently,' she continued, 'some cruel trolls have suggested that I showed a lack of judgment in making a film with Allan Forrest, a director who famously impregnated and married his own daughter. But in my defence, I really wanted a second Oscar, and felt that working with him was my best shot at that. However, regarding my comments at the time that incest is 'a private matter' and 'a family affair', I do now apologise. However, I will still accuse anyone who suggests hypocrisy on my part of being a misogynist, and sue them for all they have.'

John Smith shook his head. I mean, what was this now?! A blatant admission of the true motivation of Hollywood stars with no attempt to cover it up. He continued to wonder whether the film was just some bizarre trick to confuse them even further. The actress continued.

'Of course, my next project saw me portraying a one-legged, lesbian, trans refugee from Iran who also had AIDS and suffers the indignities of attempting to cross Europe to claim asylum in the UK...' The actress looked briefly confused, as if struggling to remember just how many minority groups her character had taken inspiration from in its shameless attempt at an Oscar-grab, then continued anyway whilst still retaining a look in her eyes suggesting she had forgotten a good two or three more. '...whilst funding the trip by working as a toilet cleaner and prostitute, and when I took this role I felt that playing such a box-ticking minority character was an absolute guarantee that I'd receive my next Academy Award, particularly when you consider how they were freely handed out for Daniel Day-Lewis portraying that spastic or Eddie Redmayne pretending to be a cripple, through to Tom Hanks getting a double whammy of Oscars in consecutive years, one for playing a man with AIDS and another for playing a mental. It is to my immense regret and personal shame, however, that just before the film was released the rules all changed and it went from being incredibly empowering and inspirational to portray minorities, and a sure-fire way to get an Oscar, to being seen as a repellent act of queer-baiting or cultural appropriation, and as a result I came in for intense criticism for portraying a minority figure when I am not part of any of those communities. In particular, I have never cleaned a toilet in my entire life.'

John Smith carefully looked around so as to try to gauge the reaction of his fellow audience members. What was this, exactly? It was presented as an apology, but the tone and the frequent casual admissions of wrongdoing without real remorse almost made it seem more like a weirdly ambiguous parody that left the viewer extremely confused as to what the actual message was. The film continued.

'Also, with regards to the rumours that the director of that film was a keen practitioner of necrophilia, allegations that have since been proven entirely true and were an open secret at the time, I now wish to apologise, not only for working with that director in the first place but for my statement at the film's premiere in which I appeared to be defending his sexual preferences by saying that necrophilia is 'a victimless crime'. In addition, I accept I was wrong to appear in a video calling for it to be legalised and for its practitioners to be recognised as a minority group and protected by law, and that it was an error of judgment for me to lead a campaign for the practice to be included in the LGBTQI initialism. To be honest, the woke thing was starting to take off in a big way even then so I was in many ways hedging my bets whilst being fully aware that there was no real logic or consistency to any of it and that it was entirely luck as to whether I ended up being seen as having been on the right or wrong side of history.'

By this point John Smith had no idea if the whole thing we was witnessing was some sort of bizarre joke. Apart from the completely contradictory and unapologetic messages, a lot of the time it seemed like the actors had simply been put in front of a camera to ramble in an inconsistent and freeform manner.

Back on the screen, the actress looked momentarily flustered before a briefly discernible change in where she was looking suggested she had remembered the autocue in front of her and was now returning to its pre-approved message. She took a deep breath, folded her hands in her lap and again stared earnestly into the camera.

'I've done a lot of soul-searching in recent years, and not just because I've had so much time on my hands after my acting roles largely dried up when I hit forty. But this is what I've come to realise: forgiveness is crucial to us moving on as a society, just as long as the person in question has generally expressed the correct views. And that is why I am campaigning to make it a crime for newspapers, websites or people on social media to accuse celebrities of hypocrisy for claiming to be woke despite having a long history of working with child abusers or massive rapists simply to further their careers.'

John Smith was even more perplexed by this point. Was this actress expressing remorse or was this a bizarre campaign video?! What had begun as an apology now seemed to be her saying that she regretted nothing, was in no way apologising for her actions and was arguing that anyone who pointed out her hypocrisy was committing a far worse transgression than the things she freely admitted to having done.

But there was more. Fortunately only a bit, though, as this section has been quite long.

'Let me assure you: Hollywood *is* woke. Hollywood *is* progressive. And if, on the many occasions we let our colleagues in Hollywood down with behaviour that perhaps falls short of the incredibly high standards we expect of everybody except ourselves, we apologise, and carry on as before whilst also continuing to criticise other people who act in exactly the same way we have but either failed to show remorse before doing it again or have never expressed the correct social or political opinions.'

She paused for a moment before adding, 'also, I've recently been leading a very public campaign to make sure that soldiers accused of rape in a warzone can still be prosecuted years later but, for clarity, I will not be campaigning for the same rules to be applied to anyone in Hollywood unless it's someone whose power within the industry has significantly diminished or, even better, has already been imprisoned due to the tireless campaigning of people far, far braver than I am.'

Her eyes lit up again, indicating she had remembered something else. 'Oh, also, some of you may remember a film where I played the wife of a murdered journalist in which I literally blacked up to portray a mixed-race person,' she went on, 'but that was way back in 2007, which was a completely different time and, anyway, I've adopted loads of kids, all the colours of the rainbow, so, weirdly, if you criticise me, even if it's for blacking up, then that actually means it's you who's racist.'

The actress again glared mournfully into the camera before concluding thus: 'Anyway, the point here is that as a woman, and in particular a woman in the public eye who speaks out on behalf of women, I am in no way responsible for my actions, and anyone who says I should be or who criticises me in any way is, of course, guilty of the repellent crime of misogyny, regardless of how valid their actual criticism may or may not be.' She pulled a sad face, looked down, and that section of the film ended.

As previously discussed, this chapter is already quite long I've decided to condense the next bit. Basically, another Hollywood star appears next and desperately tries to justify presenting himself as a woke figurehead of progressive Hollywood whilst working for a coffee company that was revealed to be using child labour, along with making films about the political situation in Syria whilst remaining pretty tight-lipped about Chinese oppression of the Uighur people. Obviously the point there is that Hollywood makes endless films about how awful the Holocaust was but even though there's something comparable to it going on today, actors are terrified of mentioning it because they don't want their latest film to be banned in China as that'll massively affect the amount of money it makes. So here are a few of the things he said in this chapter before I decided it was getting too long and cut his scene:

'Also, when it was revealed that the coffee I promoted so shamelessly was actually picked by seven year olds working for nothing other than the promise that if they picked enough coffee then they wouldn't be beaten to death in front of their co-workers, I naturally issued a vague statement about how bad it was, but neither ended my relationship with the coffee company nor handed back any of the millions of dollars I'd made from them even though the only reason they claimed they'd change their ways is because they got caught, and it's surely a sign of how dodgy they are that they did it in the first place. You may think that moving forward I might have had some moral objection to continuing to work with a company that had misled me and the public and was willing to do such a thing in the first place, and that to continue working with them based on nothing more than a vague promise that they wouldn't do it again was in some way problematic, but I do need to point out that in this situation I was paid an immense amount of money to continue to act as a spokesperson, and without that money I may have struggled to keep up the payments on my private jet. You see, people often think that us Hollywood stars aren't like the rest of you, but me having just shared my financial struggles with you shows that we really are.'

That was still a bit long, I know, but that surely proves my point that this chapter is frankly getting a bit out of hand. Also, along with this chapter being a bit long it's not *really* about the BBC, is it? Still, the BBC very much worships Hollywood stars with the correct viewpoint, so I think this is all fine. Anyway, back on screen the actor turned to the camera, whilst prominently holding up a cup of the coffee that he was paid loads to promote and continued to do so despite allegations of child labour.

'So,' he began by way of conclusion, 'when I learnt of the allegations of child labour being carried out by the manufacturers of this delicious coffee, rich and aromatic, I publically announced that I was 'saddened' and then continued as normal. So it's all fine. Did I mention my wife is a human rights lawyer? Well, she is. So I'm basically beyond reproach here. The point is that all of you are here today because you made a mistake. And the last thing I want to tell you is that everyone makes mistakes. Except me, and everyone else in Hollywood. Not only that, but with the correct apology, often really short and half-hearted, there is no mistake that cannot ultimately be forgiven, to the extent than you can simply carry on doing what you were doing before.'

He smiled and nodded at the camera, then took a sip of the child labour-employing coffee. 'Remember, it's not the actions that count in situations like this. Whilst some people accused me of being massively hypocritical, I would point out that saying something and doing something are actually different things, so it's only hypocrisy if you *say* contradictory things, not if you *say* one thing and *do* something else, as then they're unrelated. In fact, I'm petitioning for the word 'hypocrisy' to be made illegal, and for anyone who accuses a Hollywood star of being hypocritical to be prosecuted for having committed a hate crime.'

He flashed his winning smile again. John Smith raised an eyebrow. Was this satire?! He really had no idea. The whole thing could plausibly have been an arthouse prank or, more likely, a test on which their reactions would be monitored and judged. Was it even an apology? There didn't seem to be a single grain of remorse. It basically seemed that people in Hollywood, as long as they, by and large, expressed the correct opinions, could be forgiven for anything and only needed to make an extremely half-hearted and tokenistic apology before they were welcomed back into the fold.

The screen went black, the lights came back on and the curtains closed again. As they did so the Commandant strode back onto the stage with a cruelly demented glint in his eyes.
'Well!' he yelled. 'I hope that cleared things up for you all!'
John Smith looked around, helpless and confused. His fellow audience members looked just as baffled. It had cleared up nothing. It had covered a huge range of topics yet ultimately offered a bewilderingly confusing range of possible interpretations. If their minds had previously been dirty puddles only disturbed by a light breeze, the film was the equivalent of two pigeons having both a fight and a vigorous mating session in the puddle, splashing the water everywhere and, if anything, dispersing most of it. They slowly rose to their feet and, led by the guards, wandered, dazed, back into the yard.

# Chapter Eight:

# The Errors of Comedy

*In Which the Peculiar and Often Contradictory Nature of the Corporation's Comedic Output Is Discussed, Along With The Usefulness of Comedy In Manipulating People's Opinions, The Issues of Representation, Diversity and Tokenism And Whether The Word 'Fallacious' Sounds Sufficiently Like 'Fellatio' To Be Turned Into A Joke on Mrs Brown's Boys*

Dave McCreith awoke with a start. Having worked furiously for almost ten minutes he had fallen asleep from the exertion and two hours had since passed. The work itself had required immense effort and concentration as he had been adding his initials to every single page of a large document relating to BBC policy, which he had naturally not actually read and would have been utterly unable to comprehend if he had. As he started to realise where he was, he began to panic. It had started to get dark but the lights in his office had not been turned on. Cautiously, he stood up. Realising he did not know how lights were turned on, he swiftly became flustered. 'Lights turn on!' he yelled, before looking expectantly upwards, assuming that, like everything else in the Corporation, the lights would unquestioningly obey his command. When they did not he looked annoyed again and clapped his hands. Still nothing happened.

'Ball! Where are you?!' He looked around, wondering where his faithful lackey had disappeared to. 'Dave McCreith hungry!' he said aloud. 'Ball!' He wandered over to the window and briefly cast his disapproving gaze down onto the vast cardboard city of displaced council tenants who, to his great displeasure, still made their home right outside the BBC's glacial new headquarters. They had started to light fires and he briefly became indignant that they had all managed to arrange illumination whilst he had not.

Dave McCreith now weighed up his options. He could leave his office and attempt to locate his errant assistant but that was a path of action fraught with danger. He had no wish to bump into a cleaner. Nor, indeed, anyone more than two pay grades below himself. Whilst he knew that was unlikely due to security restrictions on the top seven floors of New White City meaning that only those whose salaries were in excess of two million pounds per annum (before bonuses and performance related pay) were allowed there, he knew that still meant he could bump into any of the four thousand executives whose salaries were on that level. Confused, he sat down on the floor. Then he heard footsteps down the corridor. He leapt to his feet and listened carefully. The footsteps were approaching but, disappointingly, neither of the people making them was speaking, making it impossible for him to discern who was outside his office. Taking a deep breath and puffing his chest outwards in an attempt to give himself courage, he then sharply pulled the door open, revealing an unfamiliar face holding his fist up as if about to knock.

Dave McCreith, however, interpreted this raised fist as a threat of violence. 'Don't hurt me!' he begged. 'I'll give you your own chat show!'

At that moment Terry Ball appeared just behind the visitor and Dave McCreith's shoulders dropped as he uttered a deflated sigh of relief.

'Sorry to temporarily abandon you, your grace,' said Terry Ball, 'but I had to pop down to collect some statistics to deliver to this gentleman, relating to the monitoring of brainwaves to check just how deeply the messages ingrained in our programmes are sinking into the minds of those who watch them.'

He indicated to the guest that he may enter the office, which he did, and Terry Ball then came in behind him and shut the door. The visitor was the Head of BBC Comedy. As with so many other characters I don't think it's necessarily worth giving him a name, seeing as he doesn't really play a part in the narrative and, as with so many of the chapters set in New White City, merely exists to represent and explain a particular topic. Unusually, Dave McCreith's face lit up when he entered the room, as if to say he genuinely considered the work of him and the department he led to be of value rather than being just another opportunity to overfill the Corporation with overpaid executives, even though that was something of which he was extremely supportive.

'Ah, welcome, welcome!' he began brightly. 'It's always a pleasure to welcome into my office the head of the department that has given Britain so many brilliant, classic comedy programmes over the years!'

'And Mrs Brown's Boys, too!' added Terry Ball. 'You love that programme, don't you, your grace?'

'Yes, yes, you gave us Mrs Brown's Boys! I just love that show! Particularly the bits where one of the characters says 'penis'!'

'Well, thank you, your eminence,' replied the Head of Comedy, graciously, 'we employ the very finest comedy writers on that show.' He then paused and looked confused before correcting himself. 'No, hang on, sorry, what I meant to say was that that show doesn't even have a script, and we merely get the actors to say whatever comes into their heads, just as long as they also say the word 'penis' twice per sentence. Or 'willy'. Either is fine.'

Dave McCreith uncharacteristically laughed at this point. 'Willy!' he exclaimed. 'BBC comedy at its best!' It was almost as if the merest thought of Mrs Brown's Boys had led him to regress to an infantile state.

'Thank you again, your excellence,' replied the Head of Comedy. He then looked confused once more, and corrected himself again. 'Hang on, did I say 'actors'? Obviously there are no actors in that show. It's just some random guy and his mates saying 'penis' all the way through the episode. It's actually one of the cheapest programmes for the BBC to make seeing as it has no writers nor actors involved in its entire creation.'

'Excellent, excellent!' said Dave McCreith, before sniggering again. 'Penis!' he said to himself. 'Anyway,' he continued, composing himself. 'For me, BBC Comedy is one of the most important tools in the BBC's indoctrination repertoire, for it gives the Corporation an unrivalled opportunity to instil the correct opinions, both socially and politically, into the viewing public but without them even realising it in the way they would if it were Panorama, for example, or one of those nine o'clock dramas we do about how awful it is being on benefits or something.'

'Indeed, your grace,' answered the Head of Comedy. 'We often refer to it as the 'Trojan Horse' system of indoctrination. It's a less obvious method than the ones employed on political shows or dramas, and is both extremely subtle and most powerful. And you'd be surprised how effective it is. Take, for example, how we use a Pavlovian response to condition our viewers into thinking someone is hilarious based on their worldview rather than their actual comedic ability, pushing the idea that it's some kind of scientific fact that right-wing comedians cannot be funny, only those who hold the correct opinions.'

'And they obviously fail to notice we've conditioned them to be so outraged by any comedian daring to start expressing a right-wing opinion that they don't even listen to them,' finished Dave McCreith, before pausing for a moment. 'But, of course, we do allow tokenistic right-wing representation on our programmes?'

'Yes, we allow one,' confirmed the Head of Comedy. 'It's the same principle as we use on Question Time. A token right-winger is allowed on, but we cherry-pick one who paints all members of that group in a bad light. You can see an example of this with the 'pet Tory' on the Mash Report. We deliberately chose a 'right-wing' comedian who was working class, so we could claim to be representing a minority group whilst also reinforcing the idea that white, working class people hold the incorrect opinions, then have the other 'comedians' with the correct opinions constantly tell him how wrong he is so we could *also* reinforce our oft-made claim that 'right wing comedians aren't funny'!'

'Ah, yes, diversity on comedy shows...' said Dave McCreith, thoughtfully. 'That is one of the topics I've been meaning to discuss with you. I assigned you a project to increase diversity even further. How is that going?'

'Extremely well, my liege!' replied the Head of Comedy, brightly. 'In fact, we've smashed our diversity targets by finding not one but *two* female comedians who we've deemed attractive enough to appear on our prime time comedy panel shows rather than just on Radio 4 and the occasional episode of Some News, For You, We Have!'

'Really?' replied Dave McCreith, surprised. '*Two*, you say?'

'Indeed, your excellency,' the Head of Comedy confirmed. 'But can I just check whether having then *both* on the same programme would contravene the Rule of One?'

'Oh, the Rule of One doesn't apply to white women,' Dave McCreith explained, 'and particularly not if they qualify for the Skinny Rich White Girl Club. Anyway, this is excellent news! As you know, we've been looking for some years for a woman who was both vaguely funny whilst also being slim and attractive enough to have on our Friday night comedy panel shows! But *two*?! I couldn't have dreamt such a thing was possible!'

'It is, my liege!' replied the Head of Comedy. 'Plus they both identify as feminists even thought their actual commitment to the cause is fairly tokenistic and consists of little more than inane tweets!'

Dave McCreith then looked suspicious. 'And you're quite sure they're attractive enough for prime-time TV?' he asked. 'Because normally female comedians, especially feminist ones, are simply too obese and unattractive for us to promote to proper stardom. That's why we put them on Radio 4, where no one has to actually look at them.'

'Absolutely, my liege,' confirmed the Head of Comedy.

'And you're absolutely sure they won't spend a whole half-hour banging on about feminism, and will only mention it once or twice, and even then just as an inane soundbite that is brief but can also be used in the trailer for the show in order to promote how woke it is?' asked Dave McCreith, incredulously.

'Yes, your excellency, yes!' replied the Head of Comedy, triumphantly. 'However...' he added, sadly, 'there is the possibility that one of them may go to America to launch a career.'

'Oh, I see,' replied Dave McCreith, his hope and excitement now turning to disappointment. 'It would be disappointing to lose one. We wouldn't want a female version of the Ranganathan Dilemma.'

'The Ranganathan Dilemma?' asked Terry Ball, as usual more so the characters can explain something to you, the reader, than because he didn't actually know.

'Yes,' replied Dave McCreith, as if this should be obvious. 'When we screen potential candidates to fill a given role as per the Rule of One, such as becoming our ethnic minority stand-up, it is standard practice to check they hold the correct opinions, not only to maintain consistency but because, well, can you imagine how confusing it would be to our audience if we had an Asian comedian who was pro-Brexit? They simply wouldn't be able to process it after years of us telling them that anyone who voted for Brexit, regardless of whether they say they did it for reasons of sovereignty, or fishing quotas, or farming subsidies, must actually just be racist, pure and simple.'

'Indeed,' continued the Head of Comedy, 'but then we promoted Romesh Ranganathan on many of our shows only for it to turn out he was actually quite funny, and large numbers of people liked him, and he ended up getting poached by Sky! So when we looked to replace him we made sure we found someone who not only had exactly the right opinions but also wasn't remotely funny, just to make sure he'd never leave us.'

'Nish Kumar?' speculated Terry Ball.

'Of course!' replied the Head of Comedy. 'I mean, he's going to be with us for life, isn't he?! It's not as if he's going to get given a show on a channel that relies on people actually watching it, or poached by Hollywood or HBO, is he?!'

They all laughed at this preposterous idea.

'Hmm, well, anyway,' continued Dave McCreith. 'It really sounds like we're doing an excellent job on diversity. Especially having *two* female comedians *on TV.*' Ball! Create a new inspirational diversity award, award it to me and arrange a huge ceremony for me to receive it!'

'Of course, your excellency,' replied Terry Ball, taking a note.

Perhaps on a roll now, the Director General continued with this theme. 'And disabled comedians?' he asked. 'Do you have the correct number of those? One for each disability, as usual, but only ones who do not have too severe a form of it?'

'Of course, my liege!' confirmed the Head of Comedy. 'Because a person with a specific disability naturally speaks on behalf of every person with that disability, again as per the Rule of One!'

'Only one must there be. No more and no less,' said Dave McCreith, clearly quoting from memory a line in the Clandestine Charter of the BBC Elders.

Nodding, the Head of Comedy continued. 'And, of course, they must never joke about *anything* that doesn't relate to their disability! A comedian with cerebral palsy must only be allowed to make jokes about how her hands uncontrollably shaking mean she's good at whisking pancake batter or faffing herself off, a comedian in a wheelchair must only be permitted to say things like 'well, for me the hard part of doing 'stand-up comedy' is actually standing up in the first place!' and a one-legged comedian must do a set entirely made up of saying things like 'I didn't have a leg to stand on!' and if they mention politics they must *only* do so in reference to the law surrounding their disability!'

'Well, of course,' confirmed Dave McCreith. 'I find the idea that people with the same disability could have opinions on anything that doesn't relate to their disability entirely fallacious.'

The Head of Comedy looked thoughtful at this but did not say why. 'What is it?' said Dave McCreith, impatiently.

'Oh, I was just wondering if that could be used as a joke in Mrs Brown's Boys,' said the Head of Comedy, vaguely. 'I mean, on the one hand, 'fallacious', sounds a bit like 'fellatio', making it a brilliant joke, but on the other I don't imagine many viewers of the show will even know the word so won't realise it's a play on words and just think it's the show trying to get a cheap laugh by being smutty.'

'But isn't that the entire principle upon which that show is based?' Dave McCreith pointed out.

'Well, yes,' replied the Head of Comedy, as he realised this was true. 'So, I suppose we could use it after all, as most people will just laugh because it's smutty whilst we may also finally win the critics over with such a clever piece of wordplay. Well, I'll see what the producers think.'

'Purely out of interest, your grace,' said Terry Ball, returning to the previous point, 'has it ever been considered worthwhile, at any point in the Corporation's history, to perhaps employ several people who have the same disability yet hold different opinions from each other, and who can also speak knowledgably about a subject *other* than their disability? You know, employing someone based on their ideas and opinions and talent rather than to simply tick a box?'

'That's not how the BBC works at all!' Dave McCreith spluttered, indignantly. 'They're just grateful for the work! And where else would they go? ITV?! Don't make me laugh! Anyway, if we did that, where would it end? Have you any idea what the consequences would be if we offered BBC roles based on talent and intelligence?! Ninety nine percent of the people here would lose their jobs! Did you stop to consider that?! Did you?!'

Terry Ball looked at the floor, sheepishly. 'Sorry, your grace,' he confessed, 'I admit I did not take any of those points into account.'

'Still,' said the Head of Comedy, 'you mentioned the Great Enemy, ITV, which reminds me how we recently collaborated with them on a new project in order to really mess with people's heads on the whole issue of offence.'

'Oh, yes,' replied Dave McCreith. 'We co-funded a new series of Spitting Image with them, only to immediately accuse it of sickening racism the day the first episode aired. It was rather clever, actually. Whilst celebrating as hilarious a puppet of the Prime Minister that exaggerated his features so as to give him uncontrollable hair and huge lips, when they did the same thing in their portrayal of Meghan Markle we immediately denounced it as a sickeningly vile crime of hatred that perpetuated abhorrent racial stereotypes.'

'Yes, it was very clever, your grace!' said the Head of Comedy. 'As ever, we have a hand in everything. There is not a single string behind the scenes that is not being pulled by us. As to how we constantly sow confusion... Well, you've only got to look at how the BBC has always promoted itself as a high-calibre, cultured organisation based on Reithian values, yet an astounding amount of our comedic output over the years has consisted of little more than smut, double-entendres, cross-dressing and tired slapstick.'

'Indeed, and how we ruthlessly promote our 'critically acclaimed' shows like Fleabag whilst skirting around the fact that their viewing figures are utterly dwarfed by things like Mrs Brown's Boys,' added Dave McCreith, before sniggering, presumably remembering one of his favourite episodes of that show. 'Still, I suppose, as good as it is, it's still only really a step on the journey we're taking in trying to make a programme that rivals our greatest ever show...' he added, to which Terry Ball raised a quizzical eyebrow. Well, it was him who was actually quizzical, not the eyebrow itself, but you get the point.

'You refer, of course, my liege,' said the Head of Comedy, 'to 'Allo 'Allo. A show in which we had that policeman character who was supposedly an Englishman who didn't pronounce French very well, so when he said 'passing' it sounded like 'pissing', or he could say 'that man was *wanking* at me' when he was supposed to say 'winking'... And this represented a major breakthrough, a significant step up from mere *entendre*, because what this allowed us to do was *actually have a man* using *actual swearwords* in early evening BBC programmes yet plausibly claim they weren't really there and anyone who heard them as swearwords was some sort of smutty pervert who needed their ears washing out with soap and water!'

'Indeed!' replied Dave McCreith, proudly. 'People think it's easy to come up with low-level smutty shows, but that one represented the apogee of decades of sitcom evolution, if you will! BBC Comedy had finally achieved its ultimate goal, a show consisting of little more than a man blatantly saying rude words, whilst being able to plausibly deny he was doing so, and thus claim it was good, clean family entertainment! The Holy Grail of mainstream British comedy!

'Terry Ball looked thoughtful. 'You know, I seem to recall that an entire chapter of The Book was dedicated to deconstructing and pointing out the hypocritical history of BBC comedy,' he said. 'You know... 'The Book the BBC Tried to BAN!' Er, which I've never read,' he added, remembering the Corporation's official stance on the heretical text. 'He dared to suggest there was something odd in the fact that during the 1970s it was perfectly normal to have comedians on Saturday night TV doing jokes about mothers in law or having black people for neighbours, followed by the Black and White Minstrel Show, with no one thinking there was anything wrong with that, yet the thing people actually complained about was Dave Allen or Billy Connolly poking fun at the Catholic Church, even though we now look back on them as having made good points and the old-fashioned stand-ups as being repellent.'

'Hmm, yes, well, I think the point here is that we shouldn't think about things too deeply,' replied Dave McCreith. 'That can only lead to all sorts of problems.'

'Indeed,' continued Terry Ball, 'but I suppose he was merely trying to make the point that whilst we think of offence and morality as being objective and eternal and unchanging, that's very much not the case, and not only do standards frequently change, they often switch in completely the opposite direction.'

'Hmm, so you think he was implying that morality is actually entirely personal and that no one's individual take on right and wrong will realistically stand the test of time, and as a result people should perhaps stop before they leap to be offended by everything they hear, especially if they're only really doing it to try to show everyone how amazing they are?' replied Dave McCreith.

'Yes, I think that's basically it, my liege,' replied Terry Ball.

Dave McCreith shook his head dismissively, as if the very idea itself was utterly bizarre and totally incomprehensible. 'Hmm, well, I really don't see that idea catching on,' he sniffed. 'Anyway, can we look to wrap this meeting up? I think we've covered the main themes. What do we have coming up in the autumn schedule?'

'Well, your grace,' replied the Head of Comedy, thinking. 'Again, we're marketing ourselves as being the very peak of culture whilst our actual sitcom output has somehow managed to sink quite a long way beneath the gutter. Let's see... There's a follow up to Are You Being Served?, called Mrs Slocum's Big Hairy Beaver, in which Mrs Slocum adopts a pet beaver in an extremely clumsy set up that allows us to make every single 'joke' in the show a variation on 'ooh, who's got their hands on my big, hairy beaver?' We've revived the beloved Carry On franchise with a new gay-friendly update... Carry On Up the Shitter. I mean, it's marketed as gay-friendly but it's really just the same old double-entendres. Then there's the seven hundred and forty sixth series of Mock the Week...'

Dave McCreith's face lit up at this point. 'Ah, yes! Mock the Week! Seven of the finest comedians working in Britain today, all ably assisted by a team of only twenty writers to actually come up with the terrible jokes they pretend to have just thought of on the spot, hilariously interspersed with Hugh Dennis and Dara O'Briain rolling out their tired old dad jokes!'

Terry Ball looked puzzled for a moment. I could be wrong, he thought, but isn't the show called Parody the News rather than Mock the Week? He pondered this, thinking he had surely heard it referred to by both names at different times. It was almost as two different yet similar realities had inexplicably become blended together and their histories somehow intertwined so that people could refer to things and events from either of them and everyone would still know what was being referred to. The other two, however, did not seem to have noticed this, and the Head of Comedy continued.

'Ah, on that topic, your grace, we are unfortunately having to consider axing that programme. You know how it stopped being funny when Frankie Boyle left, and since then we've had to pump laughing gas into the studio to make it look like the audience actually finds it funny? Well, that gas now accounts for almost 90% of the show's budget.'

Dave McCreith looked puzzled at this point, though it was soon apparent he was pondering a different aspect of the show. 'Well, it did briefly get funny again when we got Barry Begbie on there,' he added. 'Whatever happened to him, anyway?'

'Re-Education Camp, your grace,' replied the Head of Comedy. 'He committed one anti-BBC heresy too many. We'll probably bring him back in a few years, though, when things have changed again.'

'Very well,' replied Dave McCreith, satisfied with this reply. 'Is there anything else I need to know about your department?'

'Well, your grace,' replied the Head of Comedy, 'as it happens, we're currently finalising the line-up of terrible Radio 4 sitcoms for the autumn, all of which are the same old talentless public school actors whose only work comes from Radio 4 itself, and in which the 'humour' is entirely derived from a pun-based title. So, coming up we've got Claire in the Community, about a social worker named Claire, Tim is a Great Healer, about a doctor called Tim, Bill in A China Shop, about a man called Bill who runs a China shop... And finally... Brian Farnet from Friern Barnet!'

(Come on, 'Brian Farnet from Friern Barnet' is a much better title than 'Claire in the Community', which is actually a real Radio 4 sitcom! I reckon that even if the BBC sues me over this novel they'll still nick that name and make a sitcom out of it, which would be an irony not lost on me.)

'Hmm, that one sounds a little too clever for us, but very well,' said Dave McCreith. 'Oh, that reminds me, actually. I have an idea for a comedy show, about two detectives who, on the one hand, are notoriously corrupt, taking bribes and beating suspects left, right and centre, yet at the same time are in a homosexual relationship, meaning that not only does this contribute to our diversity quotas, but the fact they are members of a minority group places them utterly above any form of criticism, including that relating to their appalling corruption, which will serve to utterly confuse the viewer.'

'An intriguing idea, your grace,' replied the Head of Comedy. 'And the name of this show?'

''Bent Coppers',' replied Dave McCreith.

'Very good, your excellency,' said the Head of Comedy. 'I shall get our finest writers onto it immediately.'

'Or if you can't get them just get people who write for Radio 4,' replied Dave McCreith, casually. 'Anyway, it sounds like you have everything under control,' he concluded, standing up.

'Of course, your excellency,' replied the Head of Comedy, standing up to leave. 'As ever, you honour me by granting me an audience. The BBC will prevail!' Bowing as he backed towards the door, he left the office and Dave McCreith sat back down at his desk and pondered the topics they had discussed in the meeting. Then he remembered what they had opened by talking about: Mrs Brown's Boys.

'Penis!' he said, before laughing uncontrollably.

# Chapter Nine:

# A Torturous Echo Chamber

*In Which Our Hero Is Confronted for His Heresy and Forced to Suffer Unthinkable Torture That May Include Thumbscrews, Fingernail Pulling and Complete DVD Boxsets of Mrs Brown's Boys*

It was a scream from somewhere in the camp that caused John Smith to wake up with a start at what he took to be around four in the morning. There was nothing unusual in hearing a scream, and he was about to casually dismiss it as probably just Mrs Smith in cell 43 having her 4am brainwashing torture, and turn over to go back to sleep, when he stopped to reflect that it was actually quite worrying that he had started to accept the camp's abhorrent practices as being perfectly normal even though he had only been there, what, two or three days? Then he thought more carefully as he realised he actually had no idea just how long he had been incarcerated. It could have been days or it could have been months. Time no longer seemed to mean anything and it was impossible to really take any cues from anything regarding anything. Darkness no longer guaranteed that it was night time. Snow was no guarantee that it was winter. The only reality seemed to be that created by the guards and the Commandant. There was no possible way to tell truth from lies and, as he pondered this, John Smith realised that this was very much the intention. Reality had been torn from underneath their feet. There was no real consistency to anything. Well, no real consistency other than the screams.

The screaming briefly reduced in volume. John realised he did not actually know that the unfortunate victim's name was Mrs Smith, or, technically, if it was the same person he had heard being tortured or, now he thought about it, whether it did actually happen at the same time every morning. He sat up in bed and tried to clear his head and gather his thoughts. How long had he really been there? No, it was impossible to discern. Did he really have any idea where he was? The weather suggested he was still in the UK but he also reflected that his journey there had been something of a blur and it was theoretically entirely possible that he had been sedated for part of it and taken to just about any other part of the world.

Having failed to come to any satisfactory conclusions about his situation he tried to remember the life he had lived prior to his arrival in the camp. Again, exactly what had happened the night he had been taken away? He'd been watching something... But what was it? He strained his brain as hard as he could but it was no good. Could they have given him something, he wondered, could they have administered a drug currently unknown to the general public that had caused his memories of the night to be erased? It was impossible to tell. But, in any case, one of the many things he had learnt since his arrival in the camp was that human memory was fallible and unpredictable, as likely to change just as often as a BBC PR announcement. However he had spent his final night of freedom, and whatever he was supposed to have done in order to have been incarcerated in the mysterious camp where he now found himself, he simply could not recall.

At that moment the door swung upon to reveal a guard standing behind it. Here, John Smith noticed something about which he was almost certain, only to then realise with disappointment that the observation in question was so unlikely that it was surely impossible: all the guards in the camp seemed to look exactly the same. Either they had simply blurred together in his memory, and once again existed as proof that memory was no longer something on which he could realistically rely, or, as the result of some other dark science of which the BBC knew but had not made public knowledge, the guards were all, in fact, clones of one another. Realising this was a line of thought that there was no point in him pursuing, John looked up at the guard, who looked back at him with a sense of disappointment, as if looking forward to noisily waking him up and being annoyed to find him already alert and upright.

'Oh,' he said, the disappointment clear in his voice. Then, as if he had perhaps prepared something to say only to discover the situation necessary for it to make sense was not as he expected, he briefly paused then said, 'sleep well?'

John Smith looked at him suspiciously, assuming he was being sarcastic despite having an odd feeling that he was not.

'Very well, thanks!' he said, brightly, which he was able to do as a result of having been awake and thus able to start gathering his thoughts prior to the guard's arrival. The guard frowned at this then regained his train of thought, and his usual, callous and gleeful manner, before continuing.

'Anyway, I hope having some time to yourself means you've had a long, hard think about what you've done!'

John was confused again, and once more looked at the guard for any kind of cue, before attempting to give the answer he thought might possibly be expected of him. 'Er, well, there were a few moments last night when I couldn't hear any screams for up to a couple of minutes at a time, so during those moments I was able to undertake some silent contemplation...'

'Silence!' yelled the guard, his near-repetition of the second-but-last word John had said suggesting he was still not fully himself and had not quite hit his flow. 'You're making this far harder for yourself than it needs to be, you know! It's perfectly simple, really! Just as soon as you admit that what you did was wrong you're allowed to leave and return to your life! What's so complicated about that? Why can't you just do it?'

John Smith was utterly perplexed as to whether or not the guard genuinely meant this, so merely stared at him in the desperate hope that a further cue would be offered. When one was not forthcoming, he shook his head in confusion. 'Then why can't you just tell me what I did, so I can apologise for it and get on with my life?!'

The guard again threw his head back and emitted a roaring laugh. 'That would be too easy! I mean, do you have any idea what would happen if we did that for everyone?'

Again, John was far too confused to be able to discern whether this was intended as a serious question. 'Erm... It would be... Bad?' he hazarded.

The guard's face lit up. He was back in control now. 'Yes, very good! It would indeed be bad! Very bad indeed! Because then there would be no lesson learned, would there?'

'Erm, no, sir,' replied John Smith, meekly.

'Anyway,' continued the guard, now having fully warmed up into his usual demeanour, 'along with having plenty of time alone to ponder your sins, let's not forget that informative training session you had in the cinema yesterday!' The guard grinned at him maliciously. 'I hope you learnt a lot from that video!' he snarled, to which John Smith shook his head in confusion.

'No, I didn't learn anything!' he protested. 'None of it made sense! There were people sort of apologising for things whilst explaining they didn't actually regret them, and any remorse was entire tokenistic! A lot of the time even the people in the film didn't know what they were apologising for! I came out of that screening room more confused than I was when I went in!'

The guard grinned again or, more accurately, slightly expanded the grim that had been left on his face from a couple of paragraphs ago. 'Well, in that case it sounds like you need some more re-education!'

'But... What?' spluttered John Smith, bewildered. 'Are you even listening to me? I said...' But he was unable to finish his sentence as, following a shout from the guard, two more guards entered and dragged him from his bed, out of his cell and into the courtyard. 'Why can't you just tell me what I've done?!' spluttered John Smith. Yes, I know I used the word 'spluttered' at the start of this paragraph then used it again, but he continued to splutter. That's the point. If anything, when he's spluttered once he's more likely to do it again. Anyway, you try writing a book where you try to substitute the word 'said' for something else. You soon run out, I tell you.

Anyway, John was dragged out of his cell and across the courtyard, until they were approaching another building that looked just the same as all the others, a corrugated iron shed whose exterior gave not the slightest hint of the horrors that lay within. As they approached John Smith noticed Kerri Barnes-Bridge staggering out of it, with a mixed look of both terror and utter confusion on her face. When she saw John she looked like she recognised him but was so shell-shocked as to not really remember where from.

'It's too much!' she cried, once she was close enough for him to hear her. 'They asked me to recant my beliefs but I said I never really had any as I was just saying what I thought I needed to say in order to continue appearing on Radio 4 panel shows and the very occasional TV appearance! They kept asking me why, when I was appearing on Barry Begbie's show, I happily sat through his opening monologue of jokes about sexual assault but then got offended at the concept of a man marrying a hologram but not getting consent! They asked me why I didn't think that was hypocritical, and I could only tell them the truth! That I was willing to do or say anything to get on TV and maintain my career and assumed that being utterly inconsistent in your beliefs was standard BBC policy! But it wasn't enough! It wasn't enough!'

She staggered away and, noticing the uncertain, swaying way in which she walked, John Smith couldn't help but wonder if whatever monstrous torture she had been put through had served to destroy what little remaining sanity she had, before reflecting that if that were true then a similar fate surely awaited him in only a few moments. He wondered if he should console himself with the fact that she didn't appear to have suffered any obvious physical harm, or was that mere misdirection to prevent him even beginning to consider the brutal mind games and psychological torture that could be awaiting him?

But it was, in any case, a moot point as moments later he found himself inside the building, and nervously looked around for any devices or implements that could be put to some nefarious use regardless of what their original purpose was. And he did not have to look long; it was clear that this was a room where people had their opinions changed and their secrets extracted. In the middle of the dimly-lit, dusty room, was a chair fitted out with restraints, surrounded by tables and shelves containing items that could be used for any type of torture you could dare to imagine. On a trolley was what he took to be thumbscrews, surrounding a car battery, but one that had been attached to wires that appeared to have scrotal clamps fitted to the other ends of them. On a shelf there were implements that even the briefest glance at suggested had been purpose-built for pulling out fingernails and gouging eyeballs. But he almost felt his heart stop for a moment when he saw that the inventory included something he knew could be used for the most brutal type of torture imaginable: an entire DVD boxset of My Family. He shuddered as he saw this, trying not to even begin to picture the gruesome fate that awaited him. I mean, even if it had been Mrs Brown's Boys that wouldn't have been so bad, not because that programme is any better but because there were fewer episodes of it. No, there really are. You think there are loads, I know, but there were only about three or four series, even though it appears to be on BBC One every night and UK Gold about fifty seven times a day. It's all those episodes of All Round To Mrs Brown's that make you think there were more than there were. I mean, that's really the lowest of the low, isn't it? It's as if the makers of Mrs Brown's Boys accepted a bet that they couldn't make a programme that was any worse, and they won the bet by doing a tenth-rate chat show, thinking that if Mrs Merton could do it then so could they, but failing to take into account that Caroline Aherne was a very good writer and performer and could see that comedy takes more than just dressing up and saying 'penis!' fifty times an hour. I mean, it's basically Mrs Brown's Boys for which they couldn't even be bothered to write a script, and considering the standard script for Mrs Brown's Boys presumably just says 'ALL ACTORS: JUST SAY 'PENIS' AT LEAST THREE TIMES PER SENTENCE' then that's a new low even for BBC Comedy.

Phew, where was I? Oh, yes, My Family. That must have run for about ten years or more, I reckon. So upon seeing the DVD boxset John Smith not only shivered in fearful anticipation of the ordeal that was awaiting him but also wondered why anyone would actually buy the DVD boxset of that show. I mean, even if you ignore the fact it wasn't very good, it's on UK Gold all the time, literally three or four times a day. If you loved My Family then you presumably love all terrible British sitcoms so it would clearly be in your best interests to subscribe to UK Gold as it shows little else. Also, I know it's just called Gold now but it's easier to refer to it as UK Gold because I reckon a lot of people don't actually know it's changed. And on that subject, did you know that you can buy a complete DVD box set of Last of the Summer Wine?! Really! I mean, it ran for nearly forty years despite every single episode being exactly the same! And, again, it's on UK Gold at least five times a day. Also, the only people who like it are senile old people who, on the one hand, probably don't have UK Gold but, on the other hand, will they really know how to work DVD players? And my final word on that subject is this: presuming there are people who actually bought the 27-series, 642-episode (that's a guess) box set, do you think any of them ever actually manage to watch the whole thing before they die? Because I don't reckon they do. Surely the only person who'd ever buy a complete box set of Last of the Summer Wine must not just be very old but also almost certainly suffering from some form of dementia? My point here is that watching the entire run is not only a huge undertaking but also something that is surely ever only attempted by someone who's already extremely old (and senile) and must, undeniably, therefore always be doomed to failure. Okay?

Phew, sorry this chapter's gone off on a tangent. Basically, I think the issue is that the chapters featuring Dave McCreith and Terry Ball are all ending up much longer than I expected, which is creating an imbalance because these chapters in the camp featuring John Smith are the ones that contain the actual plot (yes, there's sort of a vague plot in here somewhere). Okay, so I'll get back to that right now and try to stop rambling. So, then, John Smith saw the brutal torture devices and did not need to guess exactly what monstrous, horrifying purposes they would be put to.

Attempting to pre-empt his captors, and immediately regretting it, he blurted out, 'you know what? I love My Family! Mrs Brown's Boys too! Yep, classic British sitcoms, both of them! And if I could have a cup of tea whilst watching the complete run of Not Going Out, well, that would just be marvellous!'

The guard looked at him quizzically. John managed to keep a straight face but then overdid it by freezing it in that position, intending to avoid showing any other emotions but in doing so more or less revealing that he was putting it on. Also, I should mention that he was aware of screaming happening in the next room. Whilst he had accepted that as a frequent occurrence I'm just mentioning it now as I'll be making reference to it later in this chapter. The guard threw a brief glance at another guard to see what he made of John Smith's unusual and surely implausible claim. But, because all the guards appeared the same, this guard simply shrugged back at him. Actually, I don't know if the guard who's doing all the talking in this scene is even the same one who was talking back in the cell because, after all, they're all interchangeable and it doesn't matter anyway. So, one of the guards nodded at the other two (yes, there are definitely three, I've decided) and before John knew what was happening those two guards had each grabbed one of his arms, forced him into the chair in the middle of the room and strapped his arms down to the arms of the chair, then grabbed his head and swiftly pulled another strap around his neck so that he was also unable to move his head or upper body.

Taking some deep breaths as he tried to calm down, John Smith looked around as much as he could, which is to say not very much, and soon saw another guard (by this point he had completely lost track of which one was which, as have I) approach with some sort of wire-based device, which he proceeded to fit over John Smith's head and, after some struggling, also used some protruding attachments to clamp his eyes open in a way I can't be bothered to describe in too much detail, but is basically the same as the bit in A Clockwork Orange that I'm obviously parodying or, indeed, the various times The Simpsons has also parodied it. So, the fact that he's sitting there, forced to look at a screen with his eyes clamped open is the point I'm trying to make.

'That was a bold claim you just made,' said the guard who was doing all the talking in this scene. 'But let me assure you of one thing: no matter how confident or clever you think you are when you come in here, the first thing to die in this room is a person's sense of humour.'

'I'm not surprised, if you always show them Mrs Brown's Boys and My Family,' John Smith shot back, causing the guard to immediately look annoyed at having said something he thought sounded cool and threatening but in fact lent itself to an obvious response. He then regained his composure before shaking his head slowly and admonishingly.

'Oh, for that comment, you will pay.'

'What are you going to do, strap me down and torture me?' replied John Smith contemptuously.

The guard was even more annoyed at this, irritably blurting out, 'show him the materials!'

One of the other guards now went over to the DVD player that was attached to the huge screen opposite John Smith's chair that I may not have mentioned was there but definitely was. Unable to get the DVD player to work, he solicited the help of the other two, and after about ten minutes they got it working. It's basically a comment on how at my school whenever we were going to watch a video it always took the teachers about fifteen minutes to get the thing working. Yes, really! Apparently it never occurred to them to try doing it before the lesson started or, perish the thought, to actually write down how to do it so they could remember the next time. Also, in the film adaptation of the book this bit will be a hilarious scene of slapstick, but you can't really convey slapstick in a book so you'll just have to imagine it. So they put Mrs Brown's Boys on and the episode started. Does she do a song or something? I don't know. Anyway, after a couple of minutes three or four other characters had appeared and they'd all said 'penis', 'willy' and 'bum' six or seven times each. At this point John Smith let out a short snort, though it was not one that resulted from him actually finding the programme funny but rather one of disbelief that something so bad could ever have become a fixture of national television.

'You're currently watching something made by BBC Comedy!' yelled the guard. 'You're not meant to be enjoying yourself!'

'Sorry, it's never happened before,' blurted out John. 'But that was a snort of contempt, not a laugh'. Despite his discomfort, he attempted to ignore his surroundings and concentrate on the programme in front of him. But, again, his focus was sharply broken by the guard.

'Do men have penises?' asked the guard, suddenly and unexpectedly. Whilst it was true that John Smith was more or less alert, as he had been able to gather his thoughts as a result of being woken up by the screaming prior to the guard bursting into his cell, he replied instinctively rather than carefully considering the question that was being put to him and just why he was being asked it.

'What? Of course men have penises,' he replied, casually, as if wondering why he was being asked such an obvious question. 'Same as dogs have tails and bulls have horns. Having a penis is very much one of the requirements if you're a man.' He suddenly stopped in his tracks, realising his mistake and wincing at his stupidity.

'Wrong!' replied the guard. 'There's no correlation between penis ownership and being a man, you repellent transphobe!'

'Oh, right, yes, sorry, my bad, I wasn't thinking clearly,' replied John Smith, hoping his quick apology would make up for his sickening, vile utterance, but instead it only served to encourage the guard.

'No, you have not been thinking clearly at all!' he replied, 'and that is very much part of the problem, if not *all* of the problem! And that is why we are trying to help you! To help you with your thoughts, which, as you say, are not clear, and are all wrong!'

'But you just showed me Mrs Brown's Boys, which is based on

the premise that a man doing a bad job of pretending to be a woman is utterly hilarious! How come the BBC is so obsessed with not offending pro-transgender people but still has that in its schedules?!' spluttered John, before immediately remembering that attempting to use logic or common sense when dealing with a BBC employee was an utter waste of time.

'I don't know what you're talking about!' sneered the guard. 'The main character in this show is a woman *and* has a penis, so I don't see where this supposed hypocrisy is!'

John Smith realised he sort of had a point, or at least that there was no sense in trying to reason with him. 'I'm sorry. I'll try to be more careful from now on,' he said, before attempting to turn his concentration back to the horrors that were unfolding right in front of his eyes: the entire run of Mrs Brown's Boys.

Desperately trying to look around for any form of escape, or at least anything he could focus on to lift his consciousness out of his body so as to distance himself from the horrors he was experiencing, John Smith tried in vain to avert his gaze, but it was no good. The eye clamps meant there was no way he could completely avoid seeing the episode of Mrs Brown's Boys. But then something odd happened. Perhaps it was the sleep deprivation after the days, weeks or even months at the camp. Perhaps the effects of his reprogramming had, in fact, already started to wear him down and destroy his defences and sanity, but at this point he started to actually pay attention to Mrs Brown's Boys and, in a sudden moment of zen-like perfection, his mind emptied, putting him in the perfect state to enjoy the show. In the episode in question, Mrs Brown was talking to one of the other characters, probably her daughter or something; I know, you'd think I'd know the show better than I do seeing as how much of this book is me making fun of it, and I have watched it, but I think the issue is that all the characters are pretty much the same so hardly stand out from each other anyway. So I reckon she was talking to the Randy Vicar (or is that a character from Fleabag? I can't remember) and he said 'Mrs Brown, do you eat much Italian food?' to which she replied 'no, but I am keen on trying that 'fellatio' that everyone keeps talking about!' and then the audience laughed like idiots because fellatio isn't actually Italian food, you see. That's the joke. I think that really was a joke in the episode I watched, actually, meaning my joke in the previous chapter about 'fallacious' sounding like 'fellatio' might not be that original after all. But, anyway, with his mind completely empty, something extremely strange happened.

John Smith laughed at Mrs Brown's Boys.

(That earlier one didn't count as it was a snort rather than a laugh and in any case was one of disbelief rather than genuine laughter.)

I mean, he actually 'laughed out loud', even though that's a stupid phrase because you can't laugh without doing it out loud. Thinking something is funny isn't the same as laughing at it, and if it actually was funny then you'd laugh anyway. Therefore, saying that you laughed 'out loud' is tautological. It's like going for a poo and then saying you'd just been 'shitting solids'. Because if there weren't any solids then it wasn't a poo, okay?

Anyway, the guards' faces all lit up triumphantly as they witnessed this.

'It's working!' said one of them.

'We've made a breakthrough!' said another.

'We must tell the Commandant!' said another, or possibly it was the first one again, I'm not sure.

The second one nodded his head, more slowly this time, as if fully comprehending the significance of what they had witnessed.

'It's starting to work,' he said. 'His mind is finally starting to empty. His is becoming a willing vessel.'

John Smith snapped out of his reverie and felt utterly disgusted and violated by what he had done. But he could sense the mood in the room had changed, and the guards were already unstrapping him in their rush to tell their supervisor of their breakthrough. Once they had freed him they ran out of the building, leaving John to find his own way out, which he did slowly and ponderously, wondering if what he had just experienced actually represented some worrying change from which there was no return.

John Smith staggered back outside and felt blinded by the daylight, even though the never-ending cloud meant that, at best, he was confronted with little more than a dull, grey, overcast day in which little-to-no sunlight was actually visible. His legs felt like jelly underneath him, and as he crossed the yard they gave up trying to keep him upright and he collapsed, exhausted and lay in the mud whilst attempting to regain his breath, and his sanity. After a few moments he looked up and saw a hand reaching down, offering to help him up. He took it and, with the help of the hand's owner, because it did have one and wasn't just some weird random hand floating in the air supported by nothing, got back to his feet. With his eyes having acclimatised back to daylight, he saw that the hand was that of Barry Begbie.

'And do you know what the strangest thing about of all this really is?' he asked. John Smith was still too dazed to properly consider this, but even in his dazed state knew there was an almost infinite number of entirely plausible answers. Realising just how much of an unanswerable question it was, Barry Begbie smiled and gave the reply he was thinking of. 'There are people who go through all of this, the torture, the brainwashing, the wondering if they'll ever see the outside world again, yet a few months later are back on prime-time BBC television as if nothing ever happened.' John Smith took his hand and slowly staggered to his feet, shaking his head in disbelief.

As he attempted to regain his composure, Barry Begbie tried to offer him some words of support. 'If it's any consolation, what you've just been through is mild compared to what we've heard goes on at the Manchester site.'

John Smith raised an eyebrow, struggling to comprehend how such a thing could even be possible. Barry Begbie explained.

'You see, that's the difference. At least here they believe people can be changed and released back into society in some form. Manchester is, well... Different.'

'Manchester, you say?'

'Yeah, that's right. Of course, when the BBC was forced to relocate from London to Manchester there was huge resentment because, well, BBC employees don't want to live up north, do they? Even back then they said it was a sickening infringement of their human rights and went to the European Council about it. In fact, some people even say that the reason the BBC was so relentlessly and obviously pro-EU despite claiming to be a neutral and unbiased broadcaster was actually because by staying in the EU they were clinging onto some sort of desperate hope that it would eventually rule in their favour and allow all the displaced employees to return to London on human rights grounds.'

John Smith thought about this, initially considering it somewhat far-fetched but then realising that after all he had heard and experienced it had as much chance of being true as anything else. Barry Begbie continued.

'Yes, people at the BBC never forgot that slur. Being forced to live up north, away from Ascot and the Proms and all their favourite private schools and not being able to live in Islington anymore, and having to spend almost two hours in the first class compartment of a Virgin train. So it's assumed that when they turned their former Salford Quays headquarters into the most brutal and unforgiving of all their black-op sites, the kind of place where they sent many of their enemies who'd forced the relocation in the first place... Well, it's thought to have been an ironic form of revenge.' He paused for a moment here, then added, 'plus up there they can do brutal, sickening things that most people couldn't even dream of, simply because in the highly unlikely event of the BBC losing power and its leading figures being put in trial for war crimes they could very plausibly claim to know nothing about what went on there because everyone knows no top BBC executive has ever travelled further north of Oxford.'

'Very clever,' nodded John Smith, still shaken.

'Yes...' continued Barry Begbie. 'I've heard stories about the Manchester site but it's hard to verify them. The things I heard were at least from the inside, as they were things I was told about when I was back at the BBC but, if anything, I've tried to convince myself they're only rumours and couldn't possibly be true.'

'Well, they did make me watch Mrs Brown's Boys,' replied John Smith, defensively, as if feeling that his experiences were being somewhat belittled.

'Oh, but in Manchester it's so much worse,' replied Barry Begbie, to which John Smith raised his eyebrows, partly in disbelief that such a thing were even possible but also out of concern that it may be described to him, something he was very keen to avoid. Luckily for him there was now a distraction. Also, I should add that's not me doing a lazy cop-out by avoiding describing what happens in the Manchester site, because I will be doing that in a later chapter. In fact, the reason it's only been vaguely mentioned is to build up anticipation without giving too much away too early so, if anything, it's a quite brilliant literary device.

Just then a man burst out of a room next to the one John Smith had been in. He had a mad-eyed look in, well, his eyes. The eyes are definitely the best place to have a mad-eyed look. In fact, I'd say they're the only place. But he charged by John Smith and Barry Begbie without giving any indication he had even noticed them.

'Penis!' he yelled. 'Penis, penis, willy, willy, bum-bum!!'

As he ran around the corner and out of their sight, John Smith and Barry Begbie looked at each other and nodded. 'So he was shown Mrs Brown's Boys too,' noted Barry Begbie. By the way, that man was the guy next door who I mentioned not long ago so it didn't look like I simply made him up here. Also, I'm aware of the irony of criticising Mrs Brown's Boys for obtaining what little humour it has from the endless repetition of the word 'penis', whilst also having quite a few characters here who add comic relief by saying 'penis' a lot. But at least I've got other stuff, too! I mean, that bit about him being 'mad-eyed' was reasonable, wasn't it? Or how about that line about 'laughing out loud' being the same as 'shitting solids'? That was good, too!

As Barry Begbie watched the deranged man scurry away from them, he added, 'still, so much of this is just hearsay. It's the same with rumours of there being a Resistance. Some say it's a real organisation, others that it was made up by the BBC, or at least exaggerated by them, to justify increased military patrols, or to give the public a group to hate, or even as an attempt to weed out heretics by making them think there are others like them.' He then casually surveyed the yard, a gesture that John Smith soon realised was actually in order to check whether there was anyone else within earshot. 'Still,' he continued, contemplatively, 'what if there's a weak spot? What if there was actually a way to turn the guards against each other? Could that possibly be the key to getting out of here?'

He nodded slowly then looked at the floor, thoughtfully, and John Smith realised that whilst this was not an entirely rhetorical question, it was not one he should enquire further about just yet. You should definitely remember him saying that, though, as it's an important plot point that will very much have repercussions and be referred back to in future chapters. So that's another brilliant literary device. That's two in barely a page, which I think you should appreciate.

Right, then, that's the end of this chapter.

# Chapter Ten:

# The Daily Guardians of Public Decency

*In Which Representatives of The Press Are Summoned And Given Their Instructions, With the Liberal Wing Deciding That White People Should Be Re-Branded As 'People Without Colour' and the Right-Wing Side Realising That Paddington Bear Is An Illegal Immigrant Scrounger Who Must Be Denounced*

Right then, this novel is getting much longer than I anticipated so in an attempt to keep the word count a bit lower I'm now going to format this chapter like a film script. I mean, it'll make it so much easier to read by breaking up the dialogue (of which there is a lot) and also means I can dispense with all the descriptive parts and not be having to constantly come up with different words so that you have things like 'Dave McCreith replied', 'Terry Ball pondered' or 'John Smith explained' rather than just putting 'Dave McCreith said' all the time. And all these scenes take place in the same office, anyway! Do you really need to know whereabouts they're standing? How much sunshine there was?! A lot of what novelists normally provide is either irrelevant detail or the clumsy use of the scene in order to convey other things, like if it's raining it means one of the characters is sad or something. I mean, I really think you'll see what I mean once it gets going. A whole chapter where it's not daunting blocks of text that you'll probably end up skipping anyway! And if I deem it a success I'll probably use it in other dialogue-heavy chapters, too! I don't know why I didn't think of this before!

[*Publisher's Note*: we have published this book almost exactly as we received it, as we recognised the importance of both bringing the stark warnings contained within it to the public's attention and not diluting the powerful messages of this visionary author, *however*, following advice from our lawyers we have taken the regrettable decision to change or obscure the names of some characters in this chapter, dealing as it does with the topic of journalism.

This is a result of our legal team pointing out that despite constantly banging about how freedom of speech and open debate are utterly sacrosanct and censorship of the press utterly abhorrent, or angrily railing against so-called 'cancel culture', whilst themselves constantly criticising and mocking anyone in the public eye, journalists are often hyper-sensitive, deeply vain, completely humourless and extremely litigious people who will threaten legal action against anyone who makes even the slightest criticism of them, no matter how valid, whilst utterly failing to see the irony and intense hypocrisy in them doing this.

So, bearing this in mind, and with great reluctance, we have altered the names of the journalists as they appeared in the original manuscript, and if we still end up being sued then we'll quote this disclaimer in court to make them look stupid, pointing out that by suing us they've essentially validated our argument, and also imply that their legal action was actually the result of them being offended by this disclaimer anyway.

We'd also add that this book appears to have originated from a future alternate dimension, so even if the characters are based on real people they're people who only exist in a different reality. Also, if you believe that a character whose name is 'GENERIC LIBERAL JOURNALIST' is actually meant to be you, just what does that say about how you perceive yourself?! And how sensitive would you have to be to take offence at a character you vaguely thought might be based on you in a book hardly anyone will ever read anyway?!]

So, right, this chapter starts with Dave McCreith and Terry Ball and they're obviously in Dave McCreith's office. If there are any relevant changes to their environment then I'll mention them, but I don't reckon there will be.

> DAVE MCCREITH
> (Sighing in annoyance.)
> So, I assume you've booked me yet another meeting, as if you're trying to kill me with overwork or something.

> TERRY BALL
> Ha ha, not at all, your excellence! Today is your weekly meeting with members of the press so you can issue them with their instructions. And first of all we'll be meeting [GENERIC LIBERAL JOURNALIST WHOSE NAME HAS BEEN REDACTED FOLLOWING LEGAL ADVICE], for decades one of the best-known columnists for the Custodian newspaper.

> DAVE MCCREITH
> Hmm, very well. Send her in.

TERRY BALL opens the door where, conveniently, [GENERIC LIBERAL JOURNALIST WHOSE NAME HAS BEEN REDACTED FOLLOWING LEGAL ADVICE] is waiting. I can't be bothered with a physical description, so please just imagine her as being pretty generic. And white, obviously, as she's a high up person on a liberal newspaper. She curtseys upon entering the room, approaches DAVE MCCREITH, kneels in front of him and kisses his hand when offered it, along with the expensive bejewelled BBC ring I mentioned he had a few chapters ago, before standing up.

> GENERIC LIBERAL JOURNALIST
> Your excellency! May I first of all apologise for my lateness?! I was just in the foyer and was caught short, but I noticed that, quite correctly, you have twenty seven different toilets for all the different gender identities, so it took me almost twenty minutes to read all the descriptions and decide which one resonated with me!

> DAVE MCCREITH
> Well, I hope you used the correct one, as to do otherwise

would be a hate crime.

(Thinks for a moment.)

Hang on, twenty seven gender identities? I thought it was twenty five?

TERRY BALL
Two new ones discovered yesterday, your grace.

DAVE MCCREITH
Very well. Instruct the PR department to identify anyone on the internet still referring to there being twenty five and have them publically shamed.

TERRY BALL
Consider it done, my liege.

DAVE MCCREITH
And raise the licence fee to cover the expense of ripping out all the old, hateful, incorrectly-gender confirming toilets and having them replaced.

TERRY BALL
Of course, my liege.

GENERIC LIBERAL JOURNALIST
Anyway, your excellency, it's such a pleasure to see you again! Don't worry, I won't keep you long as I've got so much to do. First of all I need to finish my latest column, 'Why Page Three was a Repellent, Monstrous Thing that Objectified Women As Sexual Objects But Also Any Man Who Ever Criticises a Woman For Having Done It Should Be Imprisoned for the Sickening Crime of 'Slut-Shaming' Because It Was Empowering And Inspiring'.

DAVE MCCREITH
Oh, that reminds me. The BBC has decided to start televising the Miss Universe pageant, so I need you to write a leader saying what a wonderful event it is.

GENERIC LIBERAL JOURNALIST
Miss Universe? But I campaigned against that for years! Isn't it a repellent, chauvinistic, sickening relic of old-school sexism that degrades women by sexually objectifying them in front of an audience of leering, lusting men?

DAVE MCCREITH
Well, yes, of course, but that was in the '80s and '90s and now it's a diverse celebration of the international sisterhood of women, an empowering event that depicts women reclaiming their sexuality against the patriarchy! Girl power!

GENERIC LIBERAL JOURNALIST
Right, I'm sorry, your grace, I wasn't aware. What's changed about it?

DAVE MCCREITH
Oh, it's still exactly the same, with near-anorexic women parading around in bikinis whilst making extremely vague and tokenistic statements about how they want to win so they can bring about world peace, only now one of the presenters is a plus-size model who's best known for going on chat shows and Twitter and expressing vague and inane soundbites about body-positivity for the unquestioning media to lap up.

GENERIC LIBERAL JOURNALIST
Oh, right, so they're invoking the Cosmo Defence?

DAVE MCCREITH
Exactly. The Cosmo Defence is where you claim to have a particular worldview, usually an inspiring, empowering and highly sanctimonious one, despite the fact that you act in a completely different way 99% of the time, *only to then* cite the very few occasions when your actions actually match your words as a way to denounce anyone who accuses you of hypocrisy. The name comes from the magazine that offers its readers an endless diet of uninspiring articles featuring skinny, attractive, white celebrities telling them to wear nice shoes and make-up and get really good at sex so that a man will

want to marry them, yet somehow claims itself a feminist magazine because once a year they run an extremely half-hearted article with a title like 'OMG, The New Feminism Is Here And It's, Like, Really Cool!'

[Note: that may seem like a harsh summary of said magazine but if you check you'll see it's entirely accurate. Well, assuming it's still going. Is it? I've no idea.]

GENERIC LIBERAL JOURNALIST
Will there be any overweight or unattractive women in this reboot?

DAVE MCCREITH
Oh, god, no. And in an irony completely lost on just about everyone, the inspiring plus-size model who presents it would be considered far too overweight to actually enter it herself.

GENERIC LIBERAL JOURNALIST
Okay, thanks for letting me know.
(Writing in her notebook.)
'Miss Universe no longer a repellent, sexist relic but a vibrant celebration of female empowerment.' Right, I'll get our Sunday supplement to commission a ten-page feature on how Miss Universe is Back But With a Feminist Twist!

TERRY BALL
Hang on, can men enter this? If they identify as women?

DAVE MCCREITH
(Worried, as if this is an idea he very much does not want anybody to entertain.)
Be quiet, Ball! Your dedication to independent though has no place at the BBC and is dangerously close to heresy!

TERRY BALL
I'm sorry, your grace.

DAVE MCCREITH

Quite right. Anyway, [GENERIC LIBERAL JOURNALIST WHOSE NAME HAS BEEN REDACTED FOLLOWING LEGAL ADVICE], write what you said you would.

GENERIC LIBERAL JOURNALIST

Of course, your grace. Tell me what to write and it shall be written! In fact, I've just finished an article that argues any man who visits a sex worker should automatically be put on the Sex Offenders' Register, whilst also arguing that sex workers themselves are engaged in noble, empowering, inspiring work because they're using their sexuality as a weapon against the patriarchy, and anyone who criticises them is committing the act of slut-shaming, and then I wrote *another* article claiming that anyone working in prostitution is only there as the result of people-trafficking and therefore it's a repellent practice and the government should be ruthlessly cracking down on it and arresting all the pimps! And we're going to run them all on the same day!

DAVE MCCREITH

Hmm, well, it would seem that it's business as usual at your newspaper. I'm pleased that the Custodian is closely following the BBC in frequently and blatantly contradicting itself by switching its moral codes on an almost daily basis.

GENERIC LIBERAL JOURNALIST

Well, yes, your grace, but for me having perfect morality isn't some sort of part-time commitment. I'm dedicated to fighting injustice and intolerance wherever I see them. In fact, on the way here, just as I got out of the limo, I heard a woman of colour refer to her son as a 'cheeky monkey' and I was so sickened to witness such a vile piece of casual racism that I ordered the police arrest her and take the child into care immediately.

DAVE MCCREITH

I am impressed by your dedication, but you seem to be implying that the Custodian is somehow possessing of a more superior level of wokeness than that of the Corporation.

GENERIC LIBERAL JOURNALIST
Well, I'm not trying to boast, but, well... We were being offended by everything back when you were still showing the Black and White Minstrel Show and having Jim Davidson on TV every week! Where were you when we were trying to have 'Baa Baa Black Sheep' banned for being racially inflammatory?! It was me who started a campaign to have the word 'manager' banned because the first three letters spelt 'man'! It was me who petitioned for 'Man-Size Tissues' to be withdrawn from sale for employing hateful, deeply misogynistic language by implying that men are somehow bigger and stronger than women but also for daring to suggest there are even *any* physical differences between the two! It was even me who argued that the word 'menopause' was hopelessly offensive and outdated because it started with the word 'men' and sounded a bit like 'men on pause'! It should really be called the 'womenopause'! The Custodian was doing all that years before you actually controlled us!

(She briefly looks worried, as if concerned she may
have overstepped the mark.)
But, in conclusion, your eminence, all I mean is that both my paper and I remain your most obedient servants. Just this morning I was writing a piece that celebrates the LGBTQI++ABARAFOQOE?HJGBV Community!

DAVE MCCREITH
(Glaring at her accusingly.)
I'm sorry? The what community?

GENERIC LIBERAL JOURNALIST
(Slightly confused.)
Er, the LGBTQI++ABARAFOQOE?HJGBV Community, your grace?

DAVE MCCREITH
Are you trying to get yourself killed with your repellent hate?! That initialism changed yesterday! The dogging community

decided they wanted to be recognised as a distinct sexual group so a D was added to it at 5pm! You need to update your terminology!

GENERIC LIBERAL JOURNALIST
(Rather terrified)
I'm sorry, your grace! I had no idea! I'll be sure to refer to it as the LGBTQI++ABARAFOQOE?HJGBVD community from now on, I swear!

DAVE MCCREITH
As someone who appears to value her life, I hope that you do.
(Suddenly stops and thinks; to TERRY BALL.)
Ball! What is the current initialism?

TERRY BALL
(Also rather terrified, and on the spot, he recites the following slowly.)
Er, well, it's the LGBTQI++ABA, er, RAFO, erm, QOE?... HJGBV.. And 'D' for 'Doggers', your grace!

DAVE MCCREITH
(As if annoyed he got it right.)
Hmm. Very good.

GENERIC LIBERAL JOURNALIST
(Thoughtfully.)
Hmm, actually, that change will prove quite useful. Just before I left the office today we were going through our archives to find examples of our writers having committed sickening hate crimes in articles they wrote a few weeks ago so are now, obviously, hopelessly outdated and full of terms that seem repellent to the modern day mind. It was most beneficial, because we lost another twenty million pounds in the last quarter so this allows us to get rid of a load of staff without paying them off, on the grounds that their repugnant values are totally at odds with ours.

DAVE MCCREITH

Hmm, well, we simply fire employees when they get too old, but do go on.

GENERIC LIBERAL JOURNALIST

Well, it made me think. Whilst we at the Custodian are, well, the custodians of the perfect, objective, eternal and correct worldview, we do have an issue that people sometimes call us out on things we said or wrote that later turned out to be abhorrent acts of hate.

DAVE MCCREITH

This has often been an issue for our organisation too. We used to have quite a problem with people daring to point out how often our organisation's past behaviour sat completely at odds with the image we were trying to promote.

GENERIC LIBERAL JOURNALIST

Well, I've noticed a trend amongst repellent members of the so-called 'alt-right', where they have the bare-faced audacity to point out things that those of us with the correct opinions have previously said that later turn out to actually have been incorrect, then retweet them and say 'this you?' They seem to believe this makes us in some way hypocritical, as when they retweet these views it may coincide with us attacking other people for holding exactly the same ones, though I consider it extremely unfair that they should use the modern standards of today to judge us for things we said as far back as two or three years ago.

DAVE MCCREITH

Hmm, yes... It's also been a problem for us to have people point out that we promote our currently worldview as perfect and flawless, and ruthlessly attack anyone who refuses to subscribe to it, and then have them provide undeniable evidence of how quickly, frequently and completely our own opinions change.
(Pause.)
Then again, on the many occasions when we highlight and

criticise past BBC behaviour that by today's standards would seem repellent, the public never seems to think it odd that we act as if the historic BBC is somehow a completely different, unrelated organisation rather than literally being the same one that's doing the criticism.

GENERIC LIBERAL JOURNALIST

Indeed, your grace, but, unfortunately, whilst organisations seem to be able to employ that get-out clause, individuals do not have such a luxury. I mean, a few years after the Brexit vote I wrote a column saying how wonderful it was that lots of old people had since died because that meant that if we held the referendum again then Remain would surely win it, and some cruel trolls said that my celebrating the death of hate-filled old people somehow sat at odds with my image as being a person who cared deeply about social inclusivity and the welfare of everyone!

DAVE MCCREITH

So what's your solution?

GENERIC LIBERAL JOURNALIST

Well, here's my idea: you know how we invented the term 'dead-naming', which made it a sickening act of hate to even mention that a trans person used to be a different gender, even if it was a famous person and everyone knew they'd transitioned and what their old name was?

DAVE MCCREITH

Of course. We disposed of hundreds of people using that principle during the Great Re-Structuring.

GENERIC LIBERAL JOURNALIST

Well, what if we were to introduce a hate crime similar to 'dead-naming' but call it 'dead *belief*-ing'? The idea would be that when somebody like us, who possesses correct, eternal, flawless morality, completely changes their opinion on something it would actually be a crime for anybody to dare point this out. We invent a new, abhorrent type of hate crime called 'dead belief-ing' that means you can completely change your opinion on anything but then use the term to denounce and smear anyone who dares point out your hypocrisy as a 'peddler of hate'!

### DAVE MCCREITH
'Dead belief-ing'. I like it. I like it a lot. It'll also save us a huge amount of time in going back through our web and TV archives and removing the thousands of examples of things that later turned out to be morally repugnant. We can simply prosecute anyone who dares point it out!

### GENERIC LIBERAL JOURNALIST
Well, thank you, your grace! So, just to sum it up in a handy, quotable form... 'Dead Belief-ing' is when somebody has the audacity to point out that your position on a particular topic has completely shifted, to the extent that the thing you used to believe has been reclassified as a hate crime, but you respond by shifting the blame to your accuser and saying them daring to point it out is *more* of a hate crime than the original opinion was because they are 'dead-belief-ing' you!

### DAVE MCCREITH
And we could also use it to attack and denounce anyone who points out just how many major BBC stars used to black up on their comedy programmes yet we continue to employ them! I shall instruct the Corporation to help seed this term into common usage, whilst also attacking anyone who dares to question the logic upon which it is based. From this day on, let both the BBC and Custodian destroy our enemies by accusing them of 'dead belief-ing'!

> (He pauses for a moment, as if remembering something.)

Oh, yes, and speaking of inane and meaningless words and phrases, I have a new one that I want you and your colleagues to start using.

### GENERIC LIBERAL JOURNALIST
Of course, your grace, and what is it?

DAVE MCCREITH
Well, I've invented a new word: 'Inspowering'. It's a portmanteau of 'inspiring' and 'empowering' and whilst being every bit as inane and meaningless as the two words it's made from, it uses fewer characters on Twitter, which is good because no one ever uses those two terms for any reason other than as a rather embarrassing attempt to virtue signal on social media in order to gain likes. So from now on I order you to start encouraging women to celebrate other women for being 'inspowering', okay?

GENERIC LIBERAL JOURNALIST
'Inspowering', you say? I like it. I'll start using it right away. Oh, and that reminds me. We have also come up with a new term that we would appreciate your assistance in bedding in.

DAVE MCCREITH
Yes?

GENERIC LIBERAL JOURNALIST
Well, it's not escaped our attention that all the terms for minorities change every few years, and sometimes a term once considered totally acceptable becomes a term of hate whilst words that were once insults become the accepted term, like 'queer' was an insult yet now it's part of the, er LGBTQI++ABARAFOQOE?HJGBVD initialism, or how calling someone 'black' was deemed racist and you were meant to say 'coloured' but then that changed, even though the leading American civil rights organisation continued to be called the 'National Association for the Advancement of *Colored* People', yet, weirdly, you could still refer to someone as a 'person of colour'... There's also another very relevant example: I'm currently running a campaign to have every single person who was historically employed by 'The Spastics Society' to be imprisoned for a hate crime as that term is now one of vile abuse but apparently *not one single one* of their employees took issue with it until a few years back...
        (She pauses for breath here.)
But I always felt that those of us who had the misfortune not

to be born a minority missed out on all that. Why shouldn't we have the words that describe us changing every decade or so, so we can complain about it? So here's my proposal: the Custodian and the BBC announce that as the term 'white people' has historically been one of hate, a name tainted with historical connotations of pure evil, we should now be referred to as... People *Without* Colour!

DAVE MCCREITH
I like it, I like it a lot... Perhaps we could also say that whilst 'People Without Colour' is the correct term, anyone saying 'non-coloured people' is committing an act of hate?

GENERIC LIBERAL JOURNALIST
A truly brilliant suggestion, your excellence.

DAVE MCCREITH
Indeed. Right, we'll have those terms embedded into official BBC Correct-Speak by the end of the day.

GENERIC LIBERAL JOURNALIST
You honour me, your grace. Oh, actually, there is something else... You see, our publication chose to do things differently. Our business plan was based on giving all our content away for free, whilst... Well, that was it, really. So I was wondering...

DAVE MCCREITH
(Deeply suspicious.)
Wondering what?

GENERIC LIBERAL JOURNALIST
Well, your grace... So, the thing is, our organisation haemorrhages tens of millions of pounds every year and does not have the luxury of being able to squander an almost limitless amount of licence fee money on whatever we choose.

DAVE MCCREITH
Hmm, you say that, but despite your constant pleading of poverty, to the extent of practically going door-to-door asking

for donations, you still found sufficient funds to join us in the legal action against The Book...

GENERIC LIBERAL JOURNALIST

Oh, yes, 'The Book the BBC Tried to BAN!'? Well, the point there is that whilst the Custodian is a firm believer in the importance of freedom of expression and importance of debate in a democratic society, that book contained a character who seemed to be a rather one-dimensional parody of me, so we couldn't let it stand! As bastions of liberalism we were well within our rights to request that every copy of that book be hurled on an enormous bonfire and burnt out of existence, with the author at the very top!

DAVE MCCREITH

I don't disagree with that. As I always say: the BBC is a firm believer in free speech, but free speech with strict limits, with the most severe punishments for those who choose to go beyond them! Still, I find it a little odd that a newspaper that's always pleading poverty and begging anyone who visits its website to donate to them in order to help them continue their vital, world-beating journalism at the same time as constantly banging on about the important of free speech and citing censorship in places like Saudi Arabia still managed to find enough money for a huge legal case to ban a little book that hurt its feelings.

[Note: another rather nice piece of pre-emptive action with regards to the potential for people to sue this book, I think you'll agree.]

GENERIC LIBERAL JOURNALIST

Well, we thought it was four million pounds well spent, and are sure our readers and subscribers agreed, but just to be sure we prosecuted anyone who posted comments in the comments section of our website suggesting otherwise. Anyway, bearing in mind that the values of our organisation resonate perfectly with those of yours, we wondered if you could perhaps use your influence with the government to introduce a new tax on newspapers, meaning that anyone who purchases one, regardless of whether it is actually our title or one of our repellent rivals, has a portion of that fee go to supporting the Custodian? I mean, there would be some who would argue that would give us a hugely unfair market advantage, but to those cruel trolls I would point out that our newspaper has the correct worldview, so deserves to be publically funded to an almost limitless degree.

DAVE MCCREITH

Hang on, can I just check your terminology? What exactly do you mean by the term 'troll'?

GENERIC LIBERAL JOURNALIST

Why, anyone who dares disagree with me, of course!

DAVE MCCREITH

Right... Anyway, hang on, are you saying that anyone who consumes a particular type of media should be forced to pay for the upkeep of a single organisation within that industry even if it's one they never personally use?! How would that make sense?! How would that be fair?!

GENERIC LIBERAL JOURNALIST

Er, well, your grace, an argument could theoretically be made that the licence fee is based on much the same principle...

DAVE MCCREITH
(Ignoring this.)

Anyway... As you pointed out earlier, you were getting offended by everything and anything decades before it was popular...

GENERIC LIBERAL JOURNALIST

Indeed we were, your grace! Did you know we once tried to get the 'Compare the Meerkat' adverts banned for being offensive to Eastern Europeans?

DAVE MCCREITH

Aren't those meerkats meant to be Russian?

GENERIC LIBERAL JOURNALIST
Russian, Eastern European, same difference...

DAVE MCCREITH
Yes, but my point is that although you very much blazed a trail by getting offended by everything you saw, you utterly failed to capitalise on that even when much of the rest of the world had come to share your unthinking woke viewpoint. I mean, that's like the whole world being morbidly obese but McDonald's failing to turn a profit!

GENERIC LIBERAL JOURNALIST
Well, your grace, as I said, our model was different, and we felt our loyal readers would support us when we made our journalism free because it had the correct worldview...

DAVE MCCREITH
And did they?

GENERIC LIBERAL JOURNALIST
No. But, your grace, I would counter by saying that even if none of our readers are willing to actually pay for the content they claim to value, my publication plays just as important a role as yours does in controlling people's thoughts, and making them accept them unquestioningly.

DAVE MCCREITH
True. The role of the news media has always been to control what the public think. For the proles we have the tabloids, and the role of your newspaper is to do that with lower-middle class people, keeping them in their place and ensuring they never question what you tell them to believe or notice the hypocrisy of it all. You know, claiming to be pro-meritocracy and anti-elitism whilst employing people almost exclusively from private schools and Oxbridge...

GENERIC LIBERAL JOURNALIST
Of course.

DAVE MCCREITH

Claiming to be environmental and anti-Big Business whilst accepting huge advertising revenues from banks and oil companies.

GENERIC LIBERAL JOURNALIST

Well, everyone needs to make a living!

DAVE MCCREITH

Banging on about diversity and representation, much like the BBC, when, also much like the BBC, your senior-level staff are almost exclusively not from minority groups...

GENERIC LIBERAL JOURNALIST

Incorrect, your grace! Our groundbreaking newspaper pioneered diversity and representation to the extent that we appointed our first female editor as far back as 2015!

DAVE MCCREITH

I stand corrected. Who can fail to be impressed by a newspaper that pioneered social justice and equality to the extent that it appointed an editor who wasn't a privately-educated, white male after only two centuries?

GENERIC LIBERAL JOURNALIST

We are rightly proud of our record and will always strive to lead the way in matters of diversity.

DAVE MCCREITH

And, based on your impressive track record, how long do you think it will be before we can expect your publication to be edited by someone from an ethnic minority background?

GENERIC LIBERAL JOURNALIST

Oh, I would think by the year 2150 at the very least.

DAVE MCCREITH

Good, and, like your organisation, the BBC has always had a firmly pro-women stance, even if, technically that didn't extend to actually having them on our Board of Directors. Or paying them the same. Or continuing to employ them once they hit fifty. But the main thing is we always promote a pro-women viewpoint, which I feel is far more important than actually giving prominent roles, or equal pay, to women.

GENERIC LIBERAL JOURNALIST
Indeed. The evil Tories may have had two female leaders and, indeed, female Prime Ministers, but whilst they may have, technically, made more progress in *actual* diversity, I strongly feel we've made more progress in campaigning for it, which I consider far more important.

DAVE MCCREITH
I absolutely share that view. The key aim of the news media is to not only tell people what to think but also to make them assume those views are their own, rather than having been put there by someone else without them ever realising it. I mean, why do people never think it odd, or even notice, that every single thing they 'believe' perfectly matches the view of their favourite newspaper?

GENERIC LIBERAL JOURNALIST
Yes, and our proudest achievement in that regard is how we've conditioned our readers to believe that grammar schools are truly sickening examples of elitism, and are utterly repellent for being 'selective', whilst distracting them from the fact we almost exclusively send our own children to private schools, or do our hardest to get them into one of the few decent comprehensives in the country, or to notice that, well, life itself is selective! They don't seem to think it at all strange that we attack grammar schools for selecting pupils based on 'academic ability', even though that's obviously *exactly* the same principle used by all universities and the professions!

DAVE MCCREITH
And your readers have never noticed that, for which I suppose you are due credit.

GENERIC LIBERAL JOURNALIST

I think we are! We go on about how anyone should be able to become a success based on their intelligence and ability, and regardless of their background, whilst fiercely campaigning against the one thing that historically helped people like them to succeed by saying that grammar schools practise a form of discrimination worse than Apartheid!

DAVE MCCREITH

Well, yes, but, of course, the issue with grammar schools is that they, regrettably, led to large numbers of intelligent and talented people from working- and lower-middle-class backgrounds threatening to take our cushy jobs in the media through ability and intelligence rather than the traditional method of utilising one's family connections. Do you have any idea of how many people from our world lost out as a result of that?! Imagine being born into privilege and assuming you'd be given a top job at the BBC or at a newspaper only to find it had been stolen from you by someone who just happened to be more intelligent! How would that be fair?!

GENERIC LIBERAL JOURNALIST

Absolutely. That in itself was a sickening example of discrimination. I mean, we did our part by experimenting with meritocracy, but it proved too damaging to the prospects of our children, so we had to turn the country against it. We couldn't stand for them coming into our world and stealing our jobs!

DAVE MCCREITH

Yes, and if a member of the proles dares step out of place by criticising us and saying they'd have done better in life if they'd had our advantages, we dismiss them by accusing them of having a 'chip on their shoulder'!

GENERIC LIBERAL JOURNALIST

Anyway, my point is that my newspaper's obedience to the BBC has never been in question. I mean, it's a sad but undeniable truth that the 'little people', such as those who live on council estates and did not attend university, do not have the intellectual powers or critical abilities that we do, so must be protected from dangerous thoughts for their own safety. And our name itself shows that we see ourselves as the 'custodians', or 'guardians', if you will, of the little people, saving them from themselves and their dangerous, hate-filled opinions. So all I'm saying is that we would appreciate financial support from an organisation that doesn't have to worry about where its money comes from.

DAVE MCCREITH
Hmm, well, I'll think about it.

TERRY BALL
Sorry to interrupt, but as today is the day you issue instructions to all elements of the press I just wanted to let you know that the representative from Today's Post will be here shortly.

There is a knock on the door.

TERRY BALL
Ah, that'll be him now.

TERRY BALL opens the door and VINCE BIGGERTON, who isn't based on anybody, and an INTERN, who doesn't need a proper name, both enter, with VINCE BIGGERTON taking a knee in front of DAVE MCCREITH, who nods to indicate he may stand up again. GENERIC LIBERAL JOURNALIST looks at them suspiciously.

GENERIC LIBERAL JOURNALIST
Oh, hello there. I suppose you've just popped in to take a break from your rabble-rousing, populist website publishing lots of photos of teenage girls in their bikinis?

VINCE BIGGERTON
But didn't you recently feature excerpts from Emma Watson's latest Vogue photoshoot, where she had her top off?

GENERIC LIBERAL JOURNALIST
Oh, don't be ridiculous. That's completely different.

VINCE BIGGERTON
How is it different?

GENERIC LIBERAL JOURNALIST
Because she's privately educated! That makes her nudity a powerful, feminist, artistic statement whilst when you do it it's just low-level titillation!

DAVE MCCREITH
Stop pretending to argue with each other, you two! You're not on Question Time now!

GENERIC LIBERAL JOURNALIST
Oh, yes, right. Force of habit! How are the wife and kids?

VINCE BIGGERTON
Good! Your family okay?!

GENERIC LIBERAL JOURNALIST
Yes, not too bad. Actually...

At this point the INTERN jumps up with a deranged look in his eyes.

INTERN
BUSTY DISPLAY!

Other than VINCE BIGGERTON, the others look at him in confusion.

DAVE MCCREITH
Is he okay?

VINCE BIGGERTON
Oh, yes, he's fine... He's our intern, actually, the grandson of our proprietor... He's been with us for three months and normally when we have an intern it's the kid of some high-up person so we just give them easy stuff to do, like writing

columns, which we'll end up having to completely re-write before we can publish them anyway... But unfortunately there was a mix-up...

INTERN
(Again, with a deranged, frazzled look in his eyes.)
AMPLE ASSETS!

VINCE BIGGERTON
And he was sent to do the proof-reading for the so-called 'sidebar of shame' on our website... You know the one... It's just loads of celebrity stuff, and consists almost entirely of pictures of reality TV stars in various states of undress, either taken from their social media feeds or from paparazzi photos of them attending Z-list awards ceremonies...

INTERN
EYE POPPING DISPLAY!

VINCE BIGGERTON
It's a little joke we play on our readers, actually, because we run dozens of these photos every day but always accompany them with a disparaging article suggesting we very much disapprove of the celebrity in question and expect our readers to also be completely disinterested in them, even though that rather obviously raises the question of why, if that were true, we ran the photos in the first place. Some of our readers even log in so they can post in the comments section saying how uninterested they are, without managing to see the irony in that either!
(He briefly looks confused as if having lost his train of thought, before finding it again.)
Hmm, well, anyway, we have various stock phrases we use there and after he spent fourteen hours a day doing little else than typing those...

INTERN
BUSTY ASSETS!

VINCE BIGGERTON

Yes, phrases like that... It's essentially frazzled his brain. It's a form of shell-shock. The proprietor will be mad when he finds out so I've just been bringing him with me everywhere I go.

INTERN

PUTS ON A BUSTY DISPLAY!

VINCE BIGGERTON

Yeah, that's pretty much all he says now.

There is a pause as they ponder this, then the INTERN wanders off to the other end of the room, which is very convenient at it means he no longer interrupts the main dialogue with his outbursts now he has made the point that he was created to make. I suppose he still does them, though.

GENERIC LIBERAL JOURNALIST

Well, anyway, I've just written a response to your recent column about why you think we should ban the traditional African practice of female genital mutilation.

VINCE BIGGERTON

Oh, yes, the one where I said it's an abhorrent practice that shouldn't be tolerated in a civilised society?

GENERIC LIBERAL JOURNALIST

Yes, that's it! Obviously I've responded by saying it's actually a wonderful, traditional, natural practice that strengthens the bond between mother and daughter and is a powerful signifier of female empowerment, whilst attacking your take on it as being based on nothing more than sickening sexism and racism!

VINCE BIGGERTON

Okay, cool, I look forward to reading it. It's a complicated issue. Despite what we say in our respective columns. Out of interest, what's your take on circumcision?

GENERIC LIBERAL JOURNALIST
(Suddenly terrified, as if unsure what the correct answer is.)
Er, don't have one!

[Note: this bit is a quite brilliant observation on how people and media outlets always like to think of their take on morality as being consistent and objective when in practice it's often reactive, by which I mean people simply take a contrary position to those they see themselves as being opposed to, because they could never bring themselves to agree with them on a single topic. So in the crazed, future world in which the events of this book take place it was the right-wing press who came out in opposition to female genital mutilation, causing the liberal press to quickly state their support for it, and to attack anyone who didn't immediately and unquestioningly agree with them. Clever, huh?! And is that really such an implausible scenario when you consider it? If anything, if you'd told me about FGM before anyone had really heard of it, I'd have been more likely to put money on the liberal press supporting it than opposing it because the groups who practice it are those who they normally defend unquestioningly. So morality is pretty much arbitrary. That's my point here, okay? I mean, have any anti-FGM people come out against circumcision? Surely most of the arguments they use against FGM would apply there, no? Or do they simply not care about that because it's done to boys rather than girls?

Of course, many people will completely miss these brilliant and utterly valid points, and rush to be outraged because they think that by simply mentioning FGM I must be trivialising it. Still, if they've bought the book already then that's a win for me regardless. Anyway, I was originally going to claim that in the future people refer to it as 'vag-slicing' rather than FGM, so if my purpose was really just to offend people without making a point then I'd have left that in. Then they'd really have had something to complain about!]

TERRY BALL
So, just to clarify, you've both decided on the side of this argument you're going to take, and you'll both denounce anyone who doesn't blindly and completely agree with you,

without thinking it necessary to have, say, a balanced and well-reasoned debate?

They all burst out laughing at this.

> VINCE BIGGERTON
> A balanced, well-reasoned debate! Good one! No, of course not. We work in the media! So the usual rules apply: a new topic is discovered, those of us in power spend, in some cases, quite a long time um-ing and ah-ing about the pros and cons, but once we've made up our minds everyone else has to automatically and unquestioningly agree with us, with no one allowed to even consider it for themselves!

> GENERIC LIBERAL JOURNALIST
> And they'll be committing a monstrous hate crime if they do! And will have opened themselves up to legal action! I mean, the newspaper I work for is called The Custodian, partly because we've always seen ourselves as the 'guardians' of freedom of speech. Free speech is absolutely sacrosanct, and is one of the sacred pillars upon which any society that considers itself civilised should be built, but there must be limits. We believe in free speech, a democratic society and an open press, but sue anyone who refuses to share our values!

[Ooh, going back to the point about clever pre-emptive measures to protect myself from legal action, what happens if you imply someone is highly litigious and they then sue you? Surely by doing so it becomes a self-fulfilling prophecy because by suing you they've proven you were correct and rendered their own legal argument invalid? It's a question for the lawyers, but surely a good one.]

> DAVE MCCREITH
> It's a slogan here at the BBC! 'Free speech but with strict limits'! Anyway, since you're both here I just wanted to check you weren't veering away from the instructions the BBC issued you with regard to what you may and may not report, and how you must frame it. The role of the media has always been to present a view of the world that is completely

polarised, a world of absolutes, black or white, right or wrong, with nothing in between, no nuance, no ambiguity, no room for rational argument or debate, and no suggestion that the public should do anything but choose between one of the two extremes then assume an identical worldview themselves! So, bearing that in mind let's do a quick exercise. [GENERIC LIBERAL JOURNALIST WHOSE NAME HAS BEEN REDACTED FOLLOWING LEGAL ADVICE], when President Obama assassinated Bin Laden, it was...

GENERIC LIBERAL JOURNALIST
A powerful blow against terrorism, in the name of freedom, democracy and world peace!

DAVE MCCREITH
Correct. But what if Bin Laden had been killed under the orders of President Trump?

GENERIC LIBERAL JOURNALIST
Then it would have been a sickening hate crime, a cruel, brutal and callous murder of a defenceless old man!

DAVE MCCREITH
Also correct. Good.

GENERIC LIBERAL JOURNALIST
Phew! I'm glad that was an easy one. I was worried you were going to ask me to think for myself there!

DAVE MCCREITH
And you, Biggerton. How would your outlet have reported the above?

VINCE BIGGERTON
We would have reported the exact opposite, my liege.

DAVE MCCREITH
Also correct. Good. And just to check you have your priorities correct and continue to obediently follow the editorial policy

of the BBC, I'd like to pose this question: if the US bombs Iran on the same day that Taylor Swift tweets 'OMG, feminism is really cool!', which is your main news story?

GENERIC LIBERAL JOURNALIST
The Taylor Swift one, your grace!

DAVE MCCREITH
Also correct. And you?

VINCE BIGGERTON
Obviously we would prioritise the Taylor Swift story, and accompany it with as many photos of her in revealing dresses as possible, whilst doing so in a tone suggesting we were critical and dismissive of the whole thing and that we weren't remotely interested, even though if that were genuinely true then we obviously simply wouldn't have reported it in the first place.

DAVE MCCREITH
Also correct. Good. It's reassuring to know that both your newspapers are as contradictory as ever despite presenting themselves as having never-changing moral values.

VINCE BIGGERTON
Well, yes, it's not as if my newspaper, Today's Post, is any stranger to blatantly contradicting itself and knowing its readership won't notice! We'll freely change our opinions and sympathise with groups we normally demonise if it helps us to make a point. Why, despite us having spent years attacking single mothers we once ran a piece where we supported a teenage girl because an evil social worker encouraged her to have an abortion, saying what a wonderful single mother she would have been! The point is that we have a hierarchy of the groups we hate, so if we can sympathise with one in order to attack another one that's higher up in it then we will do, even if that means shifting our allegiances to side with someone we attacked only a few days before! We actually once did a piece on how a family of asylum seekers were

having to live in a Travelodge because the dopy council couldn't sort them out a council house, in which we sided with the immigrant family so we could attack a loony left council! You couldn't make it up!

GENERIC LIBERAL JOURNALIST
And, of course, we in the liberal media are no strangers to offering completely contradictory worldviews to our readers in order to utterly confuse them! For example, we preach that violence is never, ever acceptable, and if we see a single instance of it occurring during a demonstration by bald, white, working class males then we'll immediately denounce the entire protest as being utterly and unquestionably motivated by hate! But, of course, if violence is committed by those groups that we refuse to even entertain criticism of, such as participants in the 2011 riots, we'll freely defend their acts of arson, looting and murder as being a worthy form of social protest, the only outlet available to those who feel marginalised and ignored by a brutal Tory government! You see! We present our newspapers as being diametrically opposed but we're actually pretty similar when you break our belief systems down. Anyway, your grace, as ever, you honour me by the simple act of allowing me in your presence, but now I must go, as I've lots of work to catch up on! I'm about to launch a campaign arguing that as potatoes were stolen from the Native Americans by early English settlers, eating them in any form is a monstrous example of cultural appropriation!

DAVE MCCREITH
That sounds like the kind of thing the BBC could get behind unquestioningly. You have my blessing.

VINCE BIGGERTON
Yeah, I need to be off, too. It's a shame that America has been plunged into this Second Civil War, because it means that when I write my columns about how Britain is both a truly wonderful and utterly awful country I actually have to do it in my poky five-bed in Chelsea rather than my Florida mansion, as that's been taken over by the local militia! You

couldn't make it up!

DAVE MCCREITH

Hmm, well, if you need inspiration for an article, have you ever considered the real story of... Paddington Bear?

VINCE BIGGERTON

(Confused.)

Paddington Bear? Beloved icon, symbol of Britain, everyone loves him? With all due respect, my liege, I'm a serious journalist and only deal with the biggest topics facing Britain today.

DAVE MCCREITH

Perhaps... But also... Originally from Peru. Sneaks into the country on a boat, under the pretence he has some sort of right to live here simply because his aunt once met an Englishman... Sponges off a hard-working British family and never does a day's work...

VINCE BIGGERTON

(His eyes lighting up in realisation.)

My god, you're right! He's an illegal! He's a scrounger! I'll write a column denouncing him at once, your grace!

INTERN

(Who has just wandered back into view, rather conveniently.)

BUSTY DISPLAY!

VINCE BIGGERTON bows to DAVE MCCREITH, nods a farewell to TERRY BALL and GENERIC LIBERAL JOURNALIST, then grabs the INTERN and leaves the room.

GENERIC LIBERAL JOURNALIST

Also, I need to finish my article on how nepotism is a sickening poison on our society that discriminates against the most disadvantaged in society! Oh, which reminds me! I arranged with your assistant for my son to come in to meet you in a few days, as he's the Custodian's new Film and TV Critic and I think he would benefit from being told what to think by you. I mean, some cruel trolls have implied that he only got the job because he's my son, but I tried to get him into Oxford or Cambridge but they said that he couldn't go simply because he failed all his A levels, which frankly I feel was a sickening act of discrimination, so I'm actually helping a minority by employing him. Anyway, your assistant has all the details!

DAVE MCCREITH
Hmm, very well. Good day to you.

GENERIC LIBERAL JOURNALIST also bows deeply, then leaves the room. TERRY BALL has been on his phone and now looks thoughtful.

TERRY BALL
Hang on, your grace... According to this, the LGBTQI++ABARAFOQOE?HJGBV initialism has changed again.

DAVE MCCREITH
Hmm, well I suppose it has been almost twenty four hours. What's been added now?

TERRY BALL
Oh, it's the letter 'N' for 'necrophile'. It was decided that group had for too long been unfairly stigmatised for its sexual preferences, and that society should show more tolerance towards them.

DAVE MCCREITH
And about time, too. After all, it is a victimless crime.

TERRY BALL
Indeed, your grace.

So, another powerful chapter there, I think you'll agree! And what a powerful critique of the modern media! In case it needs clarifying, the main point here is that the media aren't as objective or independent as they'd like you to believe, nor do they present the broad range of opinions they would have us think they do and nor are the different supposed factions within the media really as opposed to each other as they claim. They all have their prejudices and worldviews they rarely deviate from, or rather would like us to think they do even though they change their minds more often than I change my underpants, which is to say probably about once a week. I like to think I criticised the liberal media and the right wing media equally there, but if you're wondering why I spent more time on the Custodian it's because the BBC is far less likely to criticise fellow travellers than those who don't overtly support its worldview, so I felt that needed to be balanced out. Plus, it's always more fun to criticise the Custodian, as they're not just convinced they're right about everything but incredibly po-faced about it too.

Also, if you're annoyed that the newspaper you read was attacked here but fine with a different one coming in for criticism, consider this: the thing with people is that they're only too happy to see someone they don't agree with being criticised, only to be utterly outraged when the same level of criticism is aimed at people they do agree with. Think for yourself, I say. Well, think for yourself but take some rather heavy hints from me!

And, finally, I know I keep banging on about how hypocritical it would be of people if they sue me over this book but I'd just like to once more point out that if you run a newspaper committed to free speech, and are always banging on about Amnesty International and countries with even less press freedom than this one, like Saudi Arabia or somewhere, it would be really, *really* hypocritical of you to then sue the author of a book over a light-hearted depiction of an entirely fictional woke newspaper, wouldn't it? Yes it would. So that's all cleared up.

Oh, and if all the newspapers now give terrible reviews to this book it's definitely just because their feelings were hurt by the contents of this powerful chapter.

# Chapter Eleven:

# Rat on a Stick

*In Which, Over a Delicious Meal of the Camp Delicacy, Rat On A Stick, Our Heroes Discuss The Reasons for their Incarceration, Whether The Idea of Escape Is Nothing More Than a Crazed Fantasy, And The Rumours Regarding Just What Happened to the Author of 'The Book the BBC Tried to BAN!'*

As he sat in front of a roaring fire, surrounded by people who he may have only met recently but already considered close friends and kindred spirits, John Smith briefly had the feeling of not having a single care in the world, forgetting where he actually was and instead, for a few glorious moments, thinking he was on a camping trip in the wilderness, far away from civilisation and all the unavoidable surveillance and inescapable mind control that were now just accepted as integral aspects of modern British life. But then he came crashing back to reality, as he realised that by defining his imagined scenario as being completely at odds with the nightmarish world that modern life had become, he had in doing so inadvertently reminded himself of that very thing. He sighed, disappointed at having accidentally shaken himself from his carefree reverie, but consoling himself that he at least had his Rat on a Stick to look forward to, as it was very nearly cooked.

'Well,' he said philosophically, 'whilst none of us would choose to be here, we can at least focus on how, right now, we have good company, good conversation, and enough Rat on a Stick to go around.'

Like the other inmates, John Smith had abandoned trying to eat and keep down the canteen food and had joined them in solely subsisting on the most popular form of sustenance, Rat on a Stick, which was also a key foodstuff and the most popular delicacy for those people still in the supposedly-free world.

'Mmm, you certainly do a good Rat on a Stick,' he said to the woman who had cooked them, as he took a bite.

'Well, thank you!' she replied. 'I used to do this a lot before I came here. Actually, I had the Jamie Oliver Rat on a Stick Cookbook.'

'Oh, I saw the TV show he did on that but I didn't have the book,' said Jeffrey Harding. 'Call me a traditionalist, but I always felt the best Rat on a Stick recipes were Delia Smith's ones.'

'Er, I don't know if you're all aware,' cut in Kerri Barnes-Bridge, 'but there's actually a Greggs in this camp?'

The others pulled faces of disgust.

'Please don't make me feel sick when I'm trying to eat,' said Barry Begbie, biting the head off his Rat on a Stick.

You know, I wonder what they had been talking about prior to this chapter starting? I mean, obviously if it had been that important then I'd have started the chapter then rather than now and we'd have heard it, though it does make you wonder exactly what fictional characters get up to when you're writing about other characters in other places, and also raises the question of how you'd manage if two events that were very important to the plot took place at the same time but in different places rather than everyone conveniently taking it in turns to say or do anything that's relevant to the narrative? It's a quandary, I tell you. I can only hope that if something happened in the camp whilst we were off following other people in the last chapter then someone will mention it so we don't miss out. Still, it is a bit worrying. What if they were discussing something of vital importance to the plot, and us having missed it means something happening later in the book doesn't make sense? Anyway, if anything in this book does end up not making sense or looking like a plot hole, that's the excuse I'm going to use.

So, as they sat around the fire eating their Rat on a Stick, the endless drizzle continued, though it was not something that any of them even noticed anymore, as none of them could remember it having stopped the entire time they had been in the camp. And if you think them having a fire in endless drizzle is a plot hole then I'll just say that the wood was found in some shed that kept it dry or, even better, was made up of all the books the BBC had banned, including the infamous 'The Book the BBC Tried to BAN!', which you may recall has been mentioned a few times in previous chapters. Actually, yes, that's much better, because I can turn that not only into a plot device but to highlight the hypocrisy in how people who call themselves liberal and into free speech will also desperately call for something to be censored if they don't agree with it.

A sudden gust of wind lifted something off the fire and blew it to just in front of Barry Begbie. He noticed it was the partly-burned front cover from a copy of the heretical, banned text 'The Book the BBC Tried to BAN!', which, as we just discussed, the fire was almost entirely made up of, so he picked it up and examined it. 'Anyone ever read this?' he asked.

Emmeline Moneypenny looked up. 'As a BBC employee I was forbidden to even acknowledge I'd heard of it... Being caught with a copy was, and remains, a capital offense. Though, of course, senior party members all read it when it came out. Just to decide whether or not it could be read by the lower orders without corrupting them, of course.'

'Odd, then, that there should be hundreds of copies here, in a camp where people are sent to be cleansed of their heretical, anti-BBC thoughts,' said Barry Begbie.

'Well,' continued Emmeline Moneypenny, 'I think it's yet another of their tests. They leave copies lying around to see if anyone picks them up, but also to taunt and confuse us. Anyway, they officially tell us they should only be used as fuel. Actually, their official policy was to claim that burning huge piles of books was all part of their environmental crusade as it meant fewer trees needed to be chopped down or precious fossil fuels used up.'

'I did actually read it, before it was banned,' admitted Barry Begbie. 'You know, there's actually a character who seemed to be partly based on me in it?' He sounded vaguely flattered at this. 'Well, a comedian who, like me, became famous in the mid-'00s doing supposedly 'edgy' stuff but got fed up with all the limitations on what he could say, so left the BBC only to return ten years later with a woke political show, but still ends up in a BBC Re-Education Camp. He even included the bit where I did a joke about a swimmer's nose, and that she complained and said I shouldn't have made fun of her nose because she was a sportsperson rather than a generic media celebrity, but then she had a nose job – on her nose, obviously – so she could then look acceptable enough to become a generic media celebrity.'

He paused here and looked slightly puzzled. 'I can't remember if I mentioned that earlier on. I mean, it's not as if people don't repeat themselves in real life, because they definitely do. In the same way that an author of a book could easily forget whether he'd already mentioned something in a previous chapter, I could easily forget whether I'd already said something at an earlier point in time and end up saying it again. I mean, it's not as if we're all characters in a book where everything we say is very succinct and quotable and we don't, erm, you know... Oh, what's the word? You know sometimes you just forget the word you were going to say?' He looked puzzled and frustrated for a moment, then shrugged. 'Well, anyway, my point was that it's not as if we're all characters in a book about a world where the BBC has taken over the country and put dissenters into prison camps.'

He leaned back and again examined the cover of the novel about a world in which the BBC had taken over the country and put dissenters into prison camps.

'It had me speak quite eloquently about my experience of fame, as it happens,' he continued, thoughtfully, before going on to speak quite eloquently about his experience of fame. 'And fame is a fickle mistress,' he said, before adding 'and a right old slag,' purely to annoy some of the more PC-leaning people sitting around the fire and, as intended, Kerri Barnes-Bridge looked a bit annoyed when he said it, but almost as if she only did so because she thought it was expected of her, and when she realised no one had noticed she stopped immediately.

'Actually,' Barry Begbie went on, 'the character supposedly based on me was really a sort of amalgamation of all 'edgy' mid-'00s comedians, as there were some things he said that weren't originally said by me but by other comedians, yet were seemingly put in there to make a point about the strange way that during that decade you had a load of comedians on TV all the time doing quite offensive stuff whilst at the same time many of the comedians who'd been famous from the 1970s to the 1990s had since been banned from TV for being too offensive even though the modern comedians often did jokes that were much the same.'

John thought this was getting rather confusing, so paid extra attention, which you should probably also do so the point isn't lost.

'So, in the book this character partly based on me did a few jokes on Radio 4 about gypsies and fat girls and as usual the BBC sort of apologised without actually taking any action. But then it got weird. Jim Davidson then stole one of those jokes, and when he used it all the people who'd thought it was fine when I said it were suddenly outraged at how offensive it was, even though it was exactly the same joke. It seemed to be raising the question of whether the new 'edgy' comedians were really all that different from the non-PC ones from the 1970s who'd since been discredited and banned from TV forever, and whether this idea that you could somehow justify offensive jokes by claiming there was some sort of layer of knowing irony on top of them actually had any logical or moral basis to it.'

Barry Begbie looked confused for a moment. 'Still,' he continued, thoughtfully, returning to his earlier theme of how the BBC would pick you up and drop you without any apparent consistency in its reasoning, 'I suppose the thing is that the BBC is, or at least used to be, like a sort of frumpy middle aged wife, who you knew would never leave you but felt a bit boring. ITV and the other channels were like young sluts who promised a life of excitement, but once you left your wife of twenty years, the BBC, for one of them they soon got bored and you found yourself abandoned. Sometimes the BBC takes you back, but it's never quite the same.'

He reached out to the rack that sat in front of the fire and took from it another Rat on a Stick. 'Some people have fame ripped from under their feet if it's suddenly decided their values no longer match those of the Corporation... You get people like Noel Edmunds or Jim Davidson who, within what seems like a few weeks, go from hosting a prime-time Saturday evening show to struggling to sell tickets for a performance on Skegness Pier...'

Does Skegness even have a pier? I'm not sure it does. I'm not going to check, though, but that isn't a plot hole because I'm writing this in the future, remember, so for all you know one may have been built by then and you can't prove otherwise, so there.

'Whereas sometimes the decline is so slow that you don't even notice it,' Barry Begbie continued. 'One morning it suddenly hits you that someone you used to work with has gone from being the star of a top comedy panel show to being on a crappy podcast no one ever listens to, and you didn't even notice. Yet in my case they kept toying with me, and never made it clear what I could and couldn't get away with. I mean, do you remember when that 40-year old TV presenter killed herself and all the tabloids who'd spent the weeks leading up to her death hounding her because she was facing charges of domestic violence against her 27-year old boyfriend then ran endless articles about how it was the media attention that killed her?'

John Smith nodded to acknowledge he remembered this.

'Well, not only did the tabloids escape any real criticism, they suddenly rebranded themselves as being both completely blameless and also incredibly caring, starting a campaign called 'OMG, Be Nice to People!', though even that was only something they invented so they could make money by selling t-shirts with the slogan on them.'

Barry Begbie laughed to himself here. 'So there was a boxing match on a few weeks after that where a British guy was fighting a 40-year old Russian, and I tweeted 'hey, if I wanted to watch a guy in his twenties trying to avoid being knocked out by a 40-year old I'd have spent the evening round Caroline Flack's house!"

John Smith raised an eyebrow, because he was aware that was the sort of joke that, whilst quite brilliant, would almost certainly lead to social media outrage.

'And whilst people on Twitter were outraged,' continued Barry Begbie, 'because they always are, and I pointed out it was a good joke because she was still alive in it, the same tabloids then ran pages and pages about how disgusting my joke was, as if that was the worst part of the whole affair.'

He then went on to further defend this joke, or at least contextualise it, which is really useful because it saves me from having to do it.

'To be honest, the real reason I did that joke is because I wanted to have the debate about why after she died everyone basically said it was the Crown Prosecution Service's fault for pursuing the case against her, even though the people who said that were invariably the exact same ones who'd campaigned for years for a law that would mean domestic abusers could still be prosecuted if the victim didn't want to press charges yet suddenly did a complete moral about-turn when the alleged abuser was a woman rather than a man, and said she should have been let off.'

Barry Begbie looked thoughtful before continuing. 'But obviously I was just denounced as a repellent misogynist making a sickening joke about someone who'd died, even though I also did a follow-up tweet saying she was a true pioneer of gender equality by showing that women could do domestic violence just as well as men.'

Fortunately he stopped there, as whilst the points he was making were entirely valid, or at least worthy of a rational, reasoned debate, they were the sort of thing that can get authors of books in lots of trouble from people too stupid to properly understand them.

'Still...' added Emmeline Moneypenny. 'Do you remember when we were allowed at least some degree of free thought? Before everyone got offended over everything? I mean, to be fair, the Custodian newspaper always got outraged over everything but no one really paid any attention to them, yet the world reached a point where knee-jerk, unthinking outrage somehow became the standard response. But here's the thing... I mean, we called it free speech, and freedom of thought, but how did we ever know? How could we really tell what thoughts we'd come up with ourselves and which ones had been put there by the Corporation? I mean, I used to say to people, if you're an original thinker then tell me one original thought you've ever had, and they never could. All they could do was quote whatever they'd read in that morning's edition of the Custodian, and, not only that, but the worldview they held that they'd supposedly come up with on their own never, ever deviated from that of the newspaper they read. So my point there is: maybe we never really had freedom of thought or speech after all.'

Barry Begbie nodded, then paused for a moment and picked a small rat bone from between his teeth.

'And we ended up in a world where a harmless novel led to a major broadcaster doing everything in its power to have it suppressed. You know, they say the reason the BBC was so keen to have this book banned is because it contained a hilariously comedic depiction of the Director General and he was so utterly humourless, and appalled by the idea of being made fun of, that he initiated the legal action himself, and even had people fired from the BBC for laughing at him in the corridors because of things his fictional counterpart had done.'

'Yes, I heard about that,' added Emmeline Moneypenny. 'The book implied that he'd gone mad with power, and his underlings were never entirely sure if his latest pronouncement was made in sound mind or was actually a consequence of him losing control of his mental faculties as he slowly succumbed to tertiary syphilis.'

'Oh, I heard that...' said John Smith, vaguely. 'The rumour was that the Corporation is aware of his mental decline but covering it up. That's why you don't see him in public anymore. Not even to oversee the executions.'

'Hang on, are we talking about in the book or in real life?' asked Jeffrey Harding.

'Both, as far as I'm aware,' replied John Smith.

'I heard rumours when I was still at the BBC,' added Barry Begbie, 'including that the book was supposedly written by someone who worked there and was sick of the whole organisation so decided to attack it, but knew he'd have to publish it anonymously... But they say the Director General's getting worse, according to the few people I've been in contact with. Some say he fades in and out of lucidity, sometimes coming across like a confused child and other times just as ruthless and brutal as he ever was.'

'They call him the Woke Hitler, you know,' added Emmeline Moneypenny. 'It was originally meant as an insult, or at least to point out the hypocrisy in how he's supposedly a liberal yet heads up an organisation that's become more fascist than anything we've ever seen in Britain, but apparently he actually loves that name and uses it when describing himself.'

'Yes, it's odd that a seemingly-innocuous state broadcaster should have turned out to be undertaking a sinister long-term plan to control every aspect of people's lives,' pondered John Smith. 'How could a company set up to create TV and radio programmes turn into a crazed, unquestionable woke monolith with a mad thirst to control people's every thought?'

Barry Begbie had a final look at the piece of the book he was holding then threw it back onto the fire. 'Still, it wasn't a bad portrayal, as portrayals go. I was depicted as some sort of freedom fighter who actually leads a breakout from the camp.'

The others looked at him here, as if unsure whether he was actually trying to hint that he had worked out a way for them to escape but was afraid of admitting as much in case they were being listened to. As John was the newest inmate he did not share the concern over discussing this that the others appeared to. He also remembered Barry Begbie having made vague allusions to the idea a few chapters ago.

'Has anyone ever tried to escape from here?' he asked, casually.

'Yes. Eleven at the last count,' replied Barry Begbie.

'And, er, what happened to them?' asked John Smith.

Having just finished his Rat on a Stick, Barry Begbie used the stick to point to the top of the nearby fence. On each post was impaled a human head, disconnected from its body, and quite dead. Sorry, I probably didn't need to mention they were dead there, to be honest. John looked at them for a moment, thinking it odd that he had failed to notice eleven human heads on the fence, then shivered and returned to his Rat on a Stick.

'Oh,' he said. 'Well... Even if they failed, I suppose it could still be possible...'

'It is wise,' Barry Begbie counselled, looking at him carefully, 'to not speak of such things.'

John Smith realised he was expressing much more than what he appeared to be, and nodded his understanding.

There was a pause before Emmeline Moneypenny spoke again. 'Still, some of us managed to read that book before it was banned,' she continued. 'With the benefit of hindsight, a huge amount of it now seems eerily prophetic. Almost as if it was ostensibly presenting a satirical glimpse at how the future could look, seeming far too ridiculous to ever be taken seriously, when it fact so many so-called 'predictions' in that book turned out to be exactly right, like the author had somehow managed to send a completely accurate chronicle of the times in which he lived back in time as a warning.'

'Even though, as you say, the 'warning' seemed too far-fetched for anyone to ever take seriously,' added Barry Begbie.

'Yes,' agreed Emmeline Moneypenny, thoughtfully. 'It was like some point-for-point description of exactly how things would pan out... And although the author presented it as satire that was exaggerated for comic effect, reality turned out to be more grotesque than anyone could possibly have predicted.'

'Especially for him,' added Barry Begbie. There was another pause before he continued. 'You know... They say that terrible things happened to the author of that book when he was finally apprehended. In the same way that the things depicted in that book would once have seemed far beyond our comprehension, the monstrous indignities to which he was subjected are similarly almost beyond the realms of what a decent human being would even consider possible.'

'I heard he was working on a follow up,' said John Smith. 'Did anyone hear about that?'

'I heard that too,' replied Barry Begbie. 'Something about an alternative history book that imagined a world where people were free and didn't have their every thought and action controlled by the BBC in some way or another...'

John Smith looked thoughtful at this suggestion, as if struggling to even imagine how such a world could even be possible.

'Well, one of my insider contacts said it was found in his possession when they arrested him and was used as the final piece of evidence to have him executed,' said Barry Begbie, having the final word on the subject.

'It's funny, you know,' interjected Jeffrey Harding, as he hadn't said anything for ages and you'd probably forgotten he was even there. 'But in around the year 2020, what with Brexit, the US election, pandemics and everyone getting offended about everything and threatening to kill everyone, people used to talk as if we were in the End Times... But compared to now... It seems like nothing. Of course, once the war happened...'

'Ah, aye... The war...' said Barry Begbie.

John Smith looked up in interest at this mention of 'the war'. In his case it was because he was unsure how trustworthy his memories were, suspecting that they had somehow been tampered with during or after him being rendered to the Re-Education Camp, but it should also be of interest to you, the reader, as it's something to which I have frequently had characters make sinister references to without them providing any remotely concrete details.

'The war...' repeated Barry Begbie. 'Of course, even at the time there were those who claimed it was orchestrated by the BBC as part of their plan to assume power, but naturally they dismissed all those reports as 'fake news'... Whatever happened, before long the country had fallen into disarray, and I suppose it was only natural that people agreed it was a good idea that the BBC's powers be extended so greatly in order for them to sort things out, but only too late did we realise that was all part of their power grab...'

John Smith looked unsatisfied, as if this had failed to properly explain the war beyond it being a rather vague and unsatisfactory narrative device. Barry Begbie continued.

'I mean... The whole thing about them claiming to be a great, objective British institution, untouched by political bias and which represented everyone equally and fairly... Well, what better candidate to be entrusted with the future of the country? But then...' He shook his head, as if whatever he was thinking about was too horrible to put into words, which was again annoying for anyone attempting to discover more about the war. The others all shook their heads too, except John Smith, who merely watched in annoyance at what to him seemed like a cop-out to avoid explaining the whole thing to him.

'I mean, the camps were initially set up for prisoners of war,' said Emmeline Moneypenny. 'But we weren't to know what the actual intended purpose was.'

'Yes,' agreed Jeffrey Harding. 'And they assured us that commandeering the Isle of Wight as an internment camp was only temporary.'

'And then the disappearances started, and after years of presenting a worldview so contradictory than no one had any idea of what morality was anymore, they had free reign to take away anyone they liked on any made-up charge they could think of,' added Barry Begbie.

'I gave up trying to work out the rules,' said Emmeline Moneypenny, shaking her head in disbelief. 'Though I did manage it for a long time. Constantly reversing my opinions on given subjects as fads and fashions changed. I mean, here's an example of one of them: for years I was always obediently opposed to boxing because it was brutal and no better than human cock-fighting and could lead to brutal brain damage and death, and I knew that was what I was meant to believe and that those were the real reasons and not just because it was a working-class sport, and never pondering why we didn't by the same logic ban rugby, even though it was certainly because that was a posh boy's sport.'

She then stopped, as if sensing some invisible presence had raised a question to what she had just said, and felt the need to address it. 'And yes, I know that in rugby it's not the *intention* to smash people's faces in and cause brain damage and paralysis but they nonetheless still happen, so I feel that's reason enough to argue there's a double standard there because it's a game only played by posh boys and, weirdly, all Welsh people regardless of their social class.' She paused again. 'Plus let's not forget that in rugby the players sometimes get sent off for grabbing other guys' cocks, which is just weird.'

She then looked puzzled, as if having lost her train of thought, before finding it again and getting back on it, which is presumably what you do with trains of thought, unless the correct term is 'trail of thought', in which case none of that makes sense anyway.

'Anyway, boxing. So, yes, every time someone was killed in the ring I was one of those people who voiced their belief that it was barbaric and should be banned, but then people alerted me to the fact that women were barred from boxing, so all of a sudden I had to start arguing that it was a wonderful sport yet utterly discriminatory for preventing women from participating in such a brutal, bloodthirsty spectacle.'

She paused for breath, then smiled as she sensed that her audience were well aware that she was relating a tale full of moralistic about-turns and which contained virtually nothing by way of consistency. She sighed, then continued. 'So, then it all became about a campaign for women to take up boxing, denouncing anyone who said it was too dangerous for them as a misogynist who didn't think women were equal to men. And once women were allowed to box I had the uneasy feeling that if one of them had died in the ring then a lot of people would have said what a wonderful sign of equality it was. But, of course, that wasn't enough, and then we had to start saying that a *true* sign of equality would be if men and women fought each other, because obviously anyone who said there were biological differences between men and women's bodies was committing a sickening hate crime. So women started fighting men, and female deaths in the ring become a regular occurrence and, sure enough, some people did say they were wonderful examples of gender parity. And then it was decided that weighing boxers prior to a bout, and even having different weight categories, was a sickening case of 'fat-ism' and 'body-shaming', so that all had to go, so you'd then have a seven stone woman fighting a fifteen stone man. All in the name of equality, of course. Then it was decided that disabled people should simply identify as not being disabled, and that the Paralympics were actually a repellent spectacle of discrimination on par with apartheid and that in the name of true equality, should be combined with the main Olympics...'

(If this bit seems rather long and also appears to have little or no relevance to the plot, then you should take comfort in the fact I originally had a *whole chapter* much like this, including that bit where Dave McCreith talked about Gary Lineker and football, before deciding to cut almost all of it. So it could have been much worse, okay?!)

Emmeline Moneypenny now looked traumatised as she remembered what she was now describing, yet was somehow compelled to relive it all. 'Then there was the boxing match where a man in a wheelchair who could only move his little finger was encouraged to identify as a six foot four, muscle-bound, able-bodied person so was naturally matched up with another fighter who, through no fault of his own, actually *was* a six foot four muscle-bound fighter, and I was ringside. I can still remember seeing it, but as much as I remember the bloody brutality of it all I also remember the incredible enthusiasm of the nearby BBC commentator, who witnessed what was basically a man being beaten to death whilst saying things like 'every time a blow is struck in his face, the real blow that's being struck is that of true equality!' or 'his face may have been smashed beyond recognition, but so have barriers!' and who later concluded her report by writing 'and as the defeated fighter's lifeless body was dragged out of the ring I wept tears of joy for the momentous, inclusive event I had just witnessed!' She sighed. 'And then the whole trans thing had to be factored into the equation...'

She looked down, knowing it wasn't necessary to continue explaining what had happened in the world of boxing, as everyone knew, plus, in any case, she was about to venture into the sort of territory that could see books get banned by people who don't understand the nature of satire, then looked back up and attempted to round off her story.

'So, that was the kind of stuff I had to deal with, always alert to morality changing on a daily basis, and staying one step ahead of it so they couldn't accuse me of a hate crime and use it to fire me. I mean, they'd been trying to get rid of me for a few years, partly because I refused to publically change my opinions every couple of years to fit in with whatever passing trend was in vogue that week, but partly because I was a woman nearly over fifty, so the BBC felt I had no place holding down a presenting job. Anyway, I tried to keep them confused, so rather than expressly stating support for something I maintained a level of ambiguity, meaning they were never entirely sure which side I supported...'

John Smith heard this with interest. That's a good idea, he thought: remaining ambiguous and employing an air of humour whenever discussing a topic considered controversial. It struck him as an excellent way to avoid being accused of thinking the wrong thing because people would never be entirely sure *what* he thought, so he took a mental note that if he ever found himself back in the outside world, or even did something such as write a novel, that would definitely be the method he would employ so as to at least try to ensure his safety, particularly if some of the topics being discussed looked like they were veering dangerously close to the whole trans issue...

'...and I managed to avoid censure for a long time by using that method, but I knew they'd get me eventually, and they did. They asked me into the office one day and brought my attention to a radio programme I'd produced in 2002 when I had Germaine Greer and Peter Tatchell as guests. Back then, Germaine Greer spoke out for all women and her every word was sacrosanct and unquestionable. Similarly, Peter Tatchell was the Official Spokesman of the Gays, and was also beyond reproach. However, in the near twenty years since I'd put that show together they'd both become pariahs as the rules of BBC Correct-Think had changed around them, leaving them trailing behind as tired old relics, embarrassing dinosaurs who reminded people of old opinions they used to hold that they didn't want to be reminded of. So it was pointed out to me that I'd essentially hosted a radio show dedicated to hate-mongers.'

She paused at this point to reflect on an irony she had just noticed, and certainly not in order to break up a rather long paragraph. 'Oddly, they never mentioned the times I'd had someone like Nigel Farage or Katie Hopkins on my show, you know, the kind of pantomime villains the BBC would regularly let appear so the audience could boo them and feel reassured by their presence because it clearly showed that their own contrasting opinions were the correct ones... And I couldn't deny I'd had them on my show, or that their opinions were now considered outdated or that whilst I was clearly a committed feminist I was now one of the offensive, old-fashioned feminists who hadn't completely changed their opinions over the last few years... So that was that.'

Just then, the man who'd been tortured to the point of insanity by being forced to watch endless hours of terrible BBC sitcoms walked by their campfire, stopped, yelled 'penis!' then carried on walking, which provided some convenient comic relief, unless you don't find anything inherently funny in people shouting 'penis', in which case this chapter will still seem largely serious to you.

Penis.

Oh well, even if no one ever buys or reads this novel at least I had fun writing it. Still, I bet I'll win the Nobel Prize or something in about fifty years' time. I know that may seem odd, but if in 1965 you'd have suggested that Mick Jagger would one day be a 'sir' people would have thought you were insane. Stranger things have happened. No matter how rebellious you think you are there's always a strong possibility you'll end up simply being assimilated into the Establishment. As Philip K Dick famously observed, to fight the Empire is to become infected by its derangement.

Well, I think this chapter is quite long enough. Too long, probably. But you can assume that they talked well into the night and ate more Rat on a Stick and we can only hope they didn't discuss anything that could have serious ramifications on later narrative developments, though they quite possibly did go on to discuss topics even more controversial than the ones they had already covered, topics that would almost certainly have led to death threats being made to this author from loving members of the woke community had he faithfully described them.

Still, as he lay in his cell that night, John Smith couldn't help but wonder if there had been some hidden meaning in what Barry Begbie had said when he had alluded to people escaping. And that's what you should wonder, too, as it's obviously a plot point you need to pay attention to.

# Chapter Twelve:

# Reviewing the Situation

*In Which Some Novice TV Reviewers Are Given Instructions To Ensure They Never Review Anything Based on Whether It's Any Good Or Not And Instead Only Give Glowing Reviews to Films and Programmes With the Correct Message, Being Careful To Praise Anything About The Holocaust, Poor People Struggling Against Welfare Cuts, Persecution of the Gays and Anything Featuring Disabled People Or Mentals*

Dave McCreith sat at his desk looking deeply suspicious. 'Ball!' he yelled. 'Ball! Where are you?!'

'I'm over here, your grace!' replied Terry Ball, appearing from around the corner and smiling inanely. 'I suppose you want to know...'

'Stop right there!' ordered Dave McCreith. 'Yes, you are correct in thinking I called you over to enquire as to what is in my schedule today, but rather than you telling me I want to hazard a guess.'

Terry Ball looked unsure what to say so merely shrugged as if to indicate he was happy to go along with this.

'The thing is,' continued Dave McCreith, 'it's not escaped my attention that for the last couple of weeks or so my entire schedule appears to have consisted of little more than meetings with people who always seem to represent a particular subject, such as TV licensing, PR or journalism, and the discussion we have in every single one of those meetings covers that topic in considerable depth, including a comprehensive explanation of the BBC's take on it, even though both I and the person I'm meeting with obviously already know all the things we're talking about.'

Terry Ball looked at him quizzically, unsure what his point was, so Dave McCreith continued.

'My point is that it seems a little odd to have the two top figures in a given field meet up entirely to sum up or reiterate things they both already know, with a few trendy buzzwords and pieces of management-speak thrown in, but with none of those meetings ever really leading to any new ideas being developed.'

'Hang on, your grace,' interrupted Terry Ball, 'you're saying you think there's something odd in a senior BBC executive spending his working hours doing nothing more than attending endless meetings where vague future strategies are discussed but nothing concrete is ever really decided upon?'

'Well, no, I'm obviously not saying there's anything unusual in that,' clarified Dave McCreith. 'It's more that I've noticed each meeting conveniently and comprehensively covers a single topic in its entirety, as if not so much for the benefit of those in the room, but as if to explain those topics to some sort of invisible observer. I mean, if a newcomer to the Corporation were to sit in on any of those meetings then they would end up receiving an excellent overview of every aspect of the BBC and our work and worldview, but the meetings never include such a newcomer, so exactly whose benefit are they for?'

'Oh, I see, your grace,' Terry Ball replied. 'You think it's odd that you frequently just spend a whole meeting explaining a particular aspect of the BBC's remit, even though it's usually with someone who knows it already, in a way that would prove very useful if there were a theoretical fly on the wall listening in.'

'Indeed,' Dave McCreith confirmed, with a tone of suspicion. 'And that's not all. You remember that repellent novel 'The Book the BBC Tried to BAN!'? Well, it hasn't escaped my attention how that sickening, hate-filled work employed a narrative structure much the same, in that the character supposedly based on me was constantly having meetings with people in what was clearly just a clumsy literary device that allowed the author to fully explain a given topic to the reader.'

'Hmm, I suppose it would make sense to do that in a work

of fiction, for the reason you just mentioned,' agreed Terry Ball, 'even if an author using such a method would surely leave himself open to criticism regarding just how seriously the book should be taken as a work of literature.'

They both pondered this for a moment, but came to no conclusion. Terry Ball continued. 'Well, my liege, the good news is that the people you're meeting with today are both TV reviewers for the Custodian newspaper,' he said. 'So the fact you haven't met them, and that they're both new to the job, means you'll be able to provide exposition in quite specific detail and there'll be nothing odd about that whatsoever!'

'Hmm. Very well,' replied Dave McCreith, not entirely satisfied with this explanation.

There was a knock at the door. 'Enter!' shouted Dave McCreith. The door opened and in walked the two reviewers that Dave McCreith was scheduled to meet. They're really good characters, actually, in the sense that they both represent a particular viewpoint, as we'll see. In fact, one of them is a really strong female character, so if you think a valid criticism of this book is that it's lacked those, pay attention to this chapter. So, their names were Kate and Harry, as we will shortly discover.

'Good morning, your grace,' said Kate. 'I'm Kate.'

'And I'm Harry,' replied Harry, for that was his name.

'I'm ever so sorry I'm late, your grace,' apologised Kate. 'The security guard heard my Northern accent so didn't believe I had any business at the BBC, and refused me entry until I showed him my accreditation.'

'Oh, I see,' replied Dave McCreith, disinterested, before turning to Harry. 'So why were you late?'

'Oh, I was outside at the right time,' replied Harry, 'but my anxiety means I'm too afraid to knock on doors. It's too close to clapping, you see.'

Dave McCreith looked at him suspiciously, though this was actually because he was trying to work out why this individual, clearly being the pathetic, whinging snowflake that he was, had opted to work for the Custodian rather than taking his rightful place at the BBC. Still, you have to admire the literary skill there, as in just a few short paragraphs I've established Kate as someone from a non-BBC background and Harry as a right snowflaky berk. And if that wasn't apparent, I've just explicitly stated it there.

'Harry is the son of [GENERIC LIBERAL JOURNALIST WHOSE NAME WAS REDACTED IN THE RELEVANT CHAPTER FOLLOWING LEGAL ADVICE], your grace,' added Terry Ball, helpfully, 'the journalist who we met earlier. As she mentioned, it was she who found him this job at the newspaper where she already works.'

'Yes, but that's not why I got the job,' interjected Harry, defensively. 'I actually got a First in my degree.'

Kate looked surprised. 'A First? Really?!'

'Yes,' replied Harry. 'I did a BA in Vague and Non-Triggering Studies. The professors aren't allowed to actually teach us anything in case our anxiety is triggered by hateful things like facts, history and opinions, so we spend three years being taught nothing whatsoever and at the end all get given a First!'

'I stand corrected,' replied Kate, dryly.

'Yes, it's jolly unfair, actually,' sulked Harry. 'The only job mummy could get for me was TV reviewer at the Custodian, when really I'm a stand-up comedian!'

Kate again looked at him in surprise here. 'Really?! You're a stand-up? Where have you performed?'

'Oh, well, I've never performed anywhere because comedy clubs aren't safe spaces. It would be too traumatic. People might laugh at me.'

'Probably not much chance of that,' replied Kate under her breath, which Harry failed to notice, and continued talking.

'I mean, laughing triggers my anxiety. In many ways it's a hate crime as if you do it you're making fun of someone. I'm currently doing an online campaign to make it a punishable offence, arguing that people should do 'jazz hands' instead.'

Dave McCreith nodded his sympathy. 'It's true that laughter can be a hate crime because by its very nature it must have a target, which is to say a victim, and that's why the BBC has fully committed to eradicating that abhorrent practice by continuing to commission Mock the Week and the Mash Report.'

'As it happens,' continued Harry, 'I asked Mummy if she could get me on Mock the Week because, of course, you don't need to be funny, or to even ever have tried comedy to be on that because it's all scripted anyway, but they said whilst they were doing their best to increase diversity on the show they already had a generic posh boy who wasn't very funny, called Ed Gamble. Still, I told the producer that I *identify* as funny, without actually possessing the ability to create comedic material, so she got me a job as a writer on the Mash Report because they've never used that anyway.'

'Ah, yes, well, we launched The Mash Report as part of a diversity drive,' explained Dave McCreith. 'Not for the more obvious reasons you might assume but because the programme is entirely populated by people who identify as funny without actually being so, and as such are members of the underrepresented 'Unfunny Community', whose voices so desperately needed to be heard.' He looked thoughtful then continued. 'You know, for some years the BBC was absolutely desperate to find a really snowflaky millennial stand-up comedian to tick that box and cover that demographic, regardless of how utterly unfunny they were, and if we'd have managed to do so we'd have had that person on every single programme we broadcast... I mean, everything they'd have said would have been scripted for them... They'd never have been subjected to an opinion they didn't like, as all BBC programmes are 'safe spaces'... We'd never have expected them to perform in front of anyone but a pre-screened audience with the correct opinions... But we could never find one, something that has always puzzled me. But you detailing your experience seems to have finally solved that conundrum. If anything, I would think you could claim damages for the trauma you clearly suffered.'

He turned to Kate. 'And you?' he asked. 'Which public school and Oxbridge college did you attend?'

'Er, actually, your grace, I attended a comprehensive school,' Kate replied, which made Dave McCreith's eyebrows raise so high they nearly shot off the top of his head and his face to become a mask of disgust comparable to if she had told him that she had brought a packed lunch with her that consisted entirely of dog dirt. 'Then after five years of freelancing, including running a website of film reviews, I was finally allowed to be an unpaid intern at the BBC for another three years before I was eventually given a paid role at the Custodian as part of a diversity drive.'

Dave McCreith was unsure how to respond to this bombshell but fortunately Harry spoke again and saved him the trouble. 'Er, yeah, but the thing is that people say I only got where I am today because of my background but, actually, being an upper-middle class white male means I'm the most discriminated-against demographic in the country today.'

Dave McCreith raised his eyebrows again (though not as high as before) as if to say he did not doubt this. 'Yes, it's been hard for a lot of us. Personally, I consider public schools to be the greatest bastions of equality in our society because they don't make petty judgements based on minor details such as academic ability, and often give scholarships to poorer students that allow them to enter our world, sometimes as many as two a year!' He paused before returning to his earlier issue. 'And let's not forget there will forever be a home for untalented posh boys who fancy themselves comedians despite an utter absence of comedic ability, on good old Radio 4!'

He laughed quite loud at this (much louder than he'd ever laughed at anything on Radio 4 itself) before continuing. 'Anyway, I believe you both write television reviews for the Custodian newspaper and are both quite new to it, which is why you are here so I can issue you guidance on how to do that job. You may think that reviewers have far less power and influence over public opinion than, say, political journalists or the people who write those god-awful, hand-wringing opinion pieces, but you would be wrong. The BBC has always known that culture is one of our greatest weapons of manipulation, be it comedy, drama or seemingly innocuous things like music reviews.'

Kate and Harry listened intently.

'You see, reviewers are actually in a position of great power, and with that power comes the responsibility that they must jump on literally any event, no matter how minor, and use it to promote the woke agenda, regardless of how little scrutiny that may stand up to. Let me give you a recent example. The Mercury Music Prize can only be awarded to British artists, and from its very inception has been presented to a very ethnically diverse range of recipients, however a few years back a Japanese musician complained that her ineligibility was somehow an act of discrimination. We naturally reported this as a scandal, implying that the organisers were racists and needed to change their rules, whilst obviously not stopping for a single moment to point out the prize's history suggested otherwise, or that the whole point of the award is to celebrate British music. But did the organisers dare to challenge us and point any of this out? No! They meekly apologised, and mumbled something about considering changing their eligibility criteria. Of course, the whole thing was forgotten the next day, but the main thing is that we promoted our agenda and won woke points. You see?'

Kate and Harry both nodded, as if their eyes had just been opened to something incredible.

'The next thing to bear in mind,' continued Dave McCreith, 'is that reviewers of anything, be it music, film, TV or books, need to have *quite spectacularly* low standards. So if, for example, you're a music reviewer, you need to ignore the fact that there's barely been a good album made in the last decade, and that there's such a scarcity of good music that K-Pop, for god's sake, has now become popular, or that the solo effort of a washed-up member of a boyband is treated as if it's the new Sergeant Pepper, with the artist in question splashed across every single website and men's magazine in the world, even though when the actual album comes out it's beaten to the number one spot by a gameshow host singing Sinatra songs. You need to say that *everything is brilliant*. On a weekly basis you should award new albums four or five stars, even though there obviously aren't anywhere near that many good albums coming out. Essentially, add two or three stars to the score you think it really deserves. Understand?'

The trainee critics nodded attentively.

'This is part of the system. A reviewer is nothing more than a small cog in the marketing campaign for a film, TV show, book or album, and must obediently provide the company that makes it with glowing quotes for the advert and a four or five star review.'

You may think Kate and Harry would have raised some objection to this, as they were openly being informed that in their chosen career path they would be nothing more than compliant mouthpieces for corporate interests, but they said nothing, perhaps because Kate had suspected as much all along and Harry was simply too dim to comprehend the implications of what they were being told.

'Critics are our puppets! Our obedient lapdogs!' continued Dave McCreith, perhaps unnecessarily. 'If we wish to promote a worthless, artless, wretched piece of tat we simply tell them it's brilliant, far better, deeper and more meaningful than it clearly is, and they comply! Reviewers will always see things that obviously aren't there just because we tell them to! And, equally, if we order them *not* to notice something, be it blatant nepotism in the film industry, the whole diversity thing being little more than a tokenistic gesture, or how there's barely been a film or TV show released in recent memory that wasn't riddled with plot holes, they will obligingly block all that out! Reviewers will obediently ignore something that's completely obvious if they're instructed to do so by us!'

Now, what I hope you'll notice here is that, apart from how true all the above is, what I've actually done is pre-empt any poor reviews of this book by pointing out that the very practice of criticism is fundamentally flawed in the first place. Clever, huh?! So when all the critics say this is terrible, I can just say they only said that because they were offended by me attacking them for not having opinions of their own and for being terrified to challenge the establishment! And if you think I'm now contradicting what I said about critics giving brilliant reviews to everything, I should clarify that the point there was that critics obediently give good reviews to anything made by major corporations but would be utterly confused if asked to review something independently, without knowing what they and their fellow critics were expected to think. Critics are pack creatures who love a consensus, are almost entirely incapable of independent thought and who find nothing more utterly terrifying than being asked to give their own opinion on something without first being told what all the other critics are going to say.

I mean, if I'm wrong then I suggest the world of literature should bring in a new rule saying its reviewers must read each new book without knowing who the author is. Can you imagine how terrifying that would be for them? Having to review a book solely on what they thought of it, with the risk of ostracism for accidentally saying a novel by a woman who didn't go to Oxbridge and wasn't very good-looking was well-written? Or if they mistakenly said that the latest work by a generic Booker-prize type of author who is also one of their friends and who they were at university with was a bit crappy? Can you imagine?! But, yeah, if the critics say this book is bad it's because they're offended that I called them puppets of the literary establishment.

So, anyway, Dave McCreith continued, now getting to the most important lesson of his sermon, and making it more specific to the type of reviewing relevant to him. 'Still, the key point you *must* take away from this is the following: as a critic, no review you write should ever be based on the actual *quality* of the thing you're reviewing, such as the storytelling, direction or acting, and certainly not whether it makes any sense, or is even remotely original or entertaining, but on the *message that it presents.* So, a drama about a woman on benefits being abused by her partner is to be given five stars... A hand-wringing documentary about asylum seekers is to be given five stars... Anything about gay or trans rights... Five stars... You get the idea. I cannot stress strongly enough that as a reviewer it's very much your job to review the *message* of a programme, film or book rather than the thing itself.'

Harry looked slightly puzzled. 'Could you perhaps provide an example, your grace?' he asked.

'Of course,' replied Dave McCreith. 'In recent years The Handmaid's Tale is the best one. Why, it could even have been assembled by copying and pasting all the issues the BBC holds dear! Women's rights, how awful men are, how wonderful abortion is, how awful the Religious Right is in America and how awful it is that the Republicans are strongly linked with them... So you must praise that show unquestioningly. It is one of the best ever made.'

'Are you a fan of it?' asked Harry.

'Never seen it,' replied Dave McCreith.

Kate looked up quizzically, as if a taboo subject had been unexpectedly mentioned. 'Er, your grace, you mentioned religion there...'

'Oh, right, yes,' Dave McCreith replied. 'I should probably just provide some clarity there. In keeping with standard BBC policy that you can criticise Christianity, Mormonism or Scientology as much as you like yet criticism of any other religion is a monstrous hate crime, the same applies in fictional settings. Now, there are some hate-filled trolls who believe that there are real countries in the world today where women actually are treated in the same way that they are in the Handmaid's Tale, you know, by being banned from driving, or being publically flogged for adultery, being seen as nothing more than machines for having children, or having their hands chopped off or whatever, but, of course, but we naturally choose to minimise our coverage of such things, if they exist at all, because, er, well, you know... So, for clarity, fictional, near-future, dystopian depictions of women having their rights trampled on by religious extremists are to be given far more prominence and publicity than cases of that happening in the real world in this day and age, which, in any case, don't happen anyway. Understand?'

'Hmm, okay,' said Kate, taking a note of this but not entirely convinced.

As if to try to make things clearer, Dave McCreith added, 'I appreciate it can be hard work trying *not* to think about these blatant contradictions and hypocrisies, but as someone working in the media that's your job!' He looked thoughtful for a moment. 'Hmm, what else? Oh yes. Obviously it goes without saying that any drama or film about the Holocaust gets a five star review. Once again, you may think it's odd how that always happens, as it's surely theoretically possible to make a film about the Holocaust that's mawkish or sentimental, or badly acted, or historically inaccurate or just plain rubbish, but you'd be wrong. Five stars. You don't even need to bother watching it.'

'And they always win loads of Oscars, too,' added Kate.

'Well, precisely,' agreed Dave McCreith. 'And a reviewer doesn't want to be seen as going against the Academy, do they? Independent thought amongst reviewers is something we strongly discourage.'

'Right, that does make sense,' said Kate, as if something she had always suspected had finally been confirmed. 'It had occurred to me that the fact that Holocaust films always get brilliant views and loads of Oscars, as if to say that if you criticise them then you're criticising the Holocaust itself, does show how the idea that reviewers are actually reviewing the quality of something rather than its message doesn't really stand up to any scrutiny.'

(Yeah, so, just to clarify, this bit is very much not about Holocaust denial or anything like that but merely serves to point out how no Holocaust film has ever received a bad review or fewer than ten Oscar nominations, which is odd if films are meant to be reviewed based on how good they are rather than their message. And that seems to be the case for films covering any other worthy causes, as will now be discussed. But remember I've already addressed any potential accusations of Holocaust criticism, okay?!)

'Indeed,' continued Dave McCreith. 'And obviously that principle extends to you never giving good reviews to things with the incorrect message. So, whilst, say, Vera Drake is brilliant for depicting the wonder and beauty of abortion, and should be praised, a film like, say, Harry Brown, in which Michael Caine played a vigilante, is to be denounced as truly sickening, again because of the message.' He paused for a moment before remembering the final part of this topic. 'And, obviously, whenever Ken Loach makes a film about how awful it is being on benefits, or how awful zero-hours contracts are, or how awful the Tories are, you can automatically award it five stars without needing to watch it. Also, a film about a historic injustice, like wrongly-jailed IRA suspects, or, say, the Peterloo massacre, is to be praised. Again, tying in with the idea that you must not under any circumstances notice hypocrisy, a filmmaker who makes a film about the plight of the working man or zero-hour jobs or something whilst taking funding from Amazon is not something you may draw attention to.'

Kate and Harry both nodded at this and took notes.

'Anyway,' Dave McCreith continued, 'your obedience regarding this subject is obligatory because, as we all know, your newspaper is the printed wing of the BBC, and must therefore share its worldview in every way, particular in regards to social issues and matters such as diversity and representation.'

'Oh, a question, your grace!' said Kate. Dave McCreith nodded that she may ask it, so she did. 'What do we do when somebody we have previously never dared to question suddenly becomes a hate-figure like, say, JK Rowling?'

'Ah, a good question,' replied Dave McCreith. 'Of course, for years the BBC slavishly agreed with and retweeted every utterance by JK Rowling.' His face lit up here as he realised there were additional points he could explain to them. 'In fact, a specific term was coined to explain away how we unquestioningly supported JK Rowling when she posited herself as a leading Spokesperson of Woke despite the fact that her Harry Potter series had about as much diversity as the Royal Family do. We unquestioningly agreed with her assertion that the books were actually full of diversity, such as Dumbledore being gay, or Hermione actually being black, or Dobby the House Elf actually being an enthusiastic member of the dogging community, and that the reason she didn't feel the need to mention any of this in the actual books themselves is because it was so obvious that actually we were racist or homophobic for not automatically assuming it...'

He looked puzzled for a moment, as if having lost his train of thought, though it was also useful for breaking up the paragraph.

'Oh, yes,' he continued, 'This is called a 'Rowling Retcon': to retrospectively claim that a work you created was full of diversity, even though you never bothered to mention it at the time, then attack anyone who criticises you for that by saying they're the real racists for not just automatically assuming it was.'

Kate and Harry both wrote this term down. I think you should remember it too, as it's a good one: The Rowling Retcon. Dave McCreith now attempted to wrap up this point, though appeared confused as he did so. 'So, anyway, we were unquestioning supporters of JK Rowling for years, but then the woke generation turned against her, for reasons I confess to still not fully understanding, and we've sort of been ambiguous about her ever since, on the one hand no longer reporting her every tweet as being a news event of vital importance but also, weirdly, never questioning whether it's a bit odd that her critics on Twitter see no irony in claiming she's promoting hate whilst themselves bombarding her with death threats.'

He now offered a further example to illustrate his point even though an independent observer would probably have said he'd already said enough, and should move on to something else, and that maybe the words he was saying were now just a sort of off-piste diversion to make a point about something else, like a big-budget adaptation of a book not being particularly good.

'A more recent example of that was our adaptation of His Dark Materials. Again, the source books had basically no diversity whatsoever, so we simply did a Rowling Retcon to make loads of the characters ethnic or disabled or whatever, then implied anyone who pointed out that wasn't in the book was racist themselves. But we played two funny in-jokes on the audience to see if they noticed! First, despite banging on about diversity we made sure the lead role was played by a generic, skinny, privileged white girl who'd had an easy route into acting because her parents did it, and then one of the characters we made black was a professor at Oxford University, despite the implausibility of that happening in real life!' He paused for a moment then remembered another point. 'Also, as per my earlier point, that series was clearly critical of the Catholic Church, which is fine as that's one of the religions we freely allow and encourage criticism of whilst criticism of other, unnamed, religions is a monstrous hate crime. Again, as a critic, *it is your job not to notice these things*!'

His final point wasn't even relevant to his train of thought, something that both Kate and Harry noticed and thought a bit odd. 'Also we did that adaptation of the racially-charged novel Noughts and Crosses, constantly congratulating ourselves and virtue-signalling about it whilst not bothering to address why, if it was such a powerful story that urgently needed to be told, we waited about eighteen years after the book came out before adapting it.'

'Your grace,' began Kate, 'you will forgive me for pointing this out, but the BBC has always had a, shall we say, complicated relationship with depicting ethnic minorities on the screen...'

Dave McCreith was surprised at what he took to be someone challenging his authority. 'What are you talking about?! The BBC pioneered the representation of diversity on television! We broadcast the Black and White Minstrel Show for twenty years!'

Phew! A joke after that weird rambling bit!

'Er, your grace, I'm not sure that having an entirely white cast adopting 'black face' make up strictly counts as representation...'

'Well, maybe not if you judge it by the standards of today,' admitted Dave McCreith, begrudgingly. 'Anyway, once it was pointed out that white people donning blackface and performing slave-era songs in an exaggerated manner could be deemed offensive we took the show off the air. In 1979, I believe. Although I think we may have continued to run a stage show version until 1989...'

Yeah, Wikipedia says that's true so if you have a problem with it then contact them.

'Oh, I forgot to add,' added Dave McCreith, 'that in the mid-70s we improved the racial imbalance on the show by getting Lenny Henry to appear on it.'

Yeah, that's apparently true as well. If I'd invented that you'd think it was too implausible even for this book, but there you are. The truth is stranger than fiction indeed.

Harry looked puzzled at this revelation. 'Hang on, surely he didn't put on white face make up in order to balance things out?'

Dave McCreith shrugged. 'I don't know, it was before my time, and that's why I'm allowed to say how awful it was despite comparable things happening under my tenure.'

'Ah, yes,' replied Kate, 'are you talking about how, having got rid of blackface during the 1980s you brought it back in the noughties with Little Britain only to then, more recently, again decide it was outrageous and shift your position back to being opposed to it?'

'Well, yes, but I think you're very much failing to understand the whole issue here,' responded Dave McCreith, starting to get uncharacteristically flustered at this barrage of logic and common sense. 'The time to which you refer was 2008. It was a different era and we can't possibly be judged on those standards, even if the same people who were in charge then are largely in charge now. Anyway, we're the BBC! We're not held to the same standards as everyone else, and pointing out any such hypocrisy is heresy!'

'Right...' said Kate, somewhat confused. 'So, just to get this straight in my head, blacking up is the most sickening hate crime in the history of civilisation, but also comes in and out of fashion quite frequently?'

Dave McCreith looked annoyed again. 'Look, it's very simple! Blacking up was fine until the 1980s, when it became sickeningly offensive apart from on touring productions or in the theatre, then it was fine again from around the early to late '00s when Little Britain did it, then it was then basically okay until around 2016, *and then* it became sickeningly offensive again! What part of that are you struggling to understand?!'

'Right, okay...' replied Kate, unsurely. 'I'll, er, take a note of that to make sure I get it straight.' She looked at her notes before continuing. 'With regards to the Corporation cherry-picking shows from its past that highlighted its so-called commitment to equality whilst essentially banning those that didn't, how did you deal with accusations of hypocrisy? I mean, wasn't that Spike Milligan show 'Curry and Chips', where he browned-up and spoke with a 'comedy' Indian accent a BBC production?'

'No! That was ITV!' replied Dave McCreith. 'And anyone who suggests otherwise is committing BBC heresy!'

'Okay, well, more recently you put 'The Real McCoy' on the iPlayer, which was one of the first shows to have more diversity in comedy but even then it featured both black and Asian performers, as if to suggest that the BBC thought all people who aren't white can simply be grouped together for convenience...'

'You're not suggesting we should have made *two* programmes?!' spluttered Dave McCreith. 'One for Asians and a *separate* one for black people?! Where would that have led?! They should have been grateful we gave them a programme at all!'

'I'm not suggesting anything, your grace, merely observing that it was a little odd for the Corporation to assume that two entirely different races with completely different cultures would somehow have had enough in common to appear in the same show,' observed Kate.

'Oh, hang on,' cut in Harry, 'wasn't this the show that the BBC completely forgot about, never repeating or releasing on DVD and only bringing back when everyone was getting offended over diversity issues?'

'That's nonsense,' replied Dave McCreith curtly. 'It may technically have been unavailable for a short period of time, no more than a quarter of a century, but then when everyone went woke in 2020 we immediately dug it back out and boasted about what a jewel in our crown it had always been!' He did not care for these entirely accurate criticisms of the BBC, and continued to look annoyed.

'I mean,' continued Kate, 'there's a lot of inconsistency in things people get offended by in comedy these days. What about that show featuring a stereotypical Asian man who bumbles around going 'dearie me!' and 'goodness gracious me!'...'

Dave McCreith interrupted here. 'Ah, yes, you refer of course to the sickening character of Apu on the Simpsons, who people correctly decided to be offended by only thirty years after his first appearance, and who is an unacceptable, racist depiction of a particular nationality...'

'Ah, no, your grace,' Kate continued, 'I was actually referring to Citizen Khan, a recent BBC sitcom featuring an Asian protagonist who bumbles around going 'oh, dearie me!' and speaks in a stereotypical Asian accent...'

'Oh, well, that's entirely different,' replied Dave McCreith, defensively, 'I mean, in that programme the character is portrayed by an actor who is also Asian.'

'Yes...' agreed Kate, before continuing, 'but why does that somehow still mean it's okay to have a one-dimensional portrayal of a particular ethnic group at all? And the actor who portrays him doesn't speak like that in real life. Would it be considered okay to, say, remake those old Charlie Chan films, in which a bumbling Chinese detective was portrayed by a white actor with makeup and a comedy accent, but update it to have an ethnically Chinese actor of British or American nationality portray a character who went around going 'oh! Me so solly!'?'

Dave McCreith did not care for people coming into his office and upsetting his cosy world view with entirely valid points, and his face reflected this. 'Erm, well, I... With the Simpsons it apparently became okay once the supposedly one-dimensional racial stereotype was recast so as to be voiced by an actor of the same ethnicity, so... Hmm, this sounds like a rather complicated issue, so I need to think about it for a while, come to a conclusion, change my mind a few times, attack anyone who doesn't agree with my opinion, then change it a few more times after that.'

There was an awkward pause.

So, remember how I said what a strong female character Kate is? Well, she really is, isn't she?! I certainly didn't make her a female character in order to deflect criticism that there weren't enough of them. She was always going to be female, and has to be, as will be seen in this next bit, where she commits the ultimate heresy: admits that as a woman working in the liberal media, she thought Fleabag was a bit overrated!

'Anyway, we made Fleabag, so that shows beyond doubt what a woke, progressive organisation we are where our comedy is concerned,' said Dave McCreith, somewhat defensively. 'As TV reviewers, should you at any time not feel sufficiently inspired by whatever is on TV when you need to submit a review or have any original ideas, you may simply produce yet another article saying how utterly brilliant Fleabag was.'

'Hmm, yes, I get your point,' said Kate, and Dave McCreith again looked stunned in anticipation that she was planning on showing even more independent thought, 'but, well, don't you think Fleabag was, well, a little overrated?!'

Dave McCreith's eyes almost popped out of their sockets. 'What?!' he yelled uncontrollably. 'Let me tell you, missy, as a committed feminist, which I assume you must be as an employee of the liberal media, it is your *duty* to womankind to think that Fleabag was the greatest artistic achievement of this or any other time! The most empowering, inspirational, hilarious, brilliant programme the BBC has ever made, the very best of our culture!'

'Hmm, yes, I am aware of that,' continued Kate, 'but, well, wasn't it just a not-very-funny show where we were supposed to care about a posh, privileged girl whose so-called 'problems' centre around, well, nothing really, but it's got this layer of pseudo-feminism plastered over it...'

Dave McCreith looked utterly lost at this point, not just because of its heretical nature but because he did not understand what was being said. Realising this, Kate attempted to change tack. 'Well, my liege, it's just that I remember a series of films in the 1970s with titles like Confessions of a Driving Instructor and Confessions of a Window Cleaner, in which a randy young lad basically went around sleeping with everyone he met...'

'Those films were a repellent, sickening relic of an unenlightened time, nothing more than vile toxic masculinity masquerading as entertainment!' spluttered Dave McCreith.

'Er, yes, but my point is, your grace, that you could argue they're both basically the same, so I wonder if there's not a double standard at play...'

'Not at all!' Dave McCreith shot back, stunned at this insolence. 'Double standards aren't a thing when you're comparing men and women, even if they're in exactly the same situation! If a TV show has a highly promiscuous protagonist but said character is female then it's an inspiring tale of female empowerment, but if a man were to be depicted sleeping with loads of women then that would be a sickening, vile example of toxic masculinity! Is that not perfectly obvious?!'

'Er, well, your excellency,' continued Kate, with a persistence that led several people in the room to wonder if she had a death wish, 'there's also the issue of class. I mean, she's a generic posh girl, with her own flat and no financial worries, but are we crediting her with qualities we wouldn't do if she were from a poorer background? I mean, let's say I came up with a pitch for a programme about a girl who's insecure and sleeps with loads of men in a desperate attempt to find her place in the world...'

'Oh, that sounds like a truly empowering, inspiring tale...'

'...but she lives on a council estate...'

'Oh, well, she's just a slag then, we couldn't possibly commission that,' Dave McCreith replied.

'Is there not a double standard there?' asked Kate, innocently enough to make Dave McCreith at least answer the question, albeit somewhat irritably.

'Look, it's perfectly simple!' he responded. 'If a posh girl sleeps with loads of guys then it's an inspiring tale of female empowerment and we call it Fleabag but if a working class girl does the same then she's Vicky Pollard and she's a slag! Understood?!'

There was an awkward pause, as if to say everyone knew the point had been made but Dave McCreith was not going to admit it. 'Anyway, as I said, criticism of Fleabag is anti-BBC heresy, pure and simple,' he continued. 'We have conditioned members of the Skinny Rich White Girl Club to believe that without question, as per our policy that all correct-thinking females must share exactly the same views. And anyone who questions *them* is guilty of misogyny, pure and simple. Anyway,' he added, 'broadsheet TV critics are all from the same background as her anyway, and look up to Fleabag as the girl from school they wanted to be because she was captain of the hockey team.'

'Well, yes, but the thing is,' replied Kate, continuing to astonish Dave McCreith with her ability to think for herself, 'my issue with the modern brand of feminism is that, as with so much in the world today, it seems to be little more than an opportunity to virtue signal how amazing you are without actually doing anything, least of all critically think about the things you're supposed to believe in.'

'Now you listen to me, young lady!' replied Dave McCreith, both shocked and outraged, 'the BBC is a strong supporter of women... Well, in a non-executive capacity, of course, but I would strongly advise you to stop all this nonsense about independent thought right now! Have you not been listening to me telling you that as a critic you *do not* question anything?! This sort of attitude won't get you anywhere other than a place in a Re-Education Camp!'

'I apologise, your grace,' said Kate. 'I suppose you're a strong supporter in the BBC closing the pay gap between men and women, too?'

Dave McCreith was so shocked at this, once again, entirely fact-based accusation that he didn't even know where to look, let alone what to say. After a moment, he continued.

'Anyway, the whole point of our organisation is to seed confusion, and as our printed subsidiary, it is the duty of the Custodian to do the same. That is, is it not, why you came here? To receive instruction on how to ensure you never stray from supporting our worldview?'

They both nodded.

'Well, there you are, and it's hardly a recent thing. I mean, it's an irony not lost on me that back in the 1960s and 1970s the great British TV-watching public loved their presenters and comedians to be as camp as possible, everyone from Kenneth Williams to Larry Grayson to Frankie Howerd, yet at the same time they all slavishly read tabloid newspapers that referred to 'bum boys' and 'gay plagues' and were repulsed by the very idea of homosexuality. That's the sort of obvious contradiction that, as obedient critics, it's your duty to *never* point out.'

Kate and Harry both seemed vaguely unsure of how much of what they were being told was true or whether some of it was a type of test, but nonetheless took notes and continued to listen as Dave McCreith went on.

'Right, so we've covered how you never, ever, review anything based on how good it is, but based on the message... And how you must always be seeding confusion by frequently being offended by some things whilst turning a blind eye to others, then completely shifting position every few years...' He looked thoughtful. 'Do you review films as well?' he asked and, when they both nodded, he continued. 'Well, I know we're more about TV and that I mentioned Holocaust films and films with the correct message, but I just wanted to add two more basic rules for reviewing films. The first is that a film is to be endlessly applauded for making even the briefest, most tokenistic concession towards representation it can get away with. For example, after forty years, the closing seconds of the final Star Wars film depicted a lesbianical embrace that appeared on screen for almost a whole tenth of a second, instantly qualifying the entire series to be praised for its groundbreaking stance on diversity!'

'Or how about the spin-off film where the actor said Lando Calrission was queer even though there was no mention of that in the film *whatsoever*?' suggested Harry.

'Well, yes, that was even better,' replied Dave McCreith 'because in that case they literally did nothing to earn the woke points, and were saved the trouble of including a scene of diversity they would then have needed to cut before they could release the film in many less-tolerant overseas markets!'

'You do have to be careful these days, especially when you're a TV reviewer, as so much of it is triggering,' added Harry. 'I was so offended by the rape scene in the first episode of Game of Thrones that I only watched it for another eight years.'

'Indeed, it was a repellent show,' concurred Dave McCreith. 'As it was made by a rival network I made sure all the BBC's social media accounts criticised it for the endless rapes, incest, incestuous rapes and, more importantly, the monstrous idea that characters of colour could possibly die in a fictitious programme.'

'And did you stop watching it?'

'No, of course not.' He paused for a moment. 'Hmm, and the second rule is that critics must always give glowing reviews to anything featuring members of the Skinny Rich White Girl Club, the name we give to a group that celebrates and empowers women, promoting equality, diversity and body-positivity whilst very much not allowing any poor, overweight or unattractive girls to join. For example, a girl who got famous on EastEnders and who's slightly chubby and sort of not-too-bad-looking if she puts some makeup on can't be admitted, both for those reasons and because she obviously can't be a *true* feminist if she's from a poor background. The most effective vehicles for this group are yet more Jane Austen adaptations, or the forty-seventh version of Little Women, because making films of books like that mean they have an easy reply when it's asked why the film completely lacks diversity despite them always claiming to support it.'

He paused for a moment. 'And this rule particularly applies to Taylor Swift. It is BBC policy that any utterance by Taylor Swift, no matter how inane or insignificant, is to be reported as a major news story to take precedence on the front page of our website at least three times a week, even if it's just her whinging about the music industry or making an extremely public charitable donation. In keeping with Skinny Rich White Girl Club policy our article must completely overlook her immensely privileged background and extremely minimal talent to depict her as a survivor who has fought insurmountable odds to get where she is and a hero to all women for her somewhat belated attack on evil men in the record industry.'

He paused again. 'Oh, and obviously make sure her albums always get five star reviews. You don't need to worry about how all her songs sound exactly the same and just sort of meander along aimlessly, occasionally threatening to break into an actual tune whilst never actually coming good on that threat, or that to even 'write' those songs she relies on an army of at least fifteen co-writers, because aside from the fact that we unquestioningly support everything she does, we've also discovered that her fans tend to issue death threats to anyone who criticises her, so it's not really worth the bother.'

Dave McCreith paused for a moment, then remembered something else. 'Also, it goes without saying that you will *unquestioningly* support not just the work of members of this club, but their every utterance. Inane tweets, bland press releases about human rights, very public charity donations... All those things are to be reported as if they are the most important news stories of the week. Also, and I really cannot stress this enough, you must *particularly* do this if the girl in question is showing signs of self-doubt, such as saying how she thinks she's fat and ugly when she's clearly an eight stone hottie, though as part of your unthinking support you must *never* actually point out rather blatant contradictions like that. Similarly, your obedience is expected whenever one of its members complains of suffering from 'Imposter Syndrome'.'

'Imposter Syndrome?' asked Terry Ball, helpfully requiring Dave McCreith to give a very quotable description of the so-called 'condition', even though everyone else in the room would have known what it supposedly is.

'Yes,' replied Dave McCreith. ''Imposter Syndrome' is the term we use for when skinny, attractive, privileged white girls who've achieved a level of success far greater than their actual talent on its own would ever have got them experience a rare moment of sentience and start to wonder whether their success may actually be less a result of their 'talent' and quite a lot more to do with them being skinny, attractive and privileged.'

'Oh,' said Terry Ball. 'But surely their suspicions are entirely justified?'

'Well, of course,' confirmed Dave McCreith, 'but that must never be mentioned, and instead they must be supported with inane tweets along the lines of 'OMG, I'm here for you, you're super talented, you go, girl, follow your dreams!' And tying in to that, whenever discussing this group you must *never* raise the issue of nepotism. I mean, first of all, I know our society is built on hypocrisy but I think even the gullible public would notice something a little off at the idea of people in the *media* criticising the practice of nepotism.'

Kate slyly glanced at Harry here to gauge his reaction to this but he seemed to have failed to notice its relevance and continued listening intently.

'Anyway,' continued Dave McCreith, 'if you do find yourself having to stand up for an actor who only got where they did because of family connections you can justify it by vaguely suggesting that growing up around actors means you'll be more likely to be good at it, as if to imply that artistic talent is either hereditary or somehow picked up by the process of osmosis, even though the entirely obvious flaw in that argument is why none of the children of great musicians ever make anything of themselves when so many children of actors go into that profession. I mean, if artistic talent was hereditary then all the offspring of the Beatles and Stones would have wowed us with their amazing music rather than just being annoying socialites or self-proclaimed 'fashion designers' or whatever... I mean, how many albums have you ever bought by Sean or Julian Lennon? What have any of the Rolling Stones' offspring achieved? I rest my case.'

The others looked slightly confused at this point, as what had begun as an entirely reasonable way to support an argument seemed to have meandered off-message somewhat, almost as if he were being controlled by some sort of mysterious external force with an axe to grind (even if the points he made were extremely good ones). Dave McCreith himself paused at this point, perhaps also realising he had slightly wandered off from his intended point.

'But, yes, the point there is you need to come up with rather illogical and convoluted 'explanations' as to why the offspring of actors become actors themselves that skirt around the obvious explanation that it's nothing more than a matter of having a family member introduce you to an industry where talent itself is largely unimportant.'

Another pause seemed to indicate his meandering was over, and the topic had been covered.

'Oh, I have another question, your grace,' continued Kate, to which Dave McCreith nodded that she may proceed with it. 'Well, I'm slightly confused with regard to the rules surrounding when something we're outraged by should actually be cancelled. I mean, Harry mentioned how he was outraged by the first episode of Game of Thrones yet continued to watch it for the entire nine-year run. And he was constantly tweeting and writing about how offended he was with all the rape and incest and how the characters of colour were killed off, but without, crucially, ever calling for it to be cancelled, or actually following through on his vague and half-hearted claims that he would stop watching it.'

Whilst this was a rather blatant attack on the hypocrisy of Harry he completely failed to notice it, and listened for Dave McCreith's response with as much interest as Kate.

'Oh, it's actually quite simple,' replied the Director General. 'It depends how much money is at stake, and how much would be lost by major corporations. So if it's an individual then we can easily cancel them, and it's even better if it's someone who used to be famous but hasn't been on TV for years and has tweeted something vaguely controversial. They can be cancelled, and you do not need to seek our permission. However, you are *not* to call for any major franchises to be cancelled. So, Game of Thrones was untouchable, and so are all the other big ones. You are encouraged to make extremely vague complaints about the lack of representation in, say, Star Wars but you may *not*, under any circumstances, call for them to be cancelled. James Bond, too. Feel free to virtue signal about how the character is a sickening example of repellent toxic masculinity, but also bear in mind that we will not tolerate calls for the series to be boycotted, as that would cause immense financial hardship for major Hollywood studios.'

Kate and Harry both took notes about this before looking up again, as Dave McCreith continued. 'And, of course, the terminology here is vital: we call for something to be 'cancelled' and *not* 'banned' or 'censored', even though that is exactly what we mean. By using the word 'cancelled' instead it makes what we're doing look far more innocuous and casual, and deflects accusations, accurate or not, that we're banning culture and thoughts in exactly the same way the Nazis did. Similarly, if we call for a *person* to be 'cancelled' that makes it sound less serious than it is because by using the terminology we'd use when a TV series has reached its natural end we can detract from how what we're essentially doing is calling for someone to be inundated with death threats over a fairly innocuous tweet they did.'

'And how does JK Rowling fit into all this?' asked Kate. 'Because I notice that, as you mentioned earlier, whilst she was publically denounced in 2020 for her sickening views, whatever they were, people seemed to continue reading and watching Harry Potter with no qualms or even the slightest suggestion that it should be cancelled?'

Dave McCreith looked slightly sad at this point. 'Well, again, I mentioned earlier that having previously enthusiastically and unquestioningly supported her every utterance, we simply tried to maintain a silence when Twitter turned against her. But, again, no one dared suggest that the Harry Potter books or films themselves, or the new film spin-offs they were still making, should be affected, and that is once again because it would have been tremendously inconvenient to the studios involved.'

'So despite all the moralising, financial considerations are always the main thing?' clarified Kate.

'Exactly!' replied Dave McCreith. 'Too much at stake! That is what must always take precedent. How much money will be lost?' He looked at his notes to check what else he needed to tell them. 'Oh, and connected to that there's the whole issue surrounding the manipulation of what people are offended by, where your full co-operation is mandatory. Remember how back in 2020 there was a period where people decided that virtually everything that had ever been on TV was sickeningly offensive, and that we responded by removing great swathes of programmes from our streaming services? Well, I've decided we're going to do that again with the programmes that people inexplicably failed to notice could be seen as offensive the first time around. It'll give the Corporation an excellent opportunity to virtue-signal yet again.'

'Oh, very good, your excellency,' replied Harry. 'Which programmes were you thinking of?

'Well, there are ones that no one seemed to pick up on,' Dave McCreith replied. 'I was always surprised no one hauled up Last of the Summer Wine as being repellently sexist, seeing as how every single episode began with Compo sexually harassing Nora Batty before she chased him off with a broom.'

'I agree with how repellent that programme you're describing sounds,' replied Harry, 'but obviously no one of my generation would want to tweet about how offensive that show is because no one would know what we were talking about so we wouldn't get the woke points. In fact, I've only recognised about a tenth of the programmes you've mentioned. Despite being a trainee film and TV critic I've tried to avoid watching pretty much every film and TV programme that's ever been made because I find reality too triggering.'

'I see,' replied Dave McCreith, interested. 'Well, as it happens, we need some more programmes to appeal to snowflaky millennials in order to continue justifying our huge budget for BBC Three when it's not even a proper channel anymore.' He turned to Harry. 'I suppose you fit into that demographic so perhaps you could listen to some ideas to consider their suitability?'

Harry nodded his assent. 'Indeed. I'm seen as a spokesperson for the woke community, mainly because my family's background in the media means I've got loads of followers on social media who agree with everything I say.'

Impressed, Dave McCreith continued. 'Interesting... The BBC is, of course, always looking for nonsensical bandwagons to unquestioningly jump upon. So is there currently anything that the Corporation could highlight from the World of Woke?'

'Er, well, your grace,' replied Harry, 'I'm currently involved in an online campaign to have the Great Pyramids of Egypt demolished. They were constructed by slaves, you know, so the fact they continue to stand is nothing more than a sickening reminder and, indeed, blatant celebration of the practice, and we're calling for them to be destroyed so as to avoid triggering anxiety in my fellow millennials. The pyramids must fall!'

Impressed, Dave McCreith continued. 'Hmm, you would seem well qualified to advise on some projects we're currently working on to appeal to that demographic. Hmm, let me see... Well, we had this idea for a comedy about a self-harmer. That's all the rage now, isn't it? Obviously we wouldn't actually make it funny as they'd find it too triggering. Naturally you'd give something like that a glowing review but do you think it's something you'd actually like?'

'Well, actually...' replied Harry, with a slightly boastful air. 'I *am* a self-harmer.'

They all looked at him in surprise. 'Are you really?' said Kate. 'Don't take this the wrong way, but I thought I'd have seen some signs of it.'

'Oh, well, I *identify* as a self-harmer,' explained Harry, 'but I don't actually do it as I wouldn't want to hurt myself.'

There was a pause, during which Dave McCreith was unsure whether this made him less, or more, qualified for consultation on the idea. 'Well, we'll put that on the 'maybe' list,' he said, thoughtfully, before deciding to sum up and conclude the meeting. 'So, yes, that's basically it: tow the line, review things based on their message, question nothing, attack anyone who disagrees. Got it?'

Again, slightly confused, the trainee critics nodded and then the meeting ended with them leaving but I don't need to describe all that again, what with the bowing and everything.

So, yet another powerful chapter! See how I exposed BBC hypocrisy on stuff like the gender pay gap? And that's why the character of Kate wasn't just a concession to having strong female characters! Because it was more effective having a woman point out the many flaws in the Corporation's way of doing things! And pointing out that it shouldn't be a thought crime for a woman to question aspects of modern day feminism! And her character also served to highlight the unconscious bias of the Director General himself! This novel is turning out to be more woke than the world it's meant to be satirising!

# Chapter Thirteen:

# A Licence to Kill

*In Which, When the Re-Education Camp Is Stormed By a Rival Organisation With Even More Confusing Licensing Rules Than the BBC Itself, Our Heroes Are Finally Afforded A Window Of Opportunity For Escape, A Window That They Gratefully Attempt to Squeeze Through*

John Smith had enjoyed a relatively undisturbed night's sleep, what with only being woken up by tortured screams three times during the night, and as a result had enjoyed an unprecedented lie-in, not waking up until almost half four. However, as he slowly rose from his pit of slumber he became aware of a commotion. Whilst it had not initially been loud enough to wake him, he could now hear a general level of background noise, of panic and of people running around. I can't remember if I previously said that his cell did not offer him much of a view, but for narrative reasons I'm now going to say it allowed him to look out onto the main yard, which he did, and saw a large number of both guards and inmates running around in general alarm and confusion.

Keen to discover what was going on, John leapt out of bed and pulled on his, er... Overalls? Jumpsuit? Boiler suit? Again, I can't remember if I described what they wore in the camp but, yes, it'll have been some kind of overall type thing, I just realised now that I don't know if they have a different name. Still, I'm not going to waste time researching every minor detail, am I?! This isn't some historical novel where if I mention a character using a particular type of spoon I'll then get hundreds of letters from the British Spoon Appreciation Society giving me death threats because the spoon in question didn't exist until twenty years later. So, they basically wear linen onesies, okay? A sort of dark green colour. Is that enough?! Can I now get on with this thrilling narrative rather than getting bogged down in entirely pointless and irrelevant details?!

So anyway. John left his cell (which was unlocked; again, I don't have time to explain why. Maybe they don't lock them anyway because they think it's impossible to escape the camp? Or maybe they open them early in the morning? Or possibly whatever emergency that I may eventually get round to describing led them to open automatically or something?! This is far too late in the novel to keep getting bogged down in narrative inconsistencies). Entering the yard he saw Barry Begbie watching just about everyone rushing around, but doing so without displaying any panic himself, and almost with a sense of detachment.

'What's happening?' John asked him.

'The camp's being broken into,' replied Barry Begbie.

'Hang on, broken *into*?' repeated John Smith, in confusion.

'Yep. I know it sounds odd. All of us in here wondering if it's possible to escape, all the guards here knowing that's what we were thinking and thus trying to think of every possible way we might try to do it, but they became so preoccupied with that that it never occurred to them to consider having measures in place to stop people breaking *in*.'

John stared at him in disbelief. 'But, well, who would try to break in here?'

'It's the Royalty Protection Society,' Barry Begbie continued. 'They're not as well-known as the BBC but for over a century have collected royalties they believe are due for any use of music in workplaces. If you think the BBC has turned the collection of money for license fees into some sort of mad, illogical nightmare of Kafkaesque proportions, wait until you hear about the Royalty Protection Society!'

'Why, what do they do? Asked John Smith.

'Well, on a basic level they collect money from public music usage, such as when a song is played on the radio, or used in an advert. If a pub runs a karaoke night they charge them a fee for using the songs, or charge a cinema for showing a film because that's got music in. Or, at least, that's how they started out. But then they went mad with power. They were a monopoly, with no rivals, so there was no one to limit their behaviour or tell them how to operate. Before long they were forcing factories to fill in forms that ran to hundreds of pages, detailing the size of their premises, the number of people working each shift, the hours they listened to music for... But their insane greed just kept on growing... Before long they started charging, say, plumbers who were driving to jobs in case they heard someone else's car radio on the way there, which they said counted as music usage during working hours... Or they began forcing pub owners to take out licences to cover them in case a customer's mobile phone went off whilst in the pub and the ringtone was a copyrighted song.'

(Also, remember how this fictitious society was mentioned back in the chapter where Dave McCreith met with the Head of Licensing and I said it was later going to be an important plot point? Well, here we are.)

His face lit up as he remembered something. 'Actually, I used to deal with them. Back when I started out in comedy I ran my own club, and they somehow heard about it then began phoning me fifteen times a day saying that if I was hosting comedy then I must be using music to introduce the comedians on stage, even though I never did that, but they wouldn't believe me. I even said they could send someone out to check but they never did. Instead they kept sending me invoices, phoning me all day and eventually sent the bailiffs around. I had to close the club in the end, even though we never actually used music there.'

Barry Begbie stopped there, hoping that he had made his point, as he was aware that the organisation he was describing wasn't hugely well known to the wider public or readers of dystopian novels, so he just needed to provide enough information for those listening to get the general idea.

'But despite my historical animosity towards them,' he added, 'it was me who got word to them of what goes on here.'

John Smith raised his eyebrows, again suggesting he needed more explanation.

'I knew how ruthless they were. And whilst in here I made a contact, someone who said he'd be able to get a message to the outside world, but only one. I thought about this. I knew there was no point trying to tell our story to the press as they never dare challenge the BBC... Even if a journalist made the mistake of reporting what I'd said, everyone else would just denounce it as 'fake news'. Plus the government is believed to be controlled by them too. So what could I do? How could I make one single message count for anything?'

John Smith smiled here, as he believed he knew where this was going. Barry Begbie continued. 'So, I knew from my dealings with the RPS that they ruthlessly hunt down anyone they think is guilty of even a single use of copyrighted music outside the home and pursue them for everything they have, never letting a case go. So when I composed the message that my new contact promised he could deliver, I simply detailed all the examples of music use in this camp, from the TVs in the cells, to the films they show...'

John nodded as he began to understand his plan.

'Sadly, I never heard from my contact again, and have to believe he was killed somehow... But, from what we can see here... The message was received and understood!'

'Brilliant...' said John Smith, slowly. 'You realised that our only hope of being saved from an organisation that's gone mad with power over its efforts to collect money for license fees is to set another one on it!'

'Exactly,' replied Barry Begbie.

'Well, this is all most peculiar,' said Emmeline Moneypenny, suddenly appearing next to them. 'I've just been turfed out of my cell by two guards from the Royalty Protection Society who said I was breaching copyright because there was a TV in there but I hadn't paid them a licence to cover me for any music that gets used on the programmes it shows.'

'Can they...?' began John Smith, before realising that this was the exact sort of mad bureaucracy that Barry Begbie had been referring to. Then the other members of their group also joined them. So, it's now the three people already mentioned, plus that Jeffrey Harding guy and probably Kerri Barnes-Bridge, though if I stop mentioning her or don't give her any lines then please just assume she wandered off without explanation. I'll be sure to give lots of lines to Emmeline Moneypenny, though, just so I'm not accused of not including enough representation.

Near the gates a standoff was taking place. Both guards from the camp and members of the group who had broken into it were facing off, with the threat of imminent violence obvious to all. One of the camp guards had just put his hand on his baton when the camp Commandant came striding out of his office intently, walked straight up to the group and glared at the person he took to be in charge of the raiding party.

'What is the meaning of this?!' he yelled, furiously. 'Who are you people?'

The RPS Representative (now capitalised to show that's the name he shall now be referred by) took out a document and handed it to the camp Commandant. 'We've received numerous reports that this site is guilty of a huge number of cases of copyright infringement! You'll find all the necessary information in there.'

The camp Commandant hurled the document to the ground. 'I don't know who you think you are, but I should advise you that you are severely out of your depth,' he replied.

'Just doing my job, sir,' replied the RPS Representative. 'Just following up on reports of licensing laws being broken.'

'Breaking licensing laws?!' spluttered the Commandant. 'I represent the BBC! Do you not think we know a thing or two about licensing laws, and the enforcing of them?!'

'I know what you do,' replied the RPS Representative. He then raised an eyebrow and added, sardonically, 'in a way, our respective organisations are quite alike.'

The camp Commandant stared at him again, briefly lost for words at this outrageous slur. 'No! Our organisations are *nothing* alike!' he shot back. 'You and your people burst in here because you believe there's been a violation of some licensing law that you all but made up yourselves! How can a civilised society expect to exist under principles such as that?!'

'Well, regardless of what you may think,' replied the RPS Representative, 'the document you just so casually flung to the floor contains over three hundred indictments against these premises relating to the usage of copyrighted music for which you have not obtained the required licence.'

'And, as you so accurately observed,' replied the camp Commandant, 'I threw that document into the mud to show you just how much I think of it!'

The RPS Representative turned to the guards who made up his invading force. 'You've all read the charges,' he said. 'I want you to tear this place to the ground and take a note of all unauthorised music usage you find. TVs, cinematic equipment, mobile phones with ringtones that are famous songs...'

'Yes, sir,' said one of the guards, and they all set off in different directions to carry out his orders. Confused, some of the camp guards followed them in an attempt to stop them.

'Stop this! I order you to cease this action immediately!' yelled the camp Commandant, as the RPS Representative followed his men into the camp to conduct the search. Continuing to protest, but with his own guards now confused and spread out, the camp Commandant ran after him.

As our heroes watched this from a distance, Barry Begbie looked thoughtful. He had looked around and noticed two things: a group of guards who had also observed the altercation but had yet to get involved and was now standing around uncertainly, and that amongst all the commotion nobody had remembered to close the camp's main gates. Quickly glancing around, he realised what needed to be done and raised his hand to the nearby guards.

'Excuse me, sirs, but could you possible help settle an argument between us? It's very much related to our rehabilitation, and to the sort of worldview we'll need to adopt should we wish to return to civilisation as useful and correct-thinking members of society.'

One of the guards narrowed his eyes suspiciously, annoyed at being distracted but unsure what he should be doing. 'I suppose so. What is it? And be quick!'

'Yes, of course,' replied Barry Begbie, seizing the moment. 'We were just having a discussion about gender identity as it relates to the law, but couldn't agree on this: can somebody who does not have a penis be accused of rape?'

The guards all briefly looked confused, as if they were initially unsure as to what the correct response should be but did not want to reveal that in front of their colleagues. After a pause, one of them spoke out, though with a slight air of uncertainty.

'Well, according to the legal definition, only a man can be accused of rape...'

'No,' said another, 'the legal definition says only someone with a *penis* can be accused of rape, but we all know there's no connection between penis ownership and being a man...'

'Yes,' interrupted another guard, 'what about somebody who *identifies* as a man yet doesn't technically own a penis? Can they not be accused?'

'Indeed,' added another guard. 'I mean, it would be an act of legal discrimination if somebody were not allowed to be charged with rape on a minor technicality such as not having a penis. What kind of hateful monster would deny the existence of a penis based on something as insignificant as it not actually being there?!'

'Could they perhaps get around that sickening loophole via the use of a rubber phallus?' speculated another guard, casually, warming to the theme.

'Well, that's a possibility,' added the second guard, 'but surely if women are to achieve true parity with men, and particularly if they identify as them, then they deserve the right to be classified as rapists, too?!'

'No, that's the exception to the rule!' interjected another guard. 'That is an area that should never even be considered, and certainly never debated!'

'What are you talking about?!' said another guard, glaring at his colleague accusingly. 'Have you ever even read the BBC Charter?!'

'I've read it more times than you!' retorted the first guard, angrily. 'Including the new edition that only came out yesterday and contains many updates that you may not be aware of! Including all the revisions, and the penalties for anyone who still believes whatever was in the previous edition, or that the previous edition even existed!'

Another guard, or possibly one who'd already spoken, cut in here. 'Hang on, hang on, I'm confused,' he said. 'So what would happen if a man, who had a penis and everything, was charged with rape but immediately decided to identify as a woman? Would that mean that the prosecution couldn't proceed because he no longer met the legal criteria? We all know trans women *are* women but if the prosecution *did* proceed then would the state be committing a vile act of transphobia as that would imply that the new gender identity was actually meaningless in the eyes of the law? And what would correct-thinking people, who'd previously defended someone's right to choose their gender identity and viciously attacked anyone who dared question it, do in this scenario? Would they suddenly and hypocritically decide that the state was absolutely correct to ignore someone's gender identity? Or would they accuse the state of committing a sickening act of discrimination and side with the perpetrator, deciding to see *him* as the true victim rather than the person he'd attacked, meaning that the odds would be stacked against the *actual* victim even more than usual? Because if that happened then it would be a rather obvious case of a particular group who normally vocally and fiercely campaign for true equality suddenly deciding they don't want it in cases where it would be inconvenient. Surely it would be a clear example of only wanting equality when it suits you? Essentially, you'd be seeing two of the sacred cows of the woke people, rape and the trans issue, facing off to see which one ultimately trumped the other. Which one would they side with? How would that all work?!'

There was a moment's pause here as they all tried to consider this question without admitting they had become hopelessly, utterly confused by a conundrum that seemed to have so little basis in logic or common sense as to be utterly unsolvable. And if you're looking for a single takeaway from this rather controversial section then that would be it, particularly if you've obediently got offended without actually stopping to think why. And if you *are* offended then please write an answer to the guard's question that's logical, intelligent and consistent that you are *also* confident won't lead to you receiving death threats *and* which you think will still hold up in three years' time. If you can do that then you're allowed to be offended, but I suspect you won't be able to, which is rather the point.

Anyway, the guards were all deeply bewildered here, having no idea what they were meant to think, and their attempts to out-woke each other soon boiled over into frustration. The second-from-last guard to speak, clearly annoyed at having his worldview challenged, now pushed the guard he had been replying to, and that guard stumbled back and fell over into the mud. The guard he had been disagreeing with now stepped forward and pushed the first guard. Look, I know it's going to get confusing remembering which guard said what or pushed who but it doesn't really matter because the point here is that having all failed to agree on anything here it soon descends into a full-on brawl, with batons being drawn and everything. A full-on woke war, if you will, with each combatant arrogantly trying to prove that he holds a superior world view to the others. Also, I've just noticed that I never mentioned if there were any female guards or not. I admit I'm not sure what the implications of that are, so let's just move on.

(Still, isn't it worth noting that the guards in the Re-Education Camp are all really, *really* woke? I mean, on the one hand they are following orders, the standard excuse that people at a low level of power use if they ever get called to account for their actions, but on the other hand they've clearly done their homework, haven't they? And, some pretty powerful stuff in this chapter, no? I know this novel is technically meant to be humorous but, as with all great satire, there's a point to it too! So you're being entertained whilst encouraged to think!)

Anyway, as the guards desperately rolled around in the mud, their limbs flailing about as they attempted to land blows on each other, Barry Begbie turned to the others and nodded. Scarcely able to believe they would succeed in doing so, they slowly and casually walked by the scuffle, which was now increasingly violent, and, carefully looking around to check no one could see them, whilst doing their best not to arouse suspicion, stepped out of a waking nightmare and back into a reality that could easily turn out to be every bit as bad.

The moment our heroes stepped over the threshold and left the camp John Smith stopped in astonishment as he noticed something. From the day he had first arrived at the camp the weather had been endlessly grey, with drizzle, cloud and temperatures that barely rose above fifteen degrees, as if the weather was either acting in sympathy with the mood of hopelessness that overcame every single inhabitant of the camp or, more strangely, that it was somehow being controlled by unknown forces or technology in order to inhibit and control the moods of the prisoners and reinforce their feelings of hopelessness. And now, as he looked up at the clear blue sky that existed just beyond the boundaries of the camp yet was utterly unknown within it, he couldn't shake the illogical and nonsensical suspicion that the second idea was actually true.

John Smith was so thrown by this seemingly illogical yet undeniable observation that he failed to notice something far more important: he was finally free. They were all finally free. Perhaps they should have celebrated, but, of course, their escape was only the beginning, and they needed to get to safety, or the closest thing to it that existed. Barry Begbie could never have dreamt his plan would work so had not planned much beyond getting his message out, but now he realised he would need to think quickly, so looked around for a means of making their escape more permanent. His eyes fell upon a van parked right outside the gates, with the doors open and, as a quick glance confirmed, the keys still in the ignition.

'This is the RPS Detector Van!' he announced triumphantly. 'It drives across the country, covertly listening out for evidence of unlicensed music usage and then ruthlessly persecutes anyone found doing it! So...' He smiled knowingly. 'They've helped us get out, so why not let them assist us with the rest of our escape?

The others realised he made an excellent point and piled into the van, with Emmeline Moneypenny taking the wheel and no one objecting or even thinking twice about it. So if you think there's something odd about that then that's your problem and not mine. I mean, she did briefly bang against the curb and cause some damage to the paintwork at the back but that was just because she was adjusting to a vehicle she hadn't driven before. Still, this bit's pretty daring, isn't it?!

So off they drove, into a deeply uncertain future.

# Chapter Fourteen:

# Thought Crime in New White City

*In Which the Director General Becomes Deeply Perturbed By a Politician Who Appears to Possess Some Kind of Principles and Personal Values She Refuses To Change on a Whim Or According to the Vagaries of Fashion, And Who Will Not Submit to the Will of the Corporation, For Which He Vows to Break Her*

Dave McCreith was sitting at his desk, looking most disgruntled as he scrutinised a document sitting in front of him. He shook his head as he started to read its contents aloud.

"Position Vacant: Director General of the BBC'." He sighed before continuing. "The BBC, the leading thought-control organisation in the United Kingdom and beyond, is looking for a forward-thinking, progressive Director General to lead the Corporation through the current dark age of uncertainty and well into the next. The successful candidate with be a self-motivated go-getter with a 'can-do' attitude, with a proven track record of leading a world-beating organisation and moving it forward in a ground-breaking way'...' He stopped and signed. 'Hmm, I'd say fifty percent of the words in this document are nothing more than inane, meaningless, 'management-speak' buzzwords...'

'Indeed, your grace, but the HR department will make sure that when it's released that percentage is closer to seventy five,' confirmed Terry Ball. 'The document you're reading is merely the internal one, so prior to releasing it we'll obviously bulk it up by at least another fifty percent with the inclusion of dozens of meaningless phrases about, you know, empowerment, representation, diversity, all intended to make the Corporation appear to have a powerful mission statement and inspiring values even though they're obviously meaningless, wretched, virtue-signalling clichés.'

'Good, I'm glad to hear that my proposals are being implemented,' replied Dave McCreith. He skimmed a few more paragraphs of the document and looked annoyed again. 'Well, this all appears to be in order,' he harrumphed. 'Though I really don't see why we have to go through this whole rigmarole, or why I have to waste time reading this.'

'Oh, you know the rules, your grace!' said Terry Ball. 'We announce a vacancy at the top of the organisation, release the job spec, make a huge, public fuss about how we'd really like to employ a woman or an ethnic, and even ensure we interview a few of them, then announce, to nobody's surprise, that the best person for the job is a privately-educated straight white male who went to Oxbridge! Or, more specifically, you, your grace!'

'Yes, yes, I'm aware that we must follow correct and proper practice as per the BBC Charter, but I don't see why I still have to waste my time getting involved with this whole charade, especially not now our power to silence our critics has become so immense.'

'Well, your grace, we must at least make a very half-hearted attempt to make our recruitment process look honest and fair rather than just being another tokenistic PR exercise. We have our reputation to think about, you know!' replied Terry Ball.

Dave McCreith's face suddenly changed to a mask of outrage, and he slammed his fist down on his desk. 'The ruddy nerve! Expecting me to have to submit an application for the job that was mine by birth right! People at the BBC don't have to apply for jobs like the little people do!' He slammed his fist down again before frowning in disapproval.

'No, of course not, your excellence,' Terry Ball assured him, 'but those in more high-profile roles are still required to at least pretend they do, and that it's an open and fair process.' The final phrase made Dave McCreith pull a face of disbelief.

'Hmm, well it's a poor way for me to spend my time, I have to say,' he replied, before appearing to calm down, and returning to reading the document aloud. "The BBC is fully committed to being an equal opportunities employee but please note that because we view white, middle-aged, privately-educated straight men as a persecuted minority we will give the role to one of them and therefore cannot consider any women, fatties, ethnics or big fat lezzers for the position, as whilst we do employ large numbers of those groups we are only able to do so in the capacity of panellists on piss-poor Radio 4 comedy shows.' Hang on...' He looked up at his assistant once more. 'Whilst that's obviously the main principle upon which we base our recruitment for senior level executives, we're not going to use that actual wording in the advert, are we?'

'Oh, no, your grace, that's just the internal document. Again, the PR people will change all that to make it all more palatable to the press and public, and say how desperately keen we are to employ someone from a minority in a senior role only to then announce that it was your experience and unrivalled leadership skills that made you uniquely suited to taking the Corporation forward.'

'Well, I would still question the need for all this, because even before we controlled every aspect of the media it was rare if not unheard of for a journalist to point out this apparent discrepancy in our stated intentions and our actual actions.'

Terry Ball made a face as if to suggest his employer had made a valid point, even if it was one he himself have never considered. 'Well, once it's signed off by you then we'll have undergone due diligence and can publish the advert.'

Dave McCreith looked back at the document for a final perusal. 'Okay... 'The successful candidate will also have an unparalleled track record in covering up paedo scandals, and should he or she' – well, 'he', obviously – 'end up running the Corporation into the ground, perhaps by making unfounded allegations of paedophilia against well-known public figures whilst at the same time desperately covering up decades of known acts of sexual abuse amongst long-term employees, they will receive a massive payoff and then pushed up to the Board of Directors where they will receive an even bigger salary whilst having no day-to-day responsibilities.' He looked quizzical. 'I assume we'll be rephrasing that in some way?'

'No, your grace, that's how it'll appear. I mean, we could hardly leave that part out, could we? There's only so much the public will believe before they start to find our press releases a little too implausible.'

'Hmm, well, I give my authority for this to be officially released once the re-wording on the earlier section has been carried out. Naturally when I 'apply' for this job I won't be required to do anything, as per the terms of my contract of employment?'

'Oh, of course not, my liege. Whilst anyone other than you who applies for the position will be expected to submit dozens of pages of supporting documentation, attend at least three interviews and make six or seven presentations, I can confirm that for you it will be a simple one-click process and nothing more.'

'I'm glad to hear it,' replied Dave McCreith, not so much satisfied as simply having had something confirmed to him that should have been true by right. He sighed, and pushed the document to the side of his desk before looking up at his assistant. 'Well, I'll take it as read that I'll now be having a meeting with someone who represents a particular world view, which we'll go on to discuss quite comprehensively, as if to imply that the whole meeting solely existed to explore a particular subject and tidily cover the whole thing in a single sitting.'

Terry Ball raised an eyebrow as if to say that this was an in no way inaccurate summary of what was about to take place. 'Er, well, your grace, today we're meeting with that politician. You know. The troublesome one. The one who's been an MP for decades but we've recently had problems with over her refusal to tow the line.'

'Oh, her...' said Dave McCreith, pulling a face. So, I really should point out you're about to be introduced to yet another really strong female character, one who has totally stuck to her principles in a world where very few people do, even if that is largely because they never had them in the first place. The character is also a frankly brilliant commentary on the bizarre, shifting nature of morality and how somebody who was held up as morally unquestionable for decades can suddenly be denounced as a peddler of hate even though her previously-praised views haven't actually changed.

So, anyway, the door opened and in walked Claire Bolam, a long-term politician renowned for her tireless public dedication to left-wing causes. Once she had been a regular panellist on TV discussion shows and a frequent contributor to correct-thinking newspapers, but as the power of the BBC had grown and the worldview it had imposed on the public had changed, her views had started to become unfashionable to the point of heresy. But, rather than simply change them in order to continue to be elected and employed in the media, she had stuck to her guns. Stranger still, the overwhelming majority of her constituents had continued to support her and, despite the best efforts of the BBC and other compliant sections of the media, had continued to return her to Parliament. Whilst many of the unfortunate individuals who had been summoned to meet with the much-feared Director General of the BBC would be utterly terrified at the prospect, it was quite apparent that was not the case with this visitor. She strode into the room confidently and merely offered her hand to Dave McCreith rather than dropping to one knee in deference.

Dave McCreith stared at the proffered hand with as much confusion as he would have done had she opened her top and flopped one of her breasts out, even though she wouldn't have done that so I don't even know why you're thinking about it. Baffled, he turned to Terry Ball. 'What is this?!' he demanded.

Embarrassed that his employer had directed the question towards him rather than the visitor, Terry Ball glanced at both of them before offering his explanation. 'Er, well, your grace, you may recall that when politicians used to visit the monarch it was expected that they would bow to her, though whilst it was protocol it was not actually a legal requirement, so there were cases of some of the anti-royal politicians not doing so because they refused to recognise the validity of the monarchy...'

This explanation was unsatisfactory to Dave McCreith.

'Yes, but that's only the Royal Family!' he spluttered. 'Whilst I am the Director General of the BBC!'

'If you expect me to drop to one knee and defer to you as if you are some sort of feudal lord,' said Claire Bolam, 'then you will get no such satisfaction from me.'

Dave McCreith glared at her in disbelief, but she stared back and refused to be intimidated. 'As your colleague said,' she continued, 'I am under no obligation to bow.'

'Well, perhaps not from a strictly *legal* perspective,' replied Dave McCreith, struggling for words as if being faced with insolence of a level he had previously never experienced, 'but it is the done thing!'

'You sent for me and I came,' said Claire Bolam, ignoring this. 'Whilst I doubt you have much of a busy schedule, I do, so would appreciate you making this brief.'

Dave McCreith's eyebrows again shot up at this impertinence. After a pause, during which he again glanced at Terry Ball as if seeking guidance for how to navigate these new, uncertain waters, he continued.

'Very well. You seem to be a straight-talker, so I shall do the same. You appear to be two of the things that the Corporation simply cannot tolerate, much less understand: a politician with some form of moral compass and a feminist who insists on thinking for herself.'

'Indeed, Mr McCreith,' – again, the Director General's face suggested this was the first time he had disrespectfully been referred to by his actual name rather than his many regal forms of address for months, and was again taken by surprise – 'and if I succeed in doing those things then I make no apology for it.'

'Hmm, as we agreed to both shoot straight then I shall get to the point,' responded Dave McCreith. He took a folder from his desk, opened it, and turned to a particular page, which he then ran his eyes down. 'Your rap sheet is a litany of anti-BBC heresy, Thought-Crime of the highest order... Over the last few years it's almost as if your every utterance was made for no other reason than to question and humiliate the Corporation. We allowed you a certain amount of leeway, far more than we would have done for anyone else, because we've never fully been able to understand this: once, your beliefs and values entirely echoed those of the BBC, yet now they sit in almost complete opposition to it.'

'Indeed, your grace,' confirmed Claire Bolam, 'but it is the BBC that has changed, not I.'

'Impossible,' Dave McCreith shot back. 'The BBC's worldview has never changed. If you believe that's incorrect you may check the historical records, but you will find they've all been altered to favour my assertion.'

'The reason for your confusion is undoubtedly this,' Claire Bolam continued. 'You make the mistake of assuming that I said and did the things I said and did because I thought that was necessary to stay in power, rather than because I actually believed in them. My behaviour was based on principles.'

Dave McCreith again looked confused here, as the final word was unfamiliar. Attempting to hide this, he continued. 'However, even the BBC's patience eventually wears thin, and when it did we tried everything we could to oust you from office. Normally the electorate is a dim and compliant bunch and we have no problem controlling or changing what the proles think, but in your case you've been in office so long and, unusually, done a lot for the people in your constituency so they've stuck by you and failed to respond to our many attempts to discredit you, which included everything from allegations of financial misconduct regarding your expenses to extensively and disproportionately reporting on baseless accusations of anti-Semitism made against you by your opponents. Yet somehow you managed to remain in office. It was as if your constituents continued to remember the things you had done for them and decided that our never-ending attacks on your person could not have a basis in truth, which, for a powerful mind-controlling organisation such as ours, was deeply troubling.'

'I think there's a more simple explanation for you and your Corporation's dislike of me,' replied Claire Bolam, calmly. 'You've never liked me simply because I'm old-school left-wing.'

''What' wing? There's no 'left' wing!' Dave McCreith laughed, whilst also looking at Terry Ball in confusion. 'There's *right* wing, but you can only be that or liberal. I'm afraid I don't think that thing you claim to be actually exists, or ever has, so I don't see how your argument can work when the thing you claim to be isn't actually a thing anyway.'

'It was popular for a long time until those who really controlled things decided to phase it out, hence the BBC always being so keen on moderate Labour politicians and extremely unhappy about the more traditionally-minded leftist ones,' Claire Bolam responded.

'Not at all,' replied Dave McCreith. 'This so called 'left-wing' thing, if it ever even existed, must have simply run its course and no longer been relevant in a more complicated, corporation-controlled world.'

'Hmm, well, everyone's entitled to their opinions, and I don't think that's what we're here to discuss,' said Claire Bolam.

'Very well,' replied Dave McCreith, secretly relieved. 'Anyway...' He briefly glimpsed back at the folder, 'as I mentioned, your past behaviour is little more than a list of abhorrent hate crimes. Let us examine the specific crimes that the Corporation deems unforgivable. There are, in fact, a great many charges... This document says that for over thirty years you campaigned *against* topless photos in tabloid newspapers, or 'Page 3', as it was better known.'

'I did,' replied Claire Bolam, unrepentantly. 'Because I felt then, as I do now, that Page 3 exploits and objectifies women by portraying them as sex objects and nothing else.'

'*Incorrect!*' screamed Dave McCreith. 'Page 3 is an inspirational celebration of women that empowers them against the patriarchy! To suggest otherwise is to commit the repellent act of 'slut-shaming'!'

'You see?' replied Claire Bolam. 'That's what I'm talking about. Not only have you completely reversed your view on that topic, you've even endorsed a new term that can be used to denounce anyone who still believes what you used to!'

Terry Ball cut in at this point. 'It's just a point, but do you think we should actually re-brand that term to 'slag-shaming' rather than 'slut-shaming'?'

The other two looked at him, annoyed at the interruption, before Dave McCreith reluctantly addressed his point. 'Well, when we first started using that term it was because the millennials whose favour we were so desperately trying to curry did tend to follow the American terminology... I suppose that now the United States has all but completely lost its power in the world we could change it, but that's an argument for another time.'

'Well, anyway,' continued Claire Bolam, 'my point was that along with that being a stupid term it prevents people from daring to even consider some valid points. Anyway, even within your own recent past there are examples of the BBC having committed acts of so-called 'slut-shaming'...'

'Or 'slag-shaming',' interrupted Terry Ball again, which Claire Bolam acknowledged but did not incorporate as she continued.

'I mean, what about so-called 'lad mags'? I seem to recall the BBC more or less celebrating their demise by denouncing them as a sickening, sexist relic, only to decide a few months after that that their demise was truly tragic because it decimated the livelihoods of, and I quote, the 'traditional British slags' who made a living from appearing in them.'

Terry Ball smiled slightly here, as if this proved his earlier point about terminology.

'And then, not long after that,' continued Claire Bolam, 'you decided that female pop stars whose lives involved little more than posing in barely more clothes than the girls who appeared in lads' mags did were somehow modern feminists on a par with Emmeline Pankhurst!'

'That's quite different,' cut in Dave McCreith. 'Modern female pop stars are inspiring, empowering figures, and the fact that they wear virtually nothing in every public appearance simply makes them even more so.'

'But does it really?' asked Claire Bolam. 'I mean, even if you ignore how their music is nothing but inane clichés sung over a computer beat that was assembled by a team of men at their record company, whenever they perform 'live', they're actually miming, meaning that, if you think about it, their concerts are virtually indistinguishable from, and have all the artistic integrity of, a strip show.'

'There you go again!' screamed Dave McCreith. 'Strippers are empowered, inspiring women who have weaponised their sexuality, and to imply otherwise is *yet another* case of 'slut-shaming!'

Terry Ball chose not to correct him here. But even if he had wanted to he would not have had the chance as Claire Bolam immediately tore into the DG.

'I won't be silenced on this! I spent forty years standing up for the right of women not to be leered over as sex objects! I appeared on hundreds of your programmes talking about it but now you've changed the rules and decided I'm guilty of misogyny because I don't agree that it's suddenly 'inspirational' and 'empowering' to jiggle your titties around on stage?! The act hasn't changed, the practice hasn't changed, all that's changed is the terminology! But I know what's right and wrong! You can't make me change my mind based on a few hashtags and some social media shame! I will not stop speaking out about this!'

Dave McCreith glared at her. 'I'm not really sure I follow,' he said, casually.

'Well,' continued Claire Long, 'you recently ran a story about a woman who was refused entry to a museum because her extremely low-cut dress contravened their dress code, implying the museum committing a sickening act of sexism for running an establishment where the display of huge amounts of cleavage was discouraged! I mean, if a man has gone in there wearing a pair of trousers that had been specially adapted to allow his testicles to dangle down and swing around in the breeze, would you have celebrated that as a wonderful act of male empowerment?!'

(As an interesting historical aside, that really did happen. I mean, the woman in the low cut dress and the BBC reporting on it, not the man with his testicles swinging around. But I think it's an interesting example of how it's all but impossible to tell which of the examples I provide in this book are made up and which actually happened. And that, I believe, is quite revealing. Much like the dress in question.)

Dave McCreith shook his head, as if to say she was digging herself a hole from which it was becoming increasingly difficult, if not all but impossible, to get out of. After a pause Claire Bolam continued.

'My point is that I've always been suspicious and critical of how corporations attempt to hijack feminism and turn it into something else, partly for their own gain and partly to dilute its power. I've fought for decades for a form of feminism that truly supports women rather than controlling them. Your organisation and the outlets it controls have always had a rather conflicted attitude to women in that you claim to support them, and to support feminism, whilst presenting messages that do nothing of the sort. And today there's the whole thing where you go on about representation and body-positivity and diversity, whilst almost exclusively employing skinny and attractive girls for all your presenting jobs!'

'You will not criticise the Skinny Rich White Girl Club!' yelled Dave McCreith.

'Oh, I always assumed you had a name for it,' replied Claire Bolam, interested. Emboldened by the Director General's inability to successfully debunk her arguments, she continued. 'And then there's the unquestioning way you accept any pronouncement by the – what did you call it? – Skinny Rich White Girl Club without stopping to think whether it actually makes sense. I mean, you're so desperate to support people like Emma Watson that they could literally say or do anything and claim it was a powerful feminist statement and you would unquestioningly accept that. I mean, if Emma Watson made a hard-core porn film in which five guys simultaneously took her in every orifice, but then justified it by saying it was a powerful feminist statement because she was reclaiming her sexuality against the patriarchy and the haters, you'd print those exact words without realising how ridiculous you sounded!'

Terry Ball looked inquisitive here, as if wondering whether this could be interpreted as sexist, or if it was an entirely valid point, or whether the fact it was being said by a female character meant it was all fine. Yeah, probably the last one, I reckon.

Dave McCreith shook his head in disgust. 'A woman who hates women... The very worst kind. Women should not have different opinions! They should not disagree with each other! They should be united, joined together in a feminist sisterhood of empowerment!'

'You see!' Claire Bolam retorted. 'All you do is string inane buzzwords together so you can avoid actually thinking about what you're saying!'

Dave McCreith glared at her, furious with this annoying logic. He had had enough of this. 'I've had enough of this,' he announced. There, I told you he'd had enough of this. 'Anyway...' he continued. 'We tried everything to denounce you... We tried to taint you by association with the heretics Peter Tatchell and Germaine Greer!'

'And there's another thing!' Claire Bolam interrupted. 'You claim to be supportive of feminism, but that never went beyond having Germaine Greer as the one, token spokesperson for feminism every single time you needed a 'female opinion'!'

'It wasn't our fault!' protested Dave McCreith. 'She was the only feminist we could find who wasn't too damned fat or ugly to have on TV! Did you never see Andrea Dworkin?! We had no choice but to appoint Germaine Greer as our single spokesperson for all feminists! Anyway, the audience would have been confused if we'd put *two* feminists on TV, because what if they'd disagreed over something?!'

'But now you've decided she's a hate figure even though it's the BBC that has shifted its position, not her,' pointed out Claire Bolam.

'I see no hypocrisy in having had a particular individual on BBC TV seventeen times a week for twenty five years and holding them up as perfect examples of people with the correct opinions, only to later decide they were peddlers of hate and publically denounce them!' replied Dave McCreith, defiantly. 'Yes, Germaine Greer once spoke out on behalf of all women, and Peter Tatchell was the Spokesman for the Gays, but times change, and that's why we've since reclassified them both as heretics and had them sent to Re-Education Camps!'

'You forget that some of us base our careers not on wanting to be on TV all the time, or prioritising making as much money as possible, but on principles,' replied Claire Bolam.

'That's the second time you've used that word, even though I think I made it clear the first time that I don't know what it means,' Dave McCreith replied. 'The point is that feminism has changed. It's not what it was. Modern feminists are not expected to think for themselves! They're expected to retweet inane sentiments from people like Taylor Swift! They're meant to make an extremely tokenistic statements that make them look like wonderful people, but not actually *do* anything! And we certainly don't expect to see feminists thinking for themselves, as you seem to do! And if they do we simply denounce them as 'TERFs', or 'Trans Excluding Radical Feminists', which causes the Obedience Switch to go off in our audience's heads, instructing them that they must no longer listen to the person in question!'

Had he been sitting down, and I can't remember if he was, he now stood up. If he was already standing then he remained so and stared thoughtfully at Claire Bolam.

'Anyway, it's not as if you supposed old-school feminists are completely free of accusations of hypocrisy,' he accused, accusingly, with an accusatory tone. Claire Bolam stared at him as if waiting for him to offer his evidence, which he did. 'Well, what about the way *you* hold up individuals as perfect examples of human beings only to later decide they were peddlers of hate? I mean, I get that as an obedient feminist it's your duty to think abortion is wonderful, which it is, but does it really make sense to name a prominent provider of abortions after Marie Stopes who, in keeping with many people now promoted as early feminists, was actually *against* abortion, on top of being a eugenicist who supported Hitler and whose real motivation for promoting birth control was to stop poor people with inferior genes from breeding!?'

For the first time since the meeting began, Claire Bolam was briefly lost for words, before answering, 'well... Nobody's perfect. Anyway, that organisation changed its name once the sickening link was made known. Way back in 2020, I believe.'

Dave McCreith eyed his visitor carefully and suspiciously, but with a twinge of regret and confusion. 'Of all the treachery I've experienced in my life, yours was the hardest to take,' he admitted, shaking his head sadly. 'For years we slyly promoted you as someone who held the correct opinions on every topic imaginable, bringing you out on news and current affairs programmes so often that you might as well have taken a BBC salary. You were promoted by us as the very antithesis of a 'BBC Bogeyman', as someone who could always be wheeled out on Question Time to tell someone from UKIP why they were wrong, always expressing BBC Correct-Think but doing so in a way that suggested you were independent and did not speak for the Corporation. A person we could always rely on to have the correct morality and to obediently say what the BBC wanted to be said. That was a job for life.' He shook his head again, but this time admonishingly. 'Then you had to go and ruin it all by showing signs of independent thought!'

'I had no choice!' his visitor shot back. 'You failed to understand that when I said things that happened to be the same things you believed, I wasn't doing so to please you but because I genuinely believed them. But then the BBC started to change its mind on so many things and you stopped employing me for not obediently agreeing.'

'Nonsense,' replied Dave McCreith, defensively. 'The BBC has always held itself up to the highest moral standards, and even *if* we choose to then completely change these standards then, well, that's our own business.'

Claire Bolam shook her head in disbelief. 'What?!' she spluttered. 'How can you even say that?! Your opinions change on a weekly basis, and you'd have to be a moron not to see that! I mean, what about the way the BBC and its followers claim to be pro-diversity, pro-body positivity, anti-fat shaming, pro-trans and gay representation, pro-disabled representation, repelled by the idea of women being treated as nothing more than sex objects, disgusted by coercive, manipulative behaviour in relationships, sickened by vile 'toxic masculinity' and revolted by ghosting, gaslighting and whatever other terms you've made up this week to refer to common practices in human relationships, yet when Love Island came along, a programme that not only gleefully ignored all those things but seemed to celebrate the complete opposite, the BBC, the Custodian and Twitter, the three most woke voices in Britain, all fell over themselves to gushingly say how amazing it was and ran seemingly endless coverage of it and features on its contestants despite how it rather obviously exists in opposition to just about every single value you claim to hold?!'

'Well, yes,' conceded Dave McCreith, as he could not reasonably offer a logical counter to this allegation, 'but I think you're very much missing the point there. Have you stopped to consider the alternative?! I mean, you could hardly have a series of Love Island where all the contestants were fat, ugly and disabled, could you?! Who would want to watch that?!'

Claire Bolam stared at him intently, her arms folded, making it quite clear she did not need to address his response.

'Anyway,' continued Dave McCreith, huffily, 'I fail to recognise the validity of your suggestion that there's something problematic in the BBC presenting itself as a serious news organisation whilst simultaneously falling over itself to run interviews with, and revealing pictures of, Z-list social media celebrities on an almost hourly basis like it's actual news.'

There was a pause as they both attempted to recall exactly why they were actually holding the meeting they were currently involved in. Then Dave McCreith remembered, and in doing so regained his train of thought.

'Anyway,' he said. 'the many charges we've laid against you are undeniable. Yet you seem entirely unrepentant.'

'Indeed I am, your grace,' replied Claire Bolam, 'because, as I have repeatedly pointed out, it is the BBC that keeps changing its worldview, whereas mine has remained the same.'

'I choose not to recognise that allegation,' replied Dave McCreith. 'Anyway, the point is this: we may choose to call an election soon, and as you have repeatedly make it clear that you do not intend to repent your heresy nor atone for your wrongdoings or make any efforts to amend the troublesome thoughts you keep having, *and* have steadfastly resisted our attempts to turn the electorate against you, you will leave us with little choice than to force your party to announce you're being retired and replaced with a younger, more compliant candidate.'

'How about Emma Watson, my liege?' suggested Terry Ball.

'Well, obviously not her,' replied Dave McCreith, as if this was an extremely stupid idea. 'Because modern feminism is all about making vague statements and tokenistic gestures, tweeting things and making extremely well-publicised charity donations, and someone like

Emma Watson isn't going to get involved in actually trying to change anything as that would take up a huge amount of time and require her to actually do something! So she's obviously not going to go as far as to try to become an MP!' He paused for a moment as something occurred to him. 'Well, not for another ten or fifteen years or so, when her looks are starting to fade and she's struggling for film roles, anyway. So maybe then, yes.'

Having been slightly flustered by this diversion, Dave McCreith regained his composure and returned to Claire Bolam. 'Anyway, were you to let this happen unopposed we may consider forgiving your heresy and allowing you to retire to the House of Lords, or letting you appear on Strictly, as we usually reserve a place on that show for failed former politicians attempting to redeem themselves in the eye of the public.'

'Er, but not on the next series, your grace, as we've already got Kim Jong-Un booked in for that,' interrupted Terry Ball.

'Oh, that's right,' said Dave McCreith. 'He's due to meet with me whilst he's over here so I can offer tips on controlling the thoughts of an entire population. So maybe the year after that.'

'I believe disgraced former president Donald Trump is pencilled in to fill the space that year,' added Terry Ball.

'And if I refuse, and run as an independent?' Claire Bolam enquired.

Dave McCreith did not immediately answer this, and instead sighed and shook his head. After a moment his voice changed to one of pity. 'Then you leave me no choice. Guards!'

The door burst open and three BBC paramilitaries rushed in. Claire Bolam looked around, uncertain, but realised there was no chance of escape.

'This is heresy,' continued the Director General. 'Take her away. I want her broken by the end of the week.' His calm tone suddenly disappeared, to be replaced by pure fury. 'This is THE BBC and THE BBC DOES NOT TOLERATE DISSENT!'

Claire Bolam turned to Dave McCreith. 'You think you can change me?'

Dave McCreith smiled broadly. 'I use the term 'broken' more literally than you realise. You are mistaken if you think we send people to our Manchester site to be redeemed. If we thought there was any chance of that we'd send them to one of our many other facilities, but those sent to the North are those for whom we know there is no chance of redemption. No possibility of them repenting their sickening heresy. It doesn't matter what you say once you're there, doesn't matter how much or how often you claim to have changed or to have seen the error of your ways. By the time you are there, it is too late.'

For the first time since she had entered the room Claire Bolam now looked terrified, even though the expression that revealed this quickly vanished as she attempted to maintain her composure. 'What? Manchester? I've heard the rumours of what you do there. There's no chance for rehabilitation. No one ever comes out! What you do there is murder, pure and simple!'

Dave McCreith smiled a smile of victory at her. 'It's not murder,' he corrected. 'It's just unofficial execution.' He nodded to the paramilitaries, and they each took one of Claire Bolam's arms. Hang on, did I say there were three of them? If there were then I suppose two of them grabbed the same arm, or one supervised the other two. Hmm, I think that by stopping to ponder that I may have detracted from just how powerful this bit is. Or maybe it's so dark that there needs to be some comic relief? Anyway, the point is that as Dave McCreith watched them take her away he simply uttered the word 'Manchester', then shuddered. As a BBC executive he probably shuddered at the idea of visiting Manchester long before it was a Black Ops Renditioning Site, but there you are. He returned to his desk and sat down. Claire Bolam, still attempting to maintain her composure, was led from the room, into a future about which the only thing she could be certain was that whilst it was a future of unthinkable brutality, it would at least be short.

Wow, another pretty powerful chapter, I think you'll have to agree! And wasn't I spot on when I said what a powerful female character it was going to include, too?! So, before we move on to yet another brilliant chapter I think there are two points to be addressed:

1. Continuing from my point about what an amazing, powerful female character Claire Bolam was, there will be some people who say she shouldn't have suffered such a brutal end as that reduces representation in the book, but as a response to that I would point out that it's *more* of a sign that I see all my characters as equal

that a female character could suffer a fate just as brutal as a male one, okay?

Similarly, there are people who will criticise this chapter for being anti-feminist, when it actually criticises the modern brand of pseudo-feminism, or 'Insta-Feminism', as I so brilliantly called it a few chapters ago. So that's the point: it's criticising those who jump on the modern feminist bandwagon as a way to virtue signal whilst not ever bothering to trouble themselves by actually questioning things for themselves. Okay?

2. I reckon that people from across the political spectrum will not only be utterly confused by this chapter, but will all find something to be offended by. I mean, the fact that it's supportive of an old-school feminist will lead some people to criticise me for that, but there's also the vague hint of support for old-school left-wing politics, so traditional right-wingers could get offended by that, yet there's *also* an ambiguous reference to allegations of anti-Semitism towards the traditional left! And liberals will obviously get offended by me criticising people who unthinkingly support the aforementioned Insta-feminism. Basically, it's a chapter that could potentially offend followers of *all* the traditional political positions!

So there will probably be some readers who thought they'd figured out the party political stance of this book only to now be utterly confused. Maybe there's a point there? This book has something for everyone, something for everyone to agree with and something for everyone to be offended by! So why not just let things slide, eh? Why not read something that doesn't completely echo your world view?! Think for yourselves! If you're confused by everything at this stage... Good!

# Chapter Fifteen:

# London Calling

*In Which Our Heroes Make a Desperate Attempt To Escape Their Pursuers so They Can Make An Equally Desperate, and Mad, Attempt To Reach New White City And Confront the Supreme Overlords of the BBC*

Our heroes had been on the road for barely ten minutes when Barry Begbie, who had been carefully looking out of the van's back window, made a regretful announcement.

'I wish I didn't have to say this, but we're being followed.'

John Smith leapt up and looked out of the window. Further down the road, a van similar to theirs seemed to be trailing them.

'How long?'

'Since we left the camp.'

'Is it the BBC or the RPS?'

'I can't quite tell. Their detector vans are similar and they're not close enough for me to have a proper look.'

'Who do you think it's more likely to be?'

'Again, hard to tell. The BBC won't want it to become known that anyone managed to escape from one of their camps, even though there aren't any media organisations that would even dare to run our story or even listen to it... Then again, the RPS will probably want their van back.'

Jeffrey Harding squinted out of the window. 'There's no way we can beat them in a straight fight. I mean... The issue here is that

BBC paramilitaries are amongst the most highly-trained, morally bankrupt mercenaries in the country, if not the world. They shoot first and worry about the consequences later. Like the police, they know they can do whatever they like because any ostensible investigation into their conduct will exonerate them and do little more than make vague assurances that 'the culture needs to change' and that 'lessons will be learned', Ooh, the bloody police, eh?' His final comment made the others look at him strangely, until the confusion was resolved: had he made that exact outburst on a Radio 4 comedy show it would have counted as stand-up comedy, despite the obvious lack of humorous content, because it expressed a correct opinion, in this case that the police are brutal fascists whose day-to-day duties consist of little more than persecuting ethnic minorities, even though the people in the audience who would have applauded such an opinion would be exactly the same kind of people who lived in a nice area and would unhesitatingly call the police if they saw someone hanging around who looked a bit poor. Realising his current companions were not such an audience, Jeffrey Harding looked sheepish and stopped talking.

At this point the van had got close enough for Barry Begbie to identify who was in it. 'Oh, god, no,' he said. 'They're BBC.'

John Smith looked crestfallen; Jeffrey Harding put his head in his hands. Hmm, at this point I realise I can't actually remember who was in the party that escaped from the camp. Obviously John Smith, Emmeline Moneypenny, Barry Begbie and Jeffrey Harding, but did Kerri Barnes-Bridge join them? Oh, I suppose we might as well say she did. At least that makes the gender balance of the party a bit better. 'What are we going to do?' she asked, in despair.

'We can't outrun them... And if they catch us then we're as good as dead...' pondered Barry Begbie, before looking thoughtful. 'Unless...'

The others looked at him in anticipation.

'You'll just have to trust me on this. First of all, we need to change from our camp uniforms and into these RPS uniforms that are hanging up by the weapons rack. Do it!'

Unable to think of an alternative, they all took off their filthy camp overalls and put on the RPS uniforms, which had clearly been designed not just to facilitate military usage but to strike fear into anyone who saw them plus, in what I have to say is a very useful piece of luck from a narrative perspective, covered up the face of the wearer. Sort of like a visor that made their features indistinguishable. Barry Begbie then shouted to Emmeline Moneypenny.

'In a moment I need you to quickly turn this van around and put the sirens on to make it look like *we* are pulling *them* over, so reversing the balance of power. It needs to be a quick, precise movement that makes it look like this van is being driven by RPS representatives rather than escapees.'

'That's not a problem!' she yelled back, adding, 'I drove vans like this when I was a war correspondent!' in another example of something happening that really helps me out in dealing with narrative issues and potential plot-hole problems. Anyway, why can't someone be revealed to have a skill that comes in useful that they just happened not have mentioned before? If anything, having her mention it earlier for no reason other than to set this bit up is actually lazier writing than this. So that's all sorted out then.

'Everyone else: pick up a gun and get ready to burst out with me once the van's stopped,' instructed Barry Begbie to the others.

'But I've never used a gun before!' protested Kerri Barnes-Bridge. 'I'm a pacifist!'

'It doesn't matter,' Barry Begbie assured her, 'if my plan works then you won't need to.'

He looked out of the back of the van to see how far their pursuers were behind them. A moment later he shouted to Emmeline Moneypenny. 'Now!'

Emmeline Moneypenny put on the van's sirens then performed a brilliant three point turn, even though they must have been travelling at fifty miles per hour, so if you still have an issue with me mentioning how she scraped the side of the van when she first took the wheel after they escaped, you should shut up. They came to an abrupt halt before Barry Begbie flung the doors open and leapt out, brandishing an assault rifle, with the others, somewhat uncertainly, behind him. He marched to the BBC van, which had also stopped, and motioned to its confused occupants that they should get out. There were three paramilitaries, all of whom stepped out of the van, but also all kept hold of their weapons and confronted Barry Begbie suspiciously.

'We understand you were incompetent enough to allow some of your prisoners to escape from the camp and steal one of our vans,' said Barry Begbie, in a rather clever example of a double bluff.

'We were sent out in pursuit but seem to have lost them. Are you after them, too?'

'That's right,' replied one of the paramilitaries, still suspicious. 'We believe they escaped in a van just like the one you're in.'

'That's correct,' replied Barry Begbie, doubling the bluff that the paramilitary had called, so presumably tripling it, or was it now quadrupled? I'm not sure. He looked him straight in the eyes, though it didn't really make any difference because of the visor he had on. 'One of our most valuable models, containing a lot of our most expensive equipment, which we use to detect the illegal playing of copyrighted music. We're very keen to get it back.'

'Well, we're very keen to capture the escapees,' said the paramilitary, adding, 'whichever van they may or may not be in.'

'Good,' said Barry Begbie. 'Then we all want the same thing. That's good to know. You get your escapees, we get our van.'

'Perhaps we could just check inside your van, just to ensure there are no stowaways?' enquired the paramilitary, said in a casual way but laced with accusation.

'Of course,' replied Barry Begbie, before adding, 'assuming you have the necessary warrant?'

'We're the BBC!' snapped the paramilitary. 'We do not need a warrant to enter a premises or search a vehicle if we believe it lacks the necessary TV licences or if we believe its occupants are engaged in any sort of anti-BBC activity!'

'Of course!' smiled Barry Begbie. He then casually whistled a few notes, as if thinking about something else. The paramilitaries watched him as if waiting for him to step aside. A moment after he had stopped whistling, one of the paramilitaries absent-mindedly started whistling the same tune, at which Barry Begbie's facial expression suddenly switched to one of satisfaction. Though, again, no one saw as he was wearing a visor. 'I'm sorry?' he said casually, to the paramilitary who was whistling. 'What's that tune you're whistling?'

The whistling paramilitary stopped, guiltily. 'What tune?' he said, in an attempt to sound innocent.

'The tune you whistled just then,' Barry Begbie shot back. 'It was, unless I am very mistaken, Barry Biggins' 1974 number seventeen hit, 'Ooh, Yeah, Baby, You're So Groovy'.'

'Er, might have been,' replied the whistling paramilitary. 'What does that matter?'

'What does that matter?!' yelled Barry Begbie, with a volume of voice that shocked even his friends. 'What does that matter?! I'll tell you what it matters! The composer of that song will have relied on the royalties from it as his main source of income ever since it was released! He relies on that money, and every unlicensed performance of it forces him even further into poverty and destitution!'

'What?!' replied the whistling paramilitary, looking at his colleagues uncertainly. 'Well,' he continued, 'I only whistled it for a few moments. And it wasn't even a good version. And you whistled it first!'

'It was still recognisable as a copyrighted piece of music!' Barry Begbie shot back. 'And I am *allowed* to whistle it because I represent the Royalty Protection Society, which has collected monies due for musical compositions since 1947!'

'You're quite sure that's a thing?' queried the paramilitary, suspiciously. It's a different one speaking now, by the way, I suppose the third one, which sort of mixes things up a bit, only I now realise that as they're all basically interchangeable it doesn't really make any difference, so this is a bit of a waste of time.

'Absolutely,' replied Barry Begbie. 'Page eighty four, paragraph nine, subsection 6B. 'Relating to the requirement of a music licence to cover any impromptu whistling of copyrighted songs whilst out on company business." He swiftly reached into the van and took out a large document that appeared to run to hundreds of pages, and flung it over to the paramilitary, who took it and flicked through it, without actually looking up the specific reference that had been mentioned.

'Yeah, I have heard of how much insane power these guys have,' replied a different paramilitary. 'They've got this whole system of fiendishly complicated licensing fees and rules and they'll take you to court for everything you have if you don't pay, or dare to question them.'

As to whether or not Barry Begbie had researched the Royalty Protection Society in such detail that he was able to quote the page number of their various statutes is something I haven't decided; maybe he did, or maybe he was bluffing again, which, to be fair, is pretty much what he's been doing this whole time. To be honest, much of this chapter has consisted of events that often seem to be nothing more than rather convenient occurrences that enable me to push the narrative along with precious little concern for logic or good writing. Also, I should probably stop making all these arcane references to organisations that enforce music copyright. I mean, at least when I make reference to BBC licence fees everyone knows what I'm talking about, whereas this RPS stuff is a bit niche, even if it is a rather clever narrative device.

Standing his ground, Barry Begbie smiled, but I just realised that I said their faces are covered so no one would have been able to see that anyway. Hmm, I should just stop mentioning the facial expressions of people who are wearing visors as it's a waste of time.

'So I would assume you'll already have a licence to cover you for your little outburst, otherwise there'll be a rather hefty fine coming your way,' he continued, 'because, as you must be aware, any usage of copyrighted music in any work-related scenario, including travelling to and from jobs, needs to be covered by the appropriate licence.'

The paramilitaries looked at each other, concerned, uncertain whether he was bluffing but not willing to run the risk.

'And it certainly wouldn't do to have BBC employees showing such ignorance where licencing laws are concerned, would it?'

'Hmm, yeah, well, the boss keeps all the legal paperwork back in the camp,' replied one of the paramilitaries. At this point another one of them spoke, probably the one who had done the whistling and thus had the strongest motivation to steer them away from the situation he had created and back to what he thought was a more important issue.

'Er, I don't know if you're aware but we were going to try to apprehend some dangerous Thought Criminals who escaped from our camp, so maybe that should be our priority, and maybe that's more important right now...?'

Barry Begbie immediately turned on him. 'You seem to be implying that there are more important things than ensuring everyone in the country has, and has paid for, the appropriate licences for their homes and workplaces. That sounds, to me, dangerously close to anti-BBC heresy.'

The other two paramilitaries turned on their colleague accusingly and he looked worried before agreeing, 'no, you're absolutely right, we need to sort this first.'

'Good,' replied Barry Begbie. 'Then you'll want to go back to your camp and bring us the relevant documentation to prove you're not blatantly in breach of licensing laws.'

The paramilitaries again looked at him suspiciously but did not want to risk challenging him further.

'Yes, of course,' one of them said. 'We'll go and get it right now. See you back here in ten?'

'Of course,' replied Barry Begbie, smiling. Oh, wait, I said I was going to stop mentioning his facial expressions because of the visors. 'We'll be waiting right here.'

Slowly, and with a slight air of reluctance, never taking their eyes of our heroes, the paramilitaries got back into their van, reversed it and drove back the way they had come, at which point, I suppose they did actually have to take their eyes off our heroes despite my earlier assertion that they 'never' did it. As they drove away, our heroes continued to watch them, still holding up their guns, which they had been doing all the time in case I hadn't mentioned it before. Once the van was out of sight they finally, albeit briefly, relaxed.

'Okay, we need to get moving,' said Barry Begbie. They all got back in the van and Emmeline Moneypenny drove them away, again showing great skill behind the wheel.

The escapees had been driving for about twenty minutes before John Smith noticed something. What he had previously taken to be a kind of strange atmospheric disturbance, possible fallout from the nuclear attacks of a few years ago, was in fact, he realised, sunshine. Something he had not seen during his entire tenure in the camp, which he then as now attributed to a stray comment during the first day of his incarceration about the BBC having the power to control the weather. All they had known whilst in the camp was a never-ending drab grey sky accompanied by similarly never-ending drizzle, yet now he was seeing actual sunlight for the first time in, well, he didn't even know how long, and realised that it was straining his eyes. Also, if you're wondering why he's noticing this now rather than when they confronted the BBC militiamen it's because they had the visors on, remember? I didn't actually plan that, which is fortunate, as it was a lucky coincidence that means I didn't then have to come up with yet another rather laboured attempt to plug a plot-hole. But again, he thought back to his first day in the camp, when a guard had said something about the BBC having the ability to control the weather, and once more wondered if it was actually true.

'I still don't really know where we are,' admitted Emmeline Moneypenny from the front seat. 'It's been hard to navigate since all the road signs were taken down to confuse the enemy during the war.' (Not another convenient plot point; something like that could definitely have happened and probably did in the Olden Days.)

John Smith looked thoughtful. 'The weather? You must have all noticed.'

'Yes,' said Jeffrey Harding. 'Endlessly cold and rainy in the camp yet there's been nothing but glorious sunshine since, well, pretty much the moment we escaped.'

Barry Begbie pondered this. 'I mean, it *could* be that there was just a freak weather bubble over the camp. But... Well, again, when I worked at the BBC there were rumours.'

The others looked at him. 'Rumours that the BBC could control the weather,' he explained. 'There was talk of some sort of ionising device on the roof of New White City. I don't understand the science.' (Which is convenient because neither do I. You'll just have to go along with it. Anyway, I'm writing this in what to you is the future so why shouldn't it be a thing there?!)

'For what reason?' asked John Smith.

'As far as I know, to control the mood of the population,' replied Barry Begbie. 'If they need them miserable so as to make them more malleable then the weather would be made awful for months on end in the middle of summer. Sometimes it was more simple, such as making it rain on election days so as to dissuade certain demographics, like old people, from going out and voting for the awful Tories.'

'The bloody Tories!' said Kerri Barnes-Bridge, as a sort of knee-jerk response, forgetting she was not on a Radio 4 panel show, but also to give her a rare bit of dialogue.

John Smith's face lit up (but not from the 'bloody Tories!' comment). 'Hang on... If they control the weather... And the weather here's good... Then we must be in an area where BBC people are likely to live, or at least visit. I mean, the BBC wouldn't waste its weather-controlling device on, say, ensuring the people of Grimsby had permanent sunshine, would they?'

'That is a very good point,' replied Barry Begbie. 'Also, do you notice how there don't seem to be many signs of the war here? You know how they managed to keep their favourite areas of the country safe from the fighting? The only area where BBC execs and generic BBC people live?'

Their faces lit up and, in unison, they all said 'Surrey!'

'Of course!' said Emmeline Moneypenny, as if it all seemed so obvious. 'Some BBC executives not only have it written into their contracts that they never have to visit the North, but that they don't ever have to visit anywhere outside Surrey apart from the BBC head office and, very rarely, Cornwall, if they can't get to Tuscany for some reason.'

'Of course,' repeated John Smith. 'They'd keep Surrey clean and safe, wouldn't they? They'd make sure all the fighting was confined to places they'd never visit. It's the same principle that all the nukes are kept in Scotland, as far away from London as possible.'

Having briefly taken her eyes off the road, but not in a way that was in any sense dangerous, Emmeline Moneypenny returned them to it then looked alarmed. 'Sorry, guys, but I think they've caught up with us again. I just saw a BBC van go by.'

Barry Begbie climbed to the front. 'Was it the same one?'

'I'm going to have to say not,' replied Emmeline Moneypenny. 'It was going in the other direction. However, I think they must be on alert as I believe it slowed down. It could turn back any moment and catch up with us.'

Barry Begbie looked around. 'There's a clearing over there,' he observed. 'We could slow down, go in and hope they pass us and think we've disappeared.'

Emmeline Moneypenny slowed down as they approached it. 'Perhaps,' she agreed. 'These roads are pretty narrow but at least the hedgerows could plausibly be hiding a side road we might have slipped down.'

She slowed the van down and they pulled into the clearing and waited. After a few minutes the van she had earlier spotted sped past them without giving any sign it had seen them. They waited, no one saying anything, for confirmation that this was the case.

A few moments later the van slowly returned, its occupants all glaring at them. Everyone turned to look at Barry Begbie, who slowly motioned to the weapons cache in the back of the van. He nodded at the others and, slowly but surely, they started to gather and hand out the weapons.

At this moment, another vehicle appeared, as if from nowhere. It was one of those electric people carriers. They sometimes get called 'Chelsea tractors' if the owner goes into London with them but I suppose considering this one was in Surrey it was okay as they could conceivably live on a farm. I don't know the make or model as I don't really know cars. The inhabitants were all well-dressed, with the women in proper evening dresses and the men in tuxedos. Also, they were heavily armed. By the time the BBC paramilitaries noticed this, however, it was too late: the inhabitants of the so-called 'Chelsea tractor' had gunned them down in a brutal shower of automatic gunfire.

'That's for banning 'Land of Hope and Glory' from the Proms, you woke wallies!' screamed one of them, as they drove away.

Our heroes sat in silence for a moment, slightly shaken at what they had witnessed, but aware that had it not happened then they themselves would have been forced to do exactly the same. In an attempt to break the awkward silence, Barry Begbie said, 'Well... I suppose you never think of the people of Reigate or Guildford turning to armed insurrection but then, I suppose, everyone has their breaking point.'

'There are said to be pockets of resistance all over the country,' added Emmeline Moneypenny, 'but, of course, the BBC does everything it can to avoid reporting on them. And if for some reason they end up doing something so big that it can't be covered up, the BBC usually just claims it was bald, working-class white men doing their usual far-right activities.'

So, yeah, that was a rather-too-convenient cop-out but this novel's getting pretty long now so I think I need to push it along. Anyway, hugely implausible cop-outs are a mainstay of film and TV, what with Sherlock, Star Wars, Luther or whatever using them all the time. Although, now I think about it, I don't know why I didn't just have our heroes shoot the BBC paramilitaries seeing as, you know, they had loads of guns and the outcome would have been the same, and then I could have explored the psychological effects that killing people might have had on them, and they could have pondered the very nature of good vs evil and, well, it doesn't really matter now. Emmeline Moneypenny started the engine again only to look worried.

'Hang on...' she said, listening. 'There's a technical problem with the car.'

As I mentioned, I don't even know about the makes and models of cars so I'm not going to know what technical problems they have but whatever it was had been caused by the bullets. So it's the tyres being burst, or the petrol machine being punctured or something, okay? The bullets did bad things, which Emmeline Moneypenny explained to them all in great technical details, completely erasing any accusations of sexism from that bit where she dented the van when they first stole it, and the end result was that they all had to get out.

'We should probably get off the roads,' Emmeline Moneypenny pointed out, as they emerged into daylight. 'I mean, word will have got out... Having lost radio contact with that van means they'll surely suspect something happened to the occupants, and quite possibly think we were responsible. We need to stay out of their sight.'

They looked around before John noticed that only a few yards down the road were some huge iron gates, which he initially took to be the entrance to a stately home or industrial complex until he did a double take and realised they looked familiar.

'Oh, wait,' he said, as he looked at it. 'I remember this place. It used to be a popular tourist attraction... A theme park...'

Jeffrey Harding pushed the gates experimentally and, to his surprise, found they opened easily. 'This might be the best place for us to go,' he said. 'We'll be off the roads, and this gate looks like no one's been through it in years.'

So they did that, and went inside. The amusement park had clearly been deserted for some years, and had a rather eerie air about it.

'Yes, I remember this place now,' said John Smith, as he looked around. 'It was one of the most popular visitor attractions in the area... But it fell foul of BBC rules, and the owners were forced to update the rides as they were all deemed too offensive, but once all the tradition had been taken away the visitors stopped coming and it closed down.'

'Aye,' replied Barry Begbie, using an actual Scottish word for the first time in ages, just to remind you that he's Scottish. 'Look, this ride used to be the Tunnel of Love.'

They all looked up to see that it was now called the Tunnel of Entirely Consensual Sexual Encounters With A Chaperone and A

Signed Declaration of Consent Before Entry Is Allowed.

'Oh, look, there's an Emotional Roller Coaster,' said John Smith, pointing to another ride. 'It doesn't actually move, but the people who go on it are shown all sorts of manipulative pictures of orphans in Africa so as to encourage them to pay again once they get off.'

For a few moments they silently continued their journey through the eerily deserted park. 'Wait!' said Jeffrey Harding, suddenly stopping. 'I remember this place! I used to come here as a teenager! It's suddenly all coming back to me!' He looked around. 'That ride over there? It used to be called the 'Mad House.' He strained his eyes to read the new name. 'And it's now called the Breaking Down the Stigma Surrounding Mental Illness House.'

He looked embarrassed on behalf of the park's owners, whoever they were and wherever they had ended up. They continued walking, and by the time they left the park an air of melancholy had descended over the group, as if the visit had vividly reminded them of the old world that they hadn't realised they loved so much. When they reached the gate they stopped.

'Well,' said Emmeline Moneypenny. 'We're a long way from the road, so I'd say we're safe from any scouting parties sent out to locate the missing team.'

They all stopped and fell silent for a moment. After two further moments it became a clear, if unspoken, agreement that they were all wondering the same thing.

'Hang on...' said John Smith. 'What's the plan? I mean, the BBC militiamen are all on the lookout for us. Some of you are quite well known and could be recognised by the public.' He looked at Jeffrey Harding. 'You'll probably be okay, though. But, still, we can't stay on the run forever! And we've surely seen too much for them to let us return to our old lives! And even though they won't admit we've escaped from the camps, as they don't officially acknowledge they exist, they may still say we're wanted criminals and make up some false charges against us to encourage the public to turn us in if they see us...'

Barry Begbie looked thoughtful. 'There may be only one thing for it... I mean... As you say, most of us have been on TV quite prominently. If there was some way to hijack their broadcasts and get a message of truth out there... People might listen. People might be willing to hear what's really going on...' He shook his head, realising this was all but impossible. Emmeline Moneypenny's face lit up.

'I don't know,' she added. 'I still know a few sympathisers... You'd be surprised. People who read The Book secretly still work there but, of course, they're terrified to speak out. They dare not utter a single idea that sits contrary to BBC Correct-Think. But there are a few. People like us. People who could help us.'

'Do we have any choice?' asked Jeffrey Harding. 'I mean, as you say, we're all going to be on the top-level 'wanted' lists. We either risk getting the word out, which will be dangerous, or just carry on like this for a few more days until they catch us.'

'Is there some way we can reach their headquarters without being caught?' asked Kerri Barnes-Bridge.

'Well, I suppose the best way to avoid the nuclear fallout is to follow a path that takes us through as many safe zones as possible,' mused Emmeline Moneypenny. 'So, Surbiton, Kingston, Richmond, Kew... Chiswick... Then only a brief trip through Acton, and we'll be there. I think it's doable. A lot of it avoids the roads. It'll be safer to walk anyway. Shouldn't take us much more than a day.'

'We have to do it!' said John Smith. 'We have to try!'

'Aye,' said Barry Begbie, strangely using the Scottish word for 'yes' for only the second time in ages. 'Or die trying.'

'I'm not sure we really have any choice,' said Emmeline Moneypenny. 'To New White City!'

They all marvelled at the awesome fear that this name instilled in them, for they knew the journey they were about to set out on was one from which there was very little chance of return.

# Chapter Sixteen:

# Prime Minister Questions Crimes

*In Which the Prime Minister, Horace Thompson, Has His Weekly Audience With the Most Powerful Person in the Country, The Director General of the BBC, Is Castigated for His Many and Repeated Failures Then Receives His Instructions Regarding the Changes the BBC Requires to be Made to the Law*

Dave McCreith was once more looking down from his window, with a stern expression and a furrowed brow. 'Is he still there?' he demanded of Terry Ball, who looked up from his laptop.

'Is who still there, your grace?' he asked.

'The rotting corpse of the heretic Andrew Neil, of course!' he replied, as if his answer was obvious. Terry Ball looked thoughtful.

'Well, a few bones, I believe. My informants told me that the last remnants of his rotting flesh were gnawed away about two months ago.'

'Hmm. Very well,' replied Dave McCreith, as if this was an acceptable though vaguely disappointing response. 'Obviously I'm too important to use the main entrance or, indeed, venture to a floor more than three storeys below this one. Some people said that the Director General of the BBC having his own private helicopter to ferry him to work and back was an extravagance, but I feel that without it I could end up accidentally bumping into someone more than two pay grades below me, which would trigger my anxiety in an almost uncontrollable way.' He suddenly got extremely angry, as if remembering some past outrage for which he had never satisfactorily been compensated. 'I mean, really! Andrew Neil! A non-believer at the BBC! For years he was allowed to express anti-BBC Thought-Crime on our very own programmes! Why was it permitted? Why was his heresy allowed?!'

'Well, as per the Rule of One, we allowed one 'right wing comedian' on our comedy shows and one right-wing broadcaster on all our current affairs programmes, in keeping with our commitment to tokenism and diversity,' replied Terry Ball.

'Hmm, yes, but wasn't that a misinterpretation of the Rule of One, anyway?' objected Dave McCreith. 'I mean, the point of that rule was to ensure we had exactly one from each minority group in order to meet our diversity targets, but do holders of heretical views still count towards that?'

'I confess to not being entirely sure, your grace,' replied Terry Ball, comfortingly, 'but he's gone now, remember? He's in the gibbet opposite the decaying carcass of that chap who wrote the brutally satirical and ruthlessly offensive novel about the BBC. In fact, I think there are still a few bits of him left.'

'Yes, yes, I'm really not concerned about him,' replied Dave McCreith, as if wondering why his underling had seen fit to mention another heretic when he was clearly upset discussing the first. 'Anyway, what's on my agenda for today? I really feel that I've been totally overworked in the last few weeks. It's just been meeting after meeting. Sometimes up to one meeting in a single day. Often lasting almost half an hour! I do have my own private golf course, and I feel that it will have been a real waste of licence fee payers' money if I don't use it at least a few times a week!'

'Oh, you do have a meeting shortly,' Terry Ball explained, 'but it's not with anyone important.'

'Oh, then who is it?' asked Dave McCreith.

'The Prime Minister, your excellency,' replied Terry Ball. 'The Right Honourable Horace Thompson.'

A look of disgust came over Dave McCreith's face. 'Really? Must I waste time dealing with such an insignificant figure as him? I could get another few holes of golf in if I skip it.'

'I know, my liege, I know, replied Terry Ball, comfortingly, 'but it is required that you meet with him once a week. It's an amendment of the previous law, remember? The Prime Minister used to have to meet with the monarch once a week whereas now you're the most important and powerful person in the country he's obliged to meet with you.'

Dave McCreith muttered something under his breath. 'Hmm, well, I trust we still hold the leverage over him?'

'Of course, your grace,' confirmed Terry Ball. 'He'll probably be here any moment.' He waited a moment. 'Yes, any time now, I would think, your grace.' There was another pause. Then there was a knock on the door. 'Ah, that's probably him now,' said Terry Ball, crossing over to the door and opening it.

The door swung open and, after permission to enter was given via a nod from Terry Ball, in walked Horace Thompson, the Prime Minister, who had a nice, legally-safe name to show he's definitely not based on anyone. In public the Prime Minister always projected an image of joviality and confidence but now, in private, it was clear from his body language that he was scared. He regularly met presidents, royalty and popes, yet it was undeniable that nothing scared him more than his weekly audience with the Director General and Supreme Overlord of the BBC. He nervously advanced towards Dave McCreith's desk, shuffling as he did so and staring at the floor.

'Er, good afternoon, your grace. It is, of course, time for my weekly audience with you.'

Dave McCreith walked towards him and, as he approached, the Prime Minister dropped to his knees. Dave McCreith offered his hand, and Horace Thompson kissed his ring. Oh, not his bottom, you understand. I mean the actual ring on his hand. The expensive, bejewelled one with the BBC logo on it. Still, I'm sure he would kiss his anal ring if he were ordered to do so. Actually, I now realise that was quite a brilliant metaphor and I should have just left it without the weird deconstruction. Anyway, the Prime Minister nervously cleared his throat before broaching the first topic, something he clearly wished to bring up even though he was wary of doing so.

'Er, first of all, your excellency, could I perhaps enquire as to my son?'

Dave McCreith glared at him. 'Your son is quite safe. He remains, of course, in our custody so as to ensure your continued and future cooperation but you may rest assured that no harm will come to him.' He paused at this point, as if to insinuate that what was ostensibly words of assurance was actually a thinly-veiled threat.

'You must let me see him!' blurted out the Prime Minister, before realising he had spoken out of turn, and looking down at the floor, sheepishly. Dave McCreith slammed his hand down on his desk. 'How dare you raise your voice to me! You tried to defund us! You tried to close us down! After our Great Victory did you really expect me to forget all that?!'

'No, your grace. I apologise, your grace,' replied the Prime Minister, humbly. 'You have been more than fair to me, considering everything.'

'Anyway,' continued Dave McCreith, with a mischievous glint in his eye. 'You have so many children that I'm unsure as to why you should be so concerned about a particular one of them.'

'Well, your grace,' the Prime Minister bumbled, 'whilst it's true that I have fathered an indeterminate number of offspring, that's not to say I don't care about them all equally...'

'An indeterminate number of offspring!' laughed Dave McCreith. 'That's somewhat understating things, isn't it?! You know that Jacob Rees-Mogg called his sixth child 'Sixtus'? Well, maybe you could have followed his lead and called your latest offspring 'About Thirty-Sevenus'!'

'Oh, ha, yes, jolly good...!' stumbled the PM, too terrified to be sure whether he should laugh or not.

'Anyway,' continued Dave McCreith, relishing how he clearly held sway over a man assumed by most of the public to be the most powerful in the country, 'surely you should be pleased. We're paying for his upkeep, thus saving you the expense of having to reach into your own pocket as the result of one of your many infidelities!'

'Er, yes, a good point, your eminence,' replied Horace Thompson, uncertainly. 'You honour me, you really do.'

'Indeed I do,' confirmed Dave McCreith. 'Anyway. Moving on... Any news on the war in Scotland?'

'Well, your grace,' replied the Prime Minister, guiltily, 'the war continues. We remain indebted to the BBC for its lending of a significant number of BBC Paramilitaries as we attempt to defeat the breakaway republic and bring the country back under UK, and BBC, control...'

'You absolute incompetent fool!' roared Dave McCreith. 'How could you let them break free in the first place?! The only reason we've lent you our private army is because the BBC is losing hundreds of millions of pounds a year now we can no longer claim licence fees from the Scots! Have you any idea how much of a cash cow they were for us?! We earned a fortune from them and all we had to give in return was a few programmes about bagpipes or weaving chunky sweaters on a loom or some folk music concerts! And yet this war has dragged on for months now with no sign of a conclusion!'

'Er, well, your grace, there is the matter of how the BBC spent several years campaigning for a massive reduction in the size of the UK army only for it to turn out this was all a ploy so that when the civil unrest started the BBC actually had a larger military force than the government itself, which was how it was able to so easily assume control of the country, along with the fact that some people believe that the funding of a private army is beyond the remit of a public broadcaster and, as such, is a poor use of licence payers' money...'

This only served to make Dave McCreith angrier. 'It's all your fault that Scotland declared itself independent and is now a rogue state!' yelled the Director General at the beleaguered Prime Minister. 'We had a deal! You offer them a tokenistic referendum then we claim to be impartial whilst running months and months of propaganda as to why they should remain part of the Union!'

'In all fairness, my liege,' replied Horace Thompson, meekly, 'the rebellious Scots became independent through armed uprising as opposed to our one-sided, tokenistic offers of referenda that we'd have had declared invalid if they'd come close to looking like leading to independence...'

'Useless!' screamed Dave McCreith. 'You're nothing more than a hopeless, hapless, inbred, thick, talentless, generic posh boy who's only got where he has because of his privileged background!' He suddenly looked thoughtful. 'Which makes me wonder why you chose politics rather than the much easier route of joining the BBC...' There was a moment's pause as he continued to look ponderous, and the Prime Minister did not know how to respond, before attempting to compose, then justify, himself.

'Well, your excellency, we will strive to have the Scots back under control by the end of the year. I apologise for my failure but, well, as you know I've lost my direction somewhat since the unfortunate death of Roderick...'

'Ah, yes,' said Dave McCreith, leaning back in his chair and moving his hands so that each finger touched the corresponding finger on the other hand. 'You speak, of course, of your former advisor, Roderick Hemmings. We all knew you were his puppet and nothing more. Of course, there was nothing unusual in that. But the difference was that, unlike previous Svengalis, he believed he held more power than he did. And, most unforgivably, he thought he could challenge the Corporation. I mean, correct me if I'm wrong but I believe it was he who suggested that... The BBC could be defunded...' Dave McCreith shook his head in disgust that anyone could ever have entertained such an idea.

'Yes, indeed, your grace,' replied the Prime Minister, rather shamelessly attempting to blame the previous attacks on the Corporation by his government almost entirely on his former advisor. 'It was all his idea to defund the BBC. I merely suggested that in times of austerity you might have wanted to consider making a few cuts here and there...'

'Cuts!' spluttered Dave McCreith, indignantly. 'How dare you accuse the BBC of not making cuts?! What about all the money we saved when we axed our complaints department and streamlined it into a single team of paramilitaries who identify the source of each complaint then pay them a visit in order to 'encourage' them to withdraw it?!'

'Of course, your excellence, entirely proving my belief that the Corporation needs neither advice nor interference from my government,' said the Prime Minister.

'I mean, do they think news and television should be free, like water?!' continued Dave McCreith, indignantly, before looked thoughtful for a moment. 'And on that topic, how are you progressing with the law allowing you to copyright the chemical formula for water, meaning you can charge whatever you like for it?'

'Yes, it's nearly finished, your grace!' replied the Prime Minister. 'Not long now!

'Good...' replied Dave McCreith. Then his face changed to a look of sympathy. 'Still, you know, it really was most... Unfortunate, what happened to your advisor, Roderick.'

'Yes, the accident...' agreed Horace Thompson, looking slightly scared.

'That's right. The accident...' said Dave McCreith slowly. He then paused for a moment, a pause that was rich with unspoken meaning. 'A very unfortunate accident. A shame they never found the person responsible.'

Horace Thompson avoided eye contact with Dave McCreith but nodded as if to show that he agreed with what he was being told even though they both knew it not to be true. 'Yes... The accident... Most... Unfortunate.'

(Also, please remember that I'm writing this in what, to you, is the future, with the intention of sending it back as a warning using unperfected experimental technology that could mean it ends up arriving in a different reality to my one. The point I'm making is that sometimes a brilliant piece of satire can look a bit out of date because the person it was satirising was kicked out of government before the book was published, but that doesn't mean it was any less clever. Also, in my reality there really is a government advisor called Roderick Hemmings, so if this book happens to end up in a different one where there's someone with a similar name, who may or may not still be in power, then that's just a coincidence.)

Dave McCreith glared at him and smiled menacingly. 'And, of course,' he continued, 'it's quite a coincidence that as a result of that unfortunate event your government then found itself entirely rudderless and you yourself have been incapable of making a single decision without Roderick Hemmings to tell you what to do and think.'

'Er, yes, indeed, your grace,' the Prime Minister replied, not entirely convincingly. 'In many ways it was fortunate that when the country collapsed into division and anarchy after years of tearing itself apart over just about every issue going, and with the government not strong enough to restore order, the Corporation revealed it had built up a small army of paramilitaries under the guise of them working as TV licence investigators, who were able to, er, restore law and order...'

'I would respectfully point out you are incorrect in that regard,' replied Dave McCreith, sternly. 'The BBC does *not* have a huge team of paramilitaries to carry out its every order. Those so-called 'BBC militiamen' are in fact subcontracted through private companies, meaning they are neither BBC employees nor have any direct connection to us, or at least none that can be proven in law, and any activities they happen to undertake that could be deemed heavy-handed, over-officious or murderous can simply be denied by the Corporation as something we neither knew about nor authorised. It also means we don't have to bother providing, say, sick pay or minor things like that, either.'

'Oh, right, yes, of course, your grace,' the Prime Minister corrected himself. 'I apologise if myself or my government has ever implied otherwise, as we sometimes struggle with the facts...'

'Facts? Facts?!' spluttered Dave McCreith. 'Why would the BBC be in any way concerned about facts?! What planet are you living on?'

'Er, no, your eminence, it wasn't meant as a criticism, it's just that sometimes we feel the Corporation can be rather harsh on us in government...'

Dave McCreith stared at the Prime Minister in disbelief at this accusation, but by continuing to stare at him seemed to be suggesting he should put forward his evidence. And he did.

'Er, well, it's just that you recently ran an episode of the Victoria Derbyshire programme where she interviewed a group of people living in the homeless camps that sprung up around this building after you carried out what you called 'slum clearances' in order to make space to build it, people who were already up their eyeballs in debt relating to unpaid licence fees, only to make endless claims about their poverty being the result of 'Tory-led austerity'!'

'Do you deny it was a contributory factor?!' demanded Dave McCreith, to which Horace Thompson had no immediate response, and there was another embarrassed pause before Dave McCreith continued. 'Anyway, it's not as if the media is ever genuinely hard on the government. We all know it's part of the BBC's remit to present the illusion of challenging the government whilst clearly doing nothing of the sort! You know the deal!'

'Hmm, I suppose I just preferred things the way they used to be,' the Prime Minister admitted, aware that he was expressing heresy by daring to voice such a sentiment.

'Oh, things haven't really changed that much!' Dave McCreith shot back. 'The BBC and the government have always enjoyed a cosy relationship, but the only difference is that whereas it was once the BBC that was the obedient lapdog of the government, it's now the other way around!'

The Prime Minister nodded, in acknowledgement that no one

could reasonably deny this. Dave McCreith paused for a moment, still looking annoyed, before continuing.

'I mean, an idiot could see that our supposed 'opposition' to the government was never anything more than a pose. Even when people use the whole Andrew Gilligan/dodgy dossier/WMD affair as an example of the BBC challenging the government they always blatantly fail to notice that if the BBC offered the *real* opposition to the government that we claim then that sort of thing would happen on a weekly or daily basis rather than just once in our entire history!'

'Yes, indeed, a sort of very public show of supposed disagreement to give the proles the impression of opposition,' the Prime Minister nodded.

'Indeed,' Dave McCreith replied. 'We have many such techniques at our disposal. The media gives the impression it's holding the government to account, by making shallow and toothless criticisms of it, but no one ever considers or even notices what an empty gesture that is when at the same time we brutally denounce anyone who disobeys or even dares to question the very laws and rules brought in by those exact same politicians we claim to be critical of! I mean, to pick a random example, you could look at how we ostensibly held the government to account over its lockdown laws yet at the same time attacked anyone who actually challenged them by depicting them as 'peddlers of hate' whose real motivation was racism and anti-EU sentiment!'

'Yes,' Horace Thompson admitted. 'Even I was confused at how people failed to notice that the BBC simultaneously claimed it was being critical of the government whilst conditioning its followers to attack and denounce anyone who dared challenge its actual policies.'

'Indeed,' concurred Dave McCreith. 'People simply failed to notice that we were claiming to be critical of the government whilst being one of the biggest supporters of the laws brought in by *that exact government!* And that was particularly amusing when you consider that the politicians who implemented those laws saw no reason to trouble themselves to actually obey the very rules they had brought in!'

Horace Thompson nodded in deference here, well aware that his many failings and personal indiscretions had frequently been played down or ignored by the Corporation, and that as a result he had much to be grateful for.

'I mean, there's another of our techniques at play there,' Dave McCreith continued, leading Terry Ball to ponder whether his attention had drifted away from the purpose of the meeting he was holding just so he could boast about just how proud he was of his organisation's nefarious methods. 'In a free and democratic society we've learnt that rather than actually censoring someone it's easier to humiliate them. Censorship can be a rallying cry, so if we wish to silence someone we simply make them a figure of fun instead. The sort of person that correct-thinking people should not listen to but mock! Why ban someone when you can simply train a small army of people to attack them on Twitter in a way that is neither original nor particularly amusing?! Much easier to rile up the proles against anyone who dares express an opinion of which we not approve!'

'Hmm, yes, I suppose it is easier now that the BBC controls the government and tells us exactly what to do,' conceded the Prime Minister, 'though it is odd that you continued to confuse the public by then objecting to new laws that the BBC itself has forced us to implement.'

'All part of our plan,' replied Dave McCreith, simply.

The Prime Minister made a sort of harrumphing noise that certainly doesn't mean he's based on a real-life Prime Minister, so I don't know why you'd even think that.

'Anyway,' continued Dave McCreith, finally turning to something actually relevant to the meeting, 'we want to do a fundraiser telethon type thing on poverty in the country of Africa, so we need you and your cronies at the World Bank to force the government of Africa to take on some huge loans with a massive interest rate that they can never hope to pay back, throwing them even further into poverty so we can then report on that, claim it's due to drought or guerrilla war or something, then get loads of BBC viewers to donate to it.'

'Africa? What a wonderful country! Piccaninny smiles, what, what!' replied Horace Thompson, attempting to alleviate the tension in the room by what he thought what a joke but was actually blatant racism. The real Prime Minister, who this one is definitely not based on, actually said that, so if he thinks he can sue me then he can do one. Anyway, I'm so woke that I don't even know what a piccaninny smile is.

Having been silent for ages, and certainly not because I just forgot to give him any dialogue, Terry Ball now spoke for the first time in a while.

'Er, do you think perhaps it could be accompanied by an in-depth and insightful examination of the history of Africa, looking at colonialism and its treatment by multinational organisations like banks and oil companies, along with the long-term reasons for it being in poverty like having unpayable amounts of debt levied on it, whilst studying the wider context of...?'

'No!' Dave McCreith snapped. 'The country of Africa is only ever to be depicted as a place where everybody lives in a mud hut, or a corrugated iron shack at best, and which is constantly in a state of poverty due to famines and wars! Do you want to confuse our audience by suggesting there's more to it, or just make them feel a bit sorry for Africa then feel better about themselves because they've donated to our charity collection, large amounts of which will end up lining the pockets of corrupt governments anyway!'

Whilst partly chastised, Terry Ball looked thoughtful once more and again spoke up. 'Er, sorry to correct you both but Africa's a continent, isn't it?'

The other two looked confused.

'Well, maybe from a strictly *factual* point of view it may or may not be,' replied Dave McCreith, defensively, 'but for our purposes, that is for the point of offering a desperately simplistic world view so we can encourage viewers to feel like they've made a difference without every troubling themselves to even start to attempt to understand the deeply complicated geopolitical...'

Terry Ball decided this was enough of an answer for him so uncharacteristically interrupted. 'Yes, a country, of course, your grace, my apologies for interrupting.'

'Hmm, well, anyway, I will require you to set about arranging that charity telethon I mentioned. Do all the usual stuff... Pictures of starving children and some Z-list celebrities saying how awful it is... Come up with a suitably vague and inane title, like 'Comedy Against Bad Things' or 'OMG, Help Save the Needy Children'... Source the cheapest sweatshops to manufacture the merchandise. And have the PR department prepare the necessary statements for when it's revealed all the merchandise for our charity telethon was made in said sweatshops, in which we claim we knew nothing about it and promise to do better in future.'

'At once, your grace,' replied Terry Ball.

'Good,' said Dave McCreith. 'And, naturally, collect the 'donations' to this worthy cause by taking money from people's bank accounts at the same time as we take their licence fee payments, with the Re-Education Camps for anyone who dares to object.'

'And I would assume that watching this eight-hour telethon will be mandatory?' asked Horace Thompson.

'Well, of course,' replied Dave McCreith, as if this was stupid question. 'I mean, the costs of putting on these events is immense, what with all the hotels, limos and catering for the stars involved, and their agents, and producers and social media teams, so we need to ensure we make at least thirty million if we're to cover those costs before we can even think about donating any of the additional proceeds to the charity in question.' He raised an eyebrow as he thought of an additional benefit. 'And it also means we know the entire population will be at home, and with the streets empty we can use the time to make... Changes.'

The precise nature of what he was referring to by these 'changes' was then left open, which I hope will be both tantalising and terrifying to you, the reader, as you ponder what he meant and at what point in the novel it will be explained.

'Of course, your grace,' said Terry Ball. 'I shall get all of this organised immediately.'

'Good,' replied Dave McCreith, before looking thoughtful as he decided upon their next topic. 'Hmm, well, I suppose we'll have to discuss that old mainstay of all our meetings... Law and Order...'

'Always a popular subject to really rile the public and make them easier to control!' agreed Horace Thompson.

'Indeed,' replied Dave McCreith, sounding a little bored. 'The statistic that usually works as a red rag to both sides of the political spectrum is that of the prison population. Ball, do you have the current figures?'

'Er, yes, of course, your grace,' replied Terry Ball, before looking on his organiser. 'Obviously we never make a written record of numbers for the most unforgivable heretics in the Black Ops Renditioning Camp in Manchester due to plausibility of denial, but the figure there is usually around five thousand, then just under two million for people either in prison for anti-BBC Thought-Crime, or undergoing Correct-Think rehabilitation in the Re-Education Camps, and we deliberately blur those numbers as the camps do not officially exist, then just *over* three million in the Isle of Wight Licence Fee Evaders Internment Camp...'

'Er, despite those impressive numbers,' said Horace Thompson, 'we're led to believe that the public sees us as weak on law and order.'

'How can nearly ten percent of the British population be incarcerated one way or another and the public still think you're weak on crime?' Dave McCreith demanded to know.

'Well, your grace,' replied the Prime Minister, 'there appears to be some disagreement as to whether having millions of people in prison means we're tough on crime because so many have been caught, or that we've failed on crime as so many people are clearly committing it... But, also, it would seem that significant numbers of the population do not actually consider non-payment of the BBC licence fee to be a 'crime' worthy of lifetime incarceration...'

'What?!' spluttered Dave McCreith. 'Who are these people? It sounds like they need to be locked up for anti-BBC Thought-Crime!'

'Er, well, of course, we do have their details,' said Horace Thompson, 'it's just that we're talking about twenty-odd million people here, so we simply lack the capacity to round them *all* up.'

'Well, at the moment, anyway,' replied Dave McCreith, slightly annoyed, 'though I do foresee a day when all anti-BBC heresy is punished!'

'Hmm, yes, of course, your grace,' said the Prime Minister, 'it's just that our opinion polls suggest the public does not agree with all the recent changes to law and order, particularly not with the recent statute, which you forced us to put through Parliament, that murder should no longer be counted as a proper crime, and should no longer be punishable by imprisonment. In particular, the public seems to feel that being made to go on a half-day 'murder awareness course' is insufficient punishment...'

'What are they talking about?!' spluttered Dave McCreith. 'That's not all that convicted murderers have to do! They have to write a two-page essay in which they ponder why their actions were wrong, and sign a form promising not to do it again! Anyway, we can't possibly expect to find room in prisons for perpetrators of minor crimes like murder. As a society I don't believe we can truly progress until we all agree that the only true crimes are those of licence fee evasion and anti-BBC Thought-Crime.'

'Well, obviously I do not challenge your assertion there, your excellency,' replied Horace Thompson, 'but do you not think there are at least one or two other things that should be classified as crimes, such as, oh, child abuse?'

Dave McCreith exploded at this point. 'We're the BBC! With our history on child abusers, do you really think that having them imprisoned is something we've ever cared about?!'

'Actually, your grace,' said Terry Ball, lifting his eyes from the report he was still perusing. 'This report *does* say there is an individual currently incarcerated after images of child abuse were discovered on his laptop.'

'Really?!' said Dave McCreith, in disbelief, as if such a thing was utterly inconceivable.

'Yes...' replied Terry Ball, before his expression showed he had uncovered the explanation. 'Oh, I see... His laptop was examined, and over ten thousand images of child abuse found, but following a more detailed inspection it was discovered that *not a single one* of those abusive images featured a child of colour. So it was for that he was found guilty.'

'Oh, right,' replied Dave McCreith, as if this were a perfectly rational explanation.

There was an awkward pause. After this continued for a few more moments they all stood up and walked around for a bit, to stretch their legs and break up a rather dialogue-heavy chapter.

'What's the news from America?' asked Dave McCreith, suddenly remembering a topic that had strangely been given no coverage.

'Not much, I'm afraid, my liege,' admitted Horace Thompson. 'Communications remain difficult as neither the internet nor the phones have been restored. But of course, we remain confident that the newly-elected president, President Prince Harry, will soon sort out the civil war and return the country to its former glories. Just as long as there's anyone left to rule because at the current rate that the MAGAs, and ANTIFAs and the BLMs are killing each other the population will probably be down to under ten million before the year's out.'

'Hmm, seeing as how they elected a president who's not only a foreign national but a member of the royal family, do you think it's a sign they're thinking of denouncing the Declaration of Independence and re-joining Britain?' asked Dave McCreith. 'Because then we'd be able to introduce the licence fee over there, providing us with some sorely-needed income.'

'It's hard to say, your excellency,' replied the Prime Minister, 'some reports we've managed to get hold of suggest the white supremacist opposition is making significant gains in the civil war and may depose him before the year is out.'

'Oh,' murmured Dave McCreith, seemingly having lost interest. 'Still, I don't know what I find odder: Prince Harry having become the President of the United States of America, or his main opposition coming from a white supremacist party led by Kanye West.'

'Well, I assume that he endeared himself to the white supremacists by having married a white woman, your grace.'

'Yes, in the messed up world of American politics that would seem to be as good an explanation as any.'

There was another pause before Horace Thompson's face lit up as he remembered something else.

'Oh, and I'm led to believe you dealt with the author of that heretical anti-BBC novel that was quite popular until we managed to suppress it?'

'Indeed,' replied Dave McCreith, with a slightly accusatory air. 'Did you read it?'

'Well, officially, no,' answered the Prime Minister, 'but then, of course, we all said that, but we all read it. I had particular reason to take issue with that loathsome work, as it depicted me as a bumbling, overweight, messy-haired, simple-minded woman called Doris Johnson! It turned me into a laughing stock!'

'Hmm I suppose 'Doris Johnson' sounds a *bit* like Horace Thompson, though clearly not close enough to be the grounds for legal action, even though that obviously must have been extremely hurtful for you,' replied Dave McCreith, in what sounds to me like a very strong legal argument. 'But, of course, our reasons for needing it banned were much more important than mere vanity. We needed to suppress that book for attacking a powerful state broadcaster whilst avoiding accusations of that being hypocritical seeing as how we're always banging on about the importance of press freedom in places like Russian and Saudi Arabia.'

'Well, of course, your grace! Only in a truly fascist dictatorship would a government or broadcaster launch legal action to ban a book simply for poking fun at those in power!' replied Horace Johnson, in what I think you'll agree is yet another very strong legal argument. Am I overdoing this whole thing about protecting myself from being sued? Well, better to be safe than sorry.

'Anyway,' continued Dave McCreith. 'My biggest concern was how he somehow seemed to know about some of our most secretive methods of controlling the population, including our greatest one: the Set Menu of Political Beliefs.'

'Ah, yes...' replied the Prime Minister. 'The Set Menu of Political Beliefs... The principle that at the age of around sixteen you must choose between two sets of beliefs, the liberal one or the right wing one, and then for the rest of your life that choice must dictate your view on every single topic in the world and not only must you blindly and obediently follow its dogma from that day on but the choice you make also completely defines you as a person. You must never question it, nor attempt to think for yourself. The system inexplicably means if you know what somebody thinks about, say, immigration, you will also know what they think about abortion, despite those being completely unrelated issues. We have never devised a better system for telling people what to think than that.'

'Indeed,' continued Dave McCreith. 'Of course, it was by utilising that system that we were able to easily polarise opinion regarding the EU referendum... As per the rules, once a new issue arose we simply had to decide what each group's 'opinion' on it would be, then programme them into blindly accepting it.'

Terry Ball raised an eyebrow here, as he had noticed that on several occasions his employer had pointed out that a lot of the meetings he held seemed to consist of little more than him providing long-winded, rambling exposition, only for him to go into yet another meeting and do exactly that, just as he was doing now. He also noticed just how often people, including himself, would 'raise an eyebrow' at something, then also raised an eyebrow at that.

'So despite membership of the EU undoubtedly being an extremely complicated issue,' continued Dave McCreith, his long and rambling exposition seemingly showing no signs of reaching a conclusion, 'touching on just about every aspect of our lives from defence budgets to the bendiness of bananas, we decided that those on the right should be anti-EU and those who followed the liberal agenda would be pro-EU. People who'd never even given the EU a second thought, and certainly wouldn't have said they were pro-EU as recently as 2014 all of a sudden thought it was a wonderful, caring, inclusive organisation that only a monster would want to leave. And anyone who dared criticise it, such as by questioning whether it was fair that some of the world's richest people, like the Queen or James Dyson, received millions of pounds a year in farming subsidies, was accused of simply using that argument as a front for their sickening racism!'

'Yes, we did a good job there, your grace!' replied Horace Thompson.

'You did not do a good job there!' screamed Dave McCreith. 'Your role was simple, and you failed! As with Scottish independence, the deal was that you offer a token referendum then we condition the public not to vote for it. But you kept changing your mind because you thought it would help your political ambitions! Your failure to adhere to those conditions is only one of the reasons that we, er, by which I mean, whoever killed your adviser Roderick Hemmings, did what they did!'

There was a pause as the Prime Minister attempted to work out whether this was an admission of guilt over the death of his advisor, but Dave McCreith did not give him long enough to properly ponder this and instead offered his conclusions on the author of the heretical text 'The Book The BBC Tried to BAN!'

'Anyway, he somehow identified the Set Menu of Political Beliefs as a system for social control, detailing it to readers of his pathetic book and alerting them to how they were being manipulated. Not only that but he revealed it as the method we employed in order to tear the country apart when we orchestrated the Great Terror, turning the country in upon itself by spreading mistrust, division and suspicion, tricking it into falling into a state of anarchy then using the ensuing chaos to seize control!'

'Yes, of course...' agreed the Prime Minister, questioning none of this, 'but, er, I understand you have dealt with him?' said Horace Thompson.

'Correct,' replied Dave McCreith, before adding, 'I can confirm he is no longer a problem,' but providing no further details. He paused for a moment. 'Hmm, well, I believe that concludes this week's business. Continue as instructed. And, as usual, we shall continue to support your government's efforts by assuring the public there's nothing odd in a political system that ostensibly gives everyone of voting age a say in things whilst never failing to return an Eton-educated, impossibly privileged government whose every action is in support of Big Business, with anyone who dares to question the system denounced! Unless, of course, that system of democracy returns a result we do not agree with, in which case it's a deeply flawed system for giving a vote to people who didn't go to university, so didn't know what they were voting for and by extension of that must have had their minds warped by propaganda. Democracy is sacrosanct and the decision of the electorate must always be respected, unless it's the wrong decision, in which case we must do everything in our power to reverse it!'

'Indeed, your grace,' replied the Prime Minister, 'and we remain deeply grateful for you continuing to support the obvious puppet show that is our parliamentary democracy.'

'Hmm,' replied Dave McCreith, as if this was so obvious as to not even need saying. 'Actually, I do have one more idea, though we'll discuss it in more detail some other time. Basically, I feel the party political system we've had for decades is too confusing for the proles and needs simplifying. My plan is that we rename the Tories 'the Nasty Party' and combine Labour and the Liberal Democrats into 'the Nice Party', which also removes the confusion of having three parties, as it's much easier to play them off against each other when there are only two.'

Doris Johnson, er, I mean Horace Thompson, looked a bit confused at this but Dave McCreith continued anyway.

'Then what we'll do is basically support one of these parties for around twelve years at a time before switching our support to the other, controlling which one gets elected by conditioning and manipulating the mood of the population. So when we want the proles to vote for the Nice Party we'll run lots of positive stories about the economy and when we want them to vote for the Nasty Party we'll get them really mad with endless stories about immigration. It's essentially what we do already, but in a more simplified form.'

'Oh, I see,' replied the Prime Minister, now understanding this. 'Yes, an excellent idea, your grace.'

'Of course it is,' replied Dave McCreith, as if this went without saying. 'Well, I believe we've covered everything, so you may be on your way.'

The Prime Minister dropped to one knee and bowed. 'As ever, you humble and honour me by granting me this weekly audience, and I continue to be your obedient and unquestioning servant, and thank you again for your continued support in keeping us in power.'

'Hmm, yes,' replied Dave McCreith, 'but it's actually more convenient from our perspective to have a Conservative government in power. I mean, it's much easier to go on about how wonderful a particular world view is when you know there's little chance of the government ever implementing any of it, and presenting the illusion that we're critical of the government is much simpler when it's the awful Tories rather than a centrist, liberal party whose views on everything are identical to ours.'

'Of course, your excellency,' said Horace Thompson, continuing to bow as he left the room.

# Chapter Seventeen:

# An Inquisition That Most People Expected

*In Which Our Heroes Pass Through the Pleasant Riverside Suburb of Richmond and Witness Public Show Trials and Executions for Such Anti-BBC Thought-Crime as Cultural Appropriation for Eating a Potato, Because Potatoes Were Stolen From the Native Americans, Daring To Remember A Licence Fee Advert In Which David Walliams Blacked Up As Craig David And Sickening Transphobia By Using the Term 'A Wolf In Sheep's Clothing', As That Implies That A Wolf That Identifies As a Sheep Isn't Actually A Sheep*

We now re-join our heroes on their desperate quest to reach New White City and attempt to at least try to do something about the unchallengeable, unquestionable monolith that is the BBC even though they know that the chances of them somehow making the slightest dent in its power are all but non-existent. So, a lost cause? We shall see.

But I digress. Having come up along the river via Kingston, Petersham and Twickenham, avoiding any main roads, our heroes now approached civilisation for the first time in a while and knew they needed to be careful. As they reached the bottom of Richmond Hill they were aware they were entering a heavily-populated area, one that did not seem to have suffered the decimating effects of so many parts of the country during the war.

'We need to be careful,' said Emmeline Moneypenny. 'Lots of BBC people live here. It's a long way from any poor people, it's scenic, by the river... This is one of the most well-off parts of London, so I would imagine it's still heavily populated, with many of the inhabitants being BBC Inner Party members.'

They continued cautiously, keeping their eyes open and their ears attuned for the sound of BBC vans or anyone who could conceivably be suspicious or on the lookout for them. They passed under the bridge and continued along the river, when Emmeline Moneypenny stopped.

'Hmm... It's just a thought, but we can both save time and avoid the main riverside path and main roads by cutting across the green then going through Old Deer Park then Kew Gardens. It's more direct as well as offering us more directions to flee in should we be pursued.'

None of the others really knew the area, so took her at her word that this was correct and the best way to go. I'm assuming that's true of most readers, too. I mean, it's more or less true. They nodded their assent and she continued. 'There's a short cut just this way,' she said, pointing to the right. 'We cut through a kind of Tudor type courtyard that's usually pretty quiet, then across the green.'

Again, without objection, the others followed her, and they did indeed find themselves in a Tudor type courtyard area. Look, my skills of describing things seem to have deserted me but you can just go on Google Maps and look at it. That will also serve to prove that the shortcut is valid, too. So, as they made their way through this shortcut, underneath some sort of archway thing, Emmeline Moneypenny suddenly stopped in her tracks and raised a finger as if to say the others should also stop, and do it silently. She listened for a moment before turning to them.

'Something's happening. Do you hear it?'

Eyes and ears were strained again, and it became apparent that there was a commotion on the green.

'What should we do?' asked John Smith.

'I'm not sure we have a choice,' replied Emmeline Moneypenny. 'I think it's the BBC Inquisition Trials.'

The others looked at her, worried.

'I've heard of them,' said John Smith, 'but never seen them.'

'Well, they're less common since the war. They tend to put them on only in areas that are still densely populated, and there aren't many of those left. Well, they call them 'trials'... But the people in question had their guilt decided long ago. It's just for public show.'

'What should we do?' asked Jeffrey Harding.

'If anyone sees us obviously turning back as if to avoid them then they'll suspect something,' said Emmeline Moneypenny. 'I think our only choice is to carry on this way. We may even have to watch them, and appear to be joining in, just to avoid arousing suspicion.'

The rest of the group looked at each other but could see there was no alternative.

'Just look like you agree with it, and it's normal,' Emmeline Moneypenny advised them, 'and we should be okay.'

She continued walking, up through the sort of archway thing, across the road, and to the edge of the green.

Richmond Green is a large, open space, surrounded by plush houses, a theatre, a number of pubs and I think there's a solicitor's or something there too. Again, you can look on Google Street View. This makes it an excellent place for public spectacles. I would imagine that in the olden days they did witch trials there, though don't quote me on that. But the sight greeting our heroes was surely much the same as they would have found if they had stumbled upon such a witch trial, back in 1954 or whenever it was they last did them. A scaffold had been erected. A gallows was on top of it. To the side were a number of condemned prisoners. However, before their execution they were clearly going to be subjected to a final public humiliation. A medium-sized team of BBC paramilitaries was clearly in charge. And a crowd had gathered, though it was hard to tell whether their presence was entirely voluntary, or whether they were there out of fear that their absence could have counted against them and meant that a future such spectacle could include them as the main attraction. The air was thick with fear, but it was a strange mix of fear emanating from the condemned prisoners and the fear coming from the audience who were well aware that being seen as insufficiently enthusiastic about the proceedings they were witnessing could mean it would be their turn next.

'We need to get close enough to look like we're watching, but far enough away to both not be recognised and be able to escape via a path at the top of the green,' Emmeline Moneypenny explained. Following her lead, they all made their way to the fringes of the group of perhaps two hundred people who had gathered to witness the proceedings.

After a few moments a man was dragged up the steps of the scaffold and a rope was placed around his neck. The lead paramilitary took out a clipboard and read out the charge.

'James Andrews,' he said, in a powerful, loud voice. 'You have been found guilty of a tweet, made in May of this year, when you suggested it was hypocritical of the BBC to have banged on about how monstrous it is for white people to black themselves up in order to play people of colour in comedy sketches, whilst also having run an advert in the year 2007 in which David Walliams donned brown make up to portray the mixed-race singer Craig David as part of a BBC TV licence campaign!'

'But he did!' protested the prisoner, as the hangman tightened the noose. 'I even found the clip on YouTube!'

'Oh, I remember that one,' said John Smith, to Emmeline Moneypenny, who was standing next to him, 'of course it was on the BBC but it was during one of the many times when blacking up was fine...' Emmeline Moneypenny vigorously shook her head as if to tell him not just to stop speaking but to stop thinking, as there was no place for such a seditious act here.

'You are incorrect!' yelled the lead paramilitary. 'The clip you think you saw actually featured Ant McPartlin donning the monstrous likeness, as part of a campaign for the licence fee for the Great Enemy, ITV!'

'But ITV doesn't even have a licence fee!' screamed the prisoner. 'It couldn't have been for them!'

'You are incorrect!' yelled the paramilitary again. 'The only truth is BBC Correct-Think, and you shall pay for your heresy!'

A lever was pulled and the trapdoor upon which the condemned man was standing fell open, causing him to drop through the hole, and his neck to snap with a sound comparable to someone breaking a stick of rhubarb. I mean, I imagine it sounds something like that, doesn't it? A sharp crack, maybe? Actually, you're not going to know any more than I do, so I'm sticking with that. And if you say I've made a very poor effort in researching the minor details in this book, I'd counter that accusation by saying no-one wants to have 'what sound does it make when someone is hanged?' in their Google search history, and also by how accurate the route they're taking is, which I've already said you can check and confirm using a much less alarming Google search.

Another prisoner was walked up the stairs to the top of the scaffold. At this point the group was surprised to hear a voice scream 'hang the traitor!' and turn around to see it came from Emmeline Moneypenny. She nodded at them, encouraging them to similarly get behind the ruthless spectacle. After a moment, the others found themselves, uncertainly at first, voicing similar denunciations of the condemned man, whose face was a mask of fear. 'There's been a mistake!' he insisted. 'I haven't done anything!'

The lead paramilitary glared at him, then glanced down at the charge on his clipboard. 'Our records suggest otherwise. According to this you were found guilty of the sickening hate crime of cultural appropriation.'

'Cultural appropriation isn't even a thing!' protested the condemned man. 'There's no consistency in how it's applied! People get accused of it for wearing particular clothes or listening to certain types of music! And how come the BBC on one hand tirelessly promotes so-called 'multiculturalism' only to then viciously denounce anyone who tries to experience another culture as having committed 'cultural appropriation'?!'

'We work for the BBC, so don't think outdated and quaint principles such as 'logic' and 'common sense' will work on us!' replied the paramilitary. 'According to this record, on the 4th of June, you were apprehended...'

'Yes, coming out of my local Chinese takeaway, the same one I've been going to every Friday for the last twenty five years!' shouted the prisoner, only compounding his guilt.

'So you admit not only to the charge for which you have been found guilty, but to having committed the same crime for an entire quarter century?!' spluttered the paramilitary, in disbelief.

'Well, eating food from a different culture isn't cultural appropriation!' exclaimed the man.

'As you said, it was from a 'different culture'!' replied the paramilitary, 'so it precisely fits the definition!'

'So you're saying all that Anglo-Saxon people are allowed to eat is meat and potatoes?' the prisoner protested, without realising he was making things even worse for himself.

'You admit to having eaten potatoes?' asked the paramilitary, triumphantly. 'The potato was stolen by Walter Raleigh from the Native Americans, so that's *another* case of cultural appropriation to which you have just confessed!'

'This isn't fair!' protested the man, with the certainty that there was nothing he could do to avoid his fate so he might as well give a good account of himself.

'It is entirely fair!' replied the paramilitary. 'We subjected you to a full DNA test following your arrest, which revealed your ancestry as including West African, Hungarian, Serbo-Croat, Australian Aborigine... But not a single strand of Chinese... So you are guilty!'

Before the man could protest any more the paramilitary had nodded to his colleague controlling the lever, who quickly pulled it, dispatching the man to a swift death.

John Smith shuddered, but again forced himself to clap excitedly. 'Hang the heretic!' he yelled, even though a sick feeling in the pit of his stomach told him what he was doing was truly repellent. 'Hang the traitors! The BBC will prevail!'

He screamed this last line with such gusto that his friends all looked at him in concern, before realising such action could open them up to accusations of heresy, so quickly joined in the chorus of 'hang the heretic!', 'hang the anti-BBC thought criminals!' and so on.

A woman was now brought on stage for the first time. It seemed that this briefly affected the mood of the crowd, though they quickly regained their gusto for denouncing the traitors brought in front of them, as if aware that any drop in their enthusiasm levels could leave them open to accusations of sympathising with them. As the noose was placed around her neck the lead paramilitary read the charge from his clipboard.

'You used to be a journalist,' he said. A single person in the crowd booed, only to instantly stop when he realised no one else had joined him. The paramilitary looked into the crowd suspiciously but, unable to isolate the source of the voice, continued. 'Which is normally a noble and unquestionable profession... However, in an article dated the 4th of August this year, you wrote an article in which you used the phrase 'a wolf in sheep's clothing'.'

'It's a commonly used phrase,' replied the woman, defensively.

'It *was* a commonly used phrase in a less civilised, more hate-filled time!' replied the paramilitary, furiously. 'But using the phrase 'a wolf in sheep's clothing' suggests that a wolf that identifies as a sheep is not automatically a sheep, therefore making it an act of vile transphobia for which you cannot be forgiven!'

The woman opened her mouth to respond but before she could do so the lead paramilitary had nodded to the man controlling the lever, and the journalist was silenced forever.

Anyway, you get the idea. A string of people were brought onto the scaffold and had their charges of anti-BBC Thought-Crime and anti-BBC heresy read out to them, and whilst some of them tried to defend themselves it didn't make any difference and they were swiftly dispatched. Next, a sad-looking man was brought onto the scaffold and had the noose placed around his neck, with an expression suggesting any zest for life he had ever had had been squeezed out of him years ago and, oh, hang on, you don't squeeze the zest out, do you? You squeeze the juice out, and scrape the zest off. Oh well, you still get the point. Anyway, it looked like the juice of life had been scraped off him, oh, I've got it the wrong way round again. Look, the point is that it looked like he'd lost any interest in life even before the war, and no longer cared about anything. I don't need to fill this book with metaphors and similes. The power of the story is enough. The lead paramilitary again checked his clipboard.

'Non-payment of the licence fee,' he announced. The man just looked slightly mournful, saying nothing and nodding. The paramilitary paused a moment, as if expecting him to be as troublesome as the other prisoners, but after realising the prisoner clearly just wanted to get it over with, he simply nodded to the paramilitary who was controlling the lever, which was pulled and quickly dispatched the man to what appeared to be a welcome death.

John Smith looked a bit confused. 'I'm a bit confused,' he said, though quietly enough for only his friends to hear. 'So, some people are sent to the Isle of Wight prison camp for non-payment of the licence fee, yet some appear to be publically executed, and some supposed Thought Criminals, like us, get sent to the camps? How does it work?!'

'Well, I wouldn't question it too much,' replied Barry Begbie. 'I mean, society's pretty lawless now, and I can't imagine BBC heads are too bothered about the rules being applied fairly and equally everywhere. In fact, I reckon they quite happily turn a blind eye to the paramilitary gangs dealing with things themselves even if they don't particularly follow the rules. In fact, I've heard the paramilitaries are outsourced to independent contractors, not only so that they can pay millions in consultancy fees to their mates who run the companies in question, but so they can claim the actions of the death squads have nothing to do with them as they're technically not directly employed by the BBC. Anyway, if it wasn't for the rules being applied inconsistently then we could have been executed rather than being sent to the camp, in which case none of this would have happened, so I say we don't get too bogged down in the details.'

John Smith raised an eyebrow as if to say he thought this was an entirely reasonable suggestion. Also, I should add that there are three nooses set up on the scaffold, so once a prisoner has been executed the next hanging I describe takes place on the next one along, and during this the corpse from the previous one is removed and the noose and trapdoor from that one reset, okay?

Another woman was brought forward and the noose placed around her neck. The head paramilitary checked the charge and read it aloud. 'You are hereby charged that in a tweet concerning your failure to obtain tickets to see the pop star Harold Styles live in concert you complained about the practice of 'ticket scalping', which was, of course, a sickeningly racist term as you seem to be comparing your problems to the Native American practice of slicing the top of their vanquished foes' heads off as trophies, a practice that never happened anyway because all pre-colonial societies were peaceful and lived in harmony and had never even heard of war until Europeans arrived!'

'What?!' spluttered the woman. 'Even by reading the charge aloud there you contradicted...'

The lever was pulled.

Another condemned man was dragged onto the scaffold and had a noose put around his neck. The head paramilitary again read the charges, more quickly this time, as if trying to get through the execution quicker before because he wanted to get home in time for his tea or to watch EastEnders or something. 'Kenneth Wilson, you have been found guilty of anti-BBC heresy on too many counts to list and are sentenced to death!'

The lever was pulled and the man dropped through the trapdoor, his neck snapping whilst he was in the middle of saying 'but my name's actually Mike...'

Emmeline Moneypenny had been carefully watching both the crowd, to ensure it was fully concentrating on the executions, and the BBC paramilitaries, to ensure they were all occupied in dealing with the remaining prisoners one way or another. Sensing an opportunity, she turned to the others. 'Now!' she hissed, nodding her head in the direction via which they could escape and, following her lead, they casually started to walk away.

Still cheering and applauding the brutality, our heroes continued carefully around the execution scene, across the green to a small pathway on the far northwest side, which they followed through, and which led them to a car park. They carried on walking, basically, via the route they earlier mentioned. I should probably have concluded this chapter by focusing on the general monstrousness of the public executions they had witnessed, not on them walking through a car park, now I think about it.

# Chapter Eighteen:

# Instilling the 'Propa' Opinions

*In Which It Is Finally Confirmed That the BBC Covertly Controls the Weather, a Meeting with the Head of Dark Propaganda is Held Regarding the Most Secret and Fiendish of the BBC's Foul Machinations and the Threat of the 'Minging Community' is Neutralised*

Dave McCreith looked down in disgust at the camp that surrounded New White City. 'I mean, this really is unacceptable...' he said, partly to himself, though Terry Ball heard this and looked up. 'I mean, why do they have to congregate *right outside* our shiny new headquarters and make the place look so, well... Disgusting?'

Terry Ball stood up and walked over to the window. 'Well, your grace, we did destroy the housing of many thousands of people in order to build this, so I think a lot of them had nowhere else to go.'

'What?! Well, I don't see what they're complaining about. Sure, we made tens of thousands of people homeless in order to build our headquarters, but we did interview a few of them when the Victoria Derbyshire show did a hand-wringing special feature on the perils of being poor and homeless in London today.'

'Indeed we did, your excellency, and it was most noble and gracious of you to commission it!' replied Terry Ball. 'But, and this is obviously not intended as a criticism, with so much of London now reduced to rubble after the war, this is one of the few places they can get close to electric lighting, plus the feral gangs usually don't come around here because it's so well protected. Plus there's the weather, too.'

Dave McCreith looked at him, confused, awaiting clarification.

'Well, the weather, your grace. Didn't you ever wonder why it never rains on this building?'

'Well...' Dave McCreith pondered this. 'I always assumed it was because on some level the weather obeys my command, but are you now telling me that's not the reason?'

'Almost, but not quite, your grace. This building is so high as to reach the clouds, and the reason for that is the scientists who helped design it had worked out that if the building were tall enough to actually touch the ionosphere then we would be able to control the weather. It's immensely useful, and we were able to justify it in budgetary terms by pointing out that if we had full control of the weather we'd finally be able to provide an accurate weather forecast for the first time in the Corporation's history, rather than just completely guessing and getting it wrong over and over again.'

Dave McCreith looked thoughtful, as if this was something he had never pondered before. 'Oh, I see... So our weather forecasts have been completely and utterly accurate ever since then?'

'Er, well, give or take,' conceded Terry Ball. 'I believe they're right about three quarters of the time.'

Dave McCreith again looked thoughtful, briefly wondering how the BBC could control the weather yet still not accurately predict it, but brushed this off, assuming that the department in question was headed up by someone with an impeccable background but no intelligence, as was usually the case. 'So you're telling me we can control the weather?'

'Indeed, your grace!' replied Terry Ball, cheerfully. 'Which is doubly advantageous! Not only does it mean our forecasting is slightly more accurate, but it means that we can manipulate the public mood! If, say, we want the public to be angry in order to get their support for a government bill, we make sure it rains all through July. If we want to control the type of people who vote on Election Day, we make it warm and dry or cold and wet accordingly, if, say, we do or don't want old people to go out and vote.'

'Hmm, I suppose I can see the sense in some of that,' conceded Dave McCreith.

'But that's not all, your eminence!' continued Terry Ball. 'Let's say some people want to protest in Trafalgar Square. If it's a group that we support, and who we want to portray in a good light we make sure the weather is good. If, however, it's a group expressing ideas and opinions that oppose BBC Correct-Thought, such as, well, pretty much any working class white people, such as those we suspect of having supporting Brexit, we make it rain torrentially, not only discouraging people from turning up, but so that those who do turn up are more likely to be in a bad mood so the police can claim they were looking violent and turn on them, and also so that the footage we show of them depicts them sodden, miserable and a bit pathetic-looking!'

Dave McCreith looked fairly impressed. 'Hmm, I suppose that does seem like a good idea. What was the cost of this project?'

Terry Ball looked briefly thoughtful, then took out his smartphone and looked up the details. 'Oh, your excellency, it was a bargain! On top of the original building costs for this building, just another two billion pounds!'

'Oh well, it's not as if we don't have money to throw around,' replied Dave McCreith, 'and, in any case, huge, wasteful projects like that are always useful if we need evidence of why we should double the licence fee more than twice in a single week.'

There was a pause. Then Dave McCreith looked confused again. 'Hang on, weren't we talking about why all that riff-raff is camped outside our headquarters? What does that have to do with the weather?'

'Oh, it's simple, your grace,' replied Terry Ball. 'We naturally use the technology to ensure it never rains or goes under a balmy twenty five degrees in the area immediately surrounding New White City. Even in January. I can only imagine that the residents of the displacement camp down there noticed that, and that's why they've never moved on.'

Dave McCreith looked annoyed again. 'But we can control this, you say?'

Terry Ball's expression suggested he assumed this was common knowledge. 'But of course, your grace,' he replied. 'Here, let me show you.'

Terry Ball took out his smartphone and opened an app. 'Ah, here we, your lordship! It's actually quite simple. Look!'

Terry Ball handed his phone to Dave McCreith. 'You see, you

simply select the area, then choose the temperature and type of weather. Anything you like!'

Dave McCreith looked at the app carefully, then pressed a few things. Immediately snow started to fall down by the window, and towards the camp many hundreds of metres below. Dave McCreith raised an eyebrow. 'Interesting...' he said. He then changed the settings and a powerful rainstorm started to pound down. He leaned forward to see how much of the camp he could make out, and saw people running around, distressed and confused. He smiled and turned to Terry Ball. 'And thunderstorms?'

'Of course, your grace,' said Terry Ball, and opened something on the app. Dave McCreith smiled even deeper, the sort of deranged grin of someone about to inflict great suffering on his fellow human beings, and relishing every moment of it. He pressed some things on the app and moments later a huge lightning bolt had torn through the sky, hurtling down and crashing into the middle of the camp. Even from their position far above it, the screams were audible. Mad with power, Dave McCreith repeated the trick. And again. And again. He started to cackle maniacally as he heard more screams emanating from below. Terry Ball looked somewhat worried.

'Er, your grace, we wouldn't want to risk the stability and integrity of our building...'

Dave McCreith looked annoyed, like a spoilt child being told he was having his favourite toy taken away from him as punishment. Noticing this, Terry Ball attempted to console him, whilst gently taking his phone back.

'Look, your grace, I'm sure you'll be allowed to play with it again tomorrow.'

An alert then sounded on his phone and he looked at it, then frowned. Dave McCreith glared at him expectantly. 'Well, what is it?'

'Well, your grace, it would appear that following the freak weather conditions you just brought about, a good half of BBC staff are now complaining that having to go to work when it's raining is an infringement of their human rights and could trigger their anxiety, so are requesting, well, *demanding*, the right to work from home if the temperature goes under, or over, twenty two degrees, or if it's expected to rain at any point in the next week.'

'Hang on, they didn't *unionise*, did they?!' Dave McCreith spluttered.

'Well, no, of course not, my liege. We had all the union leaders fatally 'cancelled' during the Great Re-Structuring, remember?' Terry Ball assured him.

'Yes, and quite right too,' replied Dave McCreith. 'Well, obviously here at the BBC we take mental health very seriously. So issue an internal memo saying we take their concerns very seriously and will immediately launch an inquiry into the plausibility of their suggestion, and then collect the names of everyone who complained and have every tenth person publically hanged, and their bodies left to rot outside the main entrance.'

'Very good, your excellency, I'll see that it's done,' confirmed Terry Ball. Dave McCreith looked thoughtful.

'Oh, and set up a task force to ostensibly look into their concerns. Obviously it won't actually do that but if we set it up I can get four or five of my friends on it as advisors, plus also claim another two hundred grand a year in consultancy fees for being involved.'

'Yes, your grace, I'll sort it out...' Terry Ball hesitated before continuing. 'There is just one thing, your grace...?'

'Yes?!' replied Dave McCreith, impatiently.

'Well, my liege, I'm obviously not questioning your authority where having employees killed is concerned, it's just that, well... We're the BBC, not Tesco or somewhere. By having a tenth of those who complained killed you risk executing people from wealthy and powerful families, and as such could make some powerful enemies.'

Dave McCreith looked annoyed, yet also as if he was conceding there was something in this. 'Hmm, very well. Okay, as a warning, we'll only dispense with the least important workers, so make sure you only execute the BBC employees who neither went to public school nor Oxbridge.'

Terry Ball looked quizzical. 'Both of them, your grace?'

Dave McCreith nodded sadistically. 'Yes... Though just for clarity, when I referred to BBC employees who didn't got to private school or Oxbridge I was only referring to the proper, salaried employees, not the lift attendants and toilet cleaners.'

'Of course, your grace. I'll have their bodies on public display by lunchtime.'

'Good!' answered Dave McCreith. 'Well, I think it's been a most productive day! What time is it? Eleven o'clock! Well, I think it's time for lunch!'

'Er, just a moment, your grace,' interrupted Terry Ball.

'Yes? What is it?!' replied Dave McCreith, annoyed.

'Well, my liege,' you do actually have a meeting booked in for a few minutes' time,' replied Terry Ball.

'What?! Aren't you in charge of my diary? What were you thinking?! I'll probably collapse from overwork at the rate we're going and then you'll have blood on your hands.'

'Yes, of course, my apologies, your grace, but this is a fairly important meeting. It's with the BBC Head of Propaganda.'

Dave McCreith looked thoughtful at this. 'Hang on... Didn't I already meet with him? The gentleman who works in Human Resources, the department that harvests organs for use by senior BBC executives?'

'Ah, no, your grace, I do recall that meeting, but that was actually with the head of *PR*, which you will recall stands for 'plausible revisionism'. His department deals with the more public face of BBC propaganda, whilst the gentleman you're meeting today is in charge of the much more secretive Dark Propaganda department, which is to say all the things we actually believe rather than what we present to the public. So you'll be discussing longer term strategy including the next steps in the Corporation's Great Agenda.'

'Hmm, very well,' replied Dave McCreith. 'Still, I have to admit to being utterly confused. There seem to be dozens if not hundreds of departments and roles within this organisation that have names every bit as pointless and meaningless as the departments themselves.'

'Well, yes, your grace, but that's because of the edict you issued as the first act of business upon you ascending to the role of Director General,' Terry Ball pointed out, helpfully.

'Well, yes, of course. At the time I issued that edict I actually knew of three people who *didn't* have some form of tokenistic role within the BBC that allowed them to draw a six-figure salary without ever actually doing anything, so I had to remedy that!'

'Yes, your excellency, and a very good thing too,' said Terry Ball. 'So, anyway, it's the Head of Dark Propaganda you're meeting with today. A Mr Kevin Goebbels.'

'Goebbels, eh?' said Dave McCreith, thoughtfully. 'Any relation to the great man?'

'I don't believe so, your grace,' replied Terry Ball. 'His origins are a bit of a mystery. I mean, I don't believe he attended private school or Oxbridge...' – Dave McCreith looked at him in horror at this admission – 'but I believe he made quite a name for himself in the world of advertising before, as so many of his kind do, moving over so that his unique skills of manipulating the public could be put to use beyond simply making them buy things.'

Dave McCreith continued to look concerned about the details of this man he was due to meet. 'Hmm, well I suppose you'd better hold off that execution order I issued, just in case. But, hang on... How did such a person reach such an exalted position?! Surely he didn't become successful based on *talent* as opposed to privilege and nepotism?'

'Well, not exactly, your grace,' countered Terry Ball, 'as whilst he did not attend private school or Oxbridge it would still be inaccurate to suggest his success was based on talent, as he previously worked in advertising, where the average working day consists of half an hour skimming the internet to decide which YouTube clips are going to be stolen and turned into TV ads, and the rest of the time snorting industrial quantities of cocaine.'

At that exact moment there was a knock on the door. Terry Ball opened it and behind it stood Kevin Goebbels, the BBC's Head of Dark Propaganda. He looked like a typical adman: slick, slimy and amoral. Instead of dropping to his knees and taking Dave McCreith's hand to kiss upon entering the room he pointed both his fingers at the confused Director General and made a clicking noise by way of greeting, as if they were old friends. Dave McCreith stared blankly in disbelief at this insolence, forcing Terry Ball to break the ice.

'Ah, your grace, this is Kevin Goebbels, head of the BBC's Dark Propaganda Department.'

'Davey Boy!' said Kevin Goebbels, stunning the beleaguered Dave McCreith even further, and extending his hand, which the DG was still too confused to do anything other than robotically shake it.

'Head of Propaganda! And the reason we call it 'propaganda' is because it instils the 'proper' opinions!' said Kevin Goebbels, with Dave McCreith still far too baffled to work out whether this was his genuine opinion or intended as a joke. 'Have a 'ganders' at that!' he added. Dave McCreith slowly began to regain his composure and soon realised that he did not like this man. He stank of new money.

Extremely new money. Having been in his company for no more than a few seconds, Dave McCreith could already tell that he was from working class stock, that his father probably ran a market stall in the East End and that he had almost certainly got his start in dealing stocks or advertising, the sort of places where a brash, cocky personality could effortlessly compensate for a lack of intelligence or basic common sense. An adman through and through. And whilst Dave McCreith had no issue whatsoever with people rising to exalted positions without possessing the qualities of intelligence or common sense, he did have a problem with people who did it without coming from a wealthy privileged background and with an expensive education.

Hang on, thought Dave McCreith. If he really is a former Cockney barrow boy, how is his name explained away? As his shock started to subside he noticed how odd this was. Either he genuinely was descended from Nazi war criminals but had inexplicably not chosen to even attempt to disguise this, and if that were true then he was obviously not descended from Cockney stock, or he had actually chosen the name as some kind of professional nom-de-plume, perhaps deliberately choosing a name that would shock people, like some punk singer, or because he had cynically calculated that if he wanted to succeed in the world of PR and advertising then being seen as having descended from, or at least being inspired by, a famous Nazi propagandist would prove deeply beneficial. Dave McCreith was confused again. This man must have assumed the name of a notorious war criminal because he knew that in the deeply amoral world of PR it would actually help him to rise within the ranks.

(So, perhaps you're wondering why this character has been given a name when so many others were referred to throughout as simply 'the Head of PR' or the 'Head of Comedy'. Hmm, well, I think I was just trying to make a point about how many of the dark techniques pioneered by Nazi propagandists, a group very much frowned upon these days by the so-called 'PC Brigade', were influenced by modern PR and advertising. Also, once again, I need to clarify that this character is not based on a real person, in either my reality or the one this book may end up accidentally being sent back to, okay? I mean, he really isn't. But then, of course, none of them are...

Also, if you're wondering why Dave McCreith sometimes knows

so much about a particular BBC department to the point of delivering lengthy exposition on its activities whilst at other times hasn't even heard of them, well, it's partly explained away by there being so many of them, some of which seem to do nothing and some of which seem to overlap with other ones, and partly to do with how you'll know if you've ever worked in a company that the people at the top, or anywhere near the top, never have more than an extremely vague idea about what individual departments, people and teams below them actually do. Also, remember how some characters have discussed rumours that he slips in and out of lucidity, and some people think he's going mad from tertiary syphilis? Well, maybe it's that too. Essentially, what I'm saying is that rather than being lazy writing this is actually rather clever character development and a brilliant narrative device, okay?!)

'Right, yes, propaganda,' said Dave McCreith, thoughtfully, clearly still struggling to identify the specific department from which his visitor came. 'Obviously with that being one of the Corporation's main aims there are a number of departments with a remit based on that...' His face suddenly lit up as he realised the misunderstanding. 'Oh, wait, *Dark* Propaganda! You're *that* department!'

'Yes, we're actually the oldest department in the entire Corporation,' Kevin Goebbels explained. 'We've been pulling the strings from the very beginning, dating right back to when the BBC Elders decided the best way to subtly take control of the country was to do so in the guise of a broadcaster rather than a political party, as that way no one would ever suspect them, even though they'd have an immense amount of power and influence over every aspect of the public's life without them really noticing.'

'Oh, you seem quite well-versed in Corporation lore for a newcomer,' observed Dave McCreith, not entirely sure whether he thought this was a good thing.

'Cheers, Dave, but I like to do my research!' replied Kevin Goebbels. 'Plus the department I head up is one where I need to know everything, so I was fast-tracked into being a high-level BBC Initiate quicker than usual. Of course, it was the original, highly secretive manifesto, The Clandestine Charter of the BBC Elders, setting out in great detail our plan for the country over the next hundred years, The Plan for the BBC Century, which was regrettably made public when the traitor George Orwell published it as a so-called novel, '1984'.'

'Oh, yes,' replied Dave McCreith, as he recalled this notorious incident from the BBC's history. 'You know, the usual explanation for that is that when George Orwell was a mere low-ranking BBC employee, and therefore not an Initiate who was privy to our Great Agenda, he discovered a copy of it in the toilets at Broadcasting House and, assuming it was some sort of joke, maybe a prank someone had written for a Christmas party, used most of it in his book including all of both the methodology and terminology, whilst being totally unaware of its true significance.'

'Significantly derailing our plans to actually implement it,' continued Kevin Goebbels, slightly annoying Dave McCreith at the way he referred to himself as if he were a member of the BBC by birth right, 'and meaning we then had to subtly work to disassociate ourselves from the plans and themes it revealed.'

'Oh, yes,' replied Dave McCreith, as he remembered this, too. 'Since then we've had to maintain a sort of distance from the work, and try to downplay the fact it detailed our entire plan for control of the country, much of which we've since implemented albeit in slightly different ways. It's interesting how often people cite ideas or terms in the book and say 'we're lucky this never happened!' even when it's obvious they did, what with people volunteering to have listening devices in their homes, the population being under constant CCTV surveillance or the fact that morality and even facts are constantly being revised.'

'Indeed, we've often had fun with that!' added Terry Ball, 'What with light-hearted references to the terms we came up with that were originally extremely bleak yet which we trivialised in order to dilute their true power. You know, like how we turned 'Room 101', where a person must confront their darkest fears, into a sort of chat show, or how our subsidiary, Channel Four, popularised the term 'Big Brother' and even associated it with people actually *wanting* to live under constant surveillance if it turned them into a rubbish celebrity!'

'Yes, we did do a good job of obscuring the truth of the book,' agreed Dave McCreith. 'Most people don't even realise that 'BBC' originally stood for 'Big Brother Corporation' until we were forced to change the name after the traitor George Orwell stole our charter and published it as '1984'!'

'Very true, Davey Boy,' added Kevin Goebbels, 'but then he was only working from a draft copy and we made a few changes since then. I mean, '1984' referred to 'groupthink', the idea that all people must be forced to think the same way, whereas we realised it was more beneficial to employ 'two-groupthink', by conditioning everyone to choose between two sets of beliefs, and obediently and unquestioningly follow every aspect of the one they selected whilst at the same time being suspicious towards followers of the other one, allowing us to create division and chaos by playing those two groups against each other.'

'Yes, indeed, though I still think our rebranding of that as the Set Menu of Political Beliefs was better because it sounded less, well, Orwellian,' added Dave McCreith.

'Bang on,' agreed Kevin Goebbels, adding, 'anyway, we were still able to implement parts of the original manifesto in other ways, without people who had actually read the book even noticing. As we all know, the one invention that eclipsed all others in immeasurably helping us to manifest, well, our manifesto, was Twitter!'

'Yes, Twitter truly was a godsend,' agreed Dave McCreith. 'I mean, just look at the 'Two Minutes' Hate'! In the original manifesto, people would meet up to scream abuse and vitriol at a Thought-Criminal of our choosing, but thanks to Twitter we were able to not only orchestrate it there by riling up a mob to attack our chosen target, but then report upon the incident we'd set up by claiming it was actual news, even if it was something utterly trivial and unworthy like, say, a pop star being denounced for cultural appropriation because she ate some jerk chicken!'

'Only for everyone to completely forget about it half an hour later,' added Terry Ball.

Dave McCreith nodded. 'Yes, covertly taking control of Twitter for our own purposes turned out to be a more successful move than we could ever have hoped. It was particularly clever to have a limit to how many characters you can tweet because, well, exactly how many intelligent, well-nuanced arguments can you actually put forward in 280 characters or less?!'

'Yes, it's the perfect vehicle for us to promote our simplistic, limited worldview, and that's why no news report on the BBC website is complete without at least fifteen inane tweets embedded in the text!' added Kevin Goebbels.

'Plus,' added Dave McCreith, by way of concluding a part of the chapter that, whilst maybe a bit long, had made some powerful, compelling and undeniable points, 'let's not forget how we were able to use it to further the key element of the Clandestine Charter of the BBC Elders, that people should never really have the slightest idea what to think as all morality is subject to change at any time. Perhaps the best example of how completely random and illogical law and order have become is that a person can now receive a longer prison sentence for *threatening* to kill someone on Twitter than they would if they actually did it!'

They all enjoyed a good laugh at this observation that sounds mad but is weirdly not that far off the truth, and quite terrifying when you think about it.

'Ah, yes...' said Dave McCreith, slowing down after they had all got rather excited at the Corporation's many achievements in the sphere of social media, and then turning to something that I reckon you've been wanting to know more about all through this book. 'When the BBC took over the country...' He turned to Kevin Goebbels. 'I assume you know the story, and the methodology?'

'Yeah, most of it,' replied Kevin Goebbels. 'The PR company I worked for before starting here played a large part in it so even before I joined I was pretty much up to speed.'

Dave McCreith looked slightly thoughtful here, but hopefully he was not considering whether Kevin Goebbels already knowing about the thing he was about to explain would mean he shouldn't explain it anyway. And luckily he wasn't. 'Well, Twitter was a powerful tool, and its usefulness in helping us achieve our aims cannot be understated,' he continued. 'A vital weapon in our arsenal, one that allowed us to spend years stoking the suspicion, division and hatred amongst the populace that would finally allow us to ignite the civil war by turning the country against itself!'

(So, yes, it looks like you're finally going to get an actual explanation of this mysterious war that people have been referring to all through the book, so pay attention, as this next bit's quite long.)

'Of course, the Set Menu of Political Beliefs had already laid the foundations of conditioning people into believing there were only two ways of viewing the world,' Dave McCreith went on, 'so all we needed to do was build upon that, pushing the agenda of 'two group-think', which we initially did by training the public into believing that their stance on Brexit completely defined them as a person and should cause them to despise anyone who voted the opposite way. All of a sudden a topic that hardly anyone had ever given a second thought to became something you used to utterly define yourself and your world view, meaning we could use it to turn husband against wife and father against daughter! And with the population then conveniently polarised we could apply the same method to any new topic or issue that arose, telling people what to think about it by a simple process of association, and to obediently hate anyone who thought they believed the opposite, be it lockdowns, trans rights or cultural appropriation... We'd developed a way to remove all nuance, rationality or debate from an argument and instead instruct people what they should believe, and that anyone who disagreed was a 'peddler of hate' who must be denounced! And then it became a game, in which we stuck a crowbar into any crack in society and wrenched it open as far as we could! It could be anything! Why, you can condition people to think that someone who likes a different flavour of crisps to them is their greatest enemy! So we used that technique to create division, chaos and hatred wherever we liked! And before long... There were protests every day, everywhere, over whatever opinion we'd programmed people to believe they held even if we'd only done it the day before! Then the protests become skirmishes... The skirmishes become street battles... Street battles became open warfare! It was all part of the Great Agenda. Rile the public into such a state of division that before long it erupts into civil war! A bloody, mutually destructive civil war in which the only true victor was the Corporation! Divide and conquer indeed! Our greatest triumph! What better way to control the public than by turning them against each other, letting them almost destroy one another and nicely thin out the ranks of the proles before we step in and claim to be the country's saviour?!'

Kevin Goebbels nodded intently, as impressed by this piece of mass brainwashing as someone whose background was in PR should be expected to be.

'And thus began the Great Terror!' Dave McCreith went on. 'With the public, government and political parties as divided as they were, who better to restore order than the BBC, seeing as how the army had been hugely weakened as a result of us constantly campaigning for a reduction in military numbers, brainwashing the government and public into believing war and even having an armed forces was morally wrong, and with us already having a much larger military force, our own private army of BBC Paramilitaries we'd built up in the guise of them being TV licence enforcers...?'

(So, there you are, finally a vaguely satisfactory explanation of the war that people have been talking about the entire book. It's not a plothole that it's only been properly addressed here, though, as the whole point was to keep it purposefully vague, then have it as a Stunning Reveal towards the end of the book, which is what has just been done, okay?)

'Not *our* paramilitaries, Dave!' interrupted Kevin Goebbels. 'All outsourced to a private contractor, meaning they're not legally our employees, and any atrocities they may or may not commit are something we can deny any knowledge of!'

'Well, yes, of course,' admitted Dave McCreith. 'It was a simple matter of adapting the same get-out cause we used to employ when outsourced licence-fee collection agencies took people to court or threatened non-payers, where we simply said they weren't following our rules, guidelines and standards properly, even though we obviously knew what they were up to. Then, of course, once we had orchestrated The Great Terror then intervened with the paramilitaries and appeared to restore peace, assuring the public that any freedoms we took from them in doing so would be returned once the war was over, we then explained that we were *always* at war with one enemy or another and that it was then necessary to carry out The Great Re-Structuring...'

Even though everyone in the room had intimate knowledge of the Corporation, its ways and its activities, the mood slightly changed here at the mere mention of this most horrific of events from the BBC's recent history.

'The Great Re-Structuring...' repeated Dave McCreith. 'A rebranding exercise... A large-scale consultancy concerning how the Great British Public viewed its beloved state broadcaster...'

'Perhaps a disingenuous name for what we can all, in private, agree was a large-scale programme of hunting down and destroying dissent, the systematic rounding up of heretics and anti-BBC Thought-Criminals, and the torture and extermination of those who opposed us,' added Terry Ball, with an uncharacteristically dark tone. 'An innocuous name for what was actually the mass use of internment camps and capital punishment branded as a 're-structuring exercise'.'

'Yes,' agreed Dave McCreith, 'but it had to be done! Our enemies had to be punished! We *needed* to secure our position! It was imperative we won the Great Victory and guaranteed another BBC Century, another hundred years of dominance, but this time one where we did not need to hide in the shadows! Do you not think that a few million deaths is a small price to pay for the whole of Great Britain having the correct opinions?!' He then looked reflective as he remembered something else. 'Anyway, what about all the work it created for outsourced management consultants? Should all the benefits from that not be factored into the equation?!'

Both Terry Ball and Kevin Goebbels made expressions showing they had no issue with the methods the Corporation had employed when making its desperate power grab. Dave McCreith looked slightly annoyed at the mere thought anyone should think otherwise, yet continued offering evidence to support his assertion. 'I mean... All those politicians who criticised us! The heretic Andrew Neil! The anti-BBC right-wing press! They all needed to be hunted down and made to atone for their heresy! Yes, we may have destroyed three quarters of the country but we won control, dammit!'

He slammed his fist down on the desk, which I think is something he did ages ago but I then forgot could have been a character trait of his. The other two looked slightly embarrassed but then, fortunately, after gloating over the Great Victory for a few more moments, Dave McCreith regained his composure and the general mood in the room became more calm. 'So, moving forward, what will the Dark Propaganda Department be up to?' he enquired.

'I can confirm that our science wing, Imperial College London, remains faithful, and can be relied upon to immediately produce 'reports' to 'factually confirm' whatever claim we wish to make,' Kevin Goebbels replied. At this, Dave McCreith nodded in satisfaction, though Terry Ball looked momentarily confused.

'Did anyone else think it was odd that during that week in 2020 when students were getting offended by everything and deciding that any building or statue commemorating anything connected to the British Empire was sickening, not a single student of Imperial College London stopped to ponder that the name of their actual university means 'of the Empire'?' he pondered.

'Well, whilst the point you make is entirely valid from a logical and factual perspective,' explained Dave McCreith, 'the reason none of the so-called 'woke students' noticed that is because we did not instruct them to notice it, pure and simple.'

Terry Ball made a face and noise that both suggested he was satisfied with this explanation.

'And do you have any noteworthy plans with regard to rebranding words and phrases in the English language so as to manipulate and confuse?' asked Dave McCreith, casually.

'I certainly do, as in keeping with our practices!' replied Kevin Goebbels, before casually checking his organiser for any noteworthy examples of how the Corporation intended to sow linguistic uncertainty by redefining and subverting everyday words and phrases in order to utterly undermine people's confidence that even the language they used contained any element of consistency. 'I have to say that one of my favourite recent examples of us manipulating language is how we managed to turn the word 'populist' into a term of hate, in regard to political leaders who do not have the correct views. I think that was particularly clever, considering the way we constantly bang on about how vital democracy is and how all countries should have it, even though the *one single thing* a leader in a democracy needs to be is 'popular'!

'Yes, that was a good one,' agreed Dave McCreith. 'Obviously we'll take it as read that we turned the words 'hate' and 'hate crime' into generic terms for anyone guilty of anti-BBC Thought-Crime, even if we use them to denounce people who believe in something that blatantly has nothing to do with 'hate' like, I don't know, thinking that mobile phone signals can give you diseases.'

'And let's not forget that we've not just programmed our followers to obediently switch their brains off whenever they hear a topic referred to as 'hate speech', but at the same time conditioned them to believe there are certain groups who should *never* be accused of hate speech, even if, say, they've formed a mob and are calling for someone to be killed over a few cartoons!' added Kevin Goebbels.

'And, on top of that, have also been hilariously conditioned to then throw the accusation of 'hate speech' at anyone *criticising* the people making the actual death threats!' added Dave McCreith, barely being able to control his mirth.

They all laughed at this quite brilliant way they had

manipulated the public.

'Oh, and on that subject, I have a new term we wish to embed into the minds of the British public, something they will soon think they always believed and never realise it was just another thing programmed into them by us,' said Dave McCreith, beginning to regain his composure. 'The new hate crime we are inventing is that of 'cyclophobia': the idea that any criticism of cycling is heresy and means the person making it is basically just a closet racist, with no consideration to be given as to whether there's any logical or factual validity to the criticisms, and certainly ignoring the hundreds of examples you see every single day of cyclists jumping red lights, going the wrong way down one-way streets, cycling along the pavement whilst watching a YouTube clip on their phones with their headphones on or ploughing into a pedestrian who had the audacity to get in their way by sitting outside a café and then insisting the pedestrian should pay for the repairs to the bike from their hospital bed.'

'Very good, Davey Boy,' nodded Kevin Goebbels. 'We've already started to lay the foundations for this belief by having Nigel Farage appear on all of our programmes complaining about cycle lanes, thus making the association clear in our viewers' minds, but this new term sounds like it will finally formalise it.'

'Indeed,' replied Dave McCreith. 'The BBC is firmly pro-cycling and believes there should be no debate about this, so rather than us having to waste our time actually addressing criticism of it, and deal with annoying principles such as common sense or evidence, we will simply denounce it as heresy, announce that cyclists are one of the most persecuted minority groups in the world and condition our followers to assume that anyone criticising them is also anti-EU, racist, anti-vaxx and so on, and should be listened to no further.'

'Right,' Kevin Goebbels agreed. 'The standard practice for discrediting an opinion we do not wish people to hold. We simply associate it with all the other things we've conditioned our followers to consider repellent, creating a link in their minds even though there's clearly no logical connection between them. Then we denounce anyone who dares to express a forbidden opinion as committing 'hate speech', a trigger term that causes our followers to obediently switch their brains off and consider the matter no further.'

'Indeed,' nodded Dave McCreith. 'And the media, of course,

will unquestioningly embrace this idea of 'cyclophobia', and obediently help us spread it amongst the population, without applying the slightest bit of objective reasoning to it, just like they did with the last similarly illogical term we invented!'

Dave McCreith was begrudgingly realising that his animosity towards Kevin Goebbels was starting to disappear, with his obvious talents making him less concerned by the informal modes of address he employed. In any case, he reassured himself, the man's apparently humble background meant he would never even be permitted to challenge for the position of Director General so, as such, posed no threat.

'What else...?' continued Kevin Goebbels, still looking at his organiser. 'Well, we continue to offer extremely conflicting and confusing signs regarding so-called 'conspiracy theories'. I mean, we continue to denounce anyone who even dares to investigate them, using Reality Check to discredit people who don't agree with us whilst never using it on people we support...'

'Oh, I did enjoy your department's work on the QAnon theory!' said Dave McCreith, brightly.

'That's the conspiracy where lots of people believe that huge numbers of well-known figures are paedophiles but their activities are being covered up by the establishment, isn't it?' interjected Terry Ball, quite helpfully.

'Yes!' replied Dave McCreith, gleefully. 'We constantly ran articles on it telling our readers to obediently ignore it! The irony was blatant, hilarious and delicious! Yes, I'll always be proud of the way the Corporation conditioned its followers not to entertain the central idea of the QAnon conspiracy. Imagine refusing to belief that a major organisation was covering up child abuse by public figures because you were told to by the BBC!'

They all had a good laugh at this, and so should you.

'Actually, that reminds me of something else,' continued Kevin Goebbels. We decided to build on that and actually invent our own conspiracy theory, which we will then spread across the internet *and then* run loads of articles saying how ridiculous it is, this theory we secretly created and spread.'

Dave McCreith stroked his chin thoughtfully at the implications of this. 'Interesting... What did you have in mind?'

'Well, Dave, we noticed how popular the 'flat earth' theory has become amongst some people in recent years, so we thought that our theory would be similar, but claim that the earth's rotation is actually slowing down but the governments of the world are keeping it quiet and building wind turbines not to generate electricity but as propellers to keep it turning.'

Impressed, Dave McCreith pondered this. 'That's good... It brings together a lot of things. The environment, questioning of authority, people being stupid enough to believe literally anything...'

'That's the idea, Dave,' explained Kevin Goebbels. 'So we'd spread it but also debunk it using Reality Check, thus denouncing those who *believe* the theory *we invented*, whilst it's also an experiment to see if the conspiratorially-minded are actually so gullible to simultaneously believe that the earth is both flat *and* a sphere that needs to be turned artificially!'

Dave McCreith had very much warmed to Kevin Goebbels by this point, even to the point that he was willing to say so. 'Well, I'm pleased to say that it sounds as if the future of the Corporation's Dark Propaganda wing is in very safe hands. Is there anything else you have planned for the future that I may need to know about?'

'Hmm, there is one more thing... Have you heard of an advocacy group called 'The Minging Community'?'

Dave McCreith pondered this then shook his head. 'The 'Minging Community', you say? No, I can't say I have. What do they do?'

'Well, the 'Minging Community' is a group of self-confessed 'mingers', or unattractive people, who seek to increase their representation in fields such as the media, film and television due to historic underrepresentation,' explained Kevin Goebbels. 'In the same way all minority groups who have traditionally been ignored on TV or in film have in recent years started campaigning to be featured more prominently in lead roles, the same is now true of ugly people.'

'Ugly people?! On TV, and in films?!' said Dave McCreith, perplexed. 'I mean... What?! How do they even think that would work?!'

'Well, I believe they just want to be more visible,' replied Kevin Goebbels. 'They're actually becoming reasonably well-known, now. A recent social media campaign saw them complain about how, for many years, attractive actors have used make-up to make themselves ugly, like, say, Charlize Theron when she played that serial killer, or Nicole Kidman when she put on a big nose to portray Virginia Woolf.

The group are saying that the act of 'minging-up' is as problematic as 'blacking-up', and that characters who are minging should only be portrayed by actual members of the Minging Community.'

Dave McCreith scratched his chin thoughtfully. 'I mean, on the one hand it seems like they're organised in the same way, and campaign along similar lines, as the usual sort of minority representation group that we would support... But, of course, the issue here is that I'm not really sure how we'd incorporate them into our working practices... I mean, they do realise we already have Radio 4 for the so-called 'Minging Community'? You know, providing regular employment for people who hold the correct opinions yet also have the misfortune to fall within the 'plain-to-ugly' spectrum of the attractiveness scale so are obviously not good-looking enough to appear on TV?' He shook his head, sadly. 'I mean... You know the saying 'they have a face for radio'? Well, that's very much still a thing... And particularly so in comedy.'

'Out of interest,' asked Terry Ball, 'do any of these less attractive comedians ever complain about how the BBC seems to be implying they're funny by having them on Radio 4 whilst, by very rarely having them on TV, also seemingly implying they're either not actually that funny or simply not attractive enough?'

'Well, no, because the BBC is the only organisation that will offer them employment anyway, so they're not going to bite the hand that feeds them,' explained Dave McCreith. 'I mean, ITV and Channel 4 also ban unattractive people from appearing on TV, but then they don't make such a sanctimonious fuss about supposedly believing in representation!' He then looked thoughtful again, as he pondered how to deal with the new threat. 'Still, with regards to this so-called 'minging community' advocacy group... There was always a risk that such a group would arise. I mean, just about all of our programmes obviously completely lacked 'minging representation' but no one ever noticed because we didn't tell them to, though it now sounds like that's no longer the case.'

'The question, Davey, is that of how to respond to this new group,' said Kevin Goebbels. 'The problem is, as you mention, that they're the sort of group we should be seen as supporting, yet if we did that we may then have to provide actual televisual employment for ugly people.'

'Yes,' replied Dave McCreith. 'This really is a conundrum...

Hmm... There must be a way around this. Could we find girls who are sort of sixes or sevens, perhaps, and give them a makeover, so they would look presentable enough for Saturday night TV but we could still promote make-up free selfies of them in which they look vaguely 'minging'?'

Kevin Goebbels looked thoughtful as he considered this, before his face lit up. '*Or* find girls who are clearly attractive but make a big thing about how they *identify* as ugly? That could work really well. No one dares challenge anyone who says they 'identify' as something, plus that means they could practice 'minging-up' when they're in a film or TV series, using prosthetics to look ugly, and no one could accuse them of anything because we'd just say they were simply adopting the appearance of the thing they identify as being!'

'That is *quite* brilliant!' replied Dave McCreith, nodding enthusiastically. 'I do believe you've cracked it! Okay, make sure you immediately set about releasing statements announcing how supportive the BBC is of the 'Minging Community' whilst also performing a comprehensive search for girls from private schools or who are 'famous' for putting scantily-clad photos of themselves on Instagram who we can promote as identifying as minging when they're actually hotties, so still give work to as presenters and actors!'

'I'll get onto it, Dave!' replied Kevin Goebbels, enthusiastically. 'And, on top of all that, if people *still* complain by pointing out that our supposed 'minging representation' is actually just attractive people pretending, we'll simply play the 'Imposter Syndrome' card! If anyone dares question one of the girls we've decided to use in representing the Minging Community, we'll have her speak very publically about her 'struggles', meaning she'll receive loads of sympathy as well as being personally imbued with a level of depth that really isn't there, reframing the debate to be about her being the victim and thus dismissing any criticism as a hate crime!'

'Precisely!' added Dave McCreith. 'Well, this has been a most productive day's work, wouldn't you both agree?!'

'I would, Dave!' said Kevin Goebbels, and Terry Ball also nodded his enthusiasm, for he could also see they had formulated some excellent ideas that would undoubtedly prove successful.

'Well, I think that concludes the meeting!' said Dave McCreith, satisfied, before his face changed as if to indicate he had a final question. 'Oh, there is one last thing...'

'Yes?' replied Kevin Goebbels.

'Your name...' said Dave McCreith. 'Where did it come from? Are you related to the man who inspired so many in today's world, or is it just coincidence?'

Kevin Goebbels paused for a moment before realising what the Director General was referring to. 'Oh, 'Goebbels',' he said. 'No, it's not my birth name. But in the world of advertising it's pretty cut-throat, and you need something to help you get ahead and appear more memorable, so a lot of people adopt nom-de-plumes, if you will, and I chose 'Goebbels', as a tribute to the great man who inspired so many in the world of advertising and public relations.'

'Oh,' replied Dave McCreith, entirely satisfied. Kevin Goebbels left the office, not with the traditional bow but by pointing his index finger and saying 'see you later, Davey Boy! The BBC will prevail!' but Dave McCreith had, unusually, got used to this form of address and merely nodded a farewell as he left and half-heartedly repeated the Corporation's secret slogan. He looked thoughtful for a moment before turning to Terry Ball.

'So, I assume that my schedule for the rest of the week, predictably, consists of further, seemingly endless meetings with other senior BBC figures or people from the media so we can discuss in great detail particular aspects of the Corporation's work and worldview?'

Terry Ball consulted his organiser then looked surprised. 'Oh... Well, your grace, as surprising as this may seem... No. You have no such further meetings pencilled in.'

'Oh,' replied Dave McCreith, initially surprised but then looking quite confused as to how he was going to spend his working days. 'So what will I be doing?'

'I'm not sure, at the moment, your grace,' replied Terry Ball. 'But I'm sure something will happen. Quite possibly something entirely unexpected!'

'Entirely unexpected?' said Dave McCreith. 'Oh, well, if something entirely unexpected does happen I suppose I'll just have to deal with it there and then.'

And he said that having no idea of just how true those words would turn out to be.

# Chapter Nineteen:

# Boobies

*In Which Our Heroes Arrive At the Refugee Camp Outside New White City, Encountering Kindred Spirits Who Agree To Join Their Struggle, And Also A Man Whose Sanity Was Destroyed in the BBC Re-Education Camps And Who Now Runs Around Saying Nothing But 'Boobies!', Which Provides Some Much-Needed Comic Relief In the Middle of All the Hopelessness and Brutality*

Our heroes continued their journey, following the exact route they mentioned in the chapter in which we last saw them, and still managed to evade capture. And I don't think that's unreasonable, I really don't. As I said, the route they took largely followed the river, meaning they would avoid main roads, and whilst you'll remember we did see them encounter the BBC Inquisition conducting public executions on Richmond Green they managed to blend in and continue their journey. But is their plan truly insane? Perhaps. To attempt to infiltrate one of the most heavily fortified buildings in the world, with nothing but a mad dream of a better world? Do they really think they can change anything? Or do they just know they cannot stay on the run forever, and would at least like to know why they were incarcerated in the first place? Or, perhaps, could it be so insane that it just might work?! I mean, the BBC surely wouldn't expect such an attempt on their HQ? Perhaps, for that reason, they're *not* doomed to failure after all! But all of that, and more, will be revealed! Not until the next chapter, though. Still, this one's also good, and provides a vital narrative thread into the final scenes of the book. So let's get on with it!

So, after leaving Richmond they travelled through Kew, probably via the Gardens as that would mean they avoided the main road, then crossed the Thames at Kew Bridge. But, once they crossed the river, the difference was marked: whereas the leafy riverside suburbs of Twickenham, Richmond and Kew, where it was extremely likely that top BBC stars and executives would live, had been virtually unscathed by the war, it was a different story when they reached parts of the capital in which poorer people were more likely to have lived. Brentford had clearly suffered heavy bombing, and the only attempts at rebuilding appeared to be some new riverside flats, dwellings that suggested whilst the more well-off would consider living in the unfashionable borough, they would only do so if located so far from the centre as to practically be in the next borough.

Some areas of London still seemed to be smouldering; a thick smog had enveloped distant parts of the capital, whilst in others they could see the fires still burned. Other parts were charred. As they continued to cross the wasteland it was hard to believe they were still in places that had once been thriving boroughs of the city. Staring in disbelief, they wandered through scenes that could have come from a brilliantly-written future dystopia about a post-war world entirely controlled by an all-powerful media organisation.

And as they continued they found not just further evidence of destruction to land and property but evidence of the human cost. People living in tents or in makeshift cardboard huts scraped a living where they could, yet our heroes could not ignore how many of them appeared to have had their sanity irrevocably damaged. At one point they saw a woman filling a Coke bottle with water from the filthy river, whilst chanting, quietly and mechanically to herself, 'TV licence, TV licence, I must pay my TV licence.'

But still the TV screens were inescapable. In every one of the makeshift camps they walked by they noticed there was always a huge plasma TV, too high up for the residents to destroy, damage or turn off, that was permanently tuned to either a news bulletin, or Question Time, the bloody Mash Report or probably bloody Fleabag yet again.

As they passed one such camp John Smith stopped. 'You

know... I had no idea it was like this! The BBC said there was some damage, and I know that being banned from leaving our borough meant we couldn't check things for ourselves, but I had no real idea so much of London was destroyed. I knew they were lying to us, but this?! I mean, in their mad quest for power, didn't they realise they would end up with nothing left to rule over?!'

The others merely shook their heads in disbelief, and they continued.

An hour or so later they were passing a similar camp when they heard the sound of an engine.

Quick!' yelled Barry Begbie, herding them into a conveniently placed shed or something. From inside, they watched as a BBC van pulled up at the camp and a group of paramilitaries piled out then started to enter each of the huts and drag out the terrified occupants.

'You know what we're here for!' yelled the leader of the BBC paramilitary squad, once all the inhabitants had been accounted for and brought outside. 'You're all overdue on your licence fee payments!'

'But the only TV we have is the massive one you installed up there, which we have no control over and can't even turn off, and which keeps us awake all night with your never-ending propaganda!' protested a man, receiving a blow to the back of his head for his trouble. The rest of the people, gaunt and malnourished, merely looked down, terrified to say anything, as the paramilitaries raided their huts for the few things they owned of any value, which they then took away before leaving and letting the terrified people get back to their pathetic little lives. Oh, did you think our heroes were going to mount a daring mission to stop them? I mean, first of all, that would just add unnecessary words to an already over-long book but, also, how would they even do that?! Most of them have no practical skills, certainly not fighting abilities, and have only ever led well-remunerated lives as BBC employees, so what were they going to do, somehow fight off a highly-trained group of soldiers? Don't be silly. They watched it all happen then, when the coast was clear, and the villagers were no longer outside to mock them for their entirely reasonable cowardice, continued their journey.

It was perhaps an hour later when John Smith suddenly stopped in his tracks and pointed upwards. Previously obscured by what they took to be a cloud of smog or even nuclear fallout drifting from Willesden or somewhere, they now had their first view of their ultimate destination, standing defiantly, gleaming like an incredibly expensive insult to everyone who had died in the war or been incarcerated in the camps, standing barely a mile away: New White City.

They all stood silently for a moment, realising they could turn back now and almost certainly be captured and killed, or continue and have an almost miniscule chance of saving themselves. Nonetheless, there was not a person amongst them who entertained any thought of going back.

It was approaching dusk when our heroes reached the base of the BBC's headquarters where, to their surprise, they discovered the huge camp of displaced people that's been mentioned in loads of previous chapters. Cautiously, they approached it, unsure of what or who they would encounter, or why there should be such an encampment on the doorstep of the much-feared Corporation.

The makeshift camp mainly consisted of tents or, for those who had managed to obtain more luxurious dwellings, basic huts made out of corrugated iron. But from the way they were laid out it was clear that the centre of the camp was the huge fire in the middle, which served as a meeting place for the residents. John Smith noticed that it was perhaps the only place in the camp where the inhabitants could not only avoid having to look at the massive TV screen that had been placed there but, due to the crackling of the fire, could also avoid listening to it. Around the fire sat perhaps fifty or sixty people, all talking merrily and eating the camp delicacy: Rat on a Stick. Those who were not eating their Rat on a Stick were holding it in front of the fire.

Our heroes carefully approached the fire, and as people turned around they began to recognise them, yet looked puzzled as to what they were doing there.

'You're Barry Begbie!' said one of them, surprised. 'I used to love you on Parody the News before it got all woke and full of supposed comedians who were only there because they ticked boxes!'

'Yeah, Barry Begbie! Loved all those jokes you did about Down's Syndrome and swimmers' noses!' said another person.

'I'm also a comedian!' said Jeffrey Harding, proudly. 'I was on

Radio 4 a lot!'

'Yeah, great,' replied the first man, quickly turning away from him and back to Barry Begbie. 'So what brought you here? Aren't you still on the BBC with that woke political show you do? I've never watched it myself...'

Barry Begbie shook his head. 'Ach, no,' he replied. 'They took me off the air and I ended up in one of the Re-Education Camps.'

At the mention of these most feared of locations, just about everyone else at the fire turned around to look at the new arrivals.

'You were in a BBC Re-Education Camp?' asked one of them in disbelief.

'Yeah, we all were,' Barry Begbie continued. 'But we escaped.'

'Is that possible?' asked another man.

'It's not easy, but it can be done,' Barry Begbie replied. So, if this novel were not overrunning I'd have a character who refuses to believe they actually escaped and thinks they've been sent to spy on them but, oh, that would take ages and we're heading to the end now, so let's just imagine that happened without worrying about the details, okay? They managed to somehow prove their escape was genuine, and it was all fine. Before long all suspicions had been allayed, everything was okay and they were all friends, okay?

'Well, anyway,' continued the man who'd spoken first, 'this camp was originally founded by the thousands of people who were made homeless when the BBC decided to bulldoze their homes in order to make space for its new headquarters, but since then many more of us have arrived, all of us outcasts, but we're all here for similar reasons. Here we can live freely. It's an irony not lost on us that the only place we can do that is right outside the BBC's head office, but they seem to have started leaving us alone out of concern about bad publicity.' He looked thoughtful for a moment. 'Also, the weather's unusually good, which is weird. I mean, even though we live in tents and shacks it never gets too cold, even in the middle of winter, which we struggle to understand.' He looked thoughtful again. 'Still, we did have a massive torrential downpour and all those lightning strikes the other day, though that's literally the only time it's happened since we've been here.'

'Is everyone here on the run from the BBC?' asked John Smith.

'Well, either on the run from them or were released back into the world after being rehabilitated or imprisoned only to find their houses had been repossessed or destroyed,' the man replied. 'Basically, everyone here is someone who has no life to return to after it was destroyed by the BBC.'

'And what did you do?' asked Barry Begbie.

'Oh, it was pretty mild,' replied the man, sadly. 'I did a tweet, a joke about when UK Gold changed its name so it was just 'Gold', in which I said that only one of the two words in the original title was strictly accurate but they'd kept the wrong one. Of course, twenty minutes later the paramilitaries kicked down my door...'

Just behind him sat another man who had neither said anything nor even made eye contact in the time the group had been sitting by the fire but kept shaking his head uncontrollably, as if possessed by a mad, malevolent spirit. 'Boobies!' he yelled.

'Is he all right?' asked John Smith, concerned.

'Oh...' replied the man at the fire. 'Well, he was arrested for doing a tweet saying that 'Allo 'Allo wasn't very funny, and pointing out that all the so-called 'humour' literally consisted of either someone mentioning 'the Fallen Madonna with the Big Boobies' or that policeman who was meant to be English so couldn't pronounce French properly and ended up saying things like 'I was *pissing* by the door' when he meant to say 'passing' or 'that man was *wanking* at me' when he was meant to be saying 'winking'... His punishment was deliberately chosen to be ironic. He was sat in a chair, with his eyes clamped open and forced to watch the entire run of the programme, without a break. You know it ran for ten years? And even then they showed it to him three or four times. He had water and a basic drip fed into him, and was attached to a colostomy bag, but was prevented from sleeping or even closing his eyes, and in the end spent almost an entire month without sleep, watching 'Allo 'Allo on endless repeat until it destroyed his mind. And all that is left is what you see now.'

He turned to look at the man, who quickly glanced from side to side, briefly displayed a terrified look on his face and screamed 'boobies!' again.

(Sorry, this bit is rather a lot like the public execution scene in that it's little more than descriptions of the petty and bizarre reasons people were denounced, arrested and punished by the BBC. Still, surely it's better to split them up into separate chapters, anyway? That way you'll probably remember them better than you would if they were all in the same, endlessly-long single block. Still, it's all powerful stuff. When people really do get arrested for stuff like this remember that I warned you about it all!)

A few metres away a woman leaned forward and told her story. 'Ah, before the war... It seems odd now that the time we're talking about is only a few years ago but, so much has changed since then... I was actually made homeless just before it, because even though I'd run a successful chain of tanning salons for thirty years, the BBC decided that getting a fake tan counted as a hate crime because you were essentially attempting to alter your skin tone, which counted as blacking up. So one day a group of armed BBC militias visited each of my eighteen shops and burned them all to the ground.'

John Smith remembered the introduction of this law. First of all the BBC had taken everything off their streaming services that included scenes that could remotely be construed as blacking up, and a few months before that there'd been an outcry when a high-end fashion brand had brought out a jumper that included a balaclava element that was black, because people said that was also blacking up. And before that a pop singer had brought out a range of shoes in different colours but people decided the black ones counted as blacking up your feet or something. And from then on things got even more surreal and bizarre. The rules on cultural appropriation got madder and madder, and before long the guards outside Buckingham Palace were arrested and charged with having committed a hate crime because the big furry hats they wore were said to look a bit like afro hairstyles and therefore counted as blacking up, too.

(That really could be a thing before long. It might actually be a thing by the time you read this. And this next thing, too.)

A man in late middle age had been listening to this. 'I'm Dr Peters,' he announced. 'I'm the camp doctor, or rather I try to be despite having so few supplies and so little equipment to work with. You're probably wondering why I'm here.'

The others looked at him expectantly, which he took as confirmation that they were.

'I was an oncologist. One of the best in the world. Perhaps *the* best in the world. I treated royalty, politicians, celebrities... But one day I had a new patient. He was genetically a man, but he assured me he identified as a woman and always had.'

He paused and looked down before continuing. 'Now here's the thing. You remember how after years of Little Britain being considered totally fine, and the BBC being happy to promote it and profit off it, they suddenly decided it was the most sickening programme in its entire history, and the whole country supposedly agreed, even though its stars were still allowed to continue presenting high-profile shows despite them supposedly being top-level hate mongers? Well, there was a sketch in that where David Walliams' transvestite goes to have an x-ray and the doctor hands her something to protect her testicles from the radiation, only for her to insist that it's unnecessary for her to use it because she doesn't have testicles, because she's a lady. And that's exactly what happened to me.'

He sat down and lit his pipe. Despite him being an oncologist. So I reckon that's a very clever narrative device, as it sums up the feelings of hopelessness he now has; once the world's top oncologist, he now holds so little optimism for the future that he's started smoking. 'Well, this patient came to see me, and it was necessary for me to do x-rays to monitor the spread of his cancer. Each time I strongly advised him to take the shield to protect his testicles, and each time he assured me he was a woman, so the testicles I thought I could see didn't actually exist.' He shook his head in disbelief. 'And after six months of treatment, the cancer I'd been treating him for, cancer of the liver, had cleared up, but he now had testicular cancer due to not having shielded them during the treatment. Of course, for a while he insisted it was impossible for him to have testicular cancer seeing as he didn't have testicles, but then it was pointed out to him that he could sue me for millions, at which point he decided he was a man after all and that I was guilty of medical negligence. So I was struck off. I'm not entirely sure I hadn't previously been struck off for arguing he had testicles but, well, as we all know, there's no logic to any of this. And, on top of all that, due to the cancer in the man's testicles having reached an advanced and untreatable stage, he actually had to have them removed, which was unfortunate because by that point he'd decided he was a man after all.'

The others all stopped to ponder this tale, realising it was so mad as to almost not be worth contemplating. People now seemed to be taking it in turns to lean forward and offer a very snappy summary of how their downfall had come about, often in what seemed suspiciously like it was being done in a very concise and quotable way.

A woman added her story at this point. 'My husband is Indian, and whenever I went to a wedding from his side of the family...' Before she could finish, the other people around the fire had guessed the ending and she smiled at the predictability of it all. 'Yeah, wearing a sari... The rape of another culture...' She shook her head sadly. There was another pause.

'Boobies!' shouted the crazed man again, before getting up, screaming madly, and running directly into the fire, in which he was roasted alive.

'Boobies indeed,' said the first man, nodding mournfully.

At this point the growing camaraderie of the group was broken by the intrusion of a cloying, annoying voice, the sort that was not normally heard in the camps. It was that of the type of generic posh boy who works at the BBC but tries to make his accent sound a bit rougher, but rather than endearing himself to people as a result just makes them think he's even more of a twat for trying to pretend he's something he isn't. He was evidently talking to a group of people, and a few moments later the whole group appeared by the fire. The owner of the voice was, as predicted, some type of BBC employee, and he was accompanied by a producer, director and cameraman, all of whom appeared to be involved in making a documentary about the camp's inhabitants.

'Oh, my god, look at this place!' he exclaimed. 'This is amazing! So many interesting people! This is so retro!' He could barely contain his excitement as he looked around. 'OMG, look at all these tents! This is just like Glastonbury!'

The inhabitants of the camp all glared at him silently, though he totally failed to pick up on how annoying he was, and continued to look around in excitement.

'Oh my god, you smoke roll ups!' he said to a man who was attempting to forge a makeshift cigarette using the tobacco from butts thrown from New White City's smoking area held together by a piece of newspaper. 'Wow, that's so retro!' He looked at a woman who was attempting to give water to her infant daughter using a tin can. 'Oh, amazing, you're drinking out of a tin can! I've been to a bar in Borough Market where you do that!'

A few feet away a man shot him a glance of disbelief, a look of utter incomprehension as to how somebody could see people living on skid row and think it was all a big adventure after which they could return to their lives of luxury. He shook his head in disgust and returned to waiting for the Rat on a Stick he was holding in front of the fire to finish cooking. Again, failing to pick up on this, the displaced hipster continued. 'Oh, wow, you're having Rat on a Stick! You're so on-trend! I was just reading in Vice how that's the new trend in street food! There's a new pop-up in Shoreditch where they do Rat on a Stick Fusion! You can have Burmese Rat on a Stick with Lemongrass infusions!'

The young man had spent so long marvelling at all the things he took to be validation of his shallow hipster lifestyle that he had failed to notice two things: his production team, sensing that they were unwelcome, had slowly and carefully slipped away, eager to distance themselves from his inane pronouncements, and once out of his sight had hastily departed the camp and left him on his own. He was just opening his mouth to make another inappropriate observation when he was knocked off his feet by a man with a club.

'Oh, wow!' he responded, totally unware of the true gravity of his situation. 'I've heard about this! It's one of those new underground fighting clubs, a tribute to the classic David Fincher film of 1999, isn't it?! Wow, this is just like Secret Cinema!'

Another member of the mob pulled out a huge butchers' knife and used it to tear a sizeable chunk of flesh from the unwitting documentarian's side. Again, he not only appeared to have completely failed to register any pain, he still assumed that he was involved in a happening, which would surely lead to him being immortalised on one of his favourite hipster websites. As he watched the man who had torn the flesh from his side only a few moments earlier grin psychotically at him before putting it into his mouth, he looked thrilled to be part of whatever was unravelling in front of his very eyes. 'Oh my god, are you going to do this 'ironic cannibalism' thing?! I've heard about that! Dazed and Confused have just written a feature about it!'

Anyway, you can see where I'm going with this. He ends up getting eaten yet weirdly thinks the whole thing is some kind of hipster affectation. His body was consumed, though most of those who had eaten some of it looked unconvinced by its quality.

'It's not bad,' said one woman, thoughtfully, 'but it's no Rat on a Stick.'

No one disagreed with this appraisal, but they nonetheless finished eating the unfortunate hipster, after which it was realised that conversation would need to be restarted.

'Er, are we still doing the thing where we talk about why were arrested or whatever?' asked one woman, then began her story without having received confirmation either way. 'So, I had a CD by Joss Stone...' She paused, realising she was referencing not one but two things that may well need explaining to younger people. 'Yeah, CDs were what we had music on before the internet. And Joss Stone was a white girl from Devon who sang like a black American woman. I mean, I think I'd been given the CD as a present, like for my birthday in 2004 or something... But, of course, one night the BBC jackboots burst into my flat and had a nose around, and found it, and I don't think I'd ever even listened to it more than once or twice but, of course, a white woman singing like a black American woman had long since been reclassified as an abhorrent hate crime, even though Joss Stone originally got discovered on a BBC talent show...' She shook her head in disbelief, realising she did not need to continue speaking, and leaned back, dismayed.

Another woman now leaned forward to tell her tale, despite there clearly having been enough of them, and that the book's word count was spiralling out of control as a consequence.

'I was a film critic,' she began. 'I'm here because I gave a bad review to a film that had Emma Watson in it. That's basically it.'

There was a pause, during which the others looked at her expectantly, as if to say that whilst they saw nothing unusual in what she had told them they would still like the story filled out a bit, which is annoying considering I just said how the book's getting too long.

'I mean, I just said I didn't think the film was very good. I even said that I felt she was wasted in it, making it seem like I thought she was a really good actress who was sorely underused in the film in question, even though I really thought she's just a generic, skinny, white, attractive, privileged girl whose success is solely down to those things rather than her having any actual talent. Not that I said that, of course. I can't even remember which film it was. It was probably either that version of Little Women that she was in, where all the most woke young stars of Hollywood got together to make a film so white it could have been used as Nazi propaganda. Or maybe it was the version of Beauty and the Beast she did, which seemed to carry the message that a guy who's well minging kidnapping a woman is fine, and she'll eventually fall in love with him, just as long as he's had a spell cast on him and is actually good looking, and that's the main thing, not the weird subtext about Stockholm Syndrome, coercion and manipulation. Of course, I would like to have addressed the many reports about Disney using sweatshop labour to manufacture tie-in promotional stuff, or how it's a bit weird that they keep denouncing their own back catalogue by saying how disgustingly offensive it all is, yet still leave it all on their streaming platform, as if to suggest the fact they're willing to continue profiting from it means their supposed moral concerns aren't really as strong as they'd like us to think, but no one in the film reviewing business is allowed to even consider stuff like that, much less write about it.'

She then nodded as if to say that she felt that her point had been made.

Anyway, this rather over-long and repetitive, though quite brilliantly satirical, section came to an abrupt end with the arrival of a small group of men and women who had weapons and were dressed in a way suggesting they had recently returned from a military operation. The people sitting around the fire looked at them expectantly, as if awaiting news.

'Well, we hunted and destroyed two BBC vans,' announced the apparent leader. 'They were out looting, so it should discourage others, but it's just a drop in the ocean. I know we've been safe here so far but it may not last forever. If only there was some way we could really strike at the heart of the BBC...' he sighed at the ridiculousness of the very concept, then noticed our heroes, newcomers to the community.

'Oh, hello,' he said. 'I'm Hunter. I'm sort of in charge here.'

Now, I really should mention that Hunter is black. And I'm saying that now rather than doing so years later in a desperate attempt to claim this book was full of diversity and representation. I call that a 'Rowling Retcon', remember? That's when you create something that doesn't have any diversity but then later claim that various characters were actually gay or black or whatever, despite never mentioning it in the original text, and then go on to insinuate that it's actually everyone else who's racist for not just assuming they were rather than your fault for, you know, not ever bothering to mention it in the first place. I mean, the entire Harry Potter series apparently runs to a million words or something. Would it really have been too much trouble to add three more words, those words being 'Dumbledore was gay'? Also, weirdly, when I first developed this idea JK Rowling was someone the BBC and the woke people loved, then the woke people suddenly decided that rather than loving everything she did and said they actually wanted to inundate her with death threats, and the BBC decided it no longer had an opinion, not even on the issue of the death threats, because it didn't want to upset the woke people. So, as far as I can tell, that means my entirely fair criticism, which would once have led to *me* receiving death threats, is now fine. I reckon. Maybe.

Anyway, where was I? Oh, yes. Hunter was black, and that's definitely not a desperate attempt to insert some diversity into one of the very final chapters of the book. Perhaps just imagine him looking like Idris Elba, who I also think would be an excellent choice for the role in the inevitable BBC adaptation, though I wonder if the part is actually too small for an actor of his stature to take. Anyway, our heroes introduced themselves, then the conversation immediately returned to the matter of striking at the heart of the hated BBC.

'We heard what you said about wanting to take down the Corporation,' said Emmeline Moneypenny. 'And we think that's something we could assist you with.'

'What?! How do you expect to do that?' asked Hunter, almost mockingly, before realising that he recognised Barry Begbie, though obviously not Jeffrey Harding as he'd only ever really been on Radio 4 and the occasional episode of QI. 'Oh... I know you,' he said, scrutinising him. 'You used to be on TV.'

'Actually, I was on TV quite a lot too,' added Emmeline Moneypenny.

'And I used to do Radio 4 panel shows!' said Jeffrey Harding, being ignored once again.

'The point is that a number of us have worked extensively for the BBC,' continued Emmeline Moneypenny. 'And whilst we're currently out of favour, they tend to have short memories at that organisation. If we could get inside the building we'd be able to move around quite freely and possibly reach some powerful people.'

'That's good to know,' replied Hunter, 'but it only helps us if you can get close to *one* powerful person. The Director General and Supreme Overlord of the BBC himself. The one man whose mad lust for power caused all of this.'

They all did a sort of pre-shudder in anticipation of the much-feared name even being uttered aloud.

'Dave McCreith.'

They then all did an actual shudder because it had been uttered aloud.

'Dave McCreith,' repeated Hunter, the name being no less horrible for having already been spoken. 'I mean, he's the key to all of this... But despite all that we hear about him, not everyone is convinced he's even still alive. Some say he died in the war but the BBC has hidden it from the public for fear of the uncertainty and unrest it could cause, using archive footage of him to create a hologram for whenever they need him to make a public statement.'

'Some call him the 'Woke Hitler',' added Barry Begbie. 'Yet others say he is aware of this and enjoys being called it.'

'There is little about him that we know for certain,' continued Hunter. 'Some say that in his struggle for power he suffered horrible burns and has been a recluse ever since, yet has sworn revenge on those he holds responsible. Others say he's like the Emperor in Star Wars, not just in that everyone is terrified of him, but in that he has all these weird magic powers, and is also all horrible and old and wrinkly.'

'Yet at the same time I've often wondered if he not only encourages these rumours but helped to spread them,' added Barry Begbie. 'Some say he's been slowly going mad over the years but no one dares challenge his authority. It's been suggested he suffered brain damage during the war, that he lost his mind in sheer horror at the atrocities he orchestrated, or that the mental deterioration is the result of tertiary syphilis that, again, the Corporation has covered up.'

There was another pause, as people stopped to consider these wicked yet awesome rumours. But this pause was broken by a most unexpected revelation.

'I knew him,' Emmeline Moneypenny said suddenly. 'Vaguely... I mean, we weren't close or anything, and it's been years since I saw him... But, well... If there's anything left of the man I knew... Even the smallest fragment... Then maybe...'

'Hang on, I could get you close to him!' cut in Hunter. 'And if, as you say, you constantly fall in and out of favour at the BBC, how's he going to remember whether you're currently in favour or not?

'Wait, are you saying you can get us inside?' asked John Smith, disbelievingly.

'Well, yes,' replied Hunter. 'When we're not out hunting and killing BBC paramilitaries we work as cleaners in New White City. But the fact we're strictly prohibited from going anywhere near the BBC executives means it's impossible for us to ever get close enough to kill them. But perhaps with you in our party...'

They all looked at each other, wondering whether this plan was simply too outrageous to work, yet also somehow knowing that there was a reason for them all having been brought together. It seemed like fate was encouraging them to at least attempt this frankly insane plan that was nonetheless the only course of action that could, possibly, maybe, have the very smallest of chances of finally freeing the country from the iron grip of the Broadcasting for Britain Company.

John Smith shuddered, then looked up at New White City. It was now dusky and the sun had all but set, which, combined with the smog, made the very top levels of the building difficult to make out, though this was also because they were so high up as to often be obscured by cloud.

'We have to,' he said. 'We have to try. I have to know why I was sent to the camp! We have to dream of a better world!'

'A better world,' said Hunter, wistfully, in a way that made the others unsure what he really meant.

'A better world,' repeated Emmeline Moneypenny.

'I used to be on Radio 4, you know!' added Jeffrey Harding, but everyone ignored him.

They all continued to stare up at the top floor of the BBC's headquarters. John Smith nodded.

'New White City or Bust!'

# Chapter Twenty:

# The Authorship Question

*In Which the Director General Finally Gets His Hands On The Author Of the Heretical Text 'The Book the BBC Tried to BAN!' and Brutally Interrogates Him In A Desperate Attempt To Find Out What Would Drive Someone To Write Such a Sacrilegious Work, A Chapter That Also Pretty Much Pre-Empts and Answers Any Possible Criticism Someone Might Have of His Book, Which Also Conveniently Applies To This Book Too, the One You're Reading, Right Now*

Dave McCreith stood in front of the huge trophy cabinet that ran along the side wall for almost the entire length of his office. He frowned as he surveyed its contents: dozens and dozens of similar-looking statues, all from different organisations, all congratulating him for his unrivalled achievements in the fields of chasing and meeting empty and inane targets, and all featuring his name along with an award title that invariably included variations on buzzwords such as 'inclusivity', 'diversity' and 'inspirational'. His frown deepened and he let out a loud, angry sigh. Hearing this, Terry Ball looked up at him.

'Something wrong, your grace?' he asked.

'Yes!' replied Dave McCreith. 'No new awards! Dave McCreith want new awards!'

Terry Ball stood up and walked over to the cabinet to take a look. 'Nonsense, your grace!' he countered. 'What about that award you received only last week for hitting a diversity target a full two weeks earlier than you said you would when you announced the target yourself a week before that? You know, the award you were given after announcing that to counter the fact that the entire BBC board of executives is white you'd decided to ensure that we only ever employ under-represented minority groups on the cleaning staff?!'

'Well, as you say, that was almost a week ago,' protested Dave McCreith. 'Want more,' he added, sulkily, looking hurt, like a child who'd asked for a new toy but not received it. 'Dave McCreith sad.'

'There, there, your grace,' offered Terry Ball as comfort. 'Anyway, I may have some good news for you!'

Dave McCreith's face lit up in anticipation. 'Another award?' he asked, impatiently.

'Well, we've got a visitor coming in shortly, that nice man who's been CEO of loads of different charities over the years! The BBC has given him countless awards over the years and I'd be surprised if he doesn't bring one for you, too!'

'When? Here soon?!' demanded Dave McCreith, scurrying away from his trophy cabinet towards the door.

'Yes, your excellency, don't worry!' Terry Ball assured him. 'He'll be here any minute!'

And, just like Terry Ball said, at that point there was a knock at the door. As Dave McCreith was already near it he flung it open impatiently to reveal, standing behind it, a man who works exclusively as a charity CEO and so for ease of reference shall simply be referred to as The Charity Man.

'Ah, your grace, so glad to see you again!' said the Charity Man. He was holding a golden statue in the shape of a desperately malnourished African orphan, underneath which was printed the name 'Dave McCreith' along with a selection of buzzwords including 'inspirational', 'diversity', 'quotas' and other popular clichéd and meaningless terms. Dave McCreith froze as he noticed this.

'Your excellency,' continued the Charity Man. 'Once our appointment was confirmed I knew I couldn't possibly visit you without presenting you with an award for...' Before he could continue, Dave McCreith snatched the statue greedily and ungraciously from his hands, like some sort of mad Gollum, then scuttled back to his trophy cabinet and flung it inside, as if concerned that it could be rescinded and confiscated at any moment.

'Precious awards,' he said, quietly, to himself. 'Dave McCreith like precious awards.' He then scuttled back to the door and looked directly into the Charity Man's eyes. 'And the presentation ceremony? Expensive champagne? Caviar?'

'Well, of course, my liege!' confirmed The Charity Man. 'The details have just been finalised so I'll send them across to your assistant, but I can now confirm it's taking place on Friday at 7pm. We've booked it, at almost impossible expense, at the New Savoy. You know the one, it's the hotel and restaurant complex that permanently hovers above the Thames, making it completely safe from the marauding street gangs.'

Okay, so I'm actually going to interrupt this chapter right now. You see, I did write a whole chapter that basically existed to look at the role of modern charities, and in particular how they not only pay their executives massive salaries but in recent years have come in for all sorts of criticism about spending loads of money on villas for said executives when they're in a disaster or war zone, along with plentiful prostitutes for them, or charities that supposedly help nature but are also facing claims of allowing murder and sexual assault in the reservations they're meant to be protecting, or charities trying to deal with allegations of bullying and sexual harassment amongst senior staff, just like pretty much all other organisations (and you can look up all these things), though a key point was how, much like the BBC, charities seem to think they somehow shouldn't be held up to the same standards as everyone else and should be given leeway to get away with misdeeds, and quite often find a sympathetic voice for this idea in the liberal media, *but* the novel's getting a bit long plus, objectively, it's not *entirely* relevant to the BBC and whilst the Corporation does have its public charity telethons, I already covered that (quite brilliantly, I think you'll agree) in the chapter with the Prime Minister.

It was a bit legally questionable, too. Because although in the same way that it would be massively hypocritical for the BBC to sue me over this book when they'd be using licence payers' money to do so, I wouldn't put it past major charities to sue anyone who hurt their feelings with inconvenient truths even though they would also be doing so with money donated to them, either willingly or not. Still, one of the best lines was when the Charity Man justified his organisation's murderous practices by saying: 'I mean, if we can save some endangered gorillas and only have to kill a few dozen African people in the process then surely that's good for conservation, isn't it?' Also, I can handily claim that anyone who finds that offensive is failing to understand that it's actually a very powerful criticism of so-called 'white saviour' tropes.

So, let's just pretend this meeting happened and whilst some powerful, brilliant and utterly hilarious points about hypocrisy were made you'll just have to take my word for it. So, the Charity Man left, at which point Terry Ball's phone rang and he answered it, first listening with interest before his face lit up in uncontrollable excitement.

'We've found him, your grace! We have him!'

'Who?' demanded Dave McCreith. 'That terrorist? The one who was going around in a Guy Fawkes mask thinking he was a super-vigilante saving Britain from a totalitarian government?'

'Well, no, your grace, we caught him a while ago, remember? He was one of the earliest experimental patients in our Manchester Black Ops Site. He believed that the medical procedures he was subjected to whilst there had given him superpowers such as increased strength, enhanced levels of perception, super-human fighting ability...'

'And had they?'

'No, they'd simply destroyed his mental state to the point that he merely believed himself to possess those abilities, so after one or two attempts to fight against the so-called oppressive fascist state he believed he lived in, he was quite easily beaten to death by a couple of our trainee paramilitaries. Actually, his brutal death at their hands made for a rather amusing so-called 'internet meme' that did the rounds.'

'Right, so who are you talking about then?' demanded Dave McCreith, impatiently.

'The Author, your grace! The man who wrote the heretical text known as 'The Book the BBC Tried to BAN!''

Dave McCreith leapt to his feet and stared at Terry Ball. 'What?! Where is he? Please don't tell me this is some kind of joke!'

'No joke, my liege!' confirmed Terry Ball. 'He's been captured and is in transit, guarded by our elite paramilitaries as we speak!'

'Wait, is he also being transferred to the Manchester site?'

'Well, that was the plan, your grace. After all, that facility is saved only for the very worst type of anti-BBC Thought Criminal, those guilty of heresy of the very highest order.'

Dave McCreith looked thoughtful for a moment. 'No,' he said. 'Bring him to me.'

Terry Ball flashed a quizzical look. 'Are you sure, your grace? You are, of course, aware that we maintain the Manchester Black Ops site in order to carry out the most brutal punishments, so that senior BBC executives can plausibly claim to know nothing about it on the entirely believable grounds that no BBC exec would ever dream of visiting Manchester? And, indeed, it's written into their contracts that they are exempt from visiting any part of the North.'

'I know, I know,' replied Dave McCreith, impatiently. 'But this is no ordinary Thought Criminal. He deeds, his words... Well, I can barely begin to describe them. He's on an entirely different level. That book he wrote contained such unspeakable content that I can barely, well, speak about it...'

'You're surely not suggesting we execute him without prior torture, your grace?!' asked Terry Ball, confused.

'Oh, god, no,' replied Dave McCreith. 'It's just that... Well... What sort of a mind could even conceive of such anti-BBC heresy? I have to know.'

'You wish to interrogate him yourself?' asked Terry Ball, in disbelief.

'Yes,' replied Dave McCreith. 'I must. There are things I must know. Things I have to discover in person. What sort of mind does this man possess? What could drive him to commit such blasphemy? No, there's no way around it. You must bring him here.'

'Very good, your grace,' replied Terry Ball. 'I believe we have a functional interrogation chamber in the basement from the final days of the war, before we moved that department...'

'No,' interrupted Dave McCreith. 'Bring him here. To me. To this office.'

'Er...' said Terry Ball, looking thoughtful as to whether or not this was logistically possible, 'yes, I suppose that can be arranged. Let me contact the head paramilitary and tell him the plans have changed.'

'Be sure that you do. As soon as possible,' replied Dave

McCreith, before returning to his desk. Terry Ball took out his personal organiser and left the room.

An hour or so passed, an hour that isn't really worth describing and is only there because it would be a bit implausible to say that the Author was being taken to Manchester only for him to then appear moments later in West London. It doesn't really matter what happened in that hour. Dave McCreith probably had his lunch then went for a poo. I won't actually describe that, though maybe I should, seeing as how so few novels cover details like that, which they probably should do if they're aiming for realism. But you can assume that he had his own, gold-plated toilet, and probably even a BBC intern whose sole job was to wipe his bottom.

Actually, now I think about it, I can use up some of that hour to just point out that, logically, this chapter has to take place outside the thus-far linear narrative structure of the book, as it clearly depicts the author of 'The Book The BBC Tried To BAN!' still being alive, even though we know from earlier chapters that his fate was to be executed and left in a gibbet outside New White City. So this chapter must, I suppose, be set five or six months earlier than the rest of the novel. It's basically like a prequel that tells us more about the world we've already witnessed.

Oh, and on that topic, if you think it's another example of lazy writing to have not properly integrated this chapter in the narrative of the book, I do have some counter arguments. First of all, in this chapter both the Author and Dave McCreith will make references to things that happen during the main narrative, so it's easier to not have them do that until you've actually read about the things they're talking about. Also, I think it works well to have had Dave McCreith rant about the book so many times as that then nicely sets up this confrontation. Even if within the actual timeline it happens before he did all the ranting. Plus if this chapter had happened earlier it would not only have muddled the narrative but also blunted the impact of this powerful, climactic scene that is set before the novel actually starts and features a main character who's somehow not actually in the rest of the book.

Still, his spirit haunts the entire story, doesn't it? Actually, on that subject, it strikes me that maybe I should actually have combined the characters of John Smith and the Author, because then John Smith's story arc would have been stronger, and we'd have seen two powerful characters (that one and Dave McCreith) on an unavoidable collision course with each other, like the yin and yang at the very centre of the book's soul. And if you think that admission clears up once and for all that I'm not a very good writer for not having properly worked out this clearly important plot point, I wouldn't necessarily refute that charge, but would just point out you're pretty near the end of the book now so might as well finish it.

Ooh, but wait, this is even better! I should just have vaguely hinted that John Smith *is* the author of The Book, but that he's taken to the Re-Education Camps for something else, with the BBC and its paramilitaries not even realising they already have their most wanted Thought-Criminal in their custody, so continue the search in all the wrong places. This would have added a delicious dramatic tension to his time in the camp, as he'd constantly be worried they'd find out, and would also mean this chapter would in addition act as a Big Reveal, whilst *also* being the powerful climax of his and Dave McCreith's story arcs that I just mentioned. Wouldn't that have been brilliant? Yes! Am I going to go back and re-write the whole thing? No! Anyway, isn't it the sign of truly brilliant writers that they leave clues, and allude to things, which critics and academics can then spend decades debating? Yeah, let's just leave it. Someone can write their PhD thesis on it and the internet can go mad with fan theories, even though they'll probably all just say they believed there was a homoerotic subtext in which the Author, John Smith and Dave McCreith were all bumming each other, because that's pretty much what all fan theories seem to be these days, and if you wrote a PhD thesis along those lines about just about any book you'd definitely be awarded your doctorate.

Right, anyway, getting back to the story, the reason for taking such a narrative diversion is simply to ponder what sort of a man would write a book so groundbreaking and earth-shatteringly brilliant as to dare to brutally deconstruct an organisation of the power, magnitude and influence of the BBC? Surely a truly great man, a lone voice unconcerned with petty morality, able to see beyond hype, brainwashing and group-think, with a mind and intellect so sharp, focused and uncluttered as to allow him unique insight into the peculiar times in which he lived, and to use this to present a dark vision of a world how it really was, rather than how it had been presented, despite the immense personal risks he took by doing so. A man who would risk everything by taking on one of the biggest, most powerful and most pervasive organisations the world has ever known, putting his own life on the line by daring to criticise it, and taking a scalpel to what passes for morality, exposing it for the sham that it is and creating a work so brilliant, so insightful and so incisive that it threatens to tear apart the big lie of the times in which we live and in particular force the hypocrisy and inconsistencies of one of its most powerful institutions to crumble into dust by pure logic alone.

Yes. All those things. But what would be his motivation? His justification for creating such a work? And, perhaps more importantly, what would happen to such a man? What would be the repercussions of criticising the type of power that is never normally criticised and normally goes unchallenged and unquestioned? Also, in keeping with the many brilliant literary and narrative devices I've used in this book, it's particularly clever as it allows me, the author, to address a lot of the criticisms I have no doubt people will make of this book once they read it, using my avatar, The Author, as my voice. So if you've had any issue with the book and it wasn't sufficiently addressed at the time it almost certainly will be here.

Anyway, the hour passed and Terry Ball returned, accompanied by two BBC paramilitaries, dragging with them a man who they each held by one of his arms. Or at least, he bore some of the hallmarks of once having been a man. By which I don't mean he was identifying as something else, I mean that whatever brutal torture he had been subjected to had left him a mere shell of a human being. It appeared that he was unable to stand unaided. He clearly no longer possessed many teeth. One of his eyes dangled out of its socket and swung around like a grotesque pendulum. Yet despite this, when he had been carelessly dropped onto the floor he still looked up at Dave McCreith, smiled at him and said, 'so, your grace. Finally we meet.'

He then rolled onto his side and attempted to sit upright, whilst taking the loose eye and trying to push it back into its socket, where it stayed for only a few moments before falling out again.

Noticing this, one of the paramilitaries looked rather sheepish. 'Er, sorry about the, er, minor damage, your grace. We, er, didn't realise you would wish to interrogate him yourself so had already started on the groundwork when we found out.'

'It doesn't matter,' replied Dave McCreith, clearly annoyed at having someone so low down in the BBC hierarchy have the raw nerve to even speak to him. 'Wait outside.'

'Er, are you quite sure, your grace? Despite the extensive damage to his physical form, this man remains one of the most wanted criminals on the BBC's Death List, and if we were to let him out of our sight we'd be breaking...'

'Wait outside!' yelled Dave McCreith, and the paramilitaries, whilst slightly reluctant, obeyed this command, nodding their heads in deference and beginning to head out of the office, before Dave McCreith sharply raised a finger. 'Leave your weapon,' he ordered.

One of the paramilitaries looked at Terry Ball, who nodded his assent, then took his gun from its holster and handed it to Dave McCreith, who briefly examined it before putting it in his trouser pocket. The paramilitaries then left the room, leaving only Dave McCreith, Terry Ball and the Author, still on the floor and attempting to keep himself upright. Dave McCreith took a deep breath and carefully scrutinised the figure on the floor, which, whilst physically pathetic, still exuded an aura of confidence that seemed to imply that despite his hopeless position he still felt no fear.

'So...' began Dave McCreith. 'Finally we meet. Finally I have you. All this time...' He stopped, as if conscious that he was making his excitement too obvious, and needed to play it cool. He cleared his throat before continuing. 'Well, I'm a busy man, and need to leave in half an hour for an urgent round of golf, so I won't waste time. I have one simple question for you: why?'

There was a pause. The Author looked at Dave McCreith quizzically, initially unsure whether this was a diversion or misdirection before deciding the question was genuine. He smiled again before offering his reply: 'because there needs to be balance.'

There was another pause as Dave McCreith processed this.

'I don't follow,' he admitted.

'The BBC was the most powerful organisation in the country but there was no system of checks and balances to control its power and influence. The majority of the public just accepted whatever they were told. There was no other organisation with an opposing worldview that came close to its size, so dissenting voices needed to be put out there.'

'Balance!' spluttered Dave McCreith. 'How dare you suggest the BBC doesn't have balance?! What about the comedy panel shows where every single person shares exactly the same political opinions?! How about Question Time, where journalists and politicians with the correct views are rewarded with regular appearances, and whilst we do have a few tokenistic right wing commentators, they're always portrayed as pantomime villains and framed in such a way that it's entirely obvious to the audience who they're supposed to side with, and which we really prefer not to film outside the Home Counties in case we end up with a studio audience who hold the incorrect opinions?!'

The Author merely smiled at this, as if they both knew he did not need to respond to it. Dave McCreith continued. 'Anyway... I don't believe your answer. Balance, you say? No... That's not it. There was some other reason. And I intend to find out what.'

He paused, attempting to regain his composure, before continuing more calmly. 'It would be in your best interests to tell me. Do not think you can outwit me or hide anything from me, for you cannot. I can literally see inside your mind!'

'Did it occur to you that I simply believed the things I wrote, and felt they needed saying?' challenged the Author.

'*No one* could believe the things in your spiteful book!' screamed Dave McCreith. 'The public *loves* the BBC and those who do not are *made* to love the BBC!' He then stopped as he attempted to compose himself.

'Perhaps you're overthinking this,' suggested the Author. 'I mean, when the book first become popular there were some who suggested it was the insane ramblings of an inmate in a mental asylum, were there not?'

'There were,' confirmed Dave McCreith. 'But there were many theories before your identity became known! I mean, when you released the book you spread vile rumours that it was in fact the work of a BBC insider, someone within the organisation who was disgruntled but too afraid to speak out publically, but that was just more of your misdirection, and part of your pathetic attempt to gain publicity for your pathetic little book!'

'I thought it was quite clever,' replied the Author. 'I mean, it sold ten thousand copies the week everyone thought Gary Lineker had written it.'

'It was not that clever!' screamed Dave McCreith, his frustration at The Author's refusal to submit to his questions becoming more apparent.

'Oh, I don't know,' replied the Author. 'All the misinformation I spread did wonders for the sales, as each one of those rumours I invented was far more compelling than the truth: that a worthless nobody living on benefits in a seedy bedsit managed to write a novel, bypass the usual establishment publishing industry by self-publishing it, get it into the world and into the hands of free-thinking people and show them a true alternative to the orthodoxy! And, despite what you say, it must have hit quite a nerve for you to ban it!'

'It didn't hit a nerve! How dare you even insinuate such a thing!? Anyway, we don't ban things! Once something is banned people can use that as a rallying cry, as evidence that their world view is so dangerous that it must be suppressed at all costs! No, we simply condition correct-thinking people into ignoring the opinions to which we do not wish them to be exposed. *That* is how democracy works!'

The Author smiled again here. 'Of course, your grace, I was one of the few to realise that, and even covered it in my book. Rather than openly banning things, it's much more effective to simply condition people to accept your worldview unquestioningly, to the point that they block out any thought you do not want in their heads, or at least obediently follow your orders regarding which opinions they should not even explore.'

'Well, of course,' agreed Dave McCreith. 'If you ban something it becomes a *cause celebre*, and people use that to accuse you of censorship. Our methods were much more subtle. Anyone who refuses to follow BBC Correct-Think is accused of being a 'hate group' and once we've called them that it causes the Obedience Switch to go off in people's heads, meaning they simply stop considering the objective truth of the argument. I mean, you can use the word 'hate' to denounce anyone, even if what they're doing completely fails to meet its semantic definition. Again, people don't notice! The word on its own is enough to tarnish and denounce any person or any opinion and once it's been invoked the followers of BBC Correct-Think simply switch off and think no more! That's the beauty of the system! That's what makes it so perfect!'

(You see? They're essentially summarising or expanding upon many of the things from earlier chapters. I said this chapter was best placed here.)

'And, of course,' continued Dave McCreith, 'that is what we did with your book. We ignored it for as long as we could, and when that was no longer possible we initially denounced it as worthless due to not having been released by a major publisher, then ordered the critics to write reviews in which they openly and viciously attacked it.'

'I don't know what you mean,' replied the Author, innocently. 'Didn't you read all those glowing write-ups of my book?'

'I assume that by that you're referring to those reviews that appeared on Amazon and on the paperback edition that you'd quite clearly written yourself!' Dave McCreith retorted.

'Indeed!' replied the Author, with a smile. 'But in the world of mainstream publishing, literally every single book that comes out is plastered with gushing quotes all over the cover and for four or five pages inside, yet every single one of them is written by a reviewer obediently writing what the publishers want, or by other authors who share an agent or publisher with the author of the book and who have written a quote praising it without ever troubling themselves to actually read it, meaning those quotes have as much credibility, merit and validity as the fake ones I wrote myself.'

'Hmm, but we also instructed literary critics to write hatchet jobs in broadsheet newspapers,' Dave McCreith countered, 'explaining that as a work that contains the incorrect views it must therefore be a 'book of hate' and in doing so instructing correct-thinking people that they must under no circumstances read it and certainly must not consider its arguments for themselves and make their own minds up!'

'But in the case of my book your attempts to instruct people to ignore it simply failed,' the Author pointed out. 'People were beginning to see through your propaganda and lies, my work very much caught the zeitgeist, or the public mood, if you will, and your attempts to denounce me failed. Not only that but the public saw through your attempt to claim the book was actually secretly written by the BBC as part of a covert plan to create the illusion of true resistance in order to weed out potential heretics attracted by its message!'

'Which is why we had to launch the lawsuit to *actually* ban your repellent work!' Dave McCreith yelled, clearly distressed to have had the failure of his system pointed out. 'People were starting to think for themselves! And that's the absolute worst-case scenario for the BBC! Independent thought, people challenging and questioning our every utterance! Where would that lead?!'

'As I said,' replied the Author, 'there needed to be balance. Anyway, it's an irony not lost on me that as soon as you launched your lawsuit, 'The BBC vs The Book the BBC Tried to BAN!' it led to the novel becoming far better known, and selling a great many more copies as a consequence.'

'We had to do something!' shouted Dave McCreith. 'People weren't listening to our orders not to read it! Anyway,' he gloated, 'I would suggest that the fact we took legal action very much disproved your ambitious and entirely misplaced belief that we'd somehow want to avoid embarrassing ourselves by launching a lawsuit where we tried to ban a book in the full knowledge that the lawsuit would be called 'The BBC versus The Book the BBC Tried to BAN!'"

'It made for a good headline, though,' retorted the Author.

'It would have done,' Dave McCreith corrected him, 'were it not for the fact that we instructed the media that they were not to report a single word on how we were pursuing a legal case against a book that made fun of us and, of course, the media obediently did exactly what we told them. Anyway,' he snorted, 'I think it says a lot about the lack of actual humour in your supposedly-funny book that the name of that lawsuit was the nearest it ever got to actual comedy.'

'Very harsh,' replied the Author, shaking his head in mock-offense. 'Anyway, apart from thinking the name of any potential court case would be so hilarious as to put you off pursuing legal action I was also well aware of how much negative publicity you'd get if after years of banging on about how strapped for cash you were and how vital the licence fee was, you then spent millions of pounds on a legal case to censor someone who hurt your feelings.'

'The public has no say on how we spend their supposed

money!' spluttered Dave McCreith, outraged at the very idea.

'Part of me thought that the BBC would never be stupid enough to launch an expensive lawsuit against a novel when they surely would have known it would only make them look incredibly stupid, petty, hypocritical and vain in the eyes of the public,' continued the Author. 'But, on the other hand, with no budget to promote the book, I suspected that the most effective way to make it better known would be to slyly encourage the real-life BBC to launch legal action against it, as the anti-BBC lobby would seize on the Corporation's attempts to have the courts ban it as the perfect example of its hypocrisy. Why, it never seemed to occur to the BBC, or the many other organisations and individuals I attacked in the book, that by suing me they were giving me the sort of publicity I could only have dreamt of and which money simply couldn't buy! Why, I even sent a copy to your legal department in the hope that's what you'd do!'

'Hmm, I'm not entirely convinced you really did want us to sue you,' replied Dave McCreith, raising an eyebrow quizzically. 'I think you wanted it to look that way, like you'd somehow tricked us into suing you or were trying to bluff us into not doing it, because a lot of things you wrote often seemed to be there as part of an attempt to deflect or discourage legal action. Not just in the expected name of the court case, but in how one chapter was peppered with oh-so-funny lines you'd obviously put in there so they could be quoted when we did sue you in order to make us look stupid.'

The Author shrugged. 'Perhaps,' he conceded. 'But I always knew the risks. Let's just put it this way: having written a book as powerful as the one I had, I saw a lawsuit not as a possibility, but as an inevitability. The bottom line is that when you criticise the Establishment they'll always find a way to get you, whether that's via the legal route or otherwise.' He paused for a moment before adding, 'and the irony was that when you launched the legal action I had no money anyway, meaning that not only did the Corporation become a laughing stock in the eyes of the public but you couldn't claim any damages from me... But then, as a result of all the publicity, the book did actually make me quite wealthy though, of course, by that point I had vanished.'

'Oh, yes,' replied Dave McCreith, slightly bitterly. 'Your book was tried, *in absentia*, as it were, as you were able to evade our death squads before they arrived. Though, of course, that luck would not serve you forever, as your presence here clearly attests.'

'It was quite a trial, when you consider how many people and organisations claim to love free speech in theory yet despise it in practice,' said the Author, almost taunting his captor. 'I mean, it wasn't just the BBC who took offence, was it? Joining the BBC in the legal action were just about all the other TV channels, Netflix, several world governments, representatives from a number of major sporting organisations...' He looked thoughtful before continuing. 'Let me see... Also involved were both the Custodian and Today's Post newspapers, publications supposedly on opposite ends of the political spectrum yet who finally found a common cause in their desperation to have my book removed from history. Then there were numerous Hollywood celebrities and several charities including, in an irony not lost on me, Amnesty International.'

The Author then smiled. 'It was also amusing to see all the comedians who I'd amalgamated into characters in the book joining the legal action against it.' He shook his head. 'I mean, the job of a comedian is literally to make fun of people, so who'd have thought comedians themselves would turn out to be so desperately thin-skinned that they called their lawyers the moment they even suspected someone was doing the same to them?'

(So, yes, comedians suing someone for making fun of them would really be quite staggeringly hypocritical, an irony to end all ironies, and would probably cause reality to collapse in upon itself, so that's another very strong and brilliant legal defence we'd cite in any subsequent court case against this book, okay?!)

'I did actually like some of those comedians,' continued the Author, 'but with most of them I was making the point that for all the hundreds of times they appeared on BBC TV and radio, I just didn't think many of them were that funny.'

'Comedy doesn't need to be funny if it expresses the correct opinions!' spluttered Dave McCreith, indignantly. 'Have you not seen the Mash Report?! If anything, denying someone the opportunity to appear on a BBC comedy programme due a minor detail like them not actually having any comedic talent is a form of discrimination!'

Dave McCreith composed himself before continuing. 'Anyway, the entire world wanted your book banned, no, *needed* it banned! Never in the history of literature had a single work caused so much outrage! It was a poison on society!'

'Indeed,' sighed the Author. 'Despite giving the book the name I did, and filling it with arguments as to why it would be hypocritical for people to try to ban it, I tend to take the view that if someone powerful wants to use the law to get what they want then they'll always find a way, some incredibly vague charge that can't really be proven or quantified but will be accepted by the judge if the prosecution has powerful enough lawyers. It could be something really minor, like claiming it would 'incite people to violence' or that it 'affected our corporate image', or even something ridiculous like saying the fact that there was a photo of the BBC's offices on the front cover in which their logo could be seen meant it was breaching copyright.'

'Yes, as we both know, whatever methods you thought would work were not successful,' countered Dave McCreith.

'Indeed, but I very much enjoyed that during the trial it became entirely clear that none of your lawyers had actually read the book they were being paid to prosecute,' continued the Author, 'and that the defence was able to constantly humiliate them by quoting lines from it implying that money-mad, moral-free lawyers would happily take a case without bothering to consider it properly, even if it led to them looking rather foolish. In fact, and please correct me if I'm wrong here, of the three lawyers who actually took the time to read the book in its entirety, and comprehend the full scope of its message, two of them were shortly afterwards declared insane and have not practiced since?!'

'Well, you invited legal action with the outrageous allegations you made in that book!' continued Dave McCreith, ignoring this question. 'I mean, did you expect us not to be offended when you included a chapter entitled, 'In Which an Organisation With An Unrivalled History In Covering Up Child Abuse Scandals... Offers Its Services to the Catholic Church'?!' In which the character supposedly based on me offers his skills as a consultant on that topic?! Where one of the visiting priests says, 'being an organisation with such a rich history of covering up child abuse scandals has long-since made the BBC a shining beacon of inspiration to the Catholic Church'?! And I tell them the best way to deal with such things is to announce a full investigation then ensure it ends with a few vague announcements of how 'lessons will be learnt' and 'a change in culture is overdue' before all the people involved in the cover-up are shuffled off into an easy retirement or a promotion?! And did it honestly not occur to you I might sue you for having a section in that chapter saying that the Director General's office includes a shrine to Jimmy Savile?!'

'Well, that wasn't meant to be taken literally,' replied the Author, in what Dave McCreith took to be a rather weak attempt at a legal defence. 'It was more an extreme metaphor regarding how the BBC presents itself as the very epitome of wokeness despite having some extremely questionable skeletons in, well, its closet. I mean, I deliberately made some parts of it so outlandish and outrageous that I thought it might work as a legal defence, i.e. something being so preposterous that no one could be expected to take it seriously. Anyway, he was a lifelong BBC employee and was knighted by both the Queen and the Pope, so exactly who has the moral high ground here?'

This was one reasonable point too many for Dave McCreith, and he lost his temper, striking the Author across the face with the back of his hand. 'Silence!' he screamed. 'I will not have you sit in my office and point out entirely obvious logical flaws in how the Corporation operates! I'm well aware that the BBC spent a huge amount of time, effort and money dealing with all manner of issues relating to child abuse, but just because something happens to be entirely true that doesn't mean people automatically have some sort of legal right to point it out!'

'Yes, and it's also an irony not lost on me that an organisation that for decades pointed to its proud tradition of satirising politicians on its comedy shows turned out to be so very thin-skinned when it was itself the subject of satire,' added the Author regaining his composure from the blow. 'I thought that was a fairly strong legal defence, too. I mean, what about that time Nigel Farage asked the police to look into whether his treatment on Have I Got News for You might have broken electoral law and the BBC responded with a statement justifying it by saying the BBC makes fun of everyone and that 'Britain has a proud tradition of satire'? I couldn't help but feel it was a bit rich for the BBC to have defended the use of satire only to then launch a massive lawsuit against me because I wrote a book that made fun of you.'

Dave McCreith glared back at him, as he was sick and tired of ironies being lost on him. 'That's completely different!' he shot back indignantly. 'The BBC has a proud tradition of satire but that does *not* extend to allowing people to make fun of the BBC itself!' He shook his head in disbelief. 'I mean, what's so difficult to understand about that?! It's perfectly simple: people appearing *on* BBC comedy shows are allowed to make fun of anything and everyone because they have our approval, but anyone who does it outside our jurisdiction enjoys no such protection, and *certainly* not if they're daring to mock *us*! Making fun of the government is hilarious satire but doing it to the BBC is a hate crime!'

Dave McCreith paused for a moment. 'Anyway,' he sneered, 'you refer to your book as 'satire', though I would suggest calling it that contravenes the Trade Descriptions Act by virtue of how painfully unfunny it is!'

The Author smiled. 'Well, the BBC still refers to Some News For You, We Have as 'satire', even though that programme recently celebrated a landmark anniversary, what with it being twenty five years since anyone appeared on it and actually said something funny,' he shot back. He paused for a moment before going back to his original point. 'Anyway, I did try to legally cover myself by publishing the book on Amazon's American website, meaning it was protected by their First Amendment laws. Say what you want about America but at least they have actual free speech and don't pursue legal action seeking to imprison someone over a not-very-funny tweet in which they joked about blowing up an airport.'

Dave McCreith took objection to this. 'What do you mean we don't have free speech over here?! We define free speech as the practice of fully and unequivocally supporting the rights of people who completely agree with us to say whatever they like, so by that definition no one is a greater supporter of free speech than we are! The British public has always been completely free to believe and say whatever the BBC tells it to!'

The Author reflected on this before continuing. 'But of course none of that mattered in the end, because by the time the book came to be on trial you had complete control of our legal system and were able to make whatever laws you liked, so the trial itself was a mere formality. Albeit one that became a rather public embarrassment for you.'

'The Corporation could not let your sickening slurs stand!' retorted Dave McCreith. 'Even though a great many of them were clearly exaggerated for supposedly comic effect! I mean, you depicted me as a psychotic, power-mad, crazed dictator called 'Keith Davison'! And there's another thing! Did you think you were legally covered by having characters whose names made it clear they were very thinly-veiled caricatures of real people, like the Prime Minister or even myself?! And, in particular, what made you think you'd get away with having the organisation in your book, the supposed 'British Brainwashing Company' have exactly the same initials as our corporation, the Broadcasting for Britain Company?! I mean, how did you expect *not* to be sued when your fictitious company, 'the BBC', had the same initials as the *actual* BBC?!' Did you not know we copyrighted the letters B and C to prevent anyone else from using them?!'

'No,' admitted the Author, 'but I wouldn't have minded quite so much if it wasn't for the fact the BBC also bought the rights to adapt my book for TV.'

'We weren't going to turn the book itself into a TV show!' Dave McCreith spluttered. 'We were simply going to wait about thirty years then turn your story into a big-budget, hand-wringing, miscarriage-of-justice drama focusing on how brutally you were treated by the callous BBC, but not until my successor is attempting to distance himself from my reign by claiming there's been a 'culture change' and 'everything's different under my jurisdiction', by which point I'll long since be retired on a massive BBC pension!'

Terry Ball suddenly looked confused, and turned to the Author. 'Hang on, if the fictitious organisation in your book was called the 'British Brainwashing *Company*' then why did people in that book always use the shorthand 'The Corporation' when referring to it?'

'Er, I don't know, probably just a generic term,' replied the Author, vaguely. 'Anyway, the BBC is always doing thinly-veiled portrayals of real people in its dramas, like that one 'Roadkill' that was clearly based on the Prime Minister, so why are you allowed to do that and not other people? Anyway, Viz always get away with it. They've always got cartoon strips featuring parodies of politicians, TV presenters, organisations and celebrities, *and* they use their real names! As do Private Eye and Spitting Image, so what's your justification for suing me over the Book when you didn't do the same to them over the years?'

'Well, it's much harder and more expensive to sue a well-known magazine or TV show than it is an individual author who's published a book himself, as he'll be unlikely to fight back due to being unable to afford a legal defence team or having the media connections to make the public aware he's being sued and thus bring bad publicity to those who brought about the legal action,' replied Dave McCreith, almost as if he was just speaking instinctively without realising what he was admitting.

'So, picking on the little guy, then?' the Author responded. 'Sounds like a form of bullying, if you ask me, which is particularly interesting when you consider how the BBC and Custodian are always up in arms about how bullying is one of the most abhorrent practices in the modern workplace and never stop going on about it if, say, a Home Secretary does it.'

'Stop veering away from the topic in question!' ordered Dave McCreith, realising what he had said and quickly returning to his intended line of argument. 'You clearly thought you'd be safe from legal action and you were wrong, so that concludes the matter. So why did you do it? Fame?!'

'You're forgetting I published it under a pseudonym,' the Author pointed out. 'To be honest, I never even thought you'd find me once I'd evaded you. Particularly after I used the profits to buy a castle in the lawless no-man's land that now exists between England and Scotland.'

'Well, you obviously aren't as clever as you thought, because we did!' shot back Dave McCreith. 'We found you in your remote hideaway where you clearly thought you'd be safe! Because there's not a single inch of this country that we don't monitor and control!'

The Author looked briefly sad as he reflected on this, presumably as he had thought he was safe. Dave McCreith continued.

'Yes, that's why you did it! Money, pure and simple! You did it to cash in on anti-BBC sentiment, trying to turn an easy profit by cynically attempting to appeal to those who felt disenfranchised with the so-called 'mainstream media' by producing a rabble-rousing, lowest-common-denominator piece of trash masquerading as a novel!'

'There are obviously people who do that, but you can accuse anyone who writes for a living of simply writing what their readers want to hear,' the Author pointed out. 'Both right-wing and liberal journalists have to write what their editors and readers expect, or it won't get commissioned and they won't get paid. So any professional writer is suspect in that sense. But, anyway, if that were true of me then I'd have done exactly what you said and cynically targeted one group, but that would have been too easy, which is why I wrote something that challenges everyone's beliefs and, as you'll remember, makes fun of both sides of the political spectrum and everyone from the liberal media to conspiracy theorists. Sure, I could have written a hand-wringing, Brexit-is-awful novel but instead I chose to strike at the heart of everything that correct-thinking people hold dear!'

'Yet your so-called 'work' still proved popular,' replied Dave McCreith, pointing out a flaw in this argument.

'Yes, it can go both ways, I suppose,' the Author admitted. 'I would imagine there will be both obedient followers of the BBC who will refuse to read this book simply based on the title so will never discover what it's really about, whilst there will also be many anti-BBC people who'll say it's brilliant based on the title alone, without ever really understanding the actual point. I mean, if I wanted to write a commercial book I'd have done one where the awful Tory government was the target, not the BBC, and if I'd done that then the BBC itself would have thought it was brilliant!'

Dave McCreith looked annoyed at this unfortunately entirely accurate suggestion. 'Well, yes, but those are the rules. If people think it's totally fine to criticise the government or press but are outraged by the very concept of criticising the BBC then that proves how well conditioned they've been! It's still that maternalistic, 'Auntie Beeb' mentality, that the BBC is like your master and you do everything it tells you!'

'Which is *exactly* why it must be criticised!' the Author shot back. 'If something is widely believed to be beyond criticism, that has to be the thing you criticise! We shouldn't have sacred cows! No-one is above and beyond criticism!'

'The Corporation is completely beyond reproach!' Dave McCreith yelled, outraged at this full frontal assault on all that he held dear. 'We're the BBC! A beloved institution, loved by the people of Britain as much as they love contributing to its upkeep, and if they don't want to contribute to its upkeep, why, we'll have them sent to prison! There is only the BBC now! I see the future, and all I see is the jackbooted foot of a BBC paramilitary rammed into the face of mankind!'

The Author smiled once more, as if they both knew that this

outburst entirely confirmed the depiction of the BBC as it was in his novel, as a power-mad, violence-heavy rogue state in all but name.

'Well,' continued Dave McCreith, attempting to justify that position, 'we had no choice than to resort to violence and propaganda! Our position had got ever weaker over the years! For decades no one dared to criticise the BBC! No one even thought about it! It was just one of those ever-present institutions that you'd always known to be there and wouldn't have been able to imagine life without even if you'd tried! But then things started to change. Politicians, previously our most obedient lapdogs, started to question whether the licence fee was appropriate in the twenty first century! Journalists, previously utterly terrified of questioning us in case it scuppered their chances of being a highly-paid talking head on Question Time, started to write heretical articles that examined alternative funding models! We had to do something! We had to stem the tide! We had to protect our position!'

'And I had to respond to that,' responded the Author. 'Balance, remember?'

'Balance!' spluttered Dave McCreith, indignant at the very concept. 'That has no place in the modern world.'

The Author raised an eyebrow, but it was the one above the eye that was hanging out, so the effect was minimal. Meanwhile Dave McCreith paced around his captive, unable to accept that he was being honest with him and refusing to believe that there was not some deeper truth to which he had simply been unable to dig. Like the True Believer that he was, he simply could not begin to understand how somebody who held such heretical opinions could be anything other than severely mentally ill, yet his experience with the Author suggested this was not the case. After a moment his face lit up.

'I've got it!' he yelled, in a moment of inspiration. 'Devil's advocate! That's all it was! You wanted to stir things up! Your little book was nothing more than you taking cheap shots at everyone you could think of, and whilst you claimed it to have been some sort of grand philosophical treatise that took a hammer to hypocrisy in every area of society you were just trying to offend as many people as possible and cause an outcry! That's it, isn't it?!'

The Author's expression suggested this may have played some role in his motivation but was not the driving force. 'I won't deny it played some role in my motivation,' he replied, 'but it was not the driving force. Sure, I enjoy winding people up on Twitter. When the book came out and people started tweeting that they were offended by a particular thing, I would immediately tweet back asking why they hadn't been offended by a different thing, thus turning the tables on them so that they went from seeming like they were woke to suddenly not seeming nearly woke enough. It's just sport!' He smiled with the few remaining teeth he had. 'And it was very much a vindication of my world view, and of the book, when I'd receive death threats from both gammons *and* snowflakes, equally outraged by the content.' He paused to throw up some blood. 'You know, people always complain about how awful it is to deal with internet trolls and social media abuse but I always loved it! The fun you can have! I mean, if it's such a problem, don't use social media. Why does no-one ever think of that elegant solution?! But whilst I won't deny I enjoy annoying people, that interpretation is too simplistic. I mean, if I were merely playing Devil's Advocate then I'd just have written something that was blatantly, outrageously offensive, rather than deconstructing each topic, looking at it objectively and pointing out the flaws, wouldn't I? I wouldn't have included long, expository chapters that never seem to end and appeared to consist of nothing more than two characters having a long and complicated conversation, would I?! There was always a point to my so-called 'offence'. All my points stand up to scrutiny.'

'Hmm, you seem quite proud of yourself,' replied Dave McCreith, condescendingly. 'But that chapter in which the author of the book appears as a character in order to explain and justify pretty much every point he makes *in* the book really isn't as clever as you think it is, either.'

The Author raised an eyebrow as if to dispute this. I don't know why he keeps raising eyebrows considering the damage that's been done to his eyes, really. 'Not even the way I pre-empted all the possible ways people could be offended by the book?' he asked. 'Anyway, if *you're* that clever then why didn't you just read that chapter rather than doing this, as that was basically where I defended myself in the same way I'm doing here? You could have saved yourself a lot of time.'

'It was rather an obvious literary device, I thought,' replied Dave McCreith, 'having the author in the book basically be your avatar.

Frankly, a lot of not just that but of what you've been saying to me here frequently comes across suspiciously like word-for-word defences you've already prepared in order to second-guess your critics.'

The Author looked ambiguous here, as if partly offended but also pleased his work had been read in such detail. 'Ah, but I *did* pre-empt a great many of the criticisms that were made against my book, and sometimes it *was* pretty much word-for-word! I mean, it's surely not much of an argument if the person you're arguing with knew you were going to say it even before you did, is it? Anyway, I had to do that. My work was so powerful and, as I said, challenged *everyone's* beliefs, so I knew I'd come under attack from literally everyone, and the book would be denounced for being both a danger to sacred institutions and an assault on public decency, and I needed to be prepared to defend myself. Even if, a lot of the time, the attacks were from people too dim to properly comprehend my points.'

Dave McCreith glared at him here, unable to decide whether this was a thinly-veiled criticism of him, but the Author gave no further indication and merely continued.

'Anyway, the point is that the nature of modern offence means people are outraged by everything and anything, which on the one hand renders their outrage utterly meaningless but on the other means that those who wield the power to cancel or prosecute those found guilty of it are extremely dangerous, and that has very serious consequences for supposedly democratic societies.'

Dave McCreith glared at him again, wondering whether, if there was one, single takeaway from the entire book they were discussing, this was actually it.

'I mean,' continued the Author, 'what sort of society prosecutes someone for writing a novel? Did it not occur to you that the whole thing could simply have been an exercise in free speech, and nothing more? An attempt to test the very limits of our so-called 'liberal society'? And what better way to do that than by attacking the BBC, the very bastion of liberalism and tolerance itself, to see if it's actually as supportive of freedom of expression as it claims?'

Dave McCreith glared at him yet again, or maybe it was just the same glare he had kept up, but the reason he did not interrupt was because he felt the Author's current train of thought may eventually take him to a destination where the question he wanted answering would be addressed. The Author stopped to pop his errant eye back into its socket before continuing.

'Still, I knew that anyone who set out to denounce the book would find a way to do so, no matter how many attempts I made to pre-empt them. Journalists, lawyers and particularly people on Twitter would go through it with a fine-tooth comb to find something to object to, no matter how minor or insignificant, then use that to denounce it as a 'book of hate'. It could be a throwaway sentence, or a single word, which would be quite appropriate considering one of the themes in the book is the manipulation of language. But there's literally no way of knowing. Maybe they'd notice I mentioned the QAnon conspiracy theory and claim that meant the book was supporting it, even though it was blatantly obvious that the point there was the irony of the BBC heavily pushing its readers not to even entertain the idea of well-known people being child abusers and a major organisation covering it all up.'

Dave McCreith glared at this. You know what, I've mentioned that far too often; let's just assume it is just one single glare he's sustaining until I say otherwise.

'Or they'll say it's misogynist, completely ignoring the subtleties of the arguments, such as how I critiqued the bandwagon-jumping of modern feminism rather than the principle of feminism itself, and despite the fact that several characters made explicit reference to how any criticism of a woman, no matter how valid, can be denounced by it automatically being decried as misogyny without the argument itself even needing to be considered.'

'Well, you brought that upon yourself to some extent,' Dave McCreith pointed out. 'I mean, what about that term you were apparently hoping to bring into common usage but which was always going to cause outrage? 'Femi-Gammons'?! What was that supposed to mean?!'

The Author explained: 'Femi-Gammons are feminist gammons. They're women who are the first to make fun of middle-aged, ruddy-faced men who get angry on political discussion shows at people who don't share their views, then completely fail to see the irony when they themselves hysterically scream abuse at anyone who dares to challenge their own opinions. You know, like many of them did when I first coined the phrase, clearly failing to realise that in doing so they totally proved its validity. The point I was making was that people are never quite as different as they like to think they are, though I'd long since come to realise that people never really properly understand my points.'

The Author sighed at the inevitability of all this, but at least it was better than Dave McCreith glaring again.

'Or they'll pick up on that bit where I talked about the BBC writing worried columns about how Donald Trump's followers must have somehow been brainwashed to believe everything he tells them and ignore all opposing views, and that a way must be found to break them out of their worrying state of obedience, despite that being the exact way the BBC expects its audience to be with them. They'll see that as a pro-Trump rant and denounce the whole book as sickening without understanding it's a comment on media bias rather than an expression of political support, because that implies there are only two sides to an argument, and everything is black and white rather than there being infinite shades of grey.'

He sighed again. 'So, you can see why I chose to retreat from society once I made my millions. Anyway,' he sighed again, his sighing now becoming as common as Dave McCreith's glaring had been, 'of course, the point is that it's impossible to tell, and there's simply no way of predicting what'll be selected next to be attacked by the woke mob or the other lot.'

'Ah, but that's the beauty of the system!' replied Dave McCreith, gleefully rather than glarefully, which is definitely a word. 'Offence is our greatest weapon! With that we can control everything and everyone! It's been proven time and time again that the best way to control the population is by manipulating their emotions, and that there's no better way to do that than with blind hysteria! Public shaming! Throughout human history that's how we've sought to control people and break heretics, whether it was the Salem Witch Trials, McCarthyism or, I don't know, a Gap advert where a white girl leans on the shoulder of a black girl being deemed a thousand times worse than slavery! It doesn't matter! We can work with anything! And the hilarious thing is that no one ever dares to challenge wokeness! You accuse them of something and they apologise desperately and change the supposedly offensive thing without considering for one moment whether or not it's actually offensive! No one will say, 'we think you're overreacting and this isn't really offensive'. Because they're terrified to! They know how swiftly they can be denounced! Hysteria and fear! That's all we need to ruthlessly crush debate!'

The Author looked thoughtful at this point, as if he knew all this. 'And whatever happened to perspective?' he pondered. 'The so-called woke people think that any opinion that's more than about six months old is sickeningly repellent but I don't suppose it's ever occurred to them that the same thing may be said of their supposedly flawless morality in fifty years' time. Yes, values and opinions change, but my point is maybe we should bear that in mind before hurling abuse at someone who doesn't agree with us.'

(So, I know the Author sounds smug all the time, but I think this next bit goes some way towards explaining that.)

'Yes, but do you know what?' he continued, mournfully. 'I know I come across as smug, a know-it-all who's got the answers to everything and thinks he sees deeper than everyone else, but do you know why that is? If people weren't so offended that they refused to debate things then maybe someone would have engaged with me and I'd have seen things differently. I may well have changed my mind on various topics had someone been willing to calmly debate them instead of just screaming hysterically because someone held opinions different to theirs.'

'Calmly debate things!' said Dave McCreith, laughing. 'Good luck with that!' He paused for a moment before crouching down and staring into the Author's face, directly into the one eye that was still functional and in his head. Noticing this, the Author grinned at him and lifted up his dangling eye so that he could see them both. Sickened by this insolence, Dave McCreith knocked the eye out of his hand and stood back up.

'This is all very interesting exposition, but I have to know why! Why won't you tell me why?!' screamed Dave McCreith, desperate and running out of patience. 'No one questions the BBC! It is forbidden! Everyone knows the consequences! Yet you... You! You did. Normally I'd just assume you were a mental or something but now I've met you I don't believe that to be the case! So why?! Why did you do it?! Tell me! Tell me! I must know!'

The Author looked him straight in the eye, with both eyes (holding up the dangling one again). 'I have told you,' he replied, simply.

Dave McCreith paused then looked thoughtful. He took a handkerchief from his pocket and dabbed his nose, which he realised had started bleeding.

'Everything okay?' asked the Author, with mock concern. 'It looks like you might need some medical attention.' His eye had fallen out of its socket again and he pushed it back, whilst using his other eye to perform what Dave McCreith took to be a wink, though it was impossible to tell as the other eye was no longer attached to an eyelid so there was no way of making a comparison.

Ignoring the mock concern, Dave McCreith continued. 'No one could have developed such a pathological hatred for the BBC without reason,' he mused. 'So what was yours? Was it that you were a failed comedy writer who'd had one rejection too many? Or perhaps you always wanted to work for us but knew you'd never be able to because of a comprehensive school background, and had a chip on your shoulder about that?'

'Ah!' said the Author, his face lighting up triumphantly. 'I pre-empted that accusation in my book too! I even had a part where one of the characters pointed out that privileged people always claim to believe in fairness and meritocracy yet whenever someone from a more humble background accuses them of having had everything handed to them on a plate they immediately invoke the term 'chip on your shoulder'!' He paused for a moment before quietly uttering a phrase that reflected his view that the people who end up in positions of authority inevitably seem to have got there based on their backgrounds and regardless of the fact that they rarely, if ever, possess the intelligence or creativity to do a good job in them. 'Those that have the vision don't have the power, and those that have the power don't have the vision.'

'You should feel nothing but shame for having wasted so much of your life on creating such a repellent work,' said Dave McCreith, ignoring this rather quotable utterance, as he had with so many other entirely valid points.

'It only took me two months,' replied the Author, defensively.

Dave McCreith snorted derisively. 'That long?! Anyway, what did you think you would achieve with your so-called book? Did you think your words would be enough to bring down the behemoth that is the Broadcasting for Britain Company?! It was nothing more than simplistic juvenilia passing itself off as a clever critique when all it did was make endless so-called jokes about the classic BBC sitcom Mrs Brown's Boys! Also, it wasn't even that well-written from a literary or narrative perspective. You had the chapters set in the BBC Re-

Education camps – which don't exist, by the way – that were the closest thing to a plot, which even then was quite predictable, and then there were the chapters featuring the character supposedly based on me where each one had me meeting a character who clearly only existed to illustrate a topic so that I could offer exposition on the Corporation's take on it, like TV licensing, or sport, or charity, or whatever, and it was all just a bit too convenient as once the relevant points had been made the characters just disappeared and were never seen again.'

The Author appeared unaffected by this criticism. 'Well, you could look at just about any novel and point out it's deeply unrealistic,' he responded, then paused before continuing, curiously, 'so, did you read it all the way to the end?'

'As it happens, no,' replied Dave McCreith, unsure why this was relevant. 'I think I made it to the penultimate chapter or so.'

'Interesting,' replied the Author, but offered no explanation as to why this might be, to Dave McCreith's considerable suspicion. That's a clever plot point, by the way, but you won't realise until the end. 'Anyway,' continued the Author, philosophically, 'it's not like I killed anyone. It's only a novel.'

'Hmm, well, it's not a *real* novel,' sniffed Dave McCreith, sniffily. A *real* novel is written by somebody who was privately educated and that dares to tackle the biggest issues facing us today, as long as they are the *correct* issues, and are dealt with in the correct manner, by telling the reader exactly what to believe, with no room for ambiguity! And a *real* novel, of course, is one that no one actually wants or needs to read. You simply buy them to have on your shelves so everyone can see how clever and cultured you are but if you think you may actually have to discuss it at a dinner party you just skim the Wikipedia synopsis.'

The Author smiled at this attack on the literary merit of his work, and on literature itself. 'So, you don't think questioning an unchallengeable and unquestionable media monolith that has more power than the government counts as a big theme? You don't think attempting to understand the underlying principles for what we base our moral outlook on counts as a big theme?' he asked.

'No!' Dave McCreith shot back. 'Books shouldn't be challenging! You shouldn't read a book to learn something new or to have your worldview challenged! You should read a book to be reassured that everything you believe is correct and beyond criticism! But your book did none of those things! It was often quite confusing trying to work out what you actually believed, or what you were telling your readers to believe! It was impossible to tell whether the characters were mouthpieces for your own opinions or were actually making fun of people who really do believe the things they said!'

'That's because the readers were meant to decide for themselves,' replied the Author. 'Anyway, perhaps I was making the point that having a character who says a particular thing or proposes a certain world view doesn't necessarily mean that the *author* believes such things. I mean, if someone makes a film *about* Hitler you don't automatically assume it's a *pro*-Hitler film, do you? Anyway, technically, I never really expressed my own opinion, nor made it very clear if I even had one.'

'Or was that just a lazy cop-out?' Dave McCreith shot back. 'Perhaps a lot of the controversial opinions you had your characters voice *were* actually what you believe but you used that literary technique to distance yourself from them, as a rather lazy get-out clause?'

'Ah, but if that were really a thing then I wouldn't have even mentioned it in the book, would I?'

'Well, you didn't,' replied Dave McCreith, slightly confused. 'I just mentioned it now. Still, authors should tell their readers what to think, not offer them a range of possible opinions that they're expected to weigh up and decide upon! I hate ambiguity! I hate mixed messages! I don't want complicated thoughts to exist anywhere!'

(That's a reference to George Orwell's 1984, by the way, a book that's been mentioned a few times and is almost as good as this one. I recommend you read it if this book hasn't put you off reading forever.)

'Anyway,' persevered the Author, despite knowing his cause was a lost one, 'just because you don't agree with every single point in a book doesn't mean you can't like it overall. Is there a single person in the world with whom you agree on absolutely every point of every issue? If there is then you probably need to start hanging out with more intelligent people. Anyway, if you're confident in your beliefs then you should be reading things that challenge them rather than support them, as otherwise it's nothing more than pointless reinforcement.'

'At the BBC we are fierce champions of diversity, but that does not extend to diversity of thought!' Dave McCreith snapped. 'There is no place for such a thing at the Corporation!'

'Yes, well, writers *should* be afraid that their books will get them in trouble, or they're not writing them properly!' the Author shot back. 'If you write a book expecting everyone to praise everything about it and agree with everything in it then what's the point?!'

'But there has to be more!' spluttered Dave McCreith, his frustration at failing to uncover what he believed to be a hidden truth becoming more evident. 'Nothing you have told me explains what would possess anyone to spend months coming up with a novel that runs to over a hundred thousand words unless they had compelling reason! What was it?! Revenge? Who were you after?! What was your motivation?!'

'A carefully placed full stop can change the world more than a nuclear bomb,' said The Author. 'I read that somewhere. So that makes it a quote rather than plagiarism. Things can change. The BBC may have the artillery and total control of the media, but there will always be pockets of resistance, pockets of independent thought, a few lone voices in the wilderness that people will always want to hear.'

'You are incorrect,' answered Dave McCreith. 'The Resistance will be crushed, and your book with it.'

'Everything you've said here shows why you'll never defeat the Resistance,' explained the Author. 'And that's because you can't understand it. In the same way you can't understand I didn't write this book to cynically appeal to a disenfranchised demographic, or for easy profit, or to jump on a bandwagon in exchange for sales. There was too much in my book for one person to ever agree with all of it. Around halfway through the writing process I realised I wasn't writing it for everyone. I wasn't even writing it for anyone. I wrote it for no one. I mean, what kind of person would bother to write a novel that is not only untouchable in the eyes of publishers but whose contents would be considered outrageous in one way or another by literally everyone who ever read it? When it comes down to it I now realise I wrote this book for one person, and that person was me.' He paused for a moment before conceding, 'still, it was nice when it also sold millions.'

The Author coughed up some blood and they both looked at

the small puddle in front of them with interest. It became apparent to both of them that the interrogation was reaching its natural conclusion, something that could almost certainly also be said about the Author's life, though in his case it wasn't exactly natural.

'How did you identify me, anyway?' asked the Author, casually, knowing the question was, by this point, entirely academic. 'I used a pseudonym, all the online accounts and email addresses I used to promote it were fake names... I only told a few people it was me who'd written it. But one night I was dragged from my border castle by your guards. How did you track me down?'

'Do you have any inkling?' asked Dave McCreith.

'Only one idea,' replied the Author. 'I told my parents I'd written it and they were the first two people to buy the e-book. You could have accessed Amazon's records and made the entirely reasonable assumption that the first two people to buy a self-published novel would be friends or relations of the author, but as they were the same age, lived at the same address and had the same surname it was fair to think they were the author's parents, allowing you to identify me that way.'

'Your parents bought your book?' said Dave McCreith, curiously, his surprise all but confirming the Author's theory as incorrect. 'Why do you think they did that? An act of blind devotion? Pity at the lack of prospective sales? Mere curiosity?'

'I think it was more that as I'd been telling them about it whilst I was writing it they possibly suspected I had lost my mind, so bought it just to check,' replied the Author. 'I don't know if they actually read it, though.'

'And is your repellent work *really* the sort of thing you'd want your mother to read?' asked Dave McCreith.

'Well,' replied the Author, 'if my mother were to read it, on the one hand I think there are a lot of references and points she would not get, so it's possible that specific points I was making might be completely lost on her, but on the other hand I would hope she would overlook these and just be proud that her son had written such a brilliantly provocative novel.'

'Hmm, well, your theory as to how we identified you is clever and entirely plausible, but incorrect,' replied Dave McCreith. 'It was actually pure luck. When we became aware of your repellent work we stopped at nothing to identify you, offering a reward to all BBC staff if they could assist us, despite our official position being that anyone who read it would suffer severe consequences. But somebody from our comedy department recognised some of the themes and characters from a sitcom script somebody had sent in, a script so sickeningly anti-BBC, parodying all our greatest comedy shows, that it could only have been submitted to us as some sort of prank by an individual with a particular vendetta against the Corporation. The reader in question located the script and, even though you had submitted that under a fake name, we had other records of the relevant email address being linked to you. And thus it was just a matter of locating you physically, especially after you evaded us prior to the trial. And that was done when a raiding party of our paramilitaries was travelling to Scotland to put down a rebellion and noticed signs of life in your previously-abandoned castle so naturally investigated, thinking it could be hiding insurgents, but instead stumbled upon our greatest prize.'

(Oh, and it you're wondering how Dave McCreith knows all of this when at the start of the chapter he was amazed they'd managed to locate the Author, it's because he was fully briefed about it all by Terry Ball during the hour in which he was waiting for the Author to be brought to him, something that closes an apparent plot hole and definitely isn't just another example of poor writing on my part, okay?)

The Author nodded, glad to have had his hypothesis confirmed as incorrect, but still disappointed with himself for having essentially let one of his mistakes be his downfall. For the first time during the interrogation he appeared to slow down, as if the wounds from his brutal ordeal at the hands of the BBC Paramilitaries had finally caught up with him. He continued, but slower and more philosophically, as if resigning himself to the fact that there would be no escape and all he could do now was justify his existence to himself in the guise of doing it for the benefit of another.

'Oh well,' he replied, as if accepting his fate. 'I still reckon that in fifty years' time, when all the mad hysteria has died down, my novel will be celebrated as a classic, the only one that took a truly fearless look at the bizarre times in which it was written. I mean, some people will probably still virtue-signal their offence at the content, but it'll be something I could never have anticipated, like me not explicitly stating my support for dogs having the vote or something.'

'I wouldn't be so sure,' replied Dave McCreith, clearly still annoyed at having failed to extract the single piece of information from his captive that he so desperately wanted. 'You think your wretched book will change anything? Right now we have rogue computer bots roaming each and every one of the internet's darkest corners for even the slightest mention of your repellent text, to erase it from existence forever! The joy of Kindle is that we can go in and erase the book from every single one of them now we have the means! Burn them! Burn them all!'

Terry Ball, who had not said anything for ages but had nonetheless been paying close attention to everything that had been said, looked up with interest at this point. Was he referring to books or people? Because these days e-books were more popular than printed ones, though he conceded that 'delete them! Delete them all!' would have sounded less dramatic. Again, the Author offered a reaction that was the opposite of what Dave McCreith would have hoped for or even expected. He smiled.

'And as for you,' continued Dave McCreith, clearly annoyed by this, 'you will be buried in an unmarked grave. Your pathetic life was a waste and all you have to show for it is your sordid little book that will be forgotten before your corpse has even gone cold.'

'Ah, but you can't put a bullet through an idea! And neither can you put bullets through hundreds of frankly brilliant ideas strung together into a quite brilliant narrative!' replied the Author, causing Dave McCreith to wonder why, when he was quite clearly very close to death, he not only refused to denounce his heretical text but continued to go on about just how brilliant he clearly thought it was.

'No, but we can put a bullet through the person who wrote it all, and everyone who read it, and anyone who even admits to having heard of it!' Dave McCreith retorted. This still failed to have the desired effect on the Author.

'Did you really think I was naïve enough not to know what would happen to me if I dared to mock and parody an organisation as powerful as the BBC?! That book was my suicide note! Do you think I didn't know that?! By killing me all you're doing is fulfilling the prophecy!'

Dave McCreith stared intently at his captive, and there was a moment's silence. Try as he might, he was simply unable to discern whether there was any truth to a single thing the Author had said.

Had he told him everything, or nothing at all? He crouched down in front of his captive and held up three fingers. 'The only truth is BBC Correct-Think. How many fingers am I holding up?' he demanded.

The Author glared at him, then smiled, refusing to take the bait, and scooped his loose eye into his palm before lifting it up and holding it in front of the Director General. 'How many eyes am I holding up?' he asked.

'Oh, you think you're funny! But you do not exist! I have personally cancelled you!'

'I knew as much when I was brought here,' the Author retorted. 'I knew what my fate was. And, anyway, I'm not afraid to die!'

'Well, then, that is really quite fortunate,' replied Dave McCreith, all of a sudden quite calm. 'You see too much. You see too deep.'

Then he pulled out his gun and pulled the trigger.

Phew, that was powerful stuff, wasn't it? Well, apart from the use of the word 'pulled' twice in the same sentence. Or, now I notice, that I didn't clearly mention that when Dave McCreith 'pulled out his gun and pulled the trigger' he was also pointing the gun at the Author, which he was, otherwise he might have just been shooting it into the wall or something. Still, let's not let poor writing get in the way of the brilliant points being made. Oh, I just did it again by having 'let's' and 'let' within a few words of each other. Still, I suppose the point I'm trying to make is that there are more important things to kill people over than opinions and ideas, aren't there? I reckon there are. I think it's definitely a thing that suing someone over a harmless novel really is a waste of everyone's time and, crucially, licence fee payers' money, if you get my drift. The brutal suffering that the Author underwent is surely not something that should be tolerated in a so-called civilised society, and especially not when it's carried out by an organisation supposedly dedicated to fairness, decency and equality. Okay? Also, has anyone ever stopped to consider the fact that, as there's something to offend literally everyone in this book, that makes it one of the best examples of pro-equality literature ever written? I should surely get credit for that.

# Chapter Twenty One:

# Sneaking In Through The Tradesmen's Entrance

*In Which Our Heroes Set Out on the Final Journey of Their Near-Suicidal Mission to Infiltrate New White City with Their New Friends Who Bring Some Much-Needed Diversity, Only To Very Nearly Scupper the Mission After Almost Being Caught Out Using the Wrong Toilet of the Twenty Seven Different Ones Intended To Cover All the Possible Gender Identities*

So, remember that last chapter happened ages ago and we're now back to the main narrative, okay? Right. Our heroes awoke at dawn to prepare for a mission from which they could consider themselves lucky if more than one or two of them came out of alive. After breakfasting on leftover Rat on a Stick from the night before they set about discussing how to put their audacious and near-suicidal plan into action.

'Right,' said Hunter, as he threw the stick and skellington from his Rat on a Stick onto the smouldering ashes of the previous night's fire. 'Our shift starts at five. They get us in early to make sure no executives have to glimpse any poor people even for a moment. And we have our own entrance and exits, for the same reason, so getting you in won't be a problem. We may not even see anyone. Of course, the real problem is how we'll get you to the upper levels.' He looked at his watch. 'Right, we should get going.'

'Can you wait five minutes?' asked John Smith. 'I need to go for a poo and it's probably better to do it now than to risk slowing us down once we're in there.'

'Okay, good idea,' agreed Hunter. 'Right, if anyone else needs a poo then go now so we don't have to make any unscheduled stops once we're inside.'

Following this useful advice, about half of the group went off for a poo. And I should just clarify that the party was made up of the original five who escaped from the camp plus three from the rebel group. That not only makes it easier to keep track of the characters but makes sense within the narrative because a smaller group would have a better chance of sneaking in unnoticed. Anyway, five minutes later they were all back, composed themselves and silently started out on the journey from which they knew most of them stood little chance of returning.

Also, let's remember that the group made up of our heroes was led by a woman for quite a large part of its escape, and is now being led by a black man! That'll certainly destroy any criticism that this book is some kind of alt-right manifesto hidden inside a weird, yet hilarious, Trojan horse. And, on top of that, one of the others who make up the armed rebel group, the one who's second in command, is a lesbian! I mean, she certainly looks like one, what with short hair and everything and, as shown by the fact she's in an armed rebellion, she's quite violent, giving even further credence to the idea. Let's call her Brenda, as that's a good, solid lesbian name. Still, does this mean the book is now even more woke for introducing another minority character, or truly monstrous for having one who so blatantly fits a stereotype? I don't know, I really don't. The rules are just too complicated to follow anymore. Anyway, at this point our heroes looked really cool and serious as they continued to look up at New White City, and ponder the uncertain fate that awaited them there. You could imagine David Bowie's 'Heroes' playing at this point. I'm attempting to make this a bit more like a film, as I reckon TV has ruined people's attention spans and made it harder for them to use their imaginations, so I'm just trying to make it a bit easier.

They reached the contractors' and cleaners' entrance of New White

City without encountering another soul and Hunter used his security card to let them all in. Cautiously, he kept looking around until they were all inside, then listened carefully for any signs of life.

'As I thought,' he said. 'We're pretty much the first here. The building is arranged as a hierarchy, with the most important people at the top, PR and Propaganda just beneath them, then news, then it basically drops in importance so the lower floors are people who do light entertainment or work in low-level finance, then there are loads of empty floors below that. But at the moment the only floor I'd expect to have anyone on is the sixth from the top, as that's where News 24 is based so obviously they have a night shift.'

'But can you get us to the Director General's office?' asked Emmeline Moneypenny.

Hunter stroked his chin as if pondering the best course of action, then his expression changed to one suggesting something else had dawned on him. 'Yes, but it's just occurred to me that none of the top execs really get into their offices until eleven, or half ten at the very earliest, so they won't arrive for hours... However, that can work to our advantage, as we can simply get up there without anyone seeing us then hide in an empty office until they arrive.'

The others pondered this and swiftly agreed it was the best course of action. They now made their ascent up the building, which I won't describe in too much detail as it's just a group of people climbing loads and loads of stairs or lifts where they can use them. I mean, it's a huge building, remember? The top levels are pretty much in the clouds. So they did that, sneaking by the floor where the BBC News team was, who wouldn't have thought their presence out of the ordinary anyway, and made their way to the very top floor, which, to their surprise, had a surprisingly low occupancy rate, as if the BBC had built a massive headquarters only to end up using less than a quarter of its floor space, in yet another example of BBC wastefulness. Still, in this case it was advantageous, as they managed to find what they took to be an unused office at the far end of the corridor, where they then sat around for about five hours, realising, amongst other things, that they needn't have taken the toilet break before they set out after all.

At just before eleven, having taken another careful toilet break, just in case, they got ready for their final assault.

'Are we likely to face armed resistance at this level?' asked John Smith.

'It's unlikely,' replied Hunter. 'As it's difficult, if not impossible, for anyone below senior executive level to even get up here. Even our security passes will no longer work on floors this high up after seven so, whilst on the one hand it's a good thing we got up here when we did, we may have to use other means to gain access to some rooms.'

'So what will we do?' asked Barry Begbie.

'I do have a plan,' replied Hunter. 'Just follow me, and go along with everything I say. The Director General's office is the last one on this corridor.'

He opened the door, stuck his head out and looked around cautiously before signalling for the others to follow him. Slowly and carefully, they made their way along the corridor.

Just then, two suited white men, who were obviously senior executives, emerged from an office and noticed our heroes, in particular Hunter. They looked at each other, as if wanting to check they were both thinking the same thing before they risked actually vocalising it.

'Erm, sorry, but do you work here?' one of them asked Hunter. 'I mean, this is the executive floor.'

'What are you suggesting?' asked Hunter, staring at the man accusingly.

'Er, nothing!' replied the man, obviously looking extremely embarrassed. 'It's just that, er, like I said, this is the executive floor and I assume you're a cleaner or something...'

'Are you saying there's some reason I couldn't be a senior level BBC executive?' asked Hunter, again with a strongly accusatory tone.

The BBC executive went bright red. 'Er, no, not at all, sorry. Sorry...'

Both the executives scurried away, too embarrassed to look at Hunter again until they were a few metres away, at which point one of them briefly glanced back and said, 'er, this has nothing to do with your race!' rather unconvincingly. A few moments later they had disappeared into another office. Hunter smiled.

'Works every time!' he said, triumphantly. But this triumph was to be short-lived. They stopped for a few moments and listened carefully. Hearing voices suggesting another door was about to open, Hunter indicated they should all quickly hide in the toilet that was just next to them. They did this, still listening carefully, and emerged a few moments later, only to discover their re-emergence was premature. They walked right into another BBC executive, who scrutinised their group then glanced at the sign on the toilet door.

'I'm sorry, but is that a gender-neutral toilet? Should you have been using it?'

There was a pause as everyone waited for someone else to make the next move. As it turned out, the person to actually do that was Brenda the Assumed Lesbian, who knocked the executive unconscious with a single blow. If it turns out she's not actually a lesbian I'll still use the strength she clearly has as evidence that my presumption wasn't entirely unfair. She then carried him into the toilets, again showing quite considerable strength, and placed his unconscious body in a cubicle. Once back outside they placed an 'Out of Order' sign on the main toilet door, which they had taken from the cleaners' trolley they had had with them the whole time as part of their cover but which I didn't see fit to mention until I realised I needed to use it as a plot point.

They all paused for a moment, to catch their breath and again listen carefully for signs of danger. Moments later yet another door opened, and another BBC executive emerged. It could be one we saw in a previous chapter, like the Head of PR or someone, but it really doesn't matter. He also looked suspiciously at the group, though mainly at Hunter.

'Er, can I... Help you with something?' he asked, vaguely, as if not sure whether he should say the thing he was thinking.

'We've been told a senior executive needs a kidney transplant,' replied Hunter, without missing a beat, 'and these members of the cleaning staff have been sent up here by Human Resources to see if any of them are a match.'

'Oh, right, okay,' replied the executive, slowly walking away whilst continuing to watch them before, when he was far enough away, casually taking out his mobile phone.

Hunter had noticed this just before the man disappeared around the corner.

'Okay, we may have been rumbled,' he said. 'We may not have

long.' At that point they heard the unmistakeable sound of boots marching hurriedly up the stairs. Hunter looked alarmed. 'They're on to us!' he said, shaking his head. 'It must have been those first two execs we saw... Right, we've no time to lose! Move!'

'How did they get here so quickly?' asked John Smith.

'There's a super-fast lift that runs directly from the ground floor to this one, exclusively for executives or emergencies,' replied Hunter, showing it definitely wasn't a plot hole. With him leading the way, they ran down the corridor to outside Dave McCreith's office. At this point the door at the far end of the corridor, which led through from the stairs, burst open, and six paramilitaries ran in, pointing their weapons at our heroes.

'Drop your weapons!' one of them shouted. Also, sorry, I've just realised I didn't make it clear which of our heroes had weapons. Well, it was just the three who were already part of the armed rebellion, as there wouldn't have been much point in John Smith and the others having them as they wouldn't know how to use them, would they? Anyway, the point of their mission wasn't to do a massacre. How would that make them any morally superior to the BBC itself?!

There was a tense standoff. Hunter looked around, knowing in his heart what had to be done. He turned to the others. 'Make sure you get in there, and make sure you do what needs to be done.' Before any of them could react he had pulled a handgun from each of the holsters on either side of his waist, and ran towards the paramilitaries, screaming as he did so, firing ruthlessly at them, knowing that what he did undoubtedly meant his own death but could lead to freedom for millions. He took out at least three of them but, of course, being outnumbered, there was only one way it could end. His handguns were no match for the paramilitaries' automatic weapons. He was shot to pieces, holes appearing all over his body and chunks of flesh going everywhere. There was lots of blood but it was a really powerful, cinematic scene, and would have packed a really strong emotional punch if I had properly developed the character and not just introduced him a couple of chapters ago.

(As to why no other members of our heroic team were killed or even wounded, well, that's because the BBC paramilitaries were highly trained and very much focused on the most immediate threat, so not one of their bullets missed its target, okay?)

Still, what a heroic death for one of the characters of colour! I know that the overall diversity of the book has now decreased again but I think you have to agree it was worth it. Anyway, on the topic of diversity, I never explicitly mentioned the race of any of the characters, as far as I can remember, so if you assumed they were white without me having said so then it's you who's racist. Though, I suppose, when you consider that two of the main characters are senior BBC executives you were never going to just assume they weren't white. That's one of the problems, you see: a lot of the people in this book work for or have worked for the BBC so are by that very nature going to be white. If I try to include diversity for the sake of it it's not going to be credible because of the very nature of the thing I'm satirising.

Oh, but hang on... A few things have occurred to me as I pondered all this. One of the common themes of this book has been that of organisations that present themselves as diverse when only really making a tokenistic nod towards it (as with the Rule of One) but now I've gone and introduced a black character then killed him off in what could be seen as... An entirely tokenistic gesture! Oh, damn, damn! I kept on accusing the BBC of using tokenism only to do it myself! And I've *also* just remembered that some people get annoyed if you kill someone off solely as a narrative device. This is usually when it's the main character's girlfriend or something, but they also get equally outraged if it's an ethnic minority. And, *even worse*, I've remembered that the woke people get particularly annoyed if you have minority characters who die for *any* reason! Remember how they got annoyed when Game of Thrones did it? And now I've done it too! Oh, you just can't win, you really can't. Oh well, let's just finish the story and see how things stand then, okay?

# Chapter Twenty Two:

## Confronting the Auntie-Establishment

*In Which the Author Stops Providing Synopses of What Happens In the Upcoming Chapter, As That Very Much Blunts the Power of the Narrative and Spoils the Plot Twists*

At not quite the same time as the stuff in the previous chapter was happening, Dave McCreith was standing by his window, looking down at the camp, with no idea that a number of its inhabitants were at that moment launching a daring attack upon the Corporation itself. Having had an early start and arriving in the office at 10.45, he was quite irritable and, shaking his head in disgust, stared at the camp as if it was the most disgusting thing he had ever seen.

'Well, seeing as how I inexplicably no longer seem to be holding meetings all the time, are there any other events of which I should be aware?' he asked his assistant.

'A few more food riots, your grace,' said Terry Ball, 'and, at the same time, a number of people have pointed out it's a little hypocritical of the BBC to run endless programmes and articles about how brutal Tory austerity has led to even more people becoming reliant on food banks whilst skirting around the issue that at the same time these people on the poverty line are being endlessly hounded by the BBC over their outstanding licence fee payments.'

Dave McCreith looked utterly perplexed at this. 'It's outrageous to suggest that the BBC doesn't care about poor people. I mean, by imprisoning people too impoverished to pay for their TV licence are we, or are we not, therefore *ensuring* they have a roof over their head and three square meals a day?'

'Well, I think you make an excellent point there, your grace,' concurred Terry Ball.

'Indeed,' concluded Dave McCreith, by now bored of the topic. 'Anything else of interest?'

'Oh, yes, you may wish to see this, your eminence!' said Terry Ball, switching on the giant TV that was mounted on the wall and tuning it to Fox News.

(And I know what you may be thinking here: Fox News is surely a rich source of satire, so why didn't I make fun of that along with the BBC? Well, it's quite simple: Fox News is the predictable bogeyman of middlebrow types so that would have been far too easy! This is all about challenging things that normally go unquestioned, not attacking the same old predictable targets, okay?! Plus, in any case, I don't think I've ever watched it anyway.)

So, Terry Ball put Fox News on and they watched the bulletin, beginning with a reporter in full war zone body armour, standing outside the White House.

'We're hearing reports that President Prince Harry is about to make a statement from outside the Oval Office,' he began, 'and that once the statement is over he will oversee the public execution of rebel leader Kanye West.'

'Huh, politics in America is all a puppet show these days, distracting people from the real issues,' said Dave McCreith, disinterested, and used the remote control on his desk to switch the TV back off again.

Once the TV had been switched off he looked thoughtful, as if he believed he had heard something. You see, this chapter actually partly runs in parallel with the last one rather than starting the exact moment it finished. Otherwise, how would I explain what our heroes were doing during the rather long conversation that's already taken place? So, in this chapter they're only just hearing the shouting outside and, oh, the shooting's just started right now! Hearing this deafening sound, Dave McCreith and Terry Ball stared at the door in confusion, with no idea what was going on.

'We haven't discovered *more* heretics in the PR department?' Dave McCreith asked, as if this would have been a minor convenience but nothing more. 'Those executions always give me a headache, which is why I *specifically* ordered them to not take place on the higher floors!'

'I'm not aware of anything, your grace,' Terry Ball replied.

The office door then burst open and our heroes practically fell into the room, out of breath and desperate.

'Who are you?!' demanded Dave McCreith, furious at them not having knocked, and for not being high-level BBC executives. He then noticed two of them were armed, despite not being BBC paramilitaries, and tried to get to his desk either to find a weapon or raise the alarm but was unable to do so before Brenda pointed her gun at him.

'Not so fast, your grace,' she said. 'Both of you. Step away from the desk and stand by the window where I can see you.'

Dave McCreith and Terry Ball complied, moving slowly but continuing to look around for anything they could use to get out of the predicament they found themselves in. (And if you're wondering why our heroes don't seem to be showing any sign of emotion at the death of Hunter I would suggest they're either in shock, or the adrenaline is carrying them through, or they're just trying to honour his last words, okay?) The unnamed member of the rebel group who hasn't even said anything so far now locked the door behind them and shouted to the remaining BBC paramilitaries outside.

'If you try to come in here then your beloved Director General dies!' he threatened, meaning he has now had a line.

'Who are you people?' demanded Dave McCreith.

Seizing the moment, John Smith stepped forward. 'We're the British Public.'

Dave McCreith pulled a face of disgust. 'I don't normally allow the proles to get anywhere near me,' he said. He then looked more closely at the group and realised he recognised some of them. 'Oh, hang on,' he corrected himself. 'I know some of you. Barry Begbie? Emmeline Moneypenny? I remember you. Former stars of the Corporation who refused to tow the line.'

Jeffrey Harding grinned at him expectantly. 'I used to be on Radio 4 panel shows, you know!'

Dave McCreith shook his head dismissively. 'Hmm, yes, I'm sure I'm very happy for you. What do you people want?'

'Answers,' replied John Smith, simply.

'Answers about what?' demanded Dave McCreith.

Our heroes looked at each other and, realising they all had a great many questions, John got his in first. 'Well, first of all, I want to know why I ended up in a BBC Re-Education Camp! I was there for months, I think, but they never told me why! I was never told, or even given the slightest indication, of what it was I was supposed to have done or said or thought! How could I repent if I didn't know?!'

'There are literally millions of people in our camps,' replied Dave McCreith, dismissively. 'What, you think you were so important that I personally know all the details of your case? Any anti-BBC Thought-Crime is punishable by incarceration without trial and without the guilty party even being told what they did.'

'There must be some way!' shouted John Smith. 'I have to know!'

'Er, actually, your grace, we do have access to the centralised BBC Thought-Crime Database,' interjected Terry Ball, 'so we could check on that.'

'Be quiet!' yelled Dave McCreith, evidently somewhat agitated. 'If I ask you to speak then you may but other than then I would ask you to remember you're nothing more than my bumbling assistant whose only role here is to take notes or weirdly ask all sorts of questions that force me into providing lengthy and unnecessary exposition!'

'Yes, your grace,' replied Terry Ball, clearly unhappy but choosing not to express it.

'Okay, I can find you on our system, I suppose,' replied Dave McCreith. 'But I'll need to get to my computer.'

Brenda narrowed her eyes suspiciously. 'Very well,' she said, but continued to point her weapon at him. Dave McCreith sat down at the keyboard.

'Name?'

'John Smith,' replied John Smith.

'What? Really?' said Dave McCreith, as if he was being lied to. 'There'll probably be about three thousand John Smiths on the system.' He sighed, annoyed. 'I mean, if your surname's Smith, what sort of parent then calls their son John?! For Christ's sake, call him

Cornelius or something so he stands out. Ball, can you do this? I'm not very good with computers.'

'Of course, your grace,' said Terry Ball, still annoyed from being shouted at. 'Er, I'll need to access the computer,' he said. Brenda the Assumed Lesbian looked at him suspiciously but nodded her assent.

'Okay,' she said, 'but no sudden movements.'

'Of course not,' Terry Ball assured her, slowly walking to Dave McCreith's desk, waiting for the Director General to stand up, then sitting in front of the computer before starting to type. A few moments later he looked flustered. 'Yes, there are, er, nearly three thousand. I don't suppose you know your BBC-UIN?'

'My what?' asked John Smith.

'Your 'BBC Unique Identity Number',' replied Terry Ball. 'It's a number that the BBC assigns to every single citizen of Britain so we can log everything we know about them on our system. Actually, now I remember, it's not public knowledge that we use them, so you wouldn't be expected to know yours. What's your date of birth?'

John Smith told him but this only narrowed the search down to a few hundred. Look, this bit's getting a bit long but the point is that because John Smith has such a common name it took ages to find him on the system. When he was eventually located, Terry Ball looked vaguely disappointed, as if the whole thing was something of an anti-climax. And if you also think that's the case, then, actually, that's kind of the point, okay? John Smith is not some superhero, or some rebel who can lead mankind to a better world. He's just an everyday, normal, boring guy who got caught up in all this mad, out-of-control bureaucracy. Right? Anyway, Terry Ball read out what he had found.

'Hmm, well, on the night of your arrest it says your account was flagged – because personal Twitter accounts are automatically linked by us to your BBC Unique Identity Number – after you posted an offensive tweet. Let's see... Right, at 11.17pm on the night in question, during an episode of Question Time, you tweeted, 'right, what's the next step going to be in the BBC's woke crusade?''

'But...?! What's even offensive about that?' John Smith asked. 'It's not as if it isn't common knowledge how woke the BBC is.'

'It's because the word 'crusade' is sickeningly offensive!' Dave McCreith cut in, as if this were obvious. 'It reminds of us a time in history when western so-called 'civilisation' made a truly abominable incursion into the Middle East in an attempt to brutally suppress a minority group!'

'Oh...' replied John Smith, his intense sense of anti-climax felt by everyone in the room, even, to an extent, Terry Ball and Dave McCreith, who, whilst not strictly offering consolation, gave a more cold-hearted speech that nonetheless pointed out why John Smith was foolish to think his life had special purpose.

'Don't take it personally. Everyone likes to think they're special. No one likes to think they're an insignificant cog in a huge machine. Just because you happened to make it here to speak to me, the most important and powerful person in the world, doesn't mean that your personal story automatically has some sort of huge significance or that your life journey is some sort of worthy narrative.'

John Smith looked disappointed but couldn't deny the basic logic of this. 'So that's it,' he said, crestfallen. 'I somehow thought I must have been important. To be part of this. To make it here.'

'No,' replied Dave McCreith, bluntly. 'People have this ridiculous tendency to look at the disorder that is human existence and attempt to find some sort of meaning, some sort of narrative, some sort of story... When in reality there is nothing there but chaos.'

(So, did you notice what he said there? A good story isn't that important, and it's actually foolish to expect one. Sometimes you should just accept that powerful points can be made without them necessarily having to be framed within a brilliantly-told narrative. And it's the same with characters. It doesn't matter if they're one-dimensional, ill-defined (or barely defined at all) or largely implausible as long as their existence serves to make some kind of point. Okay?!)

There was a pause. The balance of power seemed to have shifted in Dave McCreith's favour. It was as if he had become emboldened by the fact that the party supposedly there to kill or apprehend him was in fact turning out to be insignificant, a mixture of people who had been exiled from TV or were simply too unimportant to have appeared on it in the first place, and had calculated a way to turn things to his advantage. He scrutinised them in turn, then, whilst looking at Kerri Barnes-Bridge, said 'judging by your body type I have to assume you're a feminist.'

'Yes, that's right,' she replied, unsure what he was implying. He scrutinised her further.

'And, let me guess... Some sort of comedian...' Kerri Barnes-Bridge nodded, suspicious as to how he was somehow guessing all of this. 'And... You're annoyed that Radio 4 was happy to have you on every single one of its panel shows yet the only time you could ever get on TV was appearing on Parody the News or Barry Begbie's show doing your generic woke stuff.'

Kerri Barnes-Bridge nodded again. 'How do you know all this?'

'Oh, you learn to make these connections when you're the Director General,' he replied, dismissively. 'Anyway, there's no need for you to get involved in all of this. You obviously won't achieve anything here, and those of you who aren't killed the moment the guards get in will be sent to our Manchester site to be tortured to death. But I may have a place for you.'

Our heroes looked at her as if to assume even considering such an offer was inconceivable, yet her face suggested she was open to it.

'It's quite simple,' continued the Director General. 'We've been made aware of a threat to our way of doing things, taking the form of a group of unattractive activists who refer to themselves as the 'Minging Community', who object to the lack of representation amongst their number on the BBC. In order to neutralise their threat we intend to create a group under our control that claims to have the same aims but is in fact almost entirely made up of attractive people. However, in keeping with our ancient and noble tradition of The Rule of One, we would actually need one minging person to join their group, just to make it look vaguely plausible. The duties would be straightforward. You'd go on all sorts of programmes talking about your aims, and whilst you wouldn't get as many prime-time TV appearances as the more attractive members of the group, you'd still get a few, and the other members would retweet everything you ever posted out of sympathy at you not being as attractive as them, because the rules state that somehow means you're a better feminist.'

'Your Director Generalship...' replied Kerri Barnes-Bridge. 'You honour me, you really do. I accept! Oh, I'd be living the dream! Getting to join the popular girls! Proper TV appearances and not having to do crappy Radio 4 panel shows all the time! When can I start?!'

The rest of the group were surprised and appalled by this

treachery.

'What?!' said John Smith. 'I'm surprised and appalled by your treachery!'

'What do you mean?!' asked Kerri Barnes-Bridge, defensively. 'Back when we were in the camp you remember it being discussed how I claim to have morals but will happily sit through Barry doing all his stuff about Down's Syndrome and rape jokes without objecting because I'm just pleased to be on TV and don't want to rock the boat! Why is this such a surprise? When did I ever indicate I wouldn't do something like this?'

Our heroes looked at each other ponderously, only to realise that, strictly speaking, she did have a point.

'Good. Then it's decided,' said Dave McCreith. Sensing he was taking control of the situation he turned to Jeffrey Harding. 'You. I believe you said you used to be on Radio 4 too?'

'Yes, indeed, your Director Generalship,' confirmed Jeffrey Harding, bowing obsequiously. 'A loyal servant of the BBC for decades until I was kicked out for being too old and too white!'

'I believe we can find a place for you back within the Corporation,' Dave McCreith assured him, at which his face lit up. 'We're thinking that for our next direction we may actually start siding with that rather strange assertion some people make that being a white, middle aged man is the hardest thing in the world these days, and would subsequently need to increase representation amongst that most discriminated against of groups.'

'Really, your grace?' replied Jeffrey Harding, excitedly.

'Yes,' confirmed Dave McCreith. 'We always need individuals for our terrible Radio 4 comedy shows to act as if they're offering some form of opposition by constantly going on about the 'bloody Tories', even though having a BBC salary for life hardly qualifies you as an outsider figure and, when you think about it, actually makes you little more than a state-funded comedian. You could easily fill that role.'

'Yes, your grace! I could, and I will!' said Jeffrey Harding, even more excited than before. 'I accept!'

'Treacherous scum!' yelled John Smith, surprising even himself. 'Has our journey together meant nothing?!'

'What did you expect me to do?' replied Jeffrey Harding. 'I'm just a generic Radio 4 comedian! I pretend to have a strong moral compass but ultimately rely on them paying me to do unfunny stuff about how awful the Tories are! What do you think I'd do otherwise, go off to Hollywood or write a brilliant sitcom?! I'm lucky if I can even sell fifteen tickets when I do a stand-up gig! I have to do this!'

'Good,' replied Dave McCreith, before pausing very briefly then turning to Terry Ball. 'Cancel him,' he ordered.

As the conversation had drifted into offers of TV work, less attention had been paid to Terry Ball, or that by sitting at Dave McCreith's desk whilst checking the records he had been able, very carefully, to take a handgun from one of the drawers. Quite possibly the one used to shoot the Author a few chapters ago. Now, at his boss's behest, he calmly fired a bullet into the chest of Jeffrey Harding, who collapsed onto the floor, gasping. And bleeding, obviously.

Kerri Barnes-Bridge looked slightly confused. 'Er, sorry, your grace, but I notice you shot him after making an offer of employment, so does the one you made to me still stand?'

'Yes, of course,' replied Dave McCreith, to her considerable relief. 'I mean, that stuff about the Minging Community obviously made sense, but do you really think the BBC is looking to employ middle aged white men for its comedy panel shows at the moment?' He shook his head in disbelief as he looked down on the pretty-much-dead body of Jeffrey Harding. 'I mean, really... Why is the offer of working on Radio 4 so incredibly appealing to these people? I mean, I know that for a huge number of these so-called 'comedians' it's the only way they'll ever be able to make a living, but still... Why can't they show some real ambition? I mean, no one ever says 'ooh, I fancy a good laugh, I'll put on Radio 4!' do they? It's basically a thing that old, senile people have on in the background all day but never really pay attention to anyway. A lot of the time, our research shows, the majority of so-called Radio 4 'listeners' are people who leave it on in their houses if they're away for the night, as if to suggest they think any potential burglars will hear it and go 'oh, we shouldn't break in here. There are definitely people inside, as why else would they have Radio 4 on at deafening volume at three in the morning?'!'

There was some shock in the room, but not that much, as Jeffrey Harding wasn't really a major character. The main feeling now was one of uncertainty. From Terry Ball's position at the desk he had his back to the wall and everyone in our heroes' party was comfortably within the range of his weapon. There was a tense standoff, as it became apparent that Brenda the Presumed Lesbian was the only person who could get a clear shot at him.

'And you!' said Dave McCreith, looking at Brenda the Assumed Lesbian. 'We could find a role for you at the BBC. Even if you've never even considered comedy, we could get you a role for life as a Radio 4 comedian because they classify any ranting by a lesbian, no matter how unfunny it is, and particularly if it's about how awful men are, as stand-up comedy! Even if we did expect you to do a gig, it would only be in front of a carefully-selected audience in Brighton who'd think you were brilliant just for saying Brexit was bad! And you'd be able to contribute to the four thousand podcasts we release every week by hosting at least ten of your own, in keeping with our slogan 'BBC Sounds – Giving A Podcast To People Whose Voices Aren't Deemed Important, Interesting, Intelligent or Funny Enough To Appear On Proper Radio Since 2017'!'

'Are you assuming I'm a lesbian?' replied Brenda the I'm Wondering If She Is a Lesbian After All.

'Erm, no...' replied Dave McCreith, unconvincingly.

'Well, I'm not,' replied Brenda the Not a Lesbian. 'I just have my hair like this because it's easier to maintain. And why can't a woman be angry all the time without people assuming she's a lesbian?'

'I'm sure I don't care,' replied Dave McCreith, no longer concerned about what he said now that he knew he was not addressing a minority. 'I naturally retract the offer of employment I made a few moments ago. And I also retract you.'

'That doesn't really make sense...' Brenda the Non-Lesbian began to say, before Dave McCreith nodded again at Terry Ball who, taking advantage of Brenda being distracted, fired the gun again, right into her head, killing her instantly. Also, please bear in mind that it's just been established that she wasn't actually a character reflecting diversity, so apparently that means she can now be killed as quickly, casually or pointlessly as I like, which would not have been the case if she had been. Those are the rules, you know. Still, I think there's a valuable lesson to be learned, and that's to not jump to conclusions based on appearances and stereotypes. At this point, the third member of the rebel group, which is to say the last one who had a gun (also the guy who was guarding the door, remember?) tried to quickly turn to Terry Ball but was too slow and was also shot, and died. So, just to be clear, none of our heroes have guns now.

Kerri Barnes-Bridge again looked confused. 'But, just to clarify, you're *definitely* not going to shoot me?'

'No!' replied Dave McCreith, irritably. 'Like I said, we have a purpose for you, and if I was going to have you shot I'd have done it already!'

'Okay, just checking,' replied Kerri Barnes-Bridge, relieved.

An uncertain pause, during which no one was sure whether to talk, or what the next step would be, was broken unexpectedly by Terry Ball.

'Oh, and don't think any of you will get out of here alive. There's a foot pedal under this desk that alerts security, and I pressed it a few minutes ago. Thirty armed militiamen will be here in moments, so if you have any clever last words you were thinking of saying, you'd probably better say them now.'

He walked over to the door, unlocked it and flung it open, allowing the surviving paramilitaries from the previous chapter to enter and point their guns at our heroes.

Emmeline Moneypenny, Barry Begbie and John Smith looked at each other. Kerri Barnes-Bridge was no longer paying much attention and was already on Twitter boasting about how she was going to be, like, really famous.

Emmeline Moneypenny turned to Dave McCreith. 'Look, I worked for the BBC for over thirty years. But none of what I've witnessed over the last few years makes any sense. If I have just one question, it's this: why?'

Dave McCreith smiled. 'The work of the Corporation often seems contradictory, random and confusing. But there is actually an underlying law to it all. A law, or rather a rule, that has always dictated and controlled everything we do. Hmm...' He stroked his chin thoughtfully. 'You're all going to die anyway. And I always enjoy explaining all this. So, perhaps it's time I told you about... The Great Polarity.'

# Chapter Twenty Three:

# The Great Polarity

*In Which the Thing This Chapter Takes Its Name From Is Revealed So I Won't Say What It Is Here As That Would Be Stupid*

Sorry, that was probably a bad place to end a chapter. I was trying to add dramatic tension by making a reveal but then making you wait until the next chapter to find out more, except that as this is a book it was just a matter of you turning/swiping to the next page just like any other part of the book, so it entirely negated that purpose. Still, when the big budget BBC adaptation of this comes out it will be a brilliant place to finish the penultimate episode, leaving the audience spending the next week wondering just what exciting revelations will await them the following Sunday night! Unless the whole thing gets released to the iPlayer in one go, I suppose. Also, I realise that if the point of that cliff-hanger was to create tension that would be immediately resolved in the next chapter then I've ruined that too by the rambling aside I've just written. So, bearing that in mind, let's get right back to the action!

The guards summoned by Terry Ball having covertly pressed the foot pedal alarm burst into the office, making it entirely clear to our heroes that there was no escape, at least not unless they could think of a plan so brilliant, so offbeat and so original that a writer as mediocre as I am almost certainly won't be able to come up with it. Knowing the balance of power had altered dramatically and now entirely favoured him, Dave McCreith smiled and started to stroll around the room. He looked thoughtful, and walked over to the window before casting his eyes over the stunning view of the ruined London. The others waited, unsure whether he was awaiting some cue from them or was simply taking his time before making this big reveal. He then walked over to his desk and sat down.

'You all came here with questions. But there is only really one answer.' He paused yet again, savouring his ultimate triumph, his final victory. 'The Great Polarity! The one single principle upon which the BBC has always operated. The one simple rule that elegantly explains everything we have every done. The Great Polarity! It's quite simple, really. Let me explain it to you.'

'Er, your grace,' interrupted Terry Ball, 'is it such a good idea to tell these people about the BBC's Great Agenda? It seems a bit pointless, if you ask me, as we're having them killed, plus whilst I'm aware they're heavily outnumbered, there's always that very slim possibility they have an escape plan that actually works, and they then get away and are able to tell the world of our supreme plan, which you've inexplicably explained to them in great detail.'

'Nonsense,' replied Dave McCreith. 'As you said, there's little to no chance of them escaping, so I can't see what harm there is in me now explaining to them our organisation's entire motivation.'

Terry Ball looked slightly frustrated at this point. 'Well, couldn't you at least shoot them first, maybe in the leg or something, *then* explain it to them as they're dying, just to make sure?' he suggested, at which Dave McCreith got angry.

'No, worm! I am *sick* of your insolence, always thinking you know better than I do when you're nothing more than my lackey, my bumbling, dim-witted assistant! When I want a meeting arranged or a coffee made I'll let you know but until then please keep your counsel to yourself!'

Terry Ball looked uncharacteristically angry himself at this point, but attempted to hide it, simply nodding and saying, 'of course, your grace, I apologise for my insolence.'

'The Great Polarity,' continued Dave McCreith, 'is the simple rule by which the entire Corporation operates, the fundamental principle dictating that the Great British Public must always be kept in a state of utter confusion, having no idea whatsoever what they should think about anything. And just to *really* keep everyone confused, every ten, or fifteen, or twenty years, we completely shift our opinion on *everything*. Blacking up is fine, blacking up is sickening... Page Three is revolting exploitation, Page Three is incredibly empowering... Feminists are right about everything, feminists are transphobic monsters... Multiculturalism is one of the greatest success stories of modern Britain, cultural appropriation is the most sickening hate crime a person can commit... That is The Great Polarity! A one hundred and eighty degree about-turn every couple of decades! And if people ever notice this contradiction they're too terrified to say anything as we whip up hysteria to destroy anyone who challenges us and our worldview! It's all about sowing such confusion that the public literally has no idea what right and wrong are anymore! That is how we manipulate the population! War is peace! Freedom is slavery! Does anything really change? No! Only the words! We set the agenda and the public dances to our tune! All the BBC has *ever* been about was absolute control, pure and simple!'

The considerable effort that the Director General was going to in order to set out the complete agenda of the BBC did make John Smith wonder whether he really did intend to have them killed, as if he did then that would surely render his lengthy outburst something of a waste of time, but he still decided to ask a question, despite the personal risk.

'But why? Why would you ruin a man's life? Why would you destroy the life of a man who, by your own admission, was a worthless nobody whose life meant nothing?'

'Because we must always be seeding confusion, and because we *can*,' replied Dave McCreith, simply. 'And here's the other thing!' He smiled gleefully in anticipation of making another Big Reveal. 'When you stop to think about it, despite all the people on Twitter moaning about everything and making their death threats, whilst those in the liberal media are terrified to question them, did you ever once actually *meet* a woke person?'

Our heroes looked thoughtful at this, as if they were being asked to question something they had never previously considered but, now the question was asked, it raised a surprising possibility.

'There were a few people I knew at BBC Comedy who claimed to be,' admitted Barry Begbie, 'though I always strongly suspected it was just a front, part of the image they projected in order to get work.'

'Well,' added John Smith. 'I worked at a university for several years, which was full of whiney, unthinking Custodian readers but they weren't, I suppose, as extreme as the woke people we were always being told about so, well, no, I don't think I actually have.'

Emmeline Moneypenny had looked even more thoughtful than the others during this exchange. 'Hmm...' she began, as if she was experiencing even more revelations than the others, 'I kind of thought I had... But now I consider it in more detail... Well, whenever I quoted a woke person in one of my articles it was always something I'd just copied from Twitter...'

'So hang on...' said John Smith. 'Are you saying...?'

'They don't exist,' interrupted Dave McCreith. 'And they never have! Not only did we make up the whole worldview they supposedly had, but all those Twitter accounts, all those quotes? All controlled by us from the BBC Correct News factories in Macedonia! The whole 'woke' thing? It never existed. It was a scam. We invented it to utterly mess with the public's heads. Again, it was all part of our grand plan for total manipulation, total control and total dominance!'

The others continued to look puzzled, as if a huge part of their perception of the world had just been wrenched away from under their feet. Each one of them appeared to be carrying out mental calculations that involved them initially thinking what they had been told couldn't possibly be true before slowly pondering everything they thought they believed and realising that it could.

'Your eminence,' objected Terry Ball, 'I strongly believe you've revealed more than enough of our plan.'

'Insolent worm! You hold your tongue before you find yourself in a Re-Education Camp!' Dave McCreith shot back. He briefly composed himself before proceeding. 'And that's not all!' he continued, his eyes lighting up like a man possessed. 'If you think things are confusing now, just wait until we move into the next phase! The BBC's plan for the first hundred years was to assume absolute control of the country by disguising ourselves as a mere broadcaster, but we know we'll have to work even harder now that we've got it! People will be made even *more* confused!'

With a deranged look now in his eyes he now proceeded to explain the next stage of his insane plan.

'You know how we've ruthlessly promoted trans rights and denounced anyone who dares question any aspect of the issue? Well, our next Great Polarity is that we're going to announce that 'trans-racialism' is totally a thing, and just a few years after we heartily joined in when the whole world vilified a woman who claimed she identified as black despite being white we'll start saying anyone who questions whether it's a real condition is now committing a sickening hate crime! In the same way that we used the term 'dead naming' as a way to attack anyone who dared point out someone used to be a different gender, we'll introduce the term 'dead *race*-ing', making it a crime to point out someone's actual biological race if they claim to identify as a different one! And if anyone accuses *us* of hypocrisy we'll simply taint them with the charge of 'dead *belief*-ing', the monstrous idea that anyone who dares to point out that someone has completely changed their opinion is actually guilty of a hate crime themselves!'

He was slightly out of breath at this point and paused for a few moments, which is quite fortunate because that surely gives you an opportunity to take in what he just said, as it was all rather complicated. However, from the future in which I'm writing this, all of the above is actually what happened. And, depending on when you're reading this, the above paragraph will either be completely sickening, or entirely true. It really could go either way. Insane, huh? And if you think this is all confusing to the point of madness, then maybe that's the point.

During Dave McCreith's lengthy speech, Terry Ball had continued to look worried at just how much he was revealing. 'Again, your grace, I strongly feel you've said too much,' he said, now appearing to be in the early stages of agitation. 'I mean, whilst you're planning on having these people killed, what about the woman you're going to let join the Minging Community as a spokesperson?'

He pointed at Kerri Barnes-Bridge, who suddenly looked up from her phone, her expression suggesting she had no idea what was going on.

'Sorry, what?' she said. 'Sorry, I wasn't listening to any of that as I've been on Twitter the whole time. I'm finally going to be properly famous!'

Terry Ball frowned at this. 'Okay, fine, she didn't hear any of it, but I still strongly feel you should not be telling secrets of the

BBC Inner Party to all and sundry!'

Dave McCreith simply turned to him and slapped him across the face.

'One more time,' he warned. 'If you dare to question me *one more time* I will not be so forgiving.'

Terry Ball lowered his head, but whilst his body language seemed to imply he was apologetic, his facial expression suggested otherwise, though Dave McCreith did not notice this as he seemed to have worked himself up into a deranged frenzy, and the general feeling in the room was that they were not entirely sure if he was in full possession of his faculties, or whether anything he said was to be believed or was in fact part of some strange test.

John Smith, despite knowing his situation was hopeless, could not stop himself from trying to argue otherwise, even if on some level he knew his words were empty. 'Empires don't last forever! The Roman Empire fell! The Nazis were defeated! Eventually you'll suffer the same fate! The BBC will one day crumble into dust!'

'You are mistaken!' Dave McCreith corrected him. 'Our first century was about subtly building up our power, but when we orchestrated The Great Terror it was so we could present ourselves as the country's saviour, to win the Great Victory but then undertake the Great Re-Structuring, hunting down and destroying our enemies and eradicating anti-BBC Thought-Crime forever! Governments, independent television, public protests, they all tried to topple us during our first century but now we're in our second we simply cannot be overthrown! We have the technology now! We control the news! And did you know we control the weather? Well, that's not all! We control TIME! Now that all clocks are digital or on phones or whatever we can make them say whatever we want! Why, sometimes when the clocks are going back we put them back by six hours as a joke, just to disorientate the population! We have the power to delete things from people's Kindles or erase websites so they never existed! There is no reality but BBC reality! There is no truth but BBC truth!'

He looked at what he took to be his vanquished enemies, who were now kneeling on the floor at the behest of the guards, something I may have forgotten to previously mention. Also, is he *actually* mad? It's definitely been a theme but I don't know how well I developed it.

'There was no way you could ever win!' Dave McCreith assured them. 'The only future is the BBC's future! Constantly changing our world view! The complete destruction of objective reality! I see the future of the human race, and that future is a BBC jackboot in the face of every man, woman and child whilst they watch Mrs Brown's Boys repeated for the hundredth time! A world without freedom, without originality, without dissent! Our new Reich! Our new future!'

By this point Dave McCreith seemed to have been completely and irrevocably consumed by the deranged, apoplectic state he had worked himself into, but then he suddenly froze and stopped speaking, with a look of shock and confusion across his face. He slowly turned around and looked down. What he saw was a letter opener rammed into his side, and the wound already bleeding heavily, with Terry Ball standing a few feet away, glaring at him, clearly the one who had put it there.

'At the appointed hour,' Terry Ball said, quite calmly, 'I kill the king.'

# Chapter Twenty Four:

# The Great Betrayal

*In Which the Title Itself Is Already a Spoiler So I Won't Provide Any More Details Here Even Though I Now Realise the Actual Betrayal Happened In the Previous Chapter Anyway*

Dave McCreith started trying to remove the letter opener, only to see this caused the wound to bleed more. Utterly confused, he looked back at Terry Ball. 'Traitor! I am your king! Guards!' he gasped. 'Kill him! Your duty is to protect the Director General at all costs!'

'That is correct,' replied the nearest paramilitary. 'But Mr Ball is the Director General now. The rules clearly state that if the DG is incapacitated in any way, or dies, his crown passes to the next in command.'

'What?!' spluttered Dave McCreith. 'Treachery! Heresy! I am your god within this realm!'

'These men are loyal to me,' Terry Ball explained, calmly. 'And have been for a long time, since I started planning this. You've been a liability for too long but I was the only man with the vision to do something about it.'

'But...' began Dave McCreith, only for Terry Ball to interrupt him.

'Yes, I've been watching you for years. Listening... Monitoring your decline with interest and knowing when it would be time for me to usurp you... Maybe once you had some good ideas, but there's a reason the public thinks you're a joke, or mad, or dead. A 'Woke

Hitler' whose brain is half rotted by tertiary syphilis, did you know that's what they think about you? How could we possibly have a pathetic shell of a man like you in charge of a company of this magnitude and magnificence?! We're the BBC, the greatest thought-control organisation in the history of the world!'

Our heroes looked around in confusion, wondering what this meant for the organisation, for the country, and for them. But, rather than giving them any indication, Terry Ball now set off on some revelatory exposition of his own, despite having warned his then-superior about it a number of times.

'The woke thing is over. This is why I had to get rid of you! You're too damned predictable! You just wanted to push the progressive agenda when I know we can confuse people even more by going in completely the opposite direction! The time of the *true* next Great Polarity is here!'

'What are you planning, you madman?!' spluttered Dave McCreith, as he slumped to the floor, clutching his side.

'I'm going the other way! If you think it's confusing trying to work out what's fine and what's offensive at the moment, wait until I've commenced my reign of terror!' replied Terry Ball. 'I'll bring back blacking up yet also have a revived Black and White Minstrel Show where the cast is all black people wearing white face make up and singing songs from the sickeningly abhorrent musical catalogue of white people! What will the public make of that?! I'll be introducing sitcoms about people on council estates where we say it's a deeply sympathetic portrayal of noble victims of Tory austerity yet the actual show is about them kidnapping children from Primark to get more benefits and selling their excess children to paedos on the dark web! A character who drops her new-born on the floor because someone referred to it as a 'bouncing baby boy'! Jokes based on a girl's mother noticing she's got plumper lips and asking if she's had filler done only to be told her boyfriend has punched her in the mouth but assured her he only did it because he loves her! Yes! A sitcom that will make brutal jokes about domestic violence yet we'll claim is raising awareness! People will be more confused than ever before! And along with bringing back blacking up we'll go back to having transsexual characters as hilarious figures of fun like in Little Britain but *then* create another sitcom that claims to celebrate both older people and the trans community but then confuse people completely by calling it 'My Granny's a Tranny', yet *at the same time* claim that word is no longer a slur and is now the correct term, in the same way that 'queer' is apparently now okay, or how the words 'black' and 'coloured' constantly switch between being the preferred terminology and a sickening word of hate!'

Dave McCreith glared at his usurper, his weakened state meaning he failed to notice that, in delivering a rather long and rambling monologue, Terry Ball had started his new reign of terror in much the same way that he had finished his. 'You'll never get away with this,' he choked, continuing to bleed to death on the floor. He then looked worried for a moment. 'Will you continue to make Mrs Brown's Boys?'

'Even better!' replied Terry Ball, triumphantly. 'I'm going to create a spin-off called Mrs Smith's Slags, about a woman with eleven daughters who sleep with every guy they meet!'

'Will it be an inspiring, empowering celebration of the weaponisation of female sexuality, like Fleabag?' asked Dave McCreith, desperately.

'No, like I said, the characters will all be working class so they'll just be slags!' replied Terry Ball, gleefully. He then did a double take at his former boss, as if slightly surprised he was still alive. 'Also,' he continued, 'if you're wondering why I stabbed you rather than shooting you, it was so I could have the satisfaction of explaining my plan to you, safe in the knowledge you were already dying, just like I said you should have done with these people!'

'You can't mess with Mrs Brown's Boys...' said Dave McCreith, weakly. 'It's the BBC's flagship show...' Staring down at him furiously, Terry Ball took out his gun and shot him in the back.

'Nothing you say matters now!' he yelled. 'Your era is over! My era has just begun!'

'Life is slow dying,' said Dave McCreith, recalling perhaps the only line of poetry he could remember from his Oxford degree and also thinking that people would think him really clever for quoting Philip Larkin as his dying words, even though by that point to have even heard of Philip Larkin was a sickening hate crime because he was mad into porno and that.

Dave McCreith lay back, and his breathing slowed down.

'Ooh, I think I've pooped my pants,' he said, before realising that meant he had just overwritten the Philip Larkin quote as his dying words with an unnecessary observation about soiling his undergarments. He then did actually die, condemning himself to being remembered for his dying words having referenced his faecal failings. Satisfied, and seemingly entirely unaffected by the death of his former employer, Terry Ball turned back to our heroes and continued explaining the new dark era he was about to usher in.

'Politics! Remember how we manipulated the electorate with the EU referendum, choosing a topic that very few people had even thought about before, much less had an opinion on, until we told them that their view on it completely defined them as a person, and in doing so caused the country to turn upon itself?! Well, we'll do it again! This time we'll decide it's time we had a referendum on NATO membership, which is, again, something nobody has given a second thought to, but within a few months we'll have manipulated the electorate in such a way that they're fighting in the streets because they've been conditioned to think anyone who opposes NATO membership is a closet racist, whilst anyone who favours it is a wonderful, caring, tolerant person, even though we'll have taken a hugely complicated and nuanced issue and made it into a desperately simplistic, black and white one! We'll set families against each other over an issue they had no opinion on a few months before, as one generation claims they always loved NATO as it stood for peace and unity, whilst the other says it just syphoned off their taxes and stole their sovereignty! A second civil war, allowing us to grab even more power! Welcome to our new dark eon! Our new BBC Reich! Every day is a bright new apocalypse!' he threw his head back and laughed like the mad genius he possibly was. And with Dave McCreith now definitely dead he knew he was unstoppable. Apparently realising this, he looked at our heroes more carefully than he had before.

'You!' he said, pointing at Emmeline Moneypenny. 'You will be welcomed back into the fold and celebrated as one of the greatest ever feminist minds, who bravely dared to stand up to the forces of wokeness that were so cruelly imposed upon us by my predecessor! The reign of Dave McCreith will be remembered as one during which 'mistakes were made' and there was a 'culture of fear', and he will be denounced at every opportunity as the traitor to the BBC that he was, with people like you employed to publically condemn him. And you!' he yelled, pointing at Barry Begbie, 'will also be welcomed back, with your own prime-time programme where you can be as offensive as possible, with loads and loads of jokes about AIDS, gypsies, Down's Syndrome, the Queen's haunted old vag and swimmers' noses!'

He paused for a moment and looked at John Smith. 'I'm sorry,' he said, 'remind me again what it was you used to do at the BBC?'

'Oh, I was never at the BBC,' John Smith explained. 'I was just sent to the camp for a critical tweet I did.'

'Oh, right, yes,' replied Terry Ball, as he remembered. 'And, sorry, I forgot which private school and Oxbridge college you went to?'

'Er, neither of those things,' said John Smith. 'I'm really just a...'

'Silence,' Terry Ball cut in. 'We have no use for you here and you are clearly nothing more than a dangerous, free-thinking heretic.' He turned to the nearest paramilitary. 'Take him away. I want him lobotomised by the end of today. I WILL make him love the BBC!'

The paramilitary nodded. 'At once, your grace. The BBC will prevail!'

Emmeline Moneypenny and Barry Begbie looked around desperately as they tried to think of a way they could save John, but knew they were completely outnumbered and there was nothing they could do as their friend was dragged, terrified, out of the office.

'THE BBC WILL PREVAIL!' screamed Terry Ball as two paramilitaries took John Smith away, into the same dark, uncertain future that the rest of the country would soon enter.

There was now a moment of silence. Barry Begbie and Emmeline Moneypenny were still too stunned at what had happened to John to say anything, but Terry Ball was clearly thinking very carefully about not just his long-term plans but about what he needed to do as a matter of urgency in order to cement his power grab. He suddenly turned to the remaining paramilitaries.

'Take these three to their new departments,' he ordered. 'They have much to do. New programmes must be made, and statements denouncing the previous regime must be released.'

Still shocked, Barry Begbie and Emmeline Moneypenny were led out of the room, along with Kerri Barnes-Bridge, who still hadn't been paying much attention and had spent the whole time on her phone.

'Clear away these bodies,' Terry Ball ordered, 'and have the corpse of Dave McCreith placed on display in the gibbet outside the main entrance where all the other traitors are.'

As the corpses were being taken away Terry Ball started to walk over to what was now his desk before another paramilitary, apparently the one in charge, approached him.

'Er, your grace, on that subject, there is one more thing.'

'Yes?' replied Terry Ball, impatiently.

'Well, my liege, we've recently learnt that some inmates from one of the Re-Education Camps managed to escape a day or two ago. The company that runs it didn't immediately tell us because they were concerned it may affect whether their contracts were renewed.'

'I can't recall a major corporation ever penalising one of its outsourcing companies for providing a truly appalling service in return for the millions it gets paid, but do go on,' said Terry Ball, slightly annoyed.

'Right, well, the thing is, your excellence,' continued the paramilitary, 'when their photos were circulated to the camp staff, a newly-arrived paramilitary recognised one of the escapees and claimed he was actually the author of The Book. You know... 'The Book the BBC Tried to BAN!' The author believed to be in a gibbet outside this very building.'

'Impossible,' replied Terry Ball, bluntly. 'That man is dead. I was here when my predecessor shot him.'

'Well, here's the thing, my liege,' continued the paramilitary. 'We are now not *quite* sure that was him. This paramilitary was adamant that he was in the scouting party who nearly apprehended the author prior to his escape just before his book was on trial, so saw his face before he got away. His story has not been corroborated but, if true, it would seem that the author was actually later taken to the camp on an unrelated charge, with those at the facility completely unaware of his true identity. Apparently whilst incarcerated he was known by a rather half-hearted, nondescript sort of name like, oh, Mark Smith or John Jones or something, which may have been his true name or simply an identity he stole, but if it really was him that would mean we had one of the most wanted anti-BBC Thought-Criminals in our own facility without even realising it. And he double-bluffed everyone in the camp, including the other inmates, by convincingly maintaining the façade that he had no idea what he was in there for and that he was only vaguely acquainted with The Book itself.'

'What are you talking about?' demanded Terry Ball, getting more annoyed at having his time wasted with something that was clearly just an unsubstantiated theory. 'I was here when the author not only admitted writing the book but explained in great length what his motivations were, and addressing any possible criticism of it.'

'Again, my liege, we're only now piecing all this information together but it has been suggested that some people actually pretended to be him in order to protect the true author, people who were already facing most serious charges of heresy so had nothing to lose by doing so, and even that the author encouraged such condemned people to pretend to be him, and therefore confuse the Corporation as to his true identity, by offering to make payments to their surviving family members from his great personal fortune.'

Terry Ball shook his head dismissively and sighed. 'I really don't have time to waste with outlandish theories like this. As far as I'm concerned we captured the author, and dealt with him appropriately.'

'No, indeed, your grace,' replied the paramilitary, 'it is only a theory, albeit one I thought you would wish to hear.'

Terry Ball shrugged, clearly having far, and many more, important things on his mind. 'I can't say I find that theory particularly convincing,' he said. 'If anything, it sounds like exactly the kind of implausible, half-baked plot twist that author himself would have used in his pathetic little book in an attempt to make it seem cleverer than it was.'

'Perhaps, your excellency,' replied the paramilitary, clearly taking this to mean the case was closed. 'But I suppose we'll never quite be *entirely* sure.'

# Chapter Twenty Five:
# The Final Acceptance

Sitting in his padded cell in a secure mental facility, John Smith reflected on how his life had got far easier in recent weeks, or rather he would have done were it not for the fact that his lobotomy had completely robbed him of the power of independent thought. Still, it meant he was an ideal BBC viewer now, as he could sit through anything he was subjected to and think it was utterly brilliant. In between emitting bloodcurdling, torturous screams and banging his head against his cell walls, he spent his days in a comfortable chair watching BBC programmes all day long, and enjoyed whatever old crap they broadcast, from antiques shows to rubbish comedies to endless repeats of Top Gear on Dave, which still counts as the BBC as it's a subsidiary channel. What had once seemed like brutal torture, and still would to any vaguely intelligent person, now seemed to him like an entirely agreeable way to pass every single one of his waking hours.

'And now on BBC One,' said the continuity announcer on the TV, 'yet another repeat of Mrs Brown's Boys!'

'Mrs Brown's Boys!' screamed John Smith, ecstatically, which was one of the few coherent phrases his decimated brain could still form. Mrs Brown appeared on the screen and did an opening monologue that quickly included the word 'penis'.

'Ha ha! 'Penis!'' John Smith guffawed. 'PENIS, PENIS, WILLY WILLY BUM-BUM!'

As his maniacal screaming echoed down the corridors of the

asylum there was another thought that would have occurred to him were it not for the fact that his lobotomy meant he was no longer capable of such complicated mental processes:

He had finally learned to love the BBC.

# THE END

# *Author's Postscript*

Whilst the society depicted in this book is one of a dark near-future, the seeds that led to such a world becoming a terrifying reality had been firmly sown by the early years of the 2020s and so, as such, I am well aware of the perils of a world where people are offended by everything, especially that which they do not understand, which is why I took the quite brilliant precaution of actually having a chapter in the book that both pre-empted and addressed just about any possible reason people could have to object to it. As the Author himself said, if he managed to completely predict your complaint then maybe you're not as clever as you think you are! I mean, what kind of brilliant post-modern devilry was *that*?!

To be offended is to completely miss the point: this was a warning I had no choice but to send, regardless of what the consequences are for me. Still, it also strikes me that anyone who is easily offended would never have made it this far, so I probably don't need to examine the nature of offence yet again. The point is that you have dared to join me on this journey and see it through to its conclusion, for which you are to be congratulated.

Bearing in mind that the book is completely self-contained I feel there is nothing left for me to say, and if your response to that is to question why, if it's true, I've chosen to include a postscript then I think that's an entirely fair criticism.

Still, as the final word on the subject I'll add that this novel is both a satire of the BBC AND a satire of people who want it defunded, whilst *also* being a satire of people who mock those who call for the BBC to be defunded, *and* a parody of people who criticise them, too. It's also a satire on people who rigidly defend the BBC and would call for legal action against, say, a novel that satirised it.

It works on quite a lot of levels, you see, and whichever level you think you understand it on there's almost certainly another one below (or above) that one, which you hadn't noticed. I think you'll have to agree that's a pretty legally watertight case and that even the merest thought of launching legal action would be hilariously pointless, even though that's based on me assuming this novel even gets published when, for all I know, it might not, and I'll never know anyway because I sent it back from a future that was not necessarily spawned from your reality.

Also, remember that in my reality this book is actually extremely close to the truth, too, if there really is such a thing as truth. All the answers are in here. It's just down to you to decide what they are.

The only thing I have to apologise for is blowing your mind.

Oh, and all the typos. Sorry about those, too.

Oh, wait, and the plot holes. Also the poor characterisation, half-heartedly planned narrative and general lack of a story.

The book is all.

And in the process of writing it I fear I may have lost my mind.

But I know I'll find it again.

# *Publisher's Postscript*

Again, we can only reiterate that of all the implausible explanations regarding the origin of this book, the one we believe to be most likely is that it is, in fact, a true story, albeit one that occurs in an alternative future dimension, that was somehow sent back as a stark warning of the terrifying world that could await us.

We cannot know the fate of the visionary figure who dared to write this powerful work and send it to us but, nonetheless, all we can hope is that as a society we take heed of its warnings and never allows such things to happen within our own reality.